Elizabeth Je[...] a small waterfront t[...] as lived there all her [...] began writing short stories over thirty years ago, in between bringing up her three children and caring for an elderly parent. More than a hundred of her stories went on to be published or broadcast; in 1976 she won a national short story competition and her success led her onto write full-length novels for both adults and children.

*Elizabeth Jeffrey titles published by
Piatkus, in alphabetical order:*

Elizabeth JEFFREY

Cassie Jordan

piatkus

PIATKUS

First published in Great Britain in 1990 by Century Hutchinson Ltd
This paperback edition published in 2018 by Piatkus

1 3 5 7 9 10 8 6 4 2

A CIP catalogue record for this book
is available from the British Library.

ISBN 978-0-349-42149-0

Typeset in Sabon by M Rules
Printed and bound in Great Britain by
Clays Ltd, Elcograf S.p.A.

Papers used by Piatkus are from well-managed forests
and other responsible sources.

Piatkus
An imprint of
Little, Brown Book Group
Carmelite House
50 Victoria Embankment
London EC4Y 0DZ

An Hachette UK Company
www.hachette.co.uk

www.littlebrown.co.uk

To the memory of my father,
Cliff Barker

Accounts of the earthquake are based on fact.

Just after 9.15 on the morning of 22 April 1884, an earthquake struck northeast Essex. It was not a severe earthquake, although between 1000 and 1500 buildings were damaged near the epicentre to the southeast of Colchester. The tremor was felt over an area of 53,000 square miles.

Chapter One

'*Cassie!*'

At the sound of her mother's voice calling from below, Cassie tried to struggle away from the young man's hold. 'I must go, Edward,' she whispered breathlessly. 'I've told you before, I'm never supposed to be in the bedroom at the same time as a guest.'

He grinned and caught her to him again. 'But it's hardly your fault if the guest walks in when you're making his bed, is it?' He began to kiss her again, his tongue gently teasing.

'No, Edward. No!' She twisted away. 'I can't ... we mustn't ... I must go.' She went over to the mirror on the dressing table to smooth her hair and rebutton her bodice, realising with dismay that there was little she could do about her flushed face.

'Later, then. Come back later.' He came and stood behind her, lifting a strand of her thick, golden hair and kissing it, all the while his blue eyes holding her reflected gaze. 'After all, my lovely Cassie, I haven't seen you since – when was it? Last October? That's a whole six months! We've got a lot of lost time to make up.' He tried to take her in his arms again but again she broke away.

1

'No. No. It's too dangerous. Mama would be furious if she found out.' She hurried across to the door and wrenched it open.

He followed her, placing his hand over hers on the door knob. 'By my father's yacht, then. Tonight. About seven. The covers have come off today and the men have been working on her, but there'll be nobody about by that time.' *Leander*, Jonas Price-Carpenter's sailing yacht was one of the many large racing yachts that had been laid up for the winter in mud berths on the River Colne and were now, in early April, emerging from their winter rest to be made ready for the summer's racing.

'Cassie! Where are you!' Her mother's voice was rising with impatience.

Cassie looked at Edward indecisively. All through the winter her dreams – both sleeping and waking – had been of this handsome young man. He had paid just one brief visit to Wyford, and had stayed at the Falcon Inn with his father, who, as owner of *Leander*, was a frequent visitor. Nevertheless, Cassie remembered everything about Edward: the way his fair hair was parted in the middle and brushed out to the sides in the latest style, his teasing blue eyes and the wide, trim moustache that masked a long upper lip and his even teeth that were hardly stained at all from the cigars he smoked. She remembered, too, the way he had looked at her, pressed her hand and – just before he left – kissed her, full on the mouth, promising to return. No one had ever kissed her that way before, not Luke, not anybody, and although it was not the first time a guest had taken a fancy to her – that was something she had learned to deal with quite early on, extricating herself from delicate situations both speedily and tactfully – it was the first time in all her nineteen years that she had felt any urge to respond.

And now, just as he had promised, Edward had come back

to the Falcon, filling her with longing and confusion. 'I don't know. I ...'

He smiled, a teasing, confident smile. 'I'll be waiting.'

Her heart thumping, Cassie hurried down the stairs and along the passage to the kitchen where her mother was making soup with the vegetables Lizzy, the scullery maid had prepared. She wouldn't go, of course. It was out of the question. But then the vision of Edward's blue eyes, and the memory of his kisses ...

Her mother looked up as she entered. 'It took you long enough to make five beds, my girl,' she said. 'With Stella helping you it should have been done in half the time.'

'Stella's polishing the snuggery.' Cassie consoled herself that this was not a lie. Her younger sister *was* polishing the snuggery. Cassie had sent her to do it ten minutes ago when the last of the beds was finished.

'Very well.' Hannah Jordan turned to put the pan on the big iron range. 'You can make a start on the pastry for the apple pies. You've a good, light hand with shortcrust.'

Cassie gave a sigh and shot a look of exasperation in her mother's direction as she rolled up her sleeves. She hated making pastry.

It was the year 1868 and life at the Falcon Inn was hard. An old, rambling building sprawling beside the grey stone church, it was in the centre of things, less than five minutes from the railway in one direction and from the river in the other, and was always busy.

The local people thought of it as the pub, the place where all thoughts of the day-by-day struggle to exist could be drowned, but to visitors it was the village inn, where a good meal and a comfortable bed were assured. Only Hannah Jordan, who ran it with autocratic efficiency, chose to refer to it as an hotel, in an endeavour to persuade herself and her daughters that they hadn't really come down in the world when they had moved there.

Not that living at the Falcon worried Cassie and Stella; they knew no other life. They had no recollection of their yacht-captain father, nor of the house in West Street where, according to their mother, there had been several servants. The only servants the girls knew now were Lizzie, rescued from the workhouse, who did all the menial tasks like scrubbing flags and emptying slops, and Mrs Gates, who came in every day to clean and help with the laundry. And the fact that Hannah had scrimped to have them expensively educated at Miss Fanny Browne's Ladies' Seminary behind the Post Office had never stopped Cassie and Stella larking about down by the river with the other village children, who, if they went to school at all, attended the National School in the High Street.

Yet something of Hannah's dissatisfaction with her present situation had rubbed off, if not on to Stella, then on to Cassie. Even now as she made the apple pies, Cassie consoled herself that a good knowledge of domestic things was no ill store, for if nothing else it would teach her how to handle her own servants when the time came – as it most surely would. Once again her thoughts turned to Edward and in her musings she nearly burnt her hand on the oven door.

By the time Cassie finished her work for the day it was very nearly seven o'clock in the evening because not only did she and Stella have to help with the cooking, they were also expected to wait on the tables in the dining room, which was full at this time of the year. In springtime the yacht owners came to Wyford, pretending they were overseeing the fitting out of their yachts for the summer's racing, a task that in reality was the responsibility of the captains, who knew what they were doing. All the owners were really required to do was to foot the bill.

The only place the girls were not expected – in fact, were forbidden by Hannah – to work was in the bars, particularly the taproom, where neither behaviour nor language were what she considered suitable for her girls.

As soon as she had finished her work Cassie hurried up to the room she shared with her sister. This was a large room at the back of the house overlooking the yard. It was reached by its own staircase leading up from the kitchen and was quite cut off from the bedrooms in the other part of the house. Hannah had put the girls there when they were quite small, for safety's sake, and they had made the most of their proximity to the kitchen to have midnight feasts, although it was always Cassie who instigated them, raiding the pantry and cutting off chunks of pie and cheese and slices of whatever cake there was available and carrying them back upstairs. The food always tasted better, eaten sitting up in bed.

'Where are you going?' Stella came into the room a few moments later and stared at Cassie, struggling into her second-best dress. 'Why are you putting on your muslin? Aren't you coming down to the wall with the rest of us?' The wall, as it was called, was a grass-covered bank that had been built up beside the river to give the low-lying marshes some protection from flooding. It was the usual meeting place for the young people of the village.

'I might.' Cassie leaned forward, frowning, to examine her freckles in the mirror.

'Not in that dress, surely.' Stella came and stood beside her. At sixteen, three years her sister's junior, Stella was very like Cassie in colouring, but where Cassie was tall and slimly built Stella was short and inclined to be plump; and where Cassie's brown eyes

were large and set wide apart Stella's were a shade too close to
a nose that although it was the same shape as Cassie's – slightly
tip-tilted – was a trifle bigger. Her mouth was just a little smaller
than Cassie's, which was wide and generous, with full lips and
a ready smile. Her hair, too, was the same golden colour, but
where Cassie's hung in thick, shining waves Stella's was fine,
with a tendency to frizz if she tried to tame it with curlpapers.
The result was that Cassie, even with the peppering of freckles
that were the bane of her life, was beautiful enough to turn the
head of any man, whilst Stella was no more than passing pretty.

'It's warm tonight,' Cassie said, moving away from the
mirror that stood on their chest of drawers. 'And this dress is
nice and thin when the weather's hot.'

'It's not that warm,' Stella remarked sensibly. 'After all, it's
only April.' She waited a moment. 'Well, are you coming?'

'Coming where?'

'Down to the wall. I'm going. I'll wait for you if you're
not ready.'

'No, don't bother. You go on. I'll be along in a minute.'
Cassie picked up her hairbrush and began to brush her hair
with careful strokes. Suddenly, she put the brush down. 'What
are you waiting for? What are you looking at me like that for?'

Stella grinned. 'I know where you're going. You're going to
meet that nice young Mr Price-Carpenter, aren't you? I'll bet
Luke doesn't know.'

'You're not to tell.' Cassie rounded on her. 'You're not to let
anyone know. Anyway, it's nothing whatever to do with Luke,'
she finished airily. Luke Turnbull was twenty-five, and by far
the best looking of all the young men who congregated down by
the wall, with thick brown hair and deepset grey eyes that were
kind and full of humour, a wide mouth and a ready smile. All
the girls liked him, but he had eyes for no one but Cassie, a fact

that faintly irritated her, although at the same time she enjoyed the superiority it gave her over the other girls, and if she led him on it was only to make them jealous. Because she would never have dreamed of taking Luke seriously. Her sights were set far higher than a humble woodworker in her uncle's yacht yard.

Stella put her head on one side. 'You can walk with me, if you like. Then people will think you're only going along the wall to meet the others.' She smiled. It was a smug smile. 'Can I wear your pretty beads? Then I won't breathe a word.'

'No.' Then, knowing what her sister was capable of if she didn't get her own way, 'Yes, all right. But only for tonight. And don't get them broken or I'll kill you.'

They left together, going out by the back door and hurrying through the churchyard, leaving it by the little kissing-gate that gave on to the road leading to the quay.

The quay was crowded at this time of the year with the usual clutch of seamen in their dark guernseys, who every evening paced up and down, smoking their clay pipes and spitting into the river, hoping to be taken on as crew on the big yachts that would soon be off racing. They took no notice of the two Jordan girls and Cassie and Stella went on, past the row of squalid cottages known as The Folley, past Turnbull's yacht yard and out on to the wall.

Any other night Cassie would have gone with Stella to join the group sitting in a row along *Fedora's* jetty, some of them dangling their bare feet in the brownish water of the rising tide as they teased and jibed each other but tonight she simply called a greeting and hurried on, as if to catch up with the staid courting couple a little way ahead. She noticed that Luke had been saving a space for her beside him, a space Stella was quick to fill. Cassie managed to glare a warning, reminding her to keep her mouth shut.

It was a warm, early April evening and a light veil of mist was beginning to creep over the marshes. The only noise, apart from the giggles and chatter of the young people on *Fedora's* jetty, was the gentle slap of the water as the tide reached its peak, and the sound of a curlew way in the distance. The row of sleek yachts stretching downriver that were so much a part of the local scene from October to May rose and fell gently with the movement of the water. They varied from forty to nearly sixty-five feet in length and some were still shrouded in their winter covers, dark and sombre, giving no hint of the polished decks and gleaming brass that would soon be revealed.

A dark-clad figure sat on the bank, half hidden by *Leander's* jetty and Cassie hung back, waiting until the couple ahead had gone. Then she began to run. As she reached him Edward stood up and held out his arms and she was enfolded in their warmth. 'I knew you'd come, Cassie,' he said as he drew her down beside him and began to kiss her.

'I mustn't stay long. If Mama knew ...' She tried to pull away but he held her close.

'I've missed you, Cassie,' he murmured against her ear, 'but I'll often be here this summer. I'm to supervise *Leander's* fitting out so we'll have plenty of time ...' He drew away from her a little, still keeping his arm round her. 'Now, surely you can stay long enough to tell me all you've been doing while I've not been here?'

It was so quiet and peaceful in the shadow of *Leander* as she moved gently on the tide that Cassie relaxed. She smiled up at him from the circle of his arm. 'And what would I have been doing but helping my mother?' she asked. 'The Falcon takes all our time, what with people staying ...'

'Yes, and who's been staying? I want to know. I want to

8

know that nobody else has come and stolen your heart.' He smiled at her, his eyes warm.

'Oh, Edward, you know that's not possible. You know I . . .' she hesitated. Edward had never actually said that he loved her so she must be careful. 'You know I'm far too busy for anything like that,' she finished instead.

He nodded, satisfied, and pulled her head on to his shoulder so that he could stroke her long silky hair. 'Have you always lived at the Falcon?' he asked.

'No, only since I was about four. Stella was less than a year old when we moved there so she can't remember living anywhere else.'

'And can you?' He played idly with a strand of hair, stroking her neck so that it was difficult to concentrate.

She sighed. 'I'm not sure. Sometimes I *think* I can. But I'm never really sure whether I remember living in the big house in West Street or whether Mama has told me about it so often that I only think I remember it. Like I *think* I remember Papa. He was a yacht captain and there's a picture of him in his uniform in Mama's room. His yacht used to win a lot of races so we were quite rich. But then he was drowned and we had to give up the big house and move to the Falcon.'

'What about his yacht?'

'It wasn't his yacht, silly.' She twisted her head to smile up at him. 'He sailed it for somebody, like Captain Chaney sails *Leander* for your father.'

'And was it as big as *Leander*?'

She frowned. 'I don't know. I don't really know anything about it. Mama never really talks about it and somehow I've never liked to ask.'

'So you never went aboard?'

'Not that I remember.' She sighed again, wistfully. 'I've often

9

thought I'd like to go aboard one of the big yachts. Then I'd know the kind of boat Papa sailed in.'

'Not necessarily. They're not all the same. *Leander*'s what's known as a gaff-rigged cutter. *Maud,* lying beside her there, is a yawl. *Vanessa,* over there, is a schooner. Then, some have one mast, some two, some even three. Oh, there are no end of different types of yachts and rigs and they come in all sizes.' He bent his head and kissed her, tired of the conversation. 'But I can take you aboard *Leander* if you like,' he said, his mouth against hers. 'I've got a key.'

'Oh, yes, I'd like that,' she answered, hardly knowing what she was saying for the turmoil he had aroused in her.

'We'd better go now, before it's too dark to see anything,' he murmured, helping her to her feet without relinquishing his hold on her. 'Not that there's much to see, at the moment, but I'm happy to show you what there is. Careful, now, we don't want you falling off the jetty into the water, do we?' he said, holding her so close to his side that she felt weak and breathless.

Leander had a distinctive smell of tarred rope, mud and seaweed, mingled with a lingering aroma from the canvas covers that had protected her from the winter weather. The brasswork was dull and there were cobwebs in the winches and windlasses. In the gathering dusk *Leander* gave the impression of a slow awakening from a winter of hibernation.

'She needs a bit of spit and polish,' Edward said, taking Cassie's hand and leading her long the deck. 'And her topsides will have to be revarnished. Quite a lot can be done while we wait for a berth in Harvey's yard to get her bottom scraped. Anyway, I'll have all that attended to after my father has gone back.'

'You're staying, then?' Cassie stumbled a little in her eagerness, trying unsuccessfully to keep her voice casual.

'Yes. I just told you. I'll be here until *Leander* goes off to

Harwich. I might even follow her there. It depends what Father wants me to do.' He headed down the companionway and unlocked the door to the cabin as he spoke.

'I can't see much.' Cassie followed him in, squinting, trying to peer into the semi-darkness.

He laughed. 'I did warn you there wasn't much to see. This is the saloon, but naturally everything was stripped out before she was laid up. It's stripped like this for racing, too, to make the boat as light as possible.'

'Oh.' Cassie was disappointed. Some of the yachts, she knew, had saloons furnished like drawing rooms, with armchairs and settees built round the sides and that was what she had been hoping to find, not just this empty maple-panelled shell. As far as she could see the only things in it were a box of the lead that was used for ballast when the boat was racing and an empty sailbag that had somehow got left behind. 'I didn't think it would be quite as bare as this,' she said, peering around.

'It won't be in a week or two, I can assure you,' he laughed. 'Not once all the paraphernalia is brought back on board. But once that happens we shan't have the place to ourselves like this, Cassie.' His voice dropped and thickened as he drew her into his arms. 'Whereas now we shan't be disturbed.' He began to kiss her with mounting passion, one hand busy with the buttons of her bodice.

At first she returned his kisses, then suddenly she became afraid of his increasing ardour and tried to push him away. 'No, Edward. It's not right, we mustn't. Supposing . . .' But her words were lost against his mouth as he lowered her none too gently to the floor.

'Supposing what? Don't you trust me, Cassie?' His voice was no more than a whisper close to her ear.

'Yes, Edward, of course I do. You know I do.' She hardly

11

knew what she was saying. This was not what she had intended. She didn't want Edward to think she was what her mother called 'a loose woman'. Letting him kiss her and caress her a little was one thing ... more than that was quite another. For a brief moment she struggled to escape from him but her own body betrayed her and she had no will to resist his expert touch and could make no more than a token protest as he lifted her skirts and began to fumble with the string of her drawers.

It was quite dark when they left *Leander*. Edward guided her along the jetty to the safety of the sea wall.

'I'll see you here again tomorrow, at the same time?' he whispered, giving her a last kiss.

'I'm not sure ...' She broke away.

'Oh, come now, don't tell me you didn't enjoy it.'

'Yes, but ...'

He caught her to him again roughly. 'Yes, Cassie, you must come. I need you. I can't do without you.' He began to kiss her again.

'I'll come if I can get away,' she said, once again weak from his embrace.

'I'll be waiting.'

She hurried off with Edward's words, 'I can't do without you,' singing in her ears. She was so in love. And Edward loved her, there could be no doubt of it. She smiled a little in the darkness. It would please Mama to know that Jonas Price-Carpenter's son, of all people, had singled her daughter out for his attentions. Mama had always said that they'd been born to better things and that their life at the Falcon was only a temporary setback. Cassie smiled again. It looked as if she'd been right, too, because Edward was a rich man. His father owned vast estates in Buckinghamshire. Suddenly, filled with joy, she began to run.

Then, just as suddenly, the pendulum of her thoughts swung and her step slowed again as she reddened with guilt. There must be no repetition of what had happened on *Leander* tonight. It had been quite wrong and must never happen again. Not until after she and Edward were married. She was quite determined about that.

Chapter Two

There had been trouble in the taproom. A fight had broken out whilst Hannah was busy elsewhere and although Tom, the big ugly potman, had used his brawn and quelled it successfully a bench had been broken and a table smashed.

Hannah surveyed the damage grimly the next morning, before even the earliest morning drinkers had arrived. 'We must get it all seen to before the place fills up later in the day,' she said. She looked at the watch she wore hanging at her waist. 'Cassie, go along to Uncle George's yard. It's seven o'clock now so they'll all be at work. Ask him if he can lend me a carpenter for a few hours. You can tell him what's happened.' She turned back to Tom. 'He might send his nephew, young Luke. He's a good worker, not like his father.'

'He hadn't need be. That Alf Turnbull's a real waster. That was him what started the row last night. 'E's a reg'lar bruiser when 'e git a bit o' drink inside 'im.' Tom began clearing up, emptying spittoons and sweeping up the old sawdust before putting down fresh. He leant on his broom, always ready for a yarn. 'Good job you wasn't about, missus ...'

14

'It would never have begun if I'd been here,' Hannah said firmly, going off down the passage with a swish of her skirts.

'You're about right at that, missus,' Tom remarked, looking after her admiringly. He turned to Cassie. 'One look from your ma's enough to take the wind outa any man's sails, drunk or sober.' With a shake of his head he went on with his sweeping.

Cassie was glad of the short walk to Turnbull's yard. It promised to be one of those hot days in late May that sometimes heralded a good summer and it had been so stuffy indoors that she had felt quite faint. She was tired, too. Last night it had been late when she had crept home from seeing Edward. Fortunately Stella was a heavy sleeper and never heard her sister climb through the scullery window – carefully left unlatched – and creep up the stairs, sometimes at past eleven o'clock. Not that she met Edward every night. Sometimes she made him wait two, or even three nights, and once it had been a whole week. But it was hard, because she loved him very much and he was always telling her how much he needed her. And in spite of her determination not to give in to his persuasive demands again until they were married, she had several times since found herself powerless against him.

Turnbull's yard was already busy. Cassie could hear the sounds of banging and sawing as she approached. A large yacht, the *Vanessa,* was on the slip, having a final coat of varnish after repairs to her hull and topsides and there was a small yawl under construction in the open-ended boat shed. The men working about the place took no notice of her as Cassie picked her way across the yard between planks of wood propped against sawing horses, pots of paint, and the odd bits of rope and old rigging half-buried in shavings, and went up the wooden stairs to the door with *Office* scrawled on it in chalk.

'Come right in,' a voice called in answer to her knock.

George Turnbull stood at a table under the window overlooking the yard studying boat plans. A short, tubby figure, with a greying fringe of hair round a shiny bald head, his shirt sleeves were rolled up to his elbows and pencils were stuck in all his waistcoat pockets and behind his ears. His son Martin sat at another table in the corner, busily adding up columns of figures.

George looked up and beamed as Cassie entered. 'Cassie, me dear. How are you? And what brings you here at this hour of the day? Not trouble, I hope? Your Aunt Maisie was a-sayin' only yesterday that she hadn't seen her sister Hannah for a week or more.'

'Oh, Mama's all right, thank you, Uncle George,' Cassie smiled, 'but there was a spot of trouble in the taproom last night and a bench and a table got broken. Mama wondered . . .'

' . . . if I could spare somebody to repair 'em.' George nodded. ''Course I can, me dear. An' if I don't miss my mark, my brother Alf was half the cause of it. He's come into work with a rare black eye this morning, drunken lout that he is. I don't know why I keep him on, 'cause he's a lazy sod, except that I feel sorry for poor Liddy, me sister-in-law, with all them kids.' He turned and made a mark on the plans with a pencil and then replaced it behind his ear. 'You can take young Luke. He's a good lad and a fine worker. You'll find him working on the yawl.' He bent over his plans again, saying over his shoulder, 'Don't tell him his father was the one who busted the furniture, though. The poor lad has enough to put up with at home without that.'

'I wouldn't keep Alf on, if it was left to me.' Martin looked up from his work. 'He costs you far more than you get out of him you know, Dad.'

George sighed. 'Do you think I don't know that, boy?' He shook his head. 'I'm soft. I know I am. On the other hand, young Luke more than makes up for what his dad don't do. He's a real hard worker . . . '

'Is that why you've sent him off to mend Aunt Hannah's furniture, Dad?' Martin said with a smile. 'I doubt you'll get paid a lot for that.'

'Hannah'll pay me what I ask,' George said.

'And that won't be a sight,' Martin retorted with more than a tinge of exasperation.

Luke was busily planing a piece of wood when Cassie found him. Totally engrossed in what he was doing, he didn't hear her approach and she studied him for a moment before speaking. He was tall, that was evident even though he was stooped over his work, and lean, with a sinewy strength that showed in the rhythmic movement of the big jack plane. His brown hair was coarse and unruly and he had thick, curly whiskers. Already his face and arms were tanned from continually working out of doors and Cassie couldn't help contrasting him with Edward, who was pale-skinned and aesthetic and altogether more refined.

Suddenly, Luke sensed her presence and looked round at her, his grey eyes lighting up under thick black eyebrows. 'Cassie! What you doin' here?' he asked in surprise.

'I've come to ask you to do a job for my mother at the Falcon,' she replied. 'Uncle George says it's all right for you to come back with me.'

'Oh.' He looked down at the work he'd been doing. 'Yes, well, I can leave this. What is it your mother wants doin'? I need to know so I can bring along the right tools.'

'She needs a table and a bench mending. They got smashed in a brawl last night, I believe.'

Luke sighed. 'I wondered where me dad got 'is black eye from,' he said, half under his breath.

'Now, Luke, I didn't say it was your father.' Cassie's voice was full of sympathy.

'You didn't need to. I know what 'e's like.' Luke gathered together an assortment of tools and put them in a bass – a canvas toolbag – and slung it over his shoulder. 'There,' he said, looking round to make sure he hadn't forgotten anything. 'I think thass all I shall need.'

Cassie turned to go and he fell into step beside her. 'Thass more'n a week or two since you've bin down to the wall, Cassie,' he said. 'I've missed you.' He looked down at her and thought how beautiful she was with her rippling golden hair and clear skin. He had loved her ever since he could remember, but he knew she was never likely to look in his direction. Her sights would be set higher than the son of Alf Turnbull, the irresponsible gambler and drunkard. At twenty-five Luke was the oldest in the family, with nine younger brothers and sisters living and another five in their graves. He lived at home in a leaky cottage in Sun Yard that was so small that he and his brothers Joe and Charlie had to go and sleep next door in Widow Blackett's front room.

'Oh, I've been kept busy. You know how it is, Luke, at this time of the year,' Cassie said with a shrug. 'All the yacht owners come to look over their yachts and some of them stay with us at the Falcon because it's handy. We were full up last week and some of them are still there. We don't get a minute to ourselves.'

'Stella always seems to manage to find time,' he argued.

'Stella doesn't have the same responsibilities that I do,' she replied with a toss of her head.

They had come through the little alleyway known as Grant's Watch and out on to Black Buoy Hill and the little kissing-gate at the back of the churchyard. Luke held the gate so that she was imprisoned in its iron circle.

'Don't you go lettin' any o' them toffs come their ole buck with you, Cassie,' he said, half-laughing, yet serious at the same time. 'Don't forget I'm savin' hard to buy you a ruby ring. One day I'll get it for you.'

'And one day I'll sprout wings and fly. But not till I'm an angel.' She laughed up into his face, a mischievous laugh, not without affection, and planted a kiss on the end of his nose. He was so surprised that he let go of the gate and she slipped through and ran home, still laughing. 'The taproom's where you're wanted,' she called back over her shoulder.

Hannah was there almost before Luke had had a chance to undo his toolbag. 'You can see what needs to be done, Luke, can't you?' she said briskly.

'Aye, Mrs Jordan.' Luke turned over the bench. 'But I reckon I'll have to go back to the yard and get more timber if I'm going to do it properly. Look, these rails have been smashed to splinters. They made a right job of it while they were about it.'

'Tell Tom what it is you want and he can fetch it. It'll all save time. Will you be able to get it done before the men come for their midday drink?'

'I'll try, Mrs Jordan.' Luke set to work and Hannah went to fetch Tom. Moments later Stella appeared in the doorway. 'Tom'll be here in a minute, Luke,' she said, smiling at him.

He looked up. 'There's no hurry. 'I've these joints to clean out before I need the fresh timber for the rails.' He carried on with what he was doing, ignoring Stella, who remained in the doorway, knowing better than to set foot over the threshold. Hannah Jordan was adamant that neither of her girls should enter the taproom under any circumstances. If she couldn't prevent Lily and Mabel, the local prostitutes, from coming in for a drink, she made sure they did their soliciting outside and that her daughters didn't meet him. Hannah considered that it was bad enough living in a public house, without subjecting her girls to the seamier side of life.

'Are you going down to the wall tonight, Luke?' Stella asked after a while, leaning on the doorpost with her feet in the passage.

'Dunno. I might.' He didn't look up.

'Cassie might come tonight. You never know.' She looked at him wickedly and was rewarded by seeing the dull flush that crept over his face. A stab of jealousy shot through her. It wasn't fair. Cassie cared no more for Luke than she cared for a fly on the wall. But Stella did, and she often wove dreams in which she and Luke were married and living in a nice house with two, or perhaps three neat little children. Stella was not ambitious. She asked no more from life than a nice home and children. And Luke.

'Stella!' Her mother's voice calling from the kitchen roused her from her dreams.

'I'll have to go, Luke. But I expect I'll see you tonight.' She gave him one of her most winning smiles.

'What?' Luke looked up from his work. 'Oh, I didn't realise you were still there, Stella.'

'What's that banging?' Hannah's sister Maisie had called in at the Falcon after going to pay her grocery bill at the shop just opposite and the two women were now sitting in Hannah's private room over elevenses of a glass of porter apiece. It was a sunny room beside the kitchen, but it was made dark by the red plush curtains at the windows and the heavy rosewood furniture that had clearly been chosen for a somewhat larger room. Overlooking the church and the churchyard, Maisie found it a useful spot from which to watch the funerals and weddings that went in and out of the church, and she usually made an excuse to call on Hannah when she knew there was a chance of viewing either.

'Your George has lent me young Luke Turnbull to do a bit of carpentering. There was a bit of a do in the taproom last night. Alf . . .'

Maisie held up her hand. 'Don't tell me. Alf Turnbull was the cause of it.' She took a drink of porter, shaking her head as she put down her glass. 'I never saw two brothers as different as that Alf and my George. My George wouldn't hurt a fly; he's a good-living, hardworking man – though I say it as perhaps shouldn't, him belonging to me – but look how he's built that business up. Started in the back yard, he did, twenty years ago, just after we were married, building a rowing boat for old Pinker Barr – and look where he is now! Repairs yachts for all the big nobs.' She gave a little smug, self-satisfied shrug and took another drink. 'Whereas his brother! Lazy good-for-nothing! If my George didn't employ him it's a sure certain thing nobody else would. I don't believe he's done a proper day's work in all the time he's been at the yard.' She shrugged again. 'But blood's thicker than water, I suppose.'

Hannah drained her glass. She'd heard it all before, many times. She put down her glass and studied her younger sister – a short, dumpy woman with carefully crimped hair under a rice straw bonnet trimmed to match her dress and shawl of the new magenta colour, and a round, pleasant face. She and her husband George could truthfully be termed a round, pleasant couple, simple in their tastes and habits, who had come up in the world due to their own diligence and hard work. Hannah was very fond of Maisie, even though her sister was inclined to be smug about her situation. She only wished that her own life was as uncomplicated.

'It's Liddy I feel sorry for,' she said now, picking up the jug and refilling Maisie's glass and her own. 'She used to be such a pretty little thing before she married Alf.'

'Nothing pretty about the poor soul now,' Maisie said, shaking her head. 'Worn out, she is, with never being without either a child in her belly or at her breast. Shameful, I think it is, the way Alf treats her.' Another characteristic shrug. 'I'm glad to say my George has got more respect for me than to keep foisting more brats on me. One was quite enough, thank you very much.' She pursed her lips primly.

'Your Martin's a good boy,' Hannah said automatically.

Maisie gave a proud smile. 'Yes, he's twenty-five now, same age as young Luke. He might not be quite so clever on his tools as his father, or Luke if it come to that, but he's a good head on his shoulders. In fact he's better at figuring than George, although perhaps I shouldn't say so. But it's a comfort to know that the business will still go on when George ... well, when George can't work any more'.

Hannah said nothing. She gathered the glasses and put them on the tray. Maisie had stayed long enough. She'd be here all day if she wasn't gently shown the door. It was all very well for her – as the wife of George Turnbull she had a nice house in Anglesea Road with two servants to look after it, but Hannah was not so lucky. A public house needed every hand available to keep it running smoothly.

'I must go,' Maisie said, taking the hint. 'I know you've a lot to do. But I might jest pop along this afternoon for five minutes. I believe old Jacob Last is bein' buried today. Three o'clock, ain't it?'

Hannah nodded. You didn't live at the Falcon without knowing most of what went on in the village. 'That's right. I doubt there won't be many to follow him, though. Most of his family is already dead.'

'What about his son? The one that emigrated to Australia after the trouble with that girl? I wondered if he might've come back.'

'I don't know. I haven't heard so.'

'Well, if I come along this afternoon we shall see, shan't we?' Maisie heaved herself out of her chair and smiled at Hannah. 'Y'know, I never thought to see you running a pub, Annie,' she said, using Hannah's childhood name. 'Things were very different, weren't they, before Reuben was ...'

'I never thought I should come to it, either,' Hannah said, cutting her off. 'And it's an hotel, not a pub.'

Maisie lifted her eyebrows. 'Can't see the difference, meself.' She gathered up her various bags and baskets. 'I just took a few bits to Liddy on my way here,' she explained in a whisper. 'She can do with a bit of help, God knows.'

'You're a good girl, Maisie.' Hannah patted her sister's shoulder, the only sign of affection she allowed herself.

After Maisie had gone Hannah called Cassie in. 'Mr Crowther is coming today,' she announced, 'and he likes to be put in the Captain's room, so we'll have to move Mr Pargeter out and put him in the Admiral's room. That's empty, isn't it, now that Mr Price-Carpenter senior has gone?' She didn't wait for Cassie to reply but went on, 'That's right. Young Mr Price-Carpenter is still in the little room at the front, so that leaves the two rooms overlooking the back yard in case anyone else comes.' All the time she was speaking she was taking plates down from the dresser ready for the midday meal. 'Call Stella to help you,' she added, without looking round. 'What's she doing?'

'Dusting, I think.' Cassie knew perfectly well that her sister was still hanging round the taproom door watching Luke Turnbull but she wasn't prepared to tell tales because she often needed a favour from Stella.

23

Any other time she probably would have called her, if only to commiserate with her over the news that Abel Crowther was coming. They neither of them liked the man, a rather brash file manufacturer from Sheffield, although their mother always went out of her way to make him comfortable. But today Cassie had other things on her mind. More important things.

She went upstairs to Edward's room, hoping he would be there. She had to talk to him. She was worried – her monthly time for being unwell was over six weeks late and she often felt sick and faint in the morning. She couldn't understand it. These were the symptoms women complained of when they feared they were to have a child. It had never occurred to Cassie that such a thing could be the outcome of her meetings with Edward. Children, as she understood it, resulted from men being brutes. What Edward had done to her had been gentle and loving. But there could be no other explanation; her monthly had never been late before. She felt unhappy and confused. This was not what she had planned. She had never wanted to trap Edward into marrying her. She had dreamed of a proper romantic proposal and an engagement ring. She only hoped he wouldn't mind. But he had said she could trust him and she did.

Edward was not in his room. She knew he was busy, for *Leander had* been to Harvey's yard to have her bottom cleaned and polished with black lead to make her faster in the water and was now nearly ready to leave. Edward would have to check with Captain Chaney that everything was in order. The Captain had already chosen his crew from the hopeful fishermen of the village and fitted them out with blue guernseys with the name *Leander* worked across the chest in white. They also had duck trousers, black shoes and shiny black straw hats – known as 'Nab light hats' because crews of light vessels plaited many of them to supplement their pay – all at the expense of the owner.

Jonas Price-Carpenter would also receive the bill for the foul weather gear of sticky yellow oilskins, sou'westers and seaboots, as well as for each man's smart going ashore rig – a blue serge suit and black shoes. This last custom had only recently been introduced but had caught on because no yacht owner was prepared to be outdone by his rivals. Then there was the yacht to inspect, although if Captain Chaney said that he was satisfied that everything was in order Edward would be happy to take his word. Joseph Chaney ran a tight, efficient ship that sailed well and won races. His appearance mirrored his efficiency; his blue serge suit was always well-pressed, his shirt and collar crackling white and his tie knotted with precision. His cheesecutter was placed on his head firmly and squarely after he had doffed it to his superiors – it was said that he used the toe caps of his shoes as a mirror to check that it was straight.

Cassie hung about waiting for Edward, pretending to dust his room, fingering his brushes and the shaving gear on the wash-stand. At the thought that soon this could be part of her everyday life a little thrill of anticipation shot through her but eventually she realised she couldn't stay any longer without arousing suspicion. She would have to wait until tonight to tell him.

She met nobody as she hurried along the wall later that day. It was a dull evening, with heavy clouds and still, oppressive air. She wondered briefly if she should have brought an umbrella but decided that if it rained she would wait on board *Leander* until it stopped. She permitted herself a little smile. It would be quite a fitting way to announce her engagement to Edward.

He was just leaving the yacht as she reached it. 'What's the matter, Edward? I'm not late, am I?' she said, smiling at him.

'No, but we can't go aboard because Captain Chaney and the men are all there.' Edward's eyes were sparkling with excitement. 'I've something to tell you, Cassie. Come and let's sit down on the other side of the bank, under those bushes.'

'I've something to tell you, too, Edward,' she said, scrambling down behind him to where bushes grew thickly over the marshes.

He found a spot that was hidden from the view of anyone walking along the wall and pulled her down beside him. 'Now,' he said, his face close to hers, after he had settled her so that he could kiss and caress her as they talked, 'What have you got to tell me, my beautiful Cassie?'

She smiled up at him, a little uncertainly. 'I think I'm to have your child, Edward. We shall have to be married. And soon.'

His reaction was immediate. He pulled away from her as if he'd suddenly found she was contaminated with some unspeakable disease. '*Child*' he croaked. 'You're to have a child?' He turned to her, panic in his face. 'Are you quite sure?'

'I – I think so.' She hung her head, ashamed of her ignorance. 'It's possible, isn't it? After what we've . . . ?' she couldn't finish.

'Yes, yes, of course it's possible,' he said irritably. 'But I didn't think . . . '

She sat up and clutched his arm. 'You will marry me, Edward, won't you? You said I could trust you. You won't leave me in disgrace?' Her voice was filled with alarm. This was not the reaction she had expected from him.

He shook her off. 'Of course I can't marry you. There's no question of it.' His voice was agitated and distant. He picked up a stone and threw it viciously down the bank.

'Why not? You love me, don't you?' she cried shrilly.

'Keep your voice down. Captain Chaney will hear you.'

'I don't care. You do love me, Edward, don't you?'

'It's not a question of love.' He turned his head away and sent another stone hurtling after the first.

'Then why can't you marry me?' She was calmer now, but it was a calmness that verged on hysteria.

He turned and looked at her. 'Because I'm already engaged to someone else,' he said desperately.

'Then you'll have to break it off, won't you? I'm sure whoever she is won't wish to marry you knowing that I'm to have your child,' Cassie insisted.

He made an impatient gesture. 'Oh, grow up, Cassie. Of course I can't break it off. I must marry Felicity. She expects it, my parents expect it – *her* parents expect it. Why, we've been betrothed almost since we were in our cradles – we've grown up together. If I were to say I wanted to marry someone else my father would cut me off without a penny and then where should we be?'

'But what about me, Edward? What about our child?' Cassie couldn't believe this was happening. Soon she would wake up and find Edward's arms round her and his voice in her ear soft and soothing, telling her they would be together for always.

'Can't you get rid of it?' His voice was not soft and soothing at all, it was irritable and impatient. 'It can't be difficult. I'm sure there are plenty of people who'll do it for you if you pay them.' He fished in his pocket and brought out several coins. 'Here you are. This'll more than pay for what needs to be done.' He turned and put his arm round her, the first sign of tenderness he had shown. 'Lots of people do it, Cassie. It happens all the time. Don't be afraid.' He smiled winningly at her. 'And now, darling Cassie, give me a kiss because I'll be going away to Harwich tomorrow with Captain Chaney, for *Leander's* first race of the season. And then we're off to Cowes.'

She pushed him away. 'No doubt that was the exciting news you had to tell me,' she said bitterly.

'That's right. And I must get back because we're leaving on

the ebb early tomorrow morning.' He tried to draw her into his arms again and again she struggled free. 'Come on, Cassie, aren't you even going to kiss me goodbye? There's no telling when I'll be back, you know. Maybe not until next year ... '

'By which time no doubt you'll be happily married to Felicity,' she said, her voice heavy with sarcasm.

'Yes, he replied, ignoring her tone. 'As a matter of fact we're to be married in September. But what difference does that make? It certainly doesn't mean I won't want to see you, Cassie. We can still ... ' he hesitated' ... see each other when I come here. And it certainly doesn't have to stop you kissing me goodbye, does it?' He put his arm round her encouragingly.

She shook it off and stared at him. 'Edward! How can you say such things! My God, you've got a nerve.' She turned away in disgust. 'And to think I believed you loved me.' She plucked at the grass, screwing up her eyes against the threatening tears.

'I do love you, Cassie. Really I do. It's just that I can't marry you.' He took out his pocket watch and looked at it as he spoke. 'Come on, now. One last kiss and then I must go.' He tried to turn her face to his but she refused to look at him. He shrugged. 'All right,' he said with a sigh. 'Have it your own way.' He scrambled up the bank and went off to *Leander* without a backward glance.

Chapter Three

After Edward had left her Cassie made no attempt to get up. She felt sick – sick because of the child she suspected was within her, sick because of his reaction to it and sick with worry as to what would be her fate. Her thoughts shied away from her mother and the Falcon. She could hear Hannah's voice now, warning both her and Stella, 'Life at an hotel can be dangerous for young girls. Some men are quite unscrupulous. But both of you are sensible girls and I trust you to keep yourselves decent and not to allow anyone to take advantage of you.' That was the reason they slept in the room over the kitchen, inaccessible from the rest of the house, and as an added precaution Hannah had even provided them with the whistles that hung at their belts in case they should be molested by a guest as they went about their duties. Cassie fingered hers now. Hannah's parting words on the subject rang in her ears. 'Now, I've warned you. Remember what I've said, because I will not have disgrace brought on the name of Jordan. If either of you ignore what I've said and get into trouble with a man I shall turn you out of my house, make no mistake about that.'

Cassie began to cry. Her mother was not given to idle threats.

She would have no compunction in turning her out. But where would she go? What would she do? And with a baby to look after, too? Visions of the workhouse rose before her. The place at the end of the village on the Colchester Road was better than some, but Lizzy the scullery maid's tales of her treatment there made Cassie shudder. To be forced to seek refuge there . . .

Yet what Edward had suggested was wicked. Beatie Morris had died, trying to rid herself of an unwanted child and Cassie remembered now the rumours that had circulated of the unspeakable things done to Beatie with rusty knitting needles by some woman in a Colchester back street. Cassie shuddered again. She couldn't face that. But she couldn't face her mother, either. She'd die first – kill herself. Throw herself in the river. Better to die that way than under the ministrations of some filthy old hag in Vineyard Street.

Slowly, she got to her feet and began to walk away from the village in the direction of the woods that skirted the marshes, careful not to climb the bank on to the sea wall until she was well past *Leander*. Everywhere was grey and dull. The sky was leaden with impending rain and the River Colne, beginning to flow now but still little more than a stream snaking its way through the black mud flats, reflected the grey clouds. The only sounds to be heard were the weird cry of the curlew and the gentle plop of gases escaping from the oozing mud. She walked along aimlessly, clutching the five golden guineas that Edward had pressed into her hand so tightly that they hurt. She opened her palm and looked at them and suddenly a feeling of outrage filled her. What did he think she was, some common trollop, happy to be bought off with a few gold coins? Fury and revulsion rose in her throat, threatening to choke her. She didn't want his filthy money. She wanted nothing more to do with him. *Ever.* With a sob of pure disgust she lifted her hand

and threw the coins as far as she could, out into the mud. They glistened for a second against the black storm clouds as they arched through the air, then fell, hardly disturbing the surface as they sank. The first drops of rain began to fall.

Luke had been down to the creek for cockles. He'd gathered all he could while the tide was at its lowest ebb but now that it had turned, covering the cockle beds, he strapped the wicker cockle basket over his shoulder and began the two-mile walk home. The path followed the river across saltings covered with sea lavender and veined with deep gullies waiting for the tide to fill them, through sloping woods and out on to the mile-long sea wall leading back to the village. It was nearly nine o'clock and the light was fading fast, aided by the gathering storm clouds. He'd be lucky to get home without a wet shirt. He hoisted the heavy basket higher on to his shoulder and began to cover the ground in long, easy strides, anxious to reach the other side of the wood before the storm broke.

The first drops of rain fell as Luke emerged from the wood into the unreal, steely grey dusk. He scanned the sky. He'd been right, there was going to be an almighty storm. As if in agreement with his thoughts a brilliant streak of lightning forked across the sky, illuminating the river, the boats and the solitary figure of a woman standing petrified and alone on the sea wall a little distance ahead. Then it was gone in a crack of thunder that reverberated all around. The woman screamed. Luke began to run.

'Cassie!' he cried as he recognised her. 'Whatyou doin' out here? You'll catch your death. Thass gonna bucket down in a minute.'

'Oh Luke. I'm so glad to see you. I don't care about the rain, but it's the thunder. I'm so afraid of the thunder.' Tears

31

streamed down her face as she ran to him and clung, shivering with fright.

'Quick, then come with me. I know where we can shelter. You'll hev to run, mind, or we shall both be soaked, there's gonna be a rare downpour in a minute. Hitch up your skirts and follow me. Thass already comin' on harder.' He slithered down the bank and led the way across the spongy marsh, dodging the bushes to make as straight a path as he could, heading for the remains of a little thatched lean-to that had once been used for cattle fodder. He stopped now and then to wait for Cassie as she stumbled along behind him in the already blinding rain. Another streak of lightning lit up the rough, hay-strewn floor and as Luke shoved the door to, Cassie flung herself at him, covering her ears with her hands and burying her head in his rough jersey as the thunder rolled all round them.

With one arm still holding her Luke used the other to release the basket of cockles and set them down. Then he gathered her close. 'Thass all right, my pretty,' he soothed as she clung to him. 'We're safe enough in this hut an' it'll keep most of the water out.' He could feel her trembling with fear through the thin stuff of her dress clinging wetly round her, and at first his only thought was to hold her close to protect her, but as she clung to him he became increasingly aware of the soft rounded warmth of her body under the layers of damp petticoat.

Suddenly the battle that raged within him was every bit as fierce as the storm outside. To hold her, to have her cling to him the way he had so often dreamed was almost too much and it took all his will-power to loosen his hold and put her from him. But another flash, so close that it hissed in the torrential rain, accompanied immediately by a crash of thunder that shook the whole marsh sent her into his arms again.

'Hold me, Luke. Don't let me go.' She hardly knew what she

was saying. Everything else was forgotten in her terror of the storm and she clung to him, winding her arms round his neck and burying her face in his shoulder, comforted by his nearness and quite uncaring of the effect this might be having on him. The thunder died away and she lifted up her face, wet with tears and rain. 'Oh, Luke, I'm so glad you're here. I'm so frightened.'

He stroked her hair and mumbled words of comfort. Then, unable to help himself, he bent over the pale oval that was all he could see of her face in the gloom and kissed her. With that kiss the last vestige of his self-control snapped and all the pent-up longing and desire for her was unleashed. Such was his strength and the force of his passion that she had no chance to struggle and when she cried out he only gathered her to him even more closely, sparing neither her nor himself until he was spent.

Afterwards he drew away and looked at where Cassie lay, her face turned from him and her shoulders heaving with great sobs.

He closed his eyes in anguish. 'Oh, Christ, what have I done!' He knelt beside her, his head bowed. 'Cassie, I'm sorry. I never meant to harm you. God knows I wouldn't hurt a hair on your pretty head.' Gentle now, he tried to help her to her feet but she shrugged him off and turned away to straighten her clothing. 'Leave me alone,' she said, her voice dead.

He turned away and put his head in his hands. 'Oh, God, Cassie, can you ever forgive me?' he mumbled. Then, in almost the same breath, 'No, I've no right to even ask that.' He turned back to her. 'I'll stand by you, Cassie,' he said quietly. 'I won't let you down. Whatever happens ... if there should be ...' His voice tailed off. 'I'll stand by you, girl. I promise you that.'

Cassie said nothing. Her thoughts were in turmoil. She had been taken completely unawares by Luke's attack and the force of his passion had both surprised and shocked her. She felt used.

33

Degraded. And yet, a corner of her mind forced her to concede that Luke's act hadn't been entirely unprovoked. She should have predicted the effect she would have on him by clinging to him so shamelessly in her terror. Yes, even if she hadn't actually encouraged him, she had made no effort to stop him. And, knowing Luke as she did, he would have obeyed her.

Suddenly, the emotional impact of all the events of the evening hit her and she staggered to the door. 'I'm going to be sick.'

Luke waited, soberly. Then he said, 'The storm's over now, Cassie. Will you let me take you home?'

She nodded wearily. 'Yes. Take me home.'

Her mother was warming milk at the kitchen range when Cassie got in. She was wearing her best green taffeta dress and there were two spots of colour on her cheeks. That meant Abel Crowther had arrived. For once Cassie was glad of his presence, for it meant her mother would be too preoccupied to notice her sidling across the kitchen and up the stairs.

'And where do you think you've been, my girl? Coming home at this time of night looking like a drowned rat?'

Cassie met her mother's eyes in the overmantel. 'I got caught in the storm. I had to shelter.'

Hannah took the milk off the stove and poured it into two mugs, then handed the saucepan to Lizzie. 'Put that to soak, then take hot water up to the girls' room. And the hip bath. And some mustard,' she added as an afterthought. She turned to Cassie and looked her up and down, taking in the torn sodden dress, the bits of old hay sticking to her hair and her ashen tear-streaked face. Her expression softened. She knew Cassie was petrified of thunderstorms and would often hide in the cupboard under the stairs with a cushion over her head if thunder so much as rumbled in the distance. 'All by yourself, were you?'

'No. I met Luke Turnbull. He ... he looked after me.' Cassie didn't look at her mother but went to the stairs.

Hannah laced the two mugs of milk liberally with whisky. 'I'll get Stella to bring you some of this when she comes up to bed,' was all she said, but her expression was thoughtful as she left the kitchen and went through to the snuggery, empty tonight except for Abel Crowther who, never idle, sat studying ledgers while he waited.

Tom the potman stood behind the long, curved bar that served both the taproom and the saloon. He'd enlisted the help of Isaac Barker tonight. Isaac was a taproom regular who was always willing to help out if things became busy or when Hannah was otherwise engaged. And she was otherwise engaged tonight, Tom thought with a tinge of jealousy. It was always the same when that man Crowther appeared – you'd think he owned the place the way he had the missus running round, always at his beck and call. Tom sometimes wondered if she was a bit partial to the man – she always dressed up smart when she knew he was coming. He sighed. There was no accounting for taste.

He leaned on the bar and looked at the men grouped round the bull ring hanging from the ceiling, tankards in their hands. What a daft way to waste hard-earned money, betting on how many throws it would take to get the ring over the nail on the wall, and a good many with their children running barefoot and hungry.

Mind, a lot of them were celebrating tonight. If they'd been picked to crew one of the racing yachts they were all right for the season, with clothes found and the prospect of a summer spent racing round the coast and as far afield as the Mediterranean if they were lucky. *And* a share in any prize money. No wonder they were all a bit happy.

'Pint o' mild an' hev one yerself.' Bill Jones was already three sheets in the wind. 'Ah, no, I forgot – you're not a drinkin' man, are ye, Tom? Ye hevn't got a wife to nag ye into drownin' yer sorrows, lucky bugger.' He reeled off laughing, into the corner where he'd got a game of dominoes going.

Tom watched him go. He could remember Bill marrying his wife Eileen after he'd got her into trouble. Pretty girl she'd been. Still was, come to that. Kept the children neat and clean, too. Bill hadn't really a lot to complain about and he knew it. He wasn't dependent on fishing in the winter and crewing on the yachts in the summer. He had a decent job with George Turnbull and a regular wage coming in. It was only Friday nights when he got the drink in him – he never came near the place for the rest of the week.

Tom often thought it was a good thing he wasn't a drinking man. The amount he was offered he could roll home drunk to his little shanty at the back of the Falcon every night and never pay for a drop. But he'd signed the pledge years ago and never gone back on it. Not like some, who were rounded up on a Saturday night by the Salvation Army boys and taken to their citadel in Alma Street to sign the pledge, managed to keep sober all day Sunday and were back on the booze before the end of the week, ready to be picked up again on Saturday.

Cassie climbed out of the bath and dried herself; her whole body felt bruised and used. Gratefully she slipped between the sheets that Lizzy had thoughtfully warmed with a hot brick wrapped in flannel. She had thought she would never feel warm again but the hot mustard bath had set her tingling from head to toe. Yet she couldn't sleep. Her mind went over and over the events of the evening: Edward's callous rejection of her, her despair, Luke's appearance and their lovemaking in the hut.

Had that been her own fault? Had she, in the deepest recesses of her mind, seen it as a way out of her dilemma – a means of salvation? Cassie tossed on her pillow. Was is possible? She couldn't believe it was. She didn't love Luke Turnbull. He was about the last person she would choose to marry. Then another thought struck her. Luke had not been gentle. Perhaps his rough treatment followed by the hot mustard bath would rid her of this thing inside her. She put her hand on her stomach. Perhaps when she woke tomorrow she would find it had all been a dreadful nightmare. She shifted her position. Already she was sure she could detect the first signs of a dull ache in the base of her spine. Cassie's spirits lifted and she fell asleep.

She was still asleep when her sister came up to bed. Stella took one look at her and drank the milk herself, enjoying the forbidden taste of whisky in it.

The next morning Cassie woke to discover her optimism unfounded. She was still pregnant.

It was June. The yachts had gone, leaving the river and the village strangely quiet. There had been the usual last-minute flurry of activity as provisions were bought from the local grocers, final adjustments made to sails and rigging, with Ambrose Turner the sailmaker up till all hours trying to get everything done, and riggers and rope-makers rushed off their feet. Then the crews bade a fond farewell to their families before setting off eagerly for an exciting season racing. Now only the men from the shipyards paced the quay and stood on the street corner, together with the few fishermen left behind to tend the oyster beds and fish for skate and plaice outside the estuary. Even the pubs were quieter now that the air of excitement and expectancy had gone and the noise from Harvey's shipyard at one end of the quay and Turnbull's at the other seemed to take on a more leisurely pace because the feverish rush to get everything finished in time was over.

Cassie crept about feeling miserable and ill. *Leander* had gone, taking Edward away, robbing her of the last vestige of hope that he might relent and marry her. Not that she had really expected him to. He didn't really love her, could never have loved her, or he wouldn't have treated her so shamefully. Cassie reminded herself of this over and over again yet a part of her still believed in Edward and looked in vain for his return.

But Luke was still here. And Luke could be the means of her salvation. He need never even know the child wasn't his … Cassie had avoided him since the night on the marsh, but soon she would have to see him, talk to him, answer the question he was certain to ask.

Yet still she hesitated, hoping against hope for some other solution because she didn't love Luke. Marriage to a common ship's joiner was not what she had envisaged. She had hoped to marry someone with a little refinement, who could keep her if not in luxury then in the comfort her mother had taught her to expect. Her hand crept again to her stomach, still flat. Edward had been the perfect answer.

The days went by and Cassie was conscious of her mother watching her all the time, anxious, she knew, for proof that sheltering from the storm with Luke Turnbull would have no repercussions. And Stella, too. Living in such close proximity and sharing a bedroom there was not much that escaped her beady eye. Cassie had managed to hoodwink her over the missed monthlies, but she couldn't hide the fact that she was sick as soon as she stood up every morning.

'What on earth's the matter with you?' Stella asked unsympathetically after being woken for the fourth time by the sound of Cassie retching into the chamber pot.

38

'It ... must ... be ... something I've eaten.' Cassie leaned her head against the side of the bed, exhausted.

'But you haven't eaten anything different from anyone else.' Stella frowned and got up on one elbow. She studied her sister for several minutes. 'Are you better now? Or shall I fetch Mama?'

'No, don't do that!' Cassie looked up in alarm but made no attempt to stand up.

'I'm going to fetch her. It might be something catching and I don't want it.' Stella was out of bed and down the stairs before Cassie could protest.

Hannah came back with her and took one look at Cassie, who was now sitting on the bed with her head in her hands. 'How many times have you missed?' she asked tersely.

'Only once – I think.' Cassie didn't look up as she told the lie.

'Hm. Well you'd better tell Luke you're in the family way. Or does he know already?'

'Luke!' Stella almost screamed the word but neither her mother nor her sister took any notice.

'No. He doesn't know. Not yet.'

'The night of the storm, was it?'

Cassie nodded, still not looking at her mother, sick at the deception that had already begun.

'I thought as much.' Hannah pursed her lips. She stood silent for a moment, looking out of the window, a thoughtful expression on her face. Then she laid her hand briefly on Cassie's shoulder. 'Well, it's no use crying over spilt milk,' she said, her voice brisk. 'What's done is done and can't be undone. I'd have looked for better than Luke Turnbull for you but at least he's a decent man and there'll be no scandal. He'll marry you and no one will be any the wiser. You'd better tell him – today. There's no time to be lost.' She went to the door. 'Now, pull yourself together and get dressed. There's work to be done.' She went back down the stairs.

Immediately Stella turned on her sister. 'Luke! You're going to have Luke's baby! You did it to spite me, you cat!' Tears of fury and frustration were pouring down her cheeks. 'You knew I wanted him so you trapped him into marrying you. Oh, I hate you, Cassie Jordan. I hate you.' She buried her face in the pillow and sobbed.

Cassie watched her, something approaching a smile hovering round her lips although it held no vestige of mirth. Everyone was putting their own interpretation on the situation and none of them was right. It was just as well. She gave a great sigh and began to put on her clothes.

She met Luke on his way home from work and they walked along the quay together. 'I'm sorry, Cassie, truly I am,' he told her. 'But don't worry, we'll get wed as soon as ever that can be arranged. I told you I'd stand by you an' I will.' He smiled down at her. 'It's no hardship to me, girl. I've loved you as long as I can remember. You know that. I jest wish ... well, you know what I mean.'

She wished she could say the same. But having a bit of fun and a lark about along the wall with Luke Turnbull was one thing, marrying him was quite another. Even now, as she walked beside him, the smell of him – of sweat mingled with wood shavings, varnish, paint and other shipyard smells – made her delicate stomach turn.

She gave him a wintry smile. 'You're a good man, Luke.' Too good to have another man's child foisted on you, the thought came unbidden as she wallowed in self-pity. She tried to stifle the thought because what alternative was there? Fate had provided a totally unexpected solution to her dilemma and it was up to her to make the best of it. 'Mama says we can live at the

Falcon till we find somewhere of our own,' she said, trying to make her voice cheerful.

'No! I don't want ...' Luke began, but his voice died away. Where else could they go? He had no money to provide anything better. In fact, he had no money to provide anything at all. Most of his money went to his mother to help feed the little ones. 'Thass very kind of 'er,' he mumbled.

He kicked a stone into the water, furious with himself at the way things had turned out. He'd never meant to force himself on Cassie like that; he'd aimed to work hard and better himself until she would have been proud to be asked to be his wife. Only by the time he'd done that she'd have married someone else, he was realistic enough to realise that. He took her hand and looked at it small and white, lying in his, roughened and dirty from his day's work at the yard. 'I never meant it to be like this, Cassie, an' I'm sorry thass how it's got to be,' he said sombrely. 'But I'll do the best I can for you, girl. I'll make it up to you. I promise you that.'

Chapter Four

The wedding was held on the fifteenth of July, three days after Cassie's twentieth birthday. It was as quiet as any event could be that was attended by Alf Turnbull and his large family, although Alf did manage to stay sober for the ceremony in church in the expectation that beer would flow freely and free at the Falcon later. Hannah had prepared the big meeting room upstairs that was used for auctions and public meetings of all kinds, spreading the long table with a snowy cloth and piling it with hams, pork pies, roast chicken and oysters, as well as all manner of jellies and trifles. Whatever her private feelings, she was determined that nobody should be able to say she hadn't done her eldest daughter proud, even if she was only marrying Luke Turnbull.

Nineteen people sat round the table; it would have been twenty but Luke's brother William, who was twenty, had gone yachting as a hand on the *Vanessa*. Cassie, in a cream lace gown that almost matched the colour of her face, sat with Luke at the head, with Uncle George, who had given Cassie away, beside her and Stella, resplendent in pale pink satin, between Luke and the Rector, the Reverend Bates. Beyond him sat Hannah in her best blue silk and a hat with purple ostrich feathers, although she was so busy making sure everything went smoothly that she hardly sat down at all. Maisie, wearing green and with a hat like a harvest festival, sat on the other side of George with their son Martin beside her while the rest of the table was taken up with Alf and Liddy and their family. There was Jim who worked at Mr Browne's ropeworks, Alice who was about to go into service at Dr Squire's house and twelve year old Jinny, who could now take Alice's place in keeping the little ones in order. The little ones consisted of Johnny – although at ten he didn't regard himself as little – Lucy, Emma and Billy, who all wore new clothes and boots provided, everyone suspected although nothing was said, by Uncle George. It was not often the whole of the Turnbull family sat down together and the children's eyes were like saucers at the sight of so much food. Seated next to Alf so that he could keep him in order was Tom Bartlett the potman, clad in his best Sunday suit and clearly proud to be included in the celebrations.

After everyone had eaten their fill and a bit more, George, as the nearest male relative, rose to his feet to propose a toast to the happy couple – although it had to be said that Cassie didn't look particularly happy. However, nobody took any notice of that – brides were supposed to be apprehensive as their wedding night drew near.

'Well, my dears,' he began, 'I'm very happy to be here today to see you wedded. My nephew wedded to my wife's niece. What could be better? It means we only have to provide one wedding present instead of two!'

Everybody laughed, as they were meant to. They all knew George was not a mean man.

'You ain't given 'em nothin' yet, far as I can see,' Alf shouted from the other end of the table. He'd drunk enough to make him genially belligerent. Soon he would turn nasty, if someone didn't stop him.

'Quiet, Alf. You shouldn't say such things.' Liddy, done up in her best clothes of funereal black, because she attended more funerals than weddings, shifted the baby on to her other arm and looked at her husband in alarm.

'Well, thass true, ain't it? 'E ain't given 'em a brass farthin', hev 'e?' Alf replied.

'No, Alf, you're right. I ain't. But that ain't to say I'm not goin' to, is it?' George beamed round at the assembled company.

Maisie looked up at her husband, her nose a little red from the sherry Hannah had provided. She didn't know what George had in mind. Surely the pair of blankets she'd given Cassie and Luke were adequate as a present. She tugged at his sleeve. 'The blankets. We gave 'em blankets,' she whispered.

He winked down at her and felt in his pocket. 'I know about the blankets,' he nodded, 'but I've got a little suthin' else for 'em.' He turned to Luke, a broad smile on his face. 'Here y'are, Luke me boy,' he said, handing him a key, 'thass the key to your own house. Well,' he corrected himself, 'thass more of a cottage really and that don't belong to you, that belong to me 'cause I've bought it, but I'm lettin' you and Cassie live there rent free for as long as you want. How about that for a weddin' present?'

Luke got to his feet. 'Uncle George . . .' he bit his lip, 'thank you.' He looked at the key in his hand as if he couldn't believe it. Hannah had told them they could have a room at the Falcon and he'd had to agree because they'd nowhere else to go but he hadn't been happy about it. He could never make it up to Cassie properly for what he'd done with her mother there all the time. And Stella. He didn't understand Stella, making such a fuss, crying and carrying on when she was told about the wedding. And look at her now, sitting there in her pink bridesmaid's dress with a look on her face that would turn cream sour. He couldn't understand it at all. It wasn't as if he'd ever shown any interest in her, everybody knew it had always been Cassie for him. But now he wouldn't have to worry about Stella and her tantrums. A great wave of relief washed over him and he beamed with delight. 'Thank you, Uncle George. Thank you on behalf of Cassie and me,' he said again. He couldn't trust himself to say more.

'You haven't asked Uncle George where the cottage is, Luke.' Cassie tugged his sleeve, a trace of impatience in her voice.

George heard and leaned towards them. 'Thass in The \ Folley. Thass one o' my little cottages near the Yard.' He looked round the table. 'So there'll be no excuse for him bein' late for work of a mornin',' he added with a grin.

Cassie's heart sank. The cottages in The Folley were dark and pokey and the people who lived there were some of the roughest in the village. It was about the last place she would have chosen if she'd been given the choice. But choice was not very evident in her life these days so it was up to her to make the best of whatever came her way. She smiled at Uncle George. 'You're very good to us, Uncle George. I . . . I don't know how to thank you. We didn't expect to have a place of our own so soon, did we, Luke?'

'No, that we didn't,' Luke beamed. He still couldn't believe his luck.

'Well . . . ' Uncle George hooked his thumbs in the armholes of his waistcoat and threw out his not inconsiderable chest, thoroughly enjoying himself. 'Under the circumstances . . . ' He stopped at a nudge from Maisie although they all knew why the wedding had been a bit rushed, even though nothing had been said openly. 'Well,' he said again, 'you jest look after that great fella there. Give 'im plenty o' suet duff, keep 'is strength

45

up so 'e can work hard for 'is old uncle, thass all I ask. 'Cept . . . come an' give your old uncle a kiss, gal. You look as pretty as a picture an' no mistake, an' I'm always partial to kissin' a pretty gal.' He winked at the assembled company.

Cassie got up and gave him a hug and kissed his whiskery cheek. 'I'll look after Luke, don't worry, Uncle,' she said. And she meant it. It was the least she could do for him.

Cassie and Luke stayed at the Falcon for a week while the little cottage in The Folley was being made habitable. Luke's brother Jim and cousin Martin came in the evenings to help him put on a coat of fresh brown paint – supplied by Uncle George – and Cassie went there every day to scrub and clean, helped by young Jinny when she could be spared from looking after the little ones at home. Cassie worked with a will, although she loathed the place, with its beaten earth floor and peeling wallpaper that no amount of flour paste would stick back on to the damp walls. But she knew that it was little short of paradise to Luke. He had been used to eleven of them living in a place not much bigger, with the little ones sleeping under the kitchen table and he and two of his brothers going next door for a bed. But she was determined to make it clean and comfortable and so she scrubbed and swept until the whole place sparkled – insofar as this was possible – with cleanliness.

They had managed to buy a bed from Mrs Roper's secondhand emporium on Anchor Hill and Aunt Maisie had given them a spindly whatnot for which she declared she had no further use. Hannah was more practical in giving them a chest of drawers that they had difficulty in getting up the stairs. By going into work an hour early each morning, Luke had made them a kitchen table and he intended to make stools as well. Till then they would have to use a beer barrel sawn in half and upended. It was not at all what Cassie had been used to, nor what she'd expected her first home to be like. And the fact that their cottage was the cleanest, smartest and best-furnished said little for the rest of the houses in the squalid row.

Nevertheless, she was glad when the cottage was ready and they could move in because that first week had not been easy. Hannah had allotted them the little room at the front of the house overlooking the High Street in return for Luke helping Tom in the bar in the evening and Cassie dreaded every night. And not only because this was the room, the very bed, that Edward had slept in, but also because it seemed the marriage was a fiasco.

Luke was worried, too. He didn't know whether it was the fact that he was up and at work by five every morning and working in the bar till eleven every night that made him too tired for lovemaking, or whether it was the memory of how he had taken Cassie on the night of the storm and his deep sense of guilt that rendered him incapable – he just couldn't tell. He had never forgotten standing beside Cassie and listening to the introduction to the marriage service, where it had talked about men behaving like brute beasts of the field'. It had struck home. That was exactly how he had behaved and he could never forget it, nor forgive himself.

Partly, though, he was inhibited by the fact that he was lying under the same roof as Hannah Jordan, his stern, disapproving mother-in-law, who was putting such a brave face on what she plainly considered was a disaster, although she never said as much.

They moved into the cottage on the Sunday, after going to church and eating their Sunday dinner with Hannah. Cassie and Stella went to church on Sundays but Hannah never did. Nobody knew why, since she insisted on Grace before meals and always said her prayers at night. Going to church was a new experience for Luke and he took his place awkwardly beside Cassie. Stella kept to the far end of the pew. Since their marriage she had hardly spoken to either Luke or Cassie, maintaining a frozen silence or answering in monosyllables when speech was unavoidable. Disdaining walking with them, she had followed them to church, nearly making herself late in the process. Luke enjoyed the service, for he liked the hymns and found he could keep the tune and sing louder than anyone else but he fell asleep and had to be prodded awake during the sermon. On his knees during the prayers he prayed fervently that he might make Cassie a 'good husband', hoping the Good Lord would understand exactly what he meant.

George and Maisie were in their family pew with Martin, who was wearing the smart new suit he'd had made for the wedding. Martin was the same age as Luke but whereas Luke was all sinewy muscle Martin was inclined to be on the pale and flabby side. But he was clever. Everyone knew that Martin had a good head on his shoulders and that George was lucky to have him in the business.

'Movin' in today then, are you?' Uncle George said, as they all met up in the churchyard afterwards. He beamed at them both.

'That's right, Uncle George. After we've had our dinner with Mama,' Cassie replied, trying to keep the apprehension out of her voice.

'Do you want any help with moving things, Luke?' Martin asked helpfully.

'No, thass all right, Marty. Thass mostly done now. But thankee for all you've done. Helping me with the painting, and that.' Luke smiled at his cousin. 'I've only to shift Cassie's box now and I've borried a hand-cart for that.'

'I think they're very lucky. Mama gave them the chest of

drawers out of my bedroom,' Stella said waspishly. 'Now I haven't got anywhere to put my things till she gets me another one.'

Aunt Maisie patted her arm. 'I don't suppose you'll hev to wait all that long, dearie. Hannah had plenty of furniture when she left West Street. I don't know what she did with it all. Surely she didn't get rid of ...'

'Come on, Maisie me dear, time we was gettin' home for our dinner. I'm gettin' a bit peckish.' George took his wife's arm firmly and marched her up the churchyard, breaking off the conversation. To his mind Maisie was a bit too ready to rake up the past at every opportunity. Sometimes it was better to let sleeping dogs lie.

Martin followed. 'Don't forget. If you want any help ...' he called over his shoulder.

Luke raised his hand. 'Thanks, Marty. I won't forget.' He turned and offered his arm to his wife while her sister trailed sulkily after them. There had been no offers of help from *her*.

After dinner Luke piled Cassie's box of possessions on to the hand-cart and trundled it down to the cottage in The Folley. Tom and Hannah waved them goodbye – Stella was nowhere to be seen – and if Cassie hadn't been so preoccupied with making sure nothing fell off she would have seen the tears glinting in her mother's eyes. Before they left Tom gave Cassie a little china bowl. 'Thass jest a little suthin' I picked up abroad in me sea-farin' days,' he said as he gave it to her. 'I ain't got much use for it.' He didn't tell her that it was his most cherished possession.

'Thank you, Tom. I shall treasure it.' She turned away quickly and bit her lip against the sudden lump in her throat and she kept it in her hand now as she walked beside her husband to their new home.

'Thass a nice spot,' Luke said, when they arrived. 'Right

near the river, so's you can look out an' see all the boats coming in an' out.'

'Yes. We're lucky it's so near the river,' Cassie agreed, speaking just a shade too quickly in her determination to make the best of things.

She busied herself putting everything away while Luke wrestled with the tiny kitchen range. It didn't take her long and when she had finished she went over to the window and looked out at the river, at full tide and sparkling in the sunlight. Luke was right. It was a nice spot. She'd always enjoyed walking by the river. Now she was living beside it. What more could she ask?

Soon the kettle was boiling on the fire Luke had lit so she made a pot of tea. They sat on the upturned barrel halves on opposite sides of the fire with their feet on a rag rug and the tea cups on the table between them and looked at each other.

Luke took a deep breath and bowed his head. 'I'm sorry, Cassie. I'm truly sorry I've brought you to this. Thass not what I had in mind. Not what I had in mind at all. I've always wanted to marry you, you know that. But I was goin' to save up an' buy you a ruby ring an' do everything proper. I never meant . . .' He bowed his head and his voice broke. 'God knows I never meant to do you harm.' He looked up again. 'But I'll make it up to you. I swear I'll make it up to you. Only say you'll forgive me for what I did to you that night.'

Cassie picked up her cup and drank some of her tea slowly, staring into the fire. Forgive him? What right had she to withhold her forgiveness? God knew her sin against him was the greater. But he must never know that. She looked at him steadily, her eyes glistening with tears. 'We're married, Luke, and there's an end of it. Or a beginning. What's done is done and past and there's no use harping on it.' She shook her head. 'I can't say I love you, Luke, but I'm your wife now, so I'll stand by you and do the best I can for you. I'll keep your house and I'll bear your children.' She leaned forward and put her hand on his arm. 'Will that do for you, Luke?'

He covered her hand with his. 'An' thass more'n I deserve, Cassie, my girl. I thank you for it.'

That night he took her to himself, clumsily but as tenderly as he knew how. Afterwards as he lay gently snoring beside her she stared up into the darkness. He's my husband, she told herself. This is my life now. This is how it will always be. But as she remembered Edward and the passion they had shared she wept.

Each day when Luke had gone to work at the yacht yard nearby Cassie cleaned up the cottage. It didn't take long, because there wasn't much in it and she had always been used to working quickly and methodically, the way her mother had taught her. One thing for which she was grateful was that the cottage was situated on the end of the row, although it meant she had further to go to the privy. The two far end cottages had families swarming with ragged children and brawling adults, but an elderly couple lived next door to Luke and Cassie – Barny Benson, too old now to go fishing, and his wife, who was bedridden by some unspecified illness that Cassie suspected was laziness. Barny was a sprightly octogenarian, always cheerful and ready for a chat. Sometimes he was the only person Cassie spoke to all day.

After a week she could stand it no longer. She was bored with so little to do after the busy life she had led at the Falcon so as soon as she had tidied the cottage she went home, as she still thought of it.

'What do you want?' Stella asked rudely, when she walked in.

'I thought Mama might be glad of an extra pair of hands,' Cassie replied coolly.

51

'Haven't you got enough to do, looking after your *husband*?' Stella put heavy emphasis on the last word.

Hannah swept in. 'That's quite enough of that, my girl,' she reprimanded Stella before turning to Cassie. 'Come to lend a hand, have you, Cassie?'

'Yes, but I needn't stay if I'm not welcome.' Cassie looked at Stella as she spoke.

'Why can't she stay in her own house,' Stella spat back, careful not to address her directly. 'We're managing perfectly well.'

'Only because I'm doing twice as much. I haven't noticed you putting yourself out, my girl. Now, go on up and get the meeting room ready. The Vestry's meeting here tonight and you know the Rector likes everything just so.'

Stella flounced off and Hannah pushed a strand of hair back under her cap. 'If I didn't keep on at her she'd never lift a finger,' she said grimly. Then she sighed and for a moment her shoulders sagged. 'But there, if things had worked out the way they should have there'd have been no need for either of you to get your hands soiled. But it's no good dwelling on what might have been. That's all in the past now.' She gave Cassie what passed as a smile. 'Life doesn't always work out the way we expect it to, does it?'

Cassie shot her mother a look. Did she know? But clearly Hannah's thoughts were still in the past and it was with an obvious effort that she dragged her mind back to the present. 'I'm glad you've come, my girl. You've a good light hand with pastry and I want some plum pies made.'

Cassie smiled at her mother and rolled up her sleeves without a word of complaint. Even if her first task was the one she had always loathed and even if Stella resented her coming, it was good to be home.

She stayed at the Falcon until after the evening meal had

been served. Then she went back to her new home in The Folley, taking a plate of food for Luke with her. It was still not quite cold when he arrived home an hour later and he ate it with relish.

'That was a rare tasty meat pudden Cassie, girl. How did you manage that?' he asked, looking at the empty kitchen range.

'I've been home, helping Mama. I brought it back with me.' She busied herself clearing the table, not looking at him.

'This is your home now, Cassie,' he chided gently. 'Don't you find enough to occupy you here?'

'No . . .' she hesitated. If she said the cottage was too small to keep her occupied he would think she was complaining. 'Mama is always glad of a helping hand,' she said apologetically.

He shook his head, disappointed. 'I expect you'll find plenty to do here when the babby comes.'

Cassie didn't reply. She preferred not to think that far ahead.

She went to the Falcon every day after that even though she knew Luke didn't really like the idea. At the end of the week she was surprised when her mother went to the dresser and took some money out of a tin. 'Here you are, Cassie. This is for you.'

Cassie looked at the coins lying on the table. 'Why are you giving me that, Mama?'

'It's your wages,' Hannah said. 'You don't live here now, so it's not a case of working for your keep. An honest day's work is worth an honest day's pay and I'm glad of your help. After all, if you didn't come I should have to think about taking on another girl. I shall give you the same every week while you continue to come.' She began whisking eggs in a basin.

Cassie picked up the coins and looked at them. She'd never been bothered about money. There was always food on the table and Hannah had always been generous in buying new clothes because she liked her daughters to be well-dressed. So apart from a few coppers for ribbons she'd never felt she needed much. Thank you, Mama, but I didn't come to be paid. And you always feed me and give me Luke's meal to take home.'

'I know you didn't come to be paid.' Hannah cut her short. 'But you work hard so it's no more than your due, and what bit of food you take is never missed. Anyway,' she added shrewdly, 'Luke won't be so likely to grudge you coming if you take home a copper.'

Cassie went back to her cottage. It had never occurred to her that the work she did was worth being paid for. After all, it was no more than she'd always done. In truth, she'd only gone back to the Falcon because she had nowhere else to go; because it was still more her home than the cottage in The Folley: the cottage that was so small that it was swept and dusted in ten minutes. And she didn't really get on with the other people in the row, with their hordes of squalling brats and the drunken fights that took place every night. She sometimes wondered how Barny Benson stuck it all the time, day in, day out, but realised that he had no choice. He had nowhere else to go.

She didn't tell Luke this – not that he was often at home. All through the summer he worked long hours for his uncle and then stayed on to make items for the cottage – the hanging cupboard to keep the food out of the way of the rats, the stools to set round the table and an armchair that was surprisingly comfortable when she had made cushions for it. He never rested, and when he eventually came home it was only to fall asleep over the meal she had brought home for him.

Cassie never complained, either to Luke or to anyone else. She knew she had sinned and she accepted that sins had to be paid for. This was a fact of life. So she kept the cottage clean and tried hard to make it comfortable, never admitting even to herself that whatever she did could not make it feel like home.

And often, as she waited for Luke to come back she would pause from the gown or petticoat she was stitching for the coming baby to lay her hand over the growing child, the cause of all her troubles. Yet she didn't hate it, didn't feel anything much for it except disbelief that it could have happened, a disbelief that still remained even as the child began to move and her body swelled. She felt no thrill of anticipation as she stitched the tiny garments, not even when Hannah presented her with a parcel of yellowing, delicately-embroidered baby clothes.

'These were in a trunk in the attic. I had them for you and Stella. You might find something there that's useful. I kept them ... Reuben always wanted a son ... ' Hannah bit her lip and turned away, then she sniffed and added in her brisk way, 'I daresay they're a bit old-fashioned but they're all good quality.'

Cassie took the parcel and unwrapped the lace-trimmed gowns and petticoats, the embroidered jackets and bonnets, the tiny vests and binders, all made of the very best materials, silks and satins and fine lawns, and the crocheted shawl of wool as soft as swansdown.

'Oh, they're beautiful, Mama. Thank you.' She kissed her mother with gratitude although she couldn't help feeling that these things would have little place in The Folley.

Sometimes she felt she didn't understand her mother at all. Hannah had always been so adamant in warning both girls of the consequences of what she euphemistically termed 'getting into trouble', yet she had uttered no word of reproach when she discovered Cassie's condition but had simply made speedy preparations for the wedding. The only word of criticism she had spoken was to say ruefully, 'I should have thought you might have set your sights a bit higher than Luke Turnbull, my girl. But what's done is done and can't be undone.'

Cassie made no reply to that. How could she have told her

mother that she had indeed set her sights higher, but fate – and Edward Price-Carpenter – had decreed otherwise. Although, as the memory of that last evening blurred it became distorted in her mind; she almost forgot Edward's cruel gesture in suggesting that she get rid of the child in the rosy remembrance of him saying he loved her. And when September came she couldn't help wondering how the preparations for his wedding were going. Was he already married – on his honeymoon, perhaps? She shied away from that thought. She pictured Felicity, the woman he was marrying not from love but from duty, as some horsy-face creature with little to commend her but her dowry. She sighed. Poor Edward. He was as trapped as she was. If only things could have been different. If only ... But it was no use dwelling on that now. It was too late. Felicity was Edward's wife and Luke was her husband.

'Look, Cassie. Look what I've made.' It was ten o'clock one evening in late September and Luke came in at the door looking grey with fatigue. 'Light the lamp so you can see it proper, dear. Why are you settin' here in the dark?'

Cassie got up and lit the lamp. 'I hadn't realised it was so dark in here,' she said. 'I've been watching the boats come up the river. The first of the yachts has just come back. I think it's the *Christobel,* but it's too dark to see properly.'

'Yes, well, it's September so they will be comin' back, won't they? An' they'll bring plenty of work for us at the yard, too, I reckon.' Luke was kneeling on the rag rug and unwrapping the sacking from the bundle he'd brought home with him as he spoke. 'There. What do you think of that! I thought it was about time I made something for our babby.' He looked up at Cassie, eager for her approval.

Cassie got down on her knees beside him to examine the oak cradle he had made. Like everything else Luke did it was the work of a real craftsman, and on the side he had carved a boat, a racing yacht with sails billowing and a sleek, stream-lined hull. 'He might be a girl,' she said, smiling at him through unexpected tears.

'Well, thass nothin' to cry about, Cassie girl.' He smiled and put his arm round her. 'I daresay there'll be other babbies. An' one of 'em's bound to be a boy.' He looked at her anxiously. 'But do you like it? Will it do?'

'Oh, Luke, it's beautiful.' Her fingers traced the carved boat and suddenly, unexpectedly, she felt a chill right through to her soul. It was as if an icy warning finger had been laid on her heart. She stood up quickly, suppressing the shiver that ran through her. 'You must be starving. I'll get your stew – I've been keeping it warm for you between hot bricks.'

Chapter Five

The winter didn't really start until after the Christmas of 1868. Until then the weather was almost unseasonably mild and Luke didn't have to lose a single day's work.

On Christmas Day Cassie and Luke went to church and then on to the Falcon Inn for their Christmas dinner. Tom was there even though the bar wasn't open; Hannah had insisted that he shouldn't spend the day alone in his little cottage at the back of the Falcon and when he protested they compromised and he agreed to come for his dinner but then he was going home.

At last Stella had relented and was becoming more kindly disposed towards Cassie and Luke. This was largely because she was walking out with young John Jameson. John had been mate aboard the *Genesta* during the yachting season, and although he was happy to go fishing on his father's smack in the winter he made no secret of the fact that he was ambitious, an ambition quite lost on Stella, who asked for nothing more than a nice home and nice children. John was there at the Falcon and Cassie had to admit that they made quite a handsome pair, John with his dark, slightly rakish good looks and Stella, plumply pretty now that she had lost her disagreeable expression.

'You're getting very fat,' Stella whispered as she and Cassie took the plates through from the kitchen. 'If you're telling people it's not supposed to be due till March ... Aren't you afraid they'll guess?'

I'll say it's a big baby.'

Stella giggled. 'Or twins.'

Cassie made a face. 'I hope not!' But her expression was thoughtful as she went back into the dining room. However carefully she dressed there was no concealing that her pregnancy was further advanced than she admitted.

After dinner, Cassie and Luke went to visit his family. They were all there, even William the next eldest, sitting crowded round the scrubbed table because there was nowhere else to sit in the little room. William had had a good season racing and had come home with prize money, more money than he had ever seen in his life before. The Turnbulls were having their best Christmas ever, thanks to him, with turkey and plum pudding instead of the oysters and pap that was their usual fare.

Alf was sitting at the head of the table. He was reasonably sober since the pubs didn't open on Christmas Day, although he had been drinking his own home-made beer – not that even he could drink much of that, it was so unpalatable. But drunk or sober he was still belligerent.

'Good God, look who's 'ere,' he said, as Cassie and Luke walked in. 'I s'pose you saw young Jim come staggerin' home with the turkey from the baker's oven an' thought you'd come an' git your share, did you?'

'No, Dad, we've had our fill of dinner, thank you. We've just dropped in to wish you all a Merry Christmas,' Luke said pleasantly.

'Come an' sit down, Cassie,' Liddy said. 'Lucy, git off that stool an' let Cassie sit down.'

'Yes, she look as if she's got more'n 'er fill o' dinner there,' Alf said rudely.

Cassie's face darkened and Luke shot a warning glance at his father but Liddy laid a hand on her arm. 'Don't take no notice,' she said softly. ''E's bad-tempered 'cause the pubs are shut an' 'e can't get 'is beer. An' if they were open 'e'd be bad-tempered 'cause he'd drunk too much, so either way that don't make no difference.' She smiled at Cassie. 'Ain't got long to go now, hev you?'

'End of February, but I'm saying March,' Cassie said, in a low voice.

'I doubt you'll go even that long.' Liddy looked at her with practised eyes.

Luke had made every one of his family a present in wood. To his mother he gave a teapot-stand decorated with pokerwork that she declared was so pretty it was too good to stand the teapot on and she would hang it on the wall; the younger girls all had little wooden dolls and the boys had pull-along railway engines, tiny editions of the ones that snorted into the railway station from Colchester. Alice was too big for dolls now that she was in service so her present was a pokerwork trinket box while the older boys and Alf were all given tobacco boxes.

As Cassie watched her husband distributing his gifts she couldn't decide who was experiencing the most pleasure, Luke in giving or his family in receiving the gifts. Her heart softened towards him. He was a good man, there was no denying that. But he wasn't Edward.

'Thass nice to think you ain't completely forgot your family now you've got yerself married to Miss High an' Mighty, Luke boy,' said Alf, maudlin over his tobacco box.

'Thass enough o' that talk, Alf,' Liddy said ineffectually.

'Well, thass true.' Alf looked into his empty beer mug and

pushed it away in disgust. 'Who do they think they are, them Jordans? Puttin' on their airs an' graces. Reuben Jordan weren't nobody. 'E used to run round with the arse outa 'is britches same as the rest of us. Jest 'cause 'e worked 'is way up to be captain o' that yacht.' His shoulders began to heave with silent laughter. 'An' then the bugger sank an' 'e got hisself drownded, so that didn't do 'im much good in the finish, did it? Quite a come-down for Miss Hannah Oakley, who thought she'd done so well for 'erself, marryin' a yacht captain. Mind you, she's got 'erself nicely set up at the Falcon ...'

Cassie got to her feet. She could stand Alf s rudeness no longer. 'It's time we were going, Luke,' she said tersely. 'I didn't come here to have my family insulted.'

'Oh, hoity, toity, Miss.' Alf was enjoying the fact that he had annoyed her. He liked nothing better than a good row.

'Thass Christmas, Dad. Leave it be,' William said warningly.

'All the same, Cassie's right. Thass time we were goin'.' Luke was red with embarrassment. He hadn't known whether to keep quiet for his mother's sake or quarrel with his father for Cassie's. He kissed his mother briefly and taking Cassie's arm hustled her out of the door, calling 'A Merry Christmas to you all' over his shoulder as they went.

'I'm sorry, Cassie girl,' he said as they went back to their home in The Folley. 'I don't know when my father is worst, when 'e's drunk or when 'e's sober.'

But Cassie was not to be placated. 'He was very rude, Luke. And I'm sure I don't know what he meant about my mother and father.'

'No, dear, neither do I. And I don't s'pose he does, if the truth be told, so don't you worry your head about it.'

'No, I shan't worry my head about it. But I shan't go there again, although I like your mother.'

They got home and Luke lit the fire that he had cleaned out and laid before they went to church earlier in the day. When it was crackling well alight he said, 'Now I'll give you *your* present, dear.'

'And I'll give your yours.' Cassie lumbered up the narrow stairs and came down with the jersey she had knitted during the long summer evenings which she had spent alone, waiting for Luke to come home from work. She had bought the wool with the wages her mother had paid her, because she didn't think it was fair to buy Luke's Christmas present with money he had earned himself. Ever since their marriage Luke had turned most of his money over to her each week, only keeping enough back for a plug of tobacco and to pay his uncle for the timber he needed for the things he made after hours. Although Cassie had never before had any dealings with money she found she could manage quite well and had been able to buy several things to brighten up the little cottage; material that matched the cushions in the armchair to make a valance to drape round the the mantelpiece; a picture of the Queen to hang on the wall and a clock with brass weights to hang beside it. The money Hannah paid her had helped to buy these things but even so she had quite a little store of silver – put by, as she told herself, for a rainy day – but in reality in the forlorn hope that she would somehow manage to save enough so that they could move to a better house.

Luke was overjoyed with his gift and insisted on putting it on and parading in it before he gave Cassie her present. This was a necklace. A most unusual necklace of highly-polished wooden shapes, carefully graded and selected for the colour and the grain of the wood and threaded on to fine wire. 'It's beautiful, Luke,' she said as she held it in her hands. 'It must have taken you hours and hours to make.' She looked down at it. It *was* beautiful but in a way it symbolised her life; wood where there might have been diamonds. She stifled the thought almost, but not quite, before it had formed.

He leaned forward and kissed her as he fastened it round her neck. 'It was a labour of love,' he said simply.

She wished she could say the same of the jersey she had made.

If the weather had been mild before Christmas it made up for it afterwards. Snow fell on Boxing Day and stayed until the last week in January, when it rained for four days and nights without stopping, melting the snow and turning the whole village into a quagmire. With the rain came gale-force nor'easterly winds.

Luke stood looking out of the window. He couldn't go to work. George had been forced to close the yard because all hands had been brought inside the sheds to work during the snow and now this was all done and most of the work was out in the open air. But nothing could be done in such torrential rain.

'Families'll starve if this goes on an' men can't work,' he said gloomily. 'It'll be a short week for us this week, too, Cassie. We managed to keep the men workin' through the snow, but this week . . . ' He shook his head. 'You make a mark on a piece o' timber an' before you can take a saw to it the rain's washed the mark away.'

Cassie went and stood beside him, watching the relentless rain, the scene made even more bleak by the fact that the tide was out, giving the whole landscape a forlorn depressed look. 'You don't need to worry about us, Luke. I've managed to put a bit by from what I'd been earning till the snow came. Even if you can't work we shan't starve.'

He looked at her in surprise. 'Then we're luckier than most, Cassie. Things are gonna be bad for some poor hearts, because there's no tellin' how long this'll go on for. The yard's awash and so will everywhere else be if the wind stays in this quarter. I don't like it. And with the tides at springs, too.'

Cassie frowned. 'I've never really understood the tides, Luke,' she said, 'even though I've lived here all my life. Oh, I know they go in and out twice a day. But where do they go? What happens to the water when the tide goes out? Does the water all slop from one side of the world to the other and back?'

'No, Cassie, my girl, thass not what happens.' Luke roared with laughter. 'Thass all to do with the pull of the moon and the sun. They both hev a pull on the water.' He made his fist into a ball. 'Now, say thass the earth. When the sun and the moon are on the same side of the earth, like this,' he used two fingers of his other hand to demonstrate, 'thass obvious that with 'em both pullin' in the same direction the pull is stronger, so the tides come up higher and go down lower – thass at springs. Then, when the sun an' moon are pullin' in opposite directions,' he moved his fingers, 'the pull will be weaker because it's comin' from different directions. So the tides are smaller an' don't go down so low an' thass neaps. An' there are two spring tides an' two neaps every month.'

Cassie looked at him thoughtfully. 'You're very clever over some things, Luke, aren't you?'

He returned her gaze. 'Not clever enough, Cassie,' he said seriously. 'Not clever enough to make you ...' He bit his lip and said no more.

She went and sat by the fire, clasping her hands over her swollen belly. She knew what he had been going to say and she felt sorry for him. Yet she tried hard to make him a good wife, to forget Edward, to forget that it was Edward's child she carried. Maybe when the baby was born things would be different ...

Before they went to bed at ten o'clock Luke put the rag rug up against the door.

'Why are you doing that?' Cassie asked.

''Cause I reckon there's gonna be a rare high tide tonight.' He stood back and looked at what he'd done. 'I shouldn't be a bit surprised if the water comes right across The Folley. I don't envy the poor creatures livin' in Smuggler's Row, there. I reckon their downstairs rooms'll be awash before mornin'.'

Smuggler's Row was a row of old cottages standing adjacent to, and between The Folley and the river.

'It won't come this far, we shan't get flooded, shall we, Luke?' Cassie asked anxiously.

'I shouldn't think so, but we'll put as much as we can upstairs, just in case.' He smiled at her. 'You go to bed, dear, I'll see to everything.'

Cassie struggled up the stairs. She tried to conceal her advanced pregnancy as much as she could, but there was no hiding the fact that it made her awkward and ungainly as well as very tired. She eased herself on to the bed. She could hear Luke moving about downstairs and before long he carried both the stools and the armchair upstairs.

'I can't fetch the table up the stairs, they're too narrow,' he said as he clambered into bed beside her.

'But did you bring the clock? And the picture of the Queen?'

'Lawks, girl, even if the water does come in thass not likely to reach halfway up the wall.'

'All the same ...'

'All right. I'll go an' fetch 'em, jest to please you.' He got out of bed again. 'Jest hark at that wind. I don't like the sound of it. But thass stopped rainin' now, thank the Lord.'

'Oh, Luke, you don't really think the tide'll come up into the house, do you?' she asked, when once again he climbed into bed beside her.

'No, but thass always as well to be prepared.' He patted her hand as it lay beside him in the bed. 'Anyway, if it does come in you'll be safe enough up here. Thass not likely to come up this far.'

Cassie lay rigid beside her husband. Suddenly she was angry. Angry at the way fate had fooled her. Hadn't she paid enough for her mistakes? Hadn't she tried to make amends? Even though she didn't love him, hadn't she done everything she could to be a good wife to Luke? And now to be threatened with the risk of filthy, muddy river water invading the place she tried so hard to keep decent and habitable. Oh, Edward, she thought miserably, if only things had been different. She fell asleep with tears wet on her cheek.

She woke as Luke suddenly jumped out of bed. 'Luke, what is it? What's wrong?' she called.

He groped for the candle and lit it. 'I can hear somethin',' he said. Then, 'Oh, my heavens above!' as he reached the head of the stairs. 'I never thought it would ever be as bad as that.'

'What is it, Luke? Oh, God, no, not the river ...' Cassie heaved herself out of bed. Her back hurt and she felt a sudden sharp pain in her side. She groped her way over to Luke, the pain forgotten as they both looked down at the evil-smelling water, black and sinister in the pool of candlelight, lapping at the stairs. Suppressing a scream of horror she shivered at the cold, dank air that rose, filling her nostrils with the stink of mud and worse. 'What are we going to do, Luke?' she said, her voice bordering on hysteria. 'Will it come any higher?' She stared mesmerised, as almost in answer to her question, the water slid ominously across the next stair.

'There's nothin' we can do till it goes down, Cassie. At least the wind's dropped. Thass something to be thankful for.' Luke put his arm protectively round her. 'Thass a two o'clock tide, an' I should think it must be gettin' on towards two now, but I don't know.'

'Well, look at my watch. It's pinned to my blouse on the chair over there.' Cassie spoke impatiently as the pain in her side stabbed again. She must have got out of bed too quickly.

'Quarter to two. Not much longer an' it'll be on the turn.' Luke sighed. ''*Then* there'll be a mess to clear up!' He led her back into the room. 'You might as well get back to bed, Cassie girl. You can't do no good standin' about gettin' cold. I'll do what's got to be done downstairs when the time comes.'

He helped her into bed and covered her up. She flinched and gave a little cry as another pain struck her.

'What's the matter, dear? Did I hurt you?' He was immediately concerned.

'No, Luke.' She looked up at him with panic in her eyes. 'But, oh God, Luke, what are we going to do? I think the baby's coming.'

'The baby's comin'! But it can't be! Thass not even due!' He saw her wince with another pain and looked round him desperately. 'You can't, Cassie. You can't have it here with two foot of water in the house. Oh, Lord, what a time to choose.' He began pulling on his trousers.

'What are you going to do, Luke?' She heaved herself up on to one elbow and held out her hand. 'You're not going to leave me? Don't leave me, Luke.'

'I'm not gonna leave you, Cassie. I'm gonna take you off to your mother's. I can't hev you birthin' a babby in this mess. Oh, Lord,' he said again, 'I never thought to bring you to this, Cassie girl.' He pulled on his boots and handed her a shawl. 'Now, come on, dear. Can you get on my back? No, course you can't. Never mind, I'll carry you in my arms, don't worry. But you'll hev to walk down the stairs, I'm afraid. They're too narrow for me to carry you down.' He wrapped the shawl and a blanket round her and then helped her carefully down the stairs. She couldn't help crying out as her bare feet reached the icy water but by that time there was sufficient room for him to pick her up and carry her. Even so, her feet trailed in the water but she didn't cry out again. She knew he was up to his thighs in it.

'We shall hev to get out of the window, I reckon,' he said breathlessly. 'I can't get the door open. There must be somethin' jammed agin it.' He pushed open the casement and sat Cassie on the sill while he climbed through, then he picked her up again and struggled on, stumbling now and then on unseen objects under the water, shouting a reply to the white faces leaning out of upstairs windows watching the sinister, yet somehow beautiful water, stretching as far as the eye could see, shining in the light of a brilliant moon. And all the while Cassie clung to him, biting her lip against the pain and fear so that she shouldn't cry out, knowing he was making as fast a progress as he could. As the ground rose the water became shallower and his progress easier and by the time he reached Black Buoy Hill die ground was dry. From there it was only a short distance through the churchyard to the Falcon.

Cassie gave a sob of relief as she nestled into the soft warmth of the bed her mother had left to come and open the door. There would be no more sleep for Hannah that night. While Luke re-lit the stove and set water to boil she found him some dry clothes – only she knew where from – before sending him off for Betty Gribbon, the old woman who officiated in all the village births. Then she gave him a large tot of rum and told him to sleep in the chair for a few hours.

'I shan't sleep, Hannah, not with all I've got on my mind,' he said. But he did, not waking till six when Lizzy came through to start work for the day.

Two hours later the baby was born. 'He's a fine lad for all he's two months early,' Betty Gribbon remarked, with something akin to a smirk. She'd seen enough to know a full-term baby when she saw it.

'I expect it was the shock of seeing the house flooded like that brought it on early,' Hannah said smoothly, although privately she herself was surprised at the size of the child.

Cassie gazed almost fearfully at the little boy when he was placed in her arms, looking for a likeness to Edward. But to her relief she could see none. His hair was dark and his face was red and puckered. She breathed a sigh of relief and was ready to smile at Luke when he came in at the door.

He took the baby in his arms. He was no stranger to babies; there had been one in his mother's house almost perpetually ever since he could remember. 'I like the name Robert, Cassie,' he said, looking down at him. 'I should like to call him by that name.'

'Very well, Luke. Robert is what he shall be. He's your son.' With those words Cassie resolved never to even think of the life her child might have had if she had been married to his real father.

Cassie slept. When she woke she was surprised to find it was afternoon. Stella was bending over the baby.

'He's not a bit like Luke, is he?' she said, gazing at him with her head on one side.

'He's not like anybody. He's like himself,' Cassie answered a shade too quickly, shooting an anxious glance at Stella.

But Stella's expression held nothing but a certain wistfulness. 'You're lucky, Cassie,' she said. 'Lucky to be married and have your own home and now a baby.' She sighed. 'I wish John and I could be married but he says he wants to work his way up to be a captain before he takes a wife.' She sat down on the bed and began folding and re-folding a corner of the coverlet. 'I've told him I don't mind, but he says he wants to save enough money so that we can buy one of the new houses in Park Road.'

'Surely that's worth waiting for. After all, you're only just seventeen, you've plenty of time,' Cassie said briskly, trying to suppress a twinge of jealousy. 'And at least when you live there you won't have to share your house with two feet of filthy, stinking river water.' She closed her eyes against the memory. 'Oh, it was awful, Stella.' She gave a shudder. 'It came in so silently. And when we looked, there it was.' She looked up at her sister. 'Has it gone down? Has Luke been to see?'

'Oh, yes. And so have I.' Stella's expression was suddenly animated. 'I've never seen anything like it, Cassie. Men were rowing across the quay in boats rescuing people and taking food to those who are trapped in their bedrooms. The water was still about two feet deep all over the quay.'

Cassie leaned forward. 'You mean it hasn't gone down at all?'

'Well, yes, it did when the tide ebbed, but they said it was an awful mess. Thick mud over everything. Uncle George's men went to rescue what they could at the Yard, and I s'pose they did the same at the other end of the quay at Harvey's Yard. But the tide this afternoon was just as high as last night's, so they say. It's quite a sight to see, Cassie.'

'Only if you don't happen to live there,' Cassie remarked, acidly.

'Oh, yes. I'm sorry. I didn't think ...'

With a sigh Cassie leaned back against the pillows and resettled her little son in the crook of her arm. She touched his cheek with her finger and an overwhelming surge of love and protectiveness engulfed her. This baby was not born to live in that dreadful cottage in The Folley, he was born for better things. Of that she was quite sure.

'Stella!' Hannah's voice floated up the stairs.

'I'm coming, Mama.' With a sigh that equalled Cassie's, Stella got up off the bed. 'All I can say is the sooner John gets to be a captain so I can have my own house like you've got the better. I hate it here.'

Cassie raised her eyebrows. She'd never heard Stella speak like that before. She lay listening to the sounds of the Falcon; sounds that were so much a part of it that she had never even noticed them when she lived here, yet now they filled her with a nostalgia that bordered on home-sickness. First there was the brewer's dray lumbering round to the yard at the back, pulled by Major and Jack, the two great dray horses that were as gentle as kittens in spite of their size. She could hear the barrels being rolled off the dray and down the chute into the cool cellar, accompanied by shouts from Joe Sainty the drayman to Tom, who was below to receive the barrels. It seemed only weeks ago that she was six and listening to her mother's warnings. 'Now, you girls, keep away from the yard while the dray is there because the cellar doors are open.' They hadn't needed telling twice, having once looked down into the yawning black chasm and heard the mysterious banging noises echoing round down there. Cassie had convinced Stella – and very nearly herself – that there was something quite horrible chained up in a far corner, in the shadowy depths never reached by the candle Tom took with him when he went to tap the barrels. Cassie smiled to herself at the memory of how, even when she was older and sent down to the cellar for bottles of wine for the guests she would fly back up the steps as if all the devils in hell were after her – remembering the imaginary 'thing' in the corner.

The dray had only just left when there were sounds of another cart. This time footsteps came up the stairs past her bedroom to the big meeting room at the front of the house and there was the sound of voices in conversation. It was Mr Craske, the auctioneer from Colchester, bringing the items for the sale to be held the next day of goods from a shipwreck off the coast. That would mean a full house for bread and cheese and beer lunches tomorrow. After that flurry of activity was over it was quiet for a while, the only sound the church clock sounding out the hour and the drone of voices in the bar, occasionally raised, then quietened by Tom. And to think I'd never noticed all these sounds before, Cassie thought drowsily. Too busy being a part of it all to notice them, I suppose.

She stayed in her mother's bed for six days. It being the middle of winter there were not many guests at the Falcon so Hannah was happy to look after her, especially as little Robert was a good baby and gave very little trouble.

On the seventh day Hannah came bustling in. 'I'll have to move you, Cassie. You can't stay in this room any longer. Mr Crowther is coming tomorrow.'

'But this isn't his room, Mama, is it? I thought you always put him in the Captain's room, next door.'

'That's right, I do. But I can't have him disturbed by the noise of the baby crying in the night. That wouldn't do at all' Hannah looked unusually flustered. 'He might hear it through the wall,' she added, almost apologetically.

'It's all right, Mama. I don't mind moving, not a bit. Where would you like me to go?' Cassie smiled up at her mother.

Hannah looked worried. 'You shouldn't really go walking about, only six days after your confinement.'

Cassie laughed. 'Oh, don't be silly, Mama. I'm sure I'm perfectly all right. Look at some of the village women ...'

'You're not some of the village women, Cassie. You're my daughter.' Hannah pinched her lip. 'I think you'd better just go across the passage into the Marquis's room, that'll be the best thing.'

'Won't Mr Crowther be able to hear the baby just the same? Not that Robert cries much in the night.'

'No, it won't be so bad. At least there'll be the passage in between.' Hannah busied herself with the cradle.

Cassie said no more but allowed herself to be helped across the passage to the room opposite. All this fuss because of Abel Crowther, who descended on the Falcon any old time he chose and threw the whole place into confusion. And it wasn't even as if he was a yacht owner, although he spent a lot of time down by the river. Sometimes Cassie couldn't understand her mother at all.

It was nearly a month before Hannah deemed the cottage fit for Cassie and the baby to return to. By that time, in spite of heavy February rain, Luke had managed to dry it out and make it habitable again. When Cassie walked into it, apart from a faint lingering smell of mud, it was as if it had never been flooded – most of the time the light was too dim to see the tell-tale water mark on the dark brown wainscotting that no amount of scrubbing could remove. She settled down to her new life. The baby took up much of her time and she was at pains to keep the cottage as bright and homely as she could. However, the often overflowing privy disgusted her and she worried about the rats in the yard and the brawling neighbours. She never complained, but simply escaped as often as she could to the Falcon, where she knew there was always a job to be done.

Luke understood. He knew how Cassie felt about the cottage although he privately felt it was disloyal to Uncle George, who had provided it out of the kindness of his heart. Nevertheless, he wished he could provide his wife with something better. One day he would. One day ...

Chapter Six

Robert was nearly three years old and Simon had been born before Stella finally persuaded John Jameson to marry her. John was in no hurry. He'd been given command of the *Miranda,* a hundred-foot racing schooner belonging to an Italian Count and had spent a highly successful season racing her round the coast of Britain and in the Mediterranean. He couldn't resist boasting how much prize money he had won and Stella knew he was on a fat retainer from *Miranda*'s rich owner so there was no excuse. They bought a house in Park Road and were married on Christmas Eve, 1871.

Hannah did just as she had done for Cassie's wedding and prepared a spread in the meeting room upstairs in the Falcon. But this time there were upwards of fifty guests, many of them well-known in the yachting world, and there was a telegram and a handsome cheque from Count Orietti. And this time the happy couple left in a flurry of rice and good wishes for a honeymoon in London.

'Rare handsome pair they made, missus,' Tom remarked as he helped clear up the room after the last of the guests had left.

'Yes.' Hannah paused in the act of stacking glasses on to a

tray. 'They've certainly got a good start to their married life. That house in Park Road reminds me of the house we had in West Street. Good-sized, airy rooms with bay windows, a nice wide hall ...' She sniffed and continued stacking the glasses. 'I jest hope they'll be happy. That's all I can say.'

Cassie came back up the stairs, with Robert trotting along behind her. He had grown into a sturdy lad, with his mother's brown eyes and hair that had lightened to the colour of ripe corn. Everyone remarked on his likeness to Cassie, whereas young Simon, even at three months, had a distinct resemblance to Luke. 'Stella should be happy. She's got what she's been hankering after long enough,' Cassie said, catching the end of the conversation. 'And did she tell you the size of the cheque Count Orietti gave John?'

'Yes,' Hannah said. 'It was more than generous. They're very lucky.'

'That don't mean they'll be any happier than you an' Luke, Cassie gal,' Tom said, putting the benches back along the wall.

Cassie didn't reply. She hoped they would be happier than she and Luke. After three years their lives seemed to have settled into a pattern that left much to be desired. Oh, she tried very hard to be a good wife to Luke; she knew she owed him that. He had, however unwittingly, saved her from certain disaster and for that she would be eternally grateful to him. But a marriage built on a mixture of gratitude and guilt was hardly a recipe for marital bliss. She knew that Luke was still filled with guilt over the episode that in his mind had almost assumed the proportions of rape. Not that they ever discussed the matter, but every time he claimed his rights as a husband – which she never denied him – he was careful not to prolong the act, and to her extreme irritation always said thank you afterwards.

Yet she could never tell him how unhappy it made her. How

could she suggest that lovemaking should be a glorious, shared experience? She wasn't supposed to know. And when he did try to kiss and caress her something inside her seemed to freeze and however hard she tried she couldn't respond.

She picked up the tray Hannah had laden with glasses. 'I'll just take these down to Lizzy and then I'll stay in the kitchen and feed the baby.' It was a convenient excuse. Simon was a good baby but he was always ready to suck.

After she had gone Hannah sat down wearily in the big chair at the head of the long table. The white cloth she had starched so carefully was covered with crumbs and stained where beer and wine had been spilt and there was still dirty crockery to be cleared away.

'I've been thinking, Tom,' she said, resting one elbow on the table and leaning her head on her hand. 'Now that Stella's got a home of her own, I wonder if Cassie and Luke would consider coming here to live.'

Tom pinched his lip. 'Do you think that would be a good idea, missus?'

'I don't know.' Hannah shook her head. 'I'd thought – hoped – they'd make their home here after they married, but when George offered them the cottage it didn't seem right for me to interfere. Anyway, it was probably a good thing that they were on their own for the first little while ...'

Tom sat down on the bench he had just pushed against the wall. 'Well, missus,' he said. 'Young Cassie already spends more time here than she do in her own home, even now she's got the two little 'uns.' He shook his head. 'I dunno what Luke'd make of it, though.'

'I can't see that it would make that much difference to Luke,' Hannah said, with a twist to her lip. 'He's never at home, anyway. He spends all his time at the yard. He's even gone back to work now, although George and Martin both said they were going to take the rest of the day off.'

'Aye, he's conscientious, I'll give 'im that.'

'But you think he might not want to come and live under the same roof as his mother-in-law?'

Tom shook his head. 'I never said that.'

'No, but it's true, all the same.' Hannah sighed. 'I'll give it more thought. I don't want to upset their apple cart. But that cottage in The Folley is no place to bring up a family, although you never hear Cassie complain and she's made it as comfortable as anyone could. And Luke . . . ' She broke off. 'I'll ask Abel what he thinks. He'll be down next month again.'

Tom said no more but stood and resumed the clearing up. That bugger Abel Crowther had a sight too much influence over the missus to his way of thinking. He didn't like the man – never had. And he didn't like the way the missus dressed herself up when she knew he was coming. Not that he was jealous, of course . . .

It was late in January 1872 before Abel Crowther came again to the Falcon. Hannah had seriously considered writing to him over the business of Cassie and Luke but he had told her many times that she wasn't to contact him at his home in Sheffield. He had more than enough to contend with there, looking after his interests in his file-making factory, he couldn't be worried with the problems of a remote country pub.

But when Abel came to the Falcon he left the worries of the file factory in Sheffield behind and was ready to listen patiently to all her problems.

Tom met him at the station with the trap and he came in with a flurry of snow and great stamping of feet.

'By gow, it's a cold 'un, tonight,' he said, blowing on his fingers after Hannah had relieved him of his thick ulster.

'Come into my sitting room and I'll get you a little something to keep out the cold,' she said with a smile, leading the way down the hall and along the passage off to the right, past the kitchen to her cosy private sitting room.

She left him by the fire and went off, soon returning with a mug of wine that she put down in the hearth and a bowl of hot, thick soup which she handed to him. 'There, now, get that inside you while I mull this wine. There's nothing like a good mug of mulled elderberry to warm the cockles of your heart.' She pushed the poker into the fire as she spoke and when it was good and hot plunged it into the mug of wine. 'There you are, my dear. All nice and hot and spicy.' She got up off her knees and sat down in the chair opposite, studying Abel as she waited for him to finish his soup.

He was a tall man, broad and well-built, and he hadn't really changed much in the twenty years he'd been coming to the Falcon. His hair was iron grey now but it was still thick and wiry, as were the whiskers that framed his face, meeting under his chin. His face was florid, that hadn't changed, and it was reddened even more tonight by the hot soup and wine. All his features were big; he had a big nose, big thick eyebrows, piercing blue eyes that were as watchful as ever under hooded lids, and a wide mouth with fleshy lips. Only his teeth were not as good as they had once been; they had become brown and stained over the years. But he hadn't lost any. Abel was not a handsome man but his face had character and would have had a certain rugged charm, had he ever relaxed his stern expression.

'Thankee, my dear.' He pushed the tray away and wiped his mouth on his napkin. 'Now, how have things been going here? Shall I tek a look at the books?' He pronounced it *bo-ooks*.

Hannah unlocked the cupboard by the side of the fireplace and took out her ledgers. She kept all her accounts meticulously and made sure that there was never any discrepancy. Abel had shown her a simple accounting system when she first took over the Falcon and it was his custom to look at them whenever he paid a visit. Hannah didn't mind – she was proud of her book-keeping skills and liked showing them off to him.

'Hm,' he said when he had closed the last ledger. 'Tha seems to be doing quite nicely here, Hannah. Plenty going on, isn't there, besides the selling of beer?' He leaned back in his chair and picked his teeth.

'Yes, we're always busy. Too busy, sometimes.' Hannah stared into the fire. A log shifted in the silence, sending a shower of sparks up the chimney. 'You know my Stella has married and moved into Park Road,' she said at last.

'Aye. Tha told me that.' He nodded.

'I was wondering if I should suggest that Cassie and Luke come to live here, now that Stella's gone,' she said thoughtfully. 'Cassie spends nearly all her time here, anyway. She's a good help to me. And now the girls' room at the back's empty ...'

Abel pulled his whiskers. 'Haven't tha got enough to do wi'out a brood of squalling brats round tha feet all the time, woman?' he asked at last.

'They're often here, anyway. I told you, Cassie spends most of her time here. And they're good childer.' She gave a shrug. 'I'll have to get somebody in, anyway, now that Stella's gone. Not that she ever overworked herself. But Luke might be quite useful in the bar ...'

'Better house 'em in the cottage on the end, I'd have thought,' Abel said with a sniff. He was referring to Falcon Cottage, the little two-up, two-down structure that was part of the Falcon buildings.

'Oh, I couldn't do that. Tom lives there, you know that.'

'Rent free, an' all.'

'It's part of his wages. No, I couldn't turn Tom out. Anyway, where would he go?'

Abel shrugged his broad shoulders. 'Tha asked me what I thought and I've told tha.'

Hannah was silent. It had always rankled with Abel that Tom lived rent free in the cottage. 'No,' she said, after a bit. 'I couldn't turn Tom out because I couldn't risk him leaving. I don't know how I'd manage without him. In fact, I know I *couldn't* manage without him. He looks after the bar, he looks after the cellar, he keeps the bowling green, looks after the horseshoe pitching, drives the trap ...'

'Oh, spare me the details. I know tha thinks he's a bloody paragon. Tha'll be tellin' me next he's a better man in bed than I am.'

'Don't be daft.' A slow smile spread across Hannah's face. 'You're jealous, Abel. I do believe you're jealous.'

'Tha's too damned reet I'm jealous. Tha'rt a handsome woman, Hannah. Tha must be aware o' that.'

She sighed and her face grew sombre. 'You needn't worry, Abel. There's never been any other man in my bed but you since Reuben died. And there's never likely to be. I can give you my word on that.' She got to her feet and picked up the tray that had held his supper. 'It's late. I can hear Tom clearing up. You'll find everything you need in your room, Abel.'

'Except thee.' He stood up and put his arm round her.

She shrugged him off and moved away. 'Keep to the rules. Never touch me except when we're in the bedroom,' she said quickly.

He looked surprised. 'But there's nobbut us here. Tha girls are both wed.'

'It makes no difference. After all these years you shouldn't find it hard.'

'It's tha that's hard, Hannah Jordan.'

'You'll find everything you need in your room,' she repeated, firmly.

He went upstairs and Hannah hurried along to the bar where Tom was hanging up the last of the glasses. 'Everything all right, Tom?' she asked, her deceptively quick glance round the bar missing nothing.

'Yes, missus. Quiet night, tonight.' Tom yawned. 'Well, I'll be off to me bed. Goodnight, missus.'

'Goodnight, Tom.' Hannah locked the door behind him and went slowly up the stairs. For twenty years Abel Crowther had shared her bed every time he came to stay at the Falcon and nobody was any the wiser. At first she had been unhappy, unwilling, but he had given her no choice in the matter and over the years, God help her, she had come to look forward to his visits in the dead of night through the door that connected his room with hers – a door that was at all other times kept locked and the key hidden. And never once in all those twenty years had she forgotten to lock the door and hide the key because she could never have borne the shame if anyone had discovered her secret.

She undressed and washed at the wash-stand in the corner, then brushed her greying hair and twisted it into a thick plait. Then she climbed into bed and waited. Half an hour later Abel came into the room, surprisingly quietly for such a big man. 'Tha'll not object to me touching tha now, love, will tha,' he murmured with a chuckle and pulled aside her nightgown.

'So there y'are, Luke.' Uncle George straightened up and rubbed his back. 'What do you think of her?'

Luke nodded slowly as he studied the designs for the new yacht laid out on the table by the light from the gas lamp.

'Yes, I think you've got it about right, Marty,' he said to his cousin, standing beside him with a pencil in his hand. 'But I still think you've given the mast too much of a rake for a gaff-rigged cutter. I reckon she'll go better if it's a degree or so more upright. Say ... there.' He drew a line with his finger. 'I know the fashion is to lay the mast well back, but to my mind you can do too much to it.'

Martin put his head on one side. 'I've worked it out very carefully, Luke,' he said after a minute. 'Mathematically, that's how it should be, taking into consideration ... '

'I don't care about the mathematics of the thing, Marty.' Luke shook his head. 'All I know is that it don't look right. Thass all.'

'Well, we can worry about that when the time comes,' George said. 'That can always be altered if needs be. First thing to do is get the timber ordered so we can get the keel laid.' He rubbed his hands together. 'Biggest job we've done. From our own design, too.'

Martin grinned. 'I only hope she'll sail!'

'We'll be in trouble if she don't,' George laughed, quite confident in his son's draughtmanship and his nephew's skill.

Martin and Luke left the office together.

'I've been trying for ages to get Dad to move into building bigger boats,' Martin said as they went down the wooden stairs and across the yard. It was dark and the men had left for the night, leaving the place almost eerily quiet after the day's activities. He shivered and hunched his shoulders into his reefer jacket. 'By jove, it's cold tonight. I reckon there'll be a sharp frost again. Yes, as I was saying, I don't see why Harvey's should get all the new work. Dad's happy to grub around doing repairs and building the odd smack but I say we need to expand.'

'As long as you don't try to get too big too soon,' Luke warned.

Martin gave a laugh that held little mirth. 'You don't need to worry about that; not while my dad's alive. I have to fight him every inch of the way to get him to do anything different. Not that he's mean, I'd never say that of Dad, Luke, but he's certainly cautious. And suspicious of anything new.'

'Well, you can't blame 'im. He's built that business up from nothin', an' he prefers to work on his tools, doesn't he?'

'Oh, yes. He's never been very fond of all the paperwork. But he doesn't have to worry now. I take care of all that, and that's what I enjoy.' Martin thrust his hands deeper into his pockets. 'I certainly enjoyed designing that cutter. I shall do more of that, I think.' He shivered. 'Well, it's daft to stand here in the freezing cold, I'm off home. See you in the morning, Luke.'

'Yes. See you in the mornin', Marty.'

They went their separate ways, Martin, hunched up against the cold, taking a short cut along beside the gasworks home to his parents' house in Anglesea Road and Luke, who never felt the cold, loping off to his family in the cottage in The Folley. He was fond of Martin, his cousin, and had never for one moment resented the fact that Martin had always been better dressed, better fed, better schooled than he had. And it didn't give him any cause for concern that Martin would inherit his father's business and one day be a rich man. That was the way of the world and Luke accepted it. As long as Martin was happy to employ him doing what he loved doing, which was working on boats, Luke would be happy and entirely without envy, although he did sometimes wish he could do better for Cassie's sake.

Cassie had not been home long. She had lit the fire and given Robert some of the stew she had carefully carried home from the Falcon in a can and he was wiping his dish round with a piece of bread so as not to waste any of the gravy. The baby was still in the little wheeled cart Luke had made when Robert was a baby.

She ladled more of the stew into a basin for Luke and put Robert to bed while he ate it. Then she helped herself to the rest and sat down at the table.

'Ah, that was a drop o' good,' he said, pushing the basin away when he'd finished. 'Brought it home with you, didn't you?'

'Yes. I can't seem to ...' She'd been going to say that she couldn't cook on the little stove in the cottage but she bit her tongue. Luke's mother had a similar cooking range and she turned out the most delicious stews and hotpots – when she had the money for the meat scraps and vegetables.

'I guessed it was one of Hannah's. She makes a rare good stew.' He moved over to his chair by the fire and held out his hands to the blaze.

Cassie sat down opposite him and picked up the little coat she was crocheting for the baby. 'She'd like us to move into the Falcon with her, now that Stella's gone,' she said, watching carefully for his reaction.

Luke sat back in his chair, his fingers loosely locked between his knees. He'd been afraid this might happen. It was only natural that Cassie didn't want to stay in this cottage, he knew she hated it even though she was careful never to complain and she'd done wonders with it. He looked round at the bright curtains and cushions, the valance round the mantelpiece and the pretty china fairings standing on it, with more of them displayed with the Sunderland jug and the bowl Tom had given her in the cupboard he'd made that hung in the corner. And everywhere was neat as a pin. But she couldn't do anything about the constant smell of damp that pervaded the place and there was still a faint mark round the wall as a reminder of the terrible floods the year Robert was born that no amount of scrubbing could remove. There had never been quite such a high tide as that since.

He sighed. He'd never said a word but he'd been saving for something better. His ambition was to buy a nice house for her and he'd saved a few shillings here and there out of the overtime money Uncle George paid him for the extra work he did. Cassie had been adamant that he should keep his overtime money since he gave her nearly all his weekly wage and the extra money was hidden in the false bottom of his toolbox at work. There'd been ten pounds there the last time he'd looked. Luke sighed again. He'd enough sense to realise it was going to take a rare long time at the rate he was saving to get enough to buy a house, even with the extra work building the new cutter would create.

'What'll we tell Uncle George? After all, 'e said we could live here rent free for as long as we wanted.'

'I think he'd understand. The fact is, I believe Mama would be glad of us there now Stella has gone. She hasn't said as much but I think she could do with our ... support, for want of a better word.'

Luke nodded. He stared into the fire for a long time without speaking.

'We don't have to go if you don't want to, Luke,' Cassie said, after the silence had stretched beyond her endurance. 'But now the big room over the scullery is empty – that's the room I used to share with Stella ... ' She put her crocheting down in her lap and stared into the fire. 'Mama made us sleep there because she thought we'd be safe from the guests,' she smiled. 'You see you can only get to it from the stairs out of the kitchen. It's quite separate from the rest of the house.' She picked up her work again. 'Mama was always worried about us being attacked. We even carried whistles at our belts ...' She broke off, realising she was on dangerous ground.

But Luke wasn't listening. 'Did you say it was quite separate?' he asked. If that was the case it might be bearable. He remembered the first week of their marriage, when Hannah's shadow seemed to hang between them, rendering him impotent and miserable. He couldn't face a lifetime feeling like that.

'Yes. And it's a big room so there would be plenty of room for the boys as well.' She hesitated. 'It would be better all round for them, wouldn't it? The yard out there ... it's not fit ... with the rats and everything.'

He nodded. 'Yes, you're right. This isn't a place to bring up youngsters. Would you like to move back to the Falcon, Cassie?'

She didn't look up. 'Only if you'd be happy to, Luke.'

He nodded again. 'Then I should think mass the best thing to do.' But his expression was bleak.

Chapter Seven

Cassie left the cottage in The Folley without a backward glance. She was glad to be rid of the stove that wouldn't cook, the doors and windows that didn't keep out the draught however much paper she stuffed into them, and the unspeakably filthy back yard.

But she didn't tell Uncle George this when she gave him back the key. 'Mama needs someone with her at the Falcon now that Stella's gone, Uncle George,' she explained. 'And there's nobody else but Luke and me, so we have to go.'

'And quite right, too, gal. That wouldn't be right to leave your mother there with on'y Tom to give 'er a hand, good though 'e is.' George patted her arm. 'Hannah's had a hard time, she can do with a bit o' support. An' don't you worry your head about the cottage. That was on'y meant to give you a start together. I shouldn't hev wanted to see you stay there for ever. I'm on'y too pleased you've got yourselves fixed up.' He smiled at her.

Impulsively, she kissed him. 'Thank you, Uncle George. You really are a dear.'

If Luke was less happy about the move he didn't say and

Cassie was too busy and happy to notice. In any event he spent most of his time at work, poring over the designs for the new yacht with his uncle and cousin, making an alteration here, an adjustment there, helping Martin to compile lists of building materials, ordering the timber and stacking it and at last supervising the laying of the keel, a long straight-grained baulk of elm. There had been some discussion over this. George had favoured oak but Luke had set his heart on elm. 'That'll do the job a treat, Uncle,' he said, showing him the piece he had chosen. 'Elm lasts for donkey's years if you keep it either completely wet or completely dry. Well, this'll be in the water all the time and I don't reckon you'll want for better.'

George lifted his hat and scratched his bald head. 'What about the ribs, then?'

'Oh, we'll do them in oak. No question o' that.'

George sniffed. Then he nodded. 'All right, boy, hev it your way. Elm it is for the keel.'

The keel was laid and the skeleton of the boat began to take shape.

Hannah was glad to have Cassie back under the same roof. Sometimes the responsibility of the Falcon lay heavy on her shoulders and it was a relief to have someone to share the decision-making as well as the work. She loved having the children about the place, too; Robert was a biddable child and liked nothing better than to follow her about, pulling the little engine his father had fashioned for him out of wood. Fortunately Simon was a contented baby, too, but all was not well with Cassie and Luke. Hannah could see that. They shared the same meal table – when Luke wasn't late so his dinner had to be kept hot between two plates over a saucepan – and they shared the same bed. Other than that they had little in common. Or so it seemed to her.

'I hadn't realized,' she said to Tom. She had made an excuse to go down into the cellar with him to check the last delivery of barrels. He had been with her almost as long as she had been at the Falcon and she confided most of her troubles and worries to him. The only subject they never discussed was Abel Crowther. Tom didn't like Abel and made no secret of the fact. Hannah knew that jealousy was the root of his dislike and although he never uttered a word of criticism she knew he resented Abel's influence over her. But Tom didn't understand. He didn't know the whole story – nobody did. Not even her sister Maisie.

'What ha'n't you realized, missus?' Tom came across to her. 'An' you shouldn't sit on them cold steps, you'll get cold in your stummick.'

Hannah shook her head and the silver strands in her hair glinted in the pool of light thrown by the candle in the sconce on the wall. 'I hadn't realized – Cassie and Luke – they hardly speak to one another.' She put her head in her hands. 'Oh, it's this damned place. I should never have asked them to come here. Cassie was born to better than this ...'

Tom took hold of her arm. 'Now, listen to me, missus. There ain't no call for you to say sech things as that. Cassie's lived at the Falcon since she was no bigger'n a minute. She don't remember the fine house you're so fond of braggin' about. The Falcon's what she's always known an' thass a sight better'n the place she's come from in The Folley.'

Hannah nodded. 'I know, Tom. But things would have been so different if Reuben hadn't been drowned. Look at Captain Chaney's wife. Four servants she's got and a nursemaid for the children. And that nice new house at the top of the village – with a bathroom, too, I hear.' She straightened her shoulders. 'And that's what *I* should have had. Then my girls would have been looked up to, the same as Captain Ham's daughters in

Anglesea Road. And Cassie wouldn't have got herself involved with Luke Turnbull, of all people.'

'There ain't nothin' wrong with young Luke, 'cept 'e worn't born with a silver spoon in 'is mouth,' Tom said, quick to spring to his defence. ''E's a good bloke an' Cassie could've done a lot worse for 'erself. He's as hardworkin' a bloke as you'd ever wish to see, and that you can't deny. But jest because 'e ain't ambitious you don't think much of 'im. Anyway, you can't complain about the gal Stella's husband. He ain't done bad for hisself. 'E must be the youngest yacht captain hereabouts, I should think.'

Tom leaned against the whitewashed wall with his arms folded. With his black bushy hair standing perpetually on end he threw a grotesque shadow on the wall. And his features in the candlelight were hardly less grotesque. He had a long face, a swarthy complexion and great staring, bulbous eyes that were, nonetheless, full of kindness. He was ugly, no one could deny that, but it didn't bother Tom. He'd had his day. Thirty years before the mast had given him all he wanted of adventure and love, of a kind. Now he asked nothing more than to serve Hannah Jordan, whom he idolized, and to return to his spartan little cottage behind the Falcon at the end of each day.

Hannah got to her feet. 'Yes, Stella's done all right for herself. I don't have any cause to fret over her.' She bit her lip. 'No, it's Cassie ...' She sighed. 'Yet I don't see we could have done any differently.'

Tom made no reply to this remark. He could see as far through a brick wall as the next man, as he was fond of saying, and at least there had been no scandal in the family. 'Like I say, Luke's a good steady boy, missus,' he said at last. ''E ain't like 'is dad. Do you know I don't believe I've ever seen Luke touch a drop o' liquor?'

'Seeing what it's done to his father has put him off, I should think,' Hannah remarked acidly.

'Well, there y'are, then.'

She shook her head. 'No, Tom, it's not just that. It's – I don't know – it's as if there's no heart in their marriage.' She turned and mounted the stairs.

Tom followed behind. 'I reckon you're a sight too fanciful, missus,' he said. 'I doubt you wouldn't even have noticed whether she was happy or not if she'd been married to a yacht captain,' he added bluntly.

Hannah didn't answer.

Cassie had made the bedroom over the scullery quite comfortable. It was a big room, big enough for her to hang a curtain across to give her and Luke privacy from the boys. Not that this was necessary because when they were old enough the two boys would share the small bedroom at the front of the house.

They brought their own furniture with them. Luke had made a new bed so they had sold the one they had bought at Mrs Roper's second-hand shop back to her – and at a better price than they had paid for it because Luke had mended it. He had also made a little truckle bed for Robert so that Simon could have the cradle. Cassie's Christmas present from Luke two years before had been a corner wash-stand, an intricate piece of work with much fretting and crossbanding, and the next year he had made her a triple mirror to stand on the chest of drawers Hannah had given them when they married. There was plenty of room for all this and the armchair, too, in the bedroom, but the table and stools had to go in the bar because there was no room for them anywhere else.

They were well settled in by the time spring came. April brought an influx of yacht owners, paying fleeting visits to the village and staying at the Falcon for two, or perhaps three nights while they discussed yachting matters with their captains, pretending to know what they were talking about when they spoke of shrouds and runners, shifters and bobstays. But as long as there was no shortage of money to fit out both yachts and crews, together with the promise of winning prestigious trophies, both the captains and the owners were happy, although for different reasons.

Jonas Price-Carpenter came, as he did each year, to inspect *Leander*. He was very like Edward, his son, in appearance, but bustling and businesslike in his manner, which could never have been said of Edward. Edward had never been back to the Falcon and Cassie gleaned from snippets of overheard conversation that this year he would be joining *Leander* at Cowes for a holiday with his wife and daughters. She wondered if he ever thought of that spring four years ago when he had been left to supervise the fitting-out of his father's yacht ... She let her mind dwell fleetingly on what might have been – on how *she* might have been going to Cowes for a holiday with Edward and their son. She'd never been on holiday and couldn't imagine what it was like. Resolutely, she turned her mind away from such thoughts and got on with the task in hand.

Hannah was in her element, sweeping imperiously about the Falcon, giving orders and seeing that they were carried out to her satisfaction. Two new girls appeared, one to wait on the tables in the dining room – something Hannah and one of her daughters had always done before – and another to help Lizzy with the cleaning and cooking. Millie, another refugee from the workhouse, had taken Lizzy's place in the scullery.

'I don't know why Mama has taken on these extra girls, do you, Tom?' Cassie asked one evening. She often helped Tom in the bar now; Hannah had deemed that since she was respectably married she was unlikely to be corrupted. And Hannah herself no longer served in the bar at all; she considered it beneath her dignity for some unfathomable reason.

Tom leaned against the bar, idly polishing a glass. 'No, Cassie gal, I don't see the need for it meself. We've always managed before, even at this time of o' the year when things git busy.' He shrugged. 'But there y'are. She git these bees in her bonnet sometimes. I jest hope she ain't tryin' to git above 'erself. When all's said an' done, this is on'y a village pub, not some high-falutin' posh hotel, an' thass no good tryin' to pretend that it is.'

Thoughtfully, Cassie slipped under the bar counter and went to collect up the dirty glasses. She was learning to hold her own amongst the banter that inevitably went on and she had a free and easy way with the men that could nevertheless change in a twinkling if one of them dared to overstep the mark. A quick remark now to three or four round the shove ha'penny board brought a gust of laughter in which she joined before turning back to the bar.

Luke had come in and was standing watching her, his face like thunder. He'd had a hard day at the yard. Several yachts were waiting to be fitted out ready for the racing season so the cutter they were building had had to be left for a few weeks. Luke didn't mind that – better to take a bit longer and make a good job was always his maxim. *Xantha* was up on the slip and should have gone back in the water today to make way for *Firefly*. But she wasn't finished. Her bottom had still to be burnished and then, to crown it all, it had rained and the paint that had been put on this afternoon was all pitted so it would have to be rubbed down and done again tomorrow. He'd left in disgust at eight o'clock. Everyone else had gone by that time except Martin, who was still working in the office and nursing an attack of indigestion caused, no doubt, by sitting too long hunched over his desk.

Cassie came back to the bar. 'Why, Luke, you're home early tonight. It's not half past eight yet.' She gave him a dutiful smile and went to peck him on the cheek but he turned his head away in a sudden fit of jealous pique.

Joe Ellis, one of the men playing shove ha'penny, called out 'Cor, Luke, bor, I wouldn't turn my head away if she belonged to me. No, that I wouldn't!' There was a roar of laughter as he brought his fist up in a gesture everyone recognised.

Luke turned a dull red. 'Seems it's a good thing I do come home early sometimes,' he said sourly, 'the way you're carryin' on.'

'Oh, Luke, don't be silly. Of course I'm not "carrying on" as you call it. But I have to be pleasant, don't I? Nobody will come here if they don't get a friendly word.' She looked over her shoulder. 'Go and get your dinner. Lizzy kept it hot for you. I'll come and talk to you in a minute, when I've washed these glasses.'

Luke went off and she busied herself behind the bar. When she looked up again Freddie Hurst was holding out his empty glass, swaying slightly as he stood there. 'Same agin, missus,' he said, smiling fatuously. 'An' put it on the slate.'

She took the glass from him. 'You've had enough for tonight, Freddie. And I'm putting nothing more on the slate. Think of your wife and children, for goodness sake. How will Annie feed them if you drink all your wages away?'

Freddie rested his elbows on the bar and looked at her owlishly. 'Annie don't care nothin' about me,' he said, speaking slowly and carefully in a desperate effort to sound sober. 'You don't unnerstand, Missus Turnbull. Since she took in them two lodgers thass all she care about. Scrubbin' an' polishin' an' cleanin' from morn till night, she is. They've got the best bedroom; me an' the three boys hev to park in the little bedroom at the back an' she sleep downstairs in the kitchen with young Bella. Thass "Git away from the table, Lenny, Mr Marchant an' Mr Brown want their supper". An' "Clean Mr Marchant's shoes, Jack, in case 'e wanta go out". I can't see why 'e can't clean 'is own bloody shoes – beggin' yer pardon, Missus Turnbull. But there ain't no comfort for the likes o' me at number four Bath Street. Not since them two men come to live there, I can tell you.'

'I daresay you're all glad of the extra money it brings in, Freddie,' Cassie said gently.

'*She* is. That don't make no difference as far as I'm concerned. She always took me wages at the end of the week an' handed me out me spendin' money and she still do. And I don't get no extra.'

'I've noticed that the children are well-shod and they've got warm winter coats.'

'Yes, I'll grant you that. An' you should see the house. New lino on the floor an' she's talkin' about a new suite o' furniture now.' He shook his head. 'If she get that we shan't be allowed inside the house. Thass bad enough as it is, we all hev to take our shoes off afore we step inside the door. Oh, not the lodgers, mind you, that don't matter 'bout them. Their boots don't get muddy, same as the rest of us, do they.' His voice was heavy with sarcasm. 'On'y place I git any comfort is when I come here,' he said sadly.

Cassie looked at him. She remembered him marrying Annie Barnes. She had been one of a family of ten and had been as proud as a peacock to marry young Freddie Hurst, a blacksmith at Harvey's shipyard. And he'd idolized her, too. 'I don't suppose Annie's very pleased if you go home drunk every night, Freddie,' she remarked.

'If I was made a bit more comfortable at home I shouldn't

need to come here every night,' he countered. 'But while them two men sit there with their feet under my table there ain't no room for me.' He sniffed loudly. 'So I git out an' leave 'em to it.'

'You go and sit over there and have another game of crib and I'll go and see if there's a mug of tea in the pot. That'll do you more good than another pint of beer on the slate.' Cassie went off to the kitchen. She knew only too well that Freddie would never have opened his heart to her like that if he had been sober and she felt sorry for him. But there was nothing she could do. Freddie was a big, brawny man who could swing a fourteen-pound hammer from dawn till dusk with hardly a break. Yet he was a peaceable man and would do anything to avoid trouble. There was no doubt that Annie, tiny as she was, ruled the Hurst household.

In the kitchen Luke had finished his meal and pushed his plate away. He was asleep at the table with his head on his arms. Cassie paused for a minute before she picked up the teapot. Luke didn't care for life at the Falcon, she knew that although he never said as much and she wondered if she had been selfish in seizing the opportunity to move out of the cottage in The Folley even though living at the Falcon was far, far better for the boys. Not that Luke complained, but there was something not right and it was not simply that he didn't like living with Hannah; it went deeper than that. But she could never ask him, any more than she could bring herself to turn to him for love when they were together in the big bed upstairs, waiting instead for his brief attentions, which always left her sad and unsatisfied.

There was always a barrier between them, a barrier his guilt had built and hers had buttressed. With a sigh she poured a mug of tea for Freddie. He wasn't the only one who had problems.

Martin left the office and turned for home then, changing his mind, retraced his steps and headed for the Falcon.

'Luke's in the kitchen, Marty,' Cassie said with a smile as he walked into the bar. 'I expect it's him you've come to see.'

'In a way, yes.' He gave a rueful grin. 'But I'd be glad of a drop of rum and peppermint, Cassie girl. I've got a rare bout of indigestion and if I go home now all I'll get from Ma is a dose of bicarb and a hot water bottle. She's an awful fusspot'

Cassie nodded. 'I'll bring it along to you in half a minute.' She finished what she was doing and made up Martin's drink.

'Where are you going with that?' Hannah was on her way to the snuggery.

'It's for Cousin Martin. He's in the kitchen with Luke.'

Hannah sniffed. 'Well, don't be long. And when you get back to the bar you can ask Tom to control the noise level. My gentlemen in the snuggery can't hear themselves speak for the hullabaloo going on in there.'

! 'I don't think it's any worse than usual, Mama. And it's certainly not as noisy as Friday and Saturday nights,' Cassie protested. 'Most of the men are playing dominoes or cribbage. And that's quiet enough.'

'Well, I still say they're making too much noise. I won't have it in my hotel and if you won't tell them I shall come and speak to them myself.' Hannah hurried on her way.

Cassie carried on to the kitchen, frowning. Her mother had never spoken about the noise in the bar before and she wondered who it could be in the snuggery that might have complained.

Luke and Martin were sitting at the table discussing the plans for a boat spread out in front of them. Cassie handed Martin his drink and turned to her husband. 'Can I get you anything, Luke?'

'Another cuppa tea wouldn't come amiss.' Luke pushed his cup over without looking up.

'Nothing stronger?' Martin cocked an eyebrow.

'Nope.'

'Sensible bloke. I'm only drinking this for medicinal purposes.' He rubbed his own ample stomach. 'It's Ma's apple puddings that do it, you know. I love 'em and I can't resist two helpings and I always end up with dreadful guts ache.' He drained his glass and handed it to Cassie. 'But I think I could manage another dose. I'm feeling better already.'

Cassie took it. 'You'd better not go home the worse for drink, Marty. Aunt Maisie'll know where you've been and she'll have a blue fit.'

'Don't worry, Cassie. Two's my limit.' He turned back to the drawings. 'So what do you think, Luke? Do you think she'd sail?'

'Sail?' Luke gave a laugh. 'She's got beautiful lines, Marty. With a hull like that she should be a real go-er.' He put his head on one side. 'The only thing is, do you think the rudder is a bit much? I think if I was you I'd fine it down a bit. She might be a bit heavy on the helm with a rudder that size.'

Martin nodded. 'Yes, I think you may be right. About like that, do you think?' He made an adjustment with his pencil.

'Yes, that should do it.' Luke closed one eye and leaned back in his chair.

Martin put his pencil down and rubbed his hands together. 'I don't reckon there'll be a boat on the Colne to touch her when she's built.'

'And when will that be?'

Martin shrugged. 'When we can get Dad in the mind to put her on the stocks, I suppose.'

'He won't build a boat like that on spec, Marty,' Luke warned. 'She'll cost a fortune. An' all in teak, too.'

'Never mind. We'll just have to put the plans aside till we find a rich man.' Martin began to roll them up. 'I wanted to design this boat and now I've done it. The designs'll keep, I'm not worried about that. One of these days someone will come and ask for a fast cutter and there they'll be.' He looked up at the clock. 'I worked later than I'd intended to get them finished and gave myself indigestion into the bargain. But never mind, it's better now, thanks to you, Cassie.' He grinned at his cousin and stretched his legs out towards the fire. 'I should be getting along home,' he said with a yawn. But he made no attempt to move.

Cassie left the two men and went back to the bar. It was nearly eleven o'clock and the room was thick with tobacco smoke that had, over the years, turned the ceiling and the walls to a yellowing brown. Isaac Barker was behind the bar helping Tom and they were beginning to clear up, hanging the pewter tankards on to hooks in the oak beams as they were washed and stacking the glasses. Over in the corner two men were concentrating on finishing a game of dominoes, watched by three or four more, savouring the last dregs of their drink as they stood there. The cribbage game was over, the cards and cribbage board left on the table. Everyone else had left.

Cassie slipped away – they wouldn't need her there again tonight. As she passed she looked in at the snuggery. This was now her mother's domain and Hannah was talking to the only two occupants, Sir Brian Saunders, who had come down from London to look over his yacht *Shamrock* and was staying at the Falcon, and *Shamrock*'s captain, Ben Hardy. Cassie knew they would have much to discuss because Sir Brian was returning to London tomorrow and they were seated in leather armchairs deep in conversation while Hannah hovered over them, anticipating their needs and generally fussing over them when all they wanted was to be left in peace. Cassie was a little surprised. She thought her mother would have known better.

She retraced her steps to the kitchen. There was one more thing to be done. Luke and Martin were still talking and took no notice as she filled a basket with food that had been left over from the day; a little soup, a few cold boiled potatoes and turnips, half a loaf of bread and a slab of bread pudding. Then she took down the cloak with a hood that was hanging behind the door and slipped out into the night. Cassie had never forgotten the plight of her neighbours in The Folley and in Smuggler's Row and she knew that the conditions they lived in were repeated over and over in the village. There were many that would be glad to find a little parcel of food hanging from the door latch in the morning and even some who would sit up late to take it in before it could be stolen. She crept quietly from house to house. It was little enough to do to alleviate their suffering, and by keeping her ear to the ground she usually managed to discover those most in need.

Her errand didn't take long and when she got back Martin was still there. Wearily, she sat down in the Windsor chair by the window, glad to rest her feet, closing her eyes and letting the conversation of the two men wash over her. It was good to be living at the Falcon again; to be part of the hustle and bustle, the comings and goings. And to be able, if only a small way, to help those less fortunate. She sighed. She hoped Luke wasn't going to be difficult over her attitude to the men in the bar. Being friendly was an important aspect of pub life and she would never allow anyone to overstep the mark. Neither, for that matter, would Tom. He was always watchful over her. But it was important that somebody should make the taproom customers feel welcome, because her mother no longer seemed to have any regard for them. In fact, she was becoming so distant and haughty towards them that they had termed her 'The Duchess' behind her back.

Cassie was at a loss to understand her mother's changed attitude. She never used to be like that. It was only since she and Luke had moved back to the Falcon. She yawned and shifted in her chair. That was another thing. She couldn't go to bed, even though she was tired out. It was her task now to do the last rounds and to lock up after Tom had left, a task Hannah had always insisted on carrying out herself previously. But lately she had taken herself off to bed when she was ready, ringing for Lizzy to take her up whisky and milk and making a fine scene if she was kept waiting. Cassie gave an almost imperceptible smile. Maybe the men weren't so far out in calling her 'The Duchess' after all. But what on earth had given her mother such grandiose ideas?

Chapter Eight

It was September and the yachts returned from their summer's racing and cruising. Some of them lay off Brightlingsea, waiting for the big equinoctial spring tides to bring them upriver in procession, their colours and prize flags proudly fluttering in the breeze, while others were towed up, to be snugged down in the carefully dug out winter mud berths, each berth marked by a wand stuck in the mud with its yacht's name on it.

The first cutter to be built in Turnbull's Yard was finished and bought by Lord Hargreaves – she was named *Florinda*. George Turnbull and his men were well-satisfied with her and Lord Hargreaves was plainly delighted and demanded that she be dressed overall and put on show for the regatta.

Abel Crowther always came to the village for the regatta and this put Hannah even more on edge than usual. She swept about the place, countermanding Cassie's instructions to the serving girls until Cassie herself was near to tears.

'Why don't you go up to your room and make yourself look nice, Mama? Mr Crowther will be here soon,' she said at last in an effort to get rid of her mother so that she and Lizzy could finish making the pies that would be in great demand later in the day.

'There's no need to be sarcastic,' Hannah snapped.

'I'm not being sarcastic, Mama, but my patience is wearing thin. Robert, take your fingers out of that jam pot! Go and find Simon, he's crawled away somewhere. See he isn't into mischief. Millie, have you washed those pans? I'm waiting for them.' Cassie pushed a strand of hair back under her cap. 'By the time I've finished here I'll be more ready to go to bed than to watch boats racing up and down the river,' she said with a sigh.

Hannah went off but came back a few minutes later. 'The tables aren't laid in the dining room, Cassie. There'll be several ...'

'I know that, Mama.' Cassie looked up from rolling pastry. 'Perhaps you could do it.'

'Me!' Hannah's eyebrows shot up till they nearly disappeared.

'You always used to pride yourself on the way your dining room looked,' Cassie reminded her, trying to keep her voice even

'*I'm* not laying tables. What do you think I employ menials for!' Hannah sat down by the window and smoothed her shot silk skirt. 'Ah!' She got up quickly and went to the mirror over the fireplace to adjust her cap, just as Lizzy was trying to put a batch of pies in the oven. 'There's Tom now. He's been to fetch Mr Crowther from the station. I'll be in the sitting room, Cassie. Make sure luncheon's not late – Mr Crowther won't want to miss any of the races. Oh, and make some hot chocolate for him, Lizzy. He'll be glad of a little something to set him on after his journey, I'm sure.'

Cassie bent her head so that the girls helping her shouldn't see the grim set to her mouth. When she was in control again she looked up. 'Will you go and lay the tables in the dining room, Florrie,' she said to the girl who had just come through the door.

'I've done them, Mrs Cassie,' Florrie answered. 'I went an' done them while you was a-talkin' to Mrs Hannah.'

Cassie smiled at her. 'Thank you, Florrie. Then perhaps you'll make a cup of chocolate and take it in to Mr Crowther. I daresay he'll be in the sitting room with Mrs Hannah.'

At last the baking was done, a substantial luncheon had been served and cleared from a full dining room and there was a large heap of pies ready to serve from the side of the pub to any who felt in need of a snack that didn't consist of either oysters, cockles or shrimps. Tom had Isaac to help him in the bar, where there was a steady stream of customers, and Lizzy and Florrie would take it in turns with Millie to look after everything else. Cassie changed into her best Dolly Varden dress of flowered cretonne, with its red silk underskirt, put Simon in his push cart and went off with Robert and Hannah to the crowded quay. It seemed as if the whole village was there, dressed in colours as bright as the bunting that was hung from every available window and pole. Stalls selling cockles, oysters and shrimps vied for trade with each other, each stall trying to outdo its neighbour in brightness and volume as they cried their wares.

Most yacht owners, if they had come, had grandstand views from their yachts, together with their families and friends. Some had their captains with them but not many; most captains were racing their smacks, named after the yachts in which they had won the money that had paid for them. Abel Crowther was on the yawl *Maud* as the guest of her owner Sir Harry Dutton, and Stella could be seen waving from *Eagle,* the yacht her husband John now captained for a Mr Griffiths, a rich London businessman.

It was obvious that Hannah was annoyed that she had not

received an invitation to watch the proceedings from one of the yachts but this didn't worry Cassie in the slightest. She was quite happy to be with the crowd, cheering as the races began and ended. One of the highlights of the day would be the return of the smacks, which were already racing a course that would take them out into the North Sea, up to Aldburgh Point and back. But while they waited for this there were plenty of other events; rowing, sculling and small boat sailing races – and the annual race between the shipwrights and the sailors. This was raced in twenty-five foot gigs – boats normally used to take the owners aboard their yachts from the shore – each rowed by eight of the brawniest men. It was the one time of the year when the shipwrights from Harvey's and Turnbull's worked together instead of in competition, but it was not often that they managed to defeat the sailors.

'Can you see Papa, boys?' Cassie knelt down beside the two boys, Simon fastened into the pushcart and Robert tied alongside it. 'Look, there he is, rowing in the boat nearest to us. The boats are both level. Shout for Papa, boys.' She got to her feet and began to jump up and down. 'Come on, shipwrights! Oh, come on, shipwrights!'

Hannah, standing beside her and nodding graciously here and there hissed at her, 'Don't make such an exhibition of yourself, girl. Jumping up and down like that. Remember who you are, for goodness sake.'

Cassie straightened her hat. 'I'm enjoying myself, Mama. There's no crime in that. Oh, they've won! The shipwrights have won! That's the first time for three years. Clap your hands and cheer, boys. Papa's won!'

'Anybody'd think he did it single-handed,' Hannah said sourly, turning away.

Cassie took no notice. She picked Robert up. 'Look, Bobby,

can you see that man on the greasy pole out there over the water? He's trying to walk along it. If he reaches the flag at the end he'll win a joint of meat. Oh, there he goes, he's fallen in the water.' A great groan went up from the crowd followed by a whoop as a young lad managed to skid swiftly along to the end of the pole and scoop up the flag before following his friend into the river with a great splash. As he surfaced he brandished the flag. 'I've done it!' he sputtered. 'I've won the meat!' Yelling excitedly he swam for the shore.

Luke came along sweating and grinning. 'We beat 'em this year,' he said gleefully. 'Mind you, I knew we would. We had a good crew.'

Cassie smiled at him. 'Did you hear us shouting? I told the boys to shout for the shipwrights and they did, didn't you, boys?'

Luke looked at her for a minute. 'It's not often you smile at me, Cassie girl,' he said quietly. Then he turned away and scooped Robert up on to his shoulder. 'Look, Bobby, here comes "pull devil, pull baker". This'll make you laugh,' he said, jigging him up and down.

The crowd was cheering again as two large rowing dinghies pulled out into midstream. One was armed with bags of soot and the other with bags of chalk and they were fastened together with a good long length of rope. There were two men on the oars and one in the bow of each boat. The fun began. The 'devil' began pelting the other boat with soot and the 'baker' retaliated with chalk. The boats rowed round in circles; one after another fell in and climbed out again – often into the enemy's boat – while those watching from the shore screamed for their favourites. The two crews plastered each other until the bags were empty and both boats were capsized. The crowd went crazy with laughter and excitement and a roar of approval went up when the contest was declared a draw.

'We'd better go home. It'll be a busy night tonight,' Hannah said, anxious to leave.

'Oh, we can't go yet, the smacks aren't back,' Cassie protested.

'No, but they're on their way!' A great shout went up as the first of the great topsails hove into view. It would be a while before the finish of the race but there was plenty to watch in the meantime, accompanied by a steady commentary from some boys perched at a yacht's masthead. '*Elise* is ahead!' '*Sunbeam's* with 'er.' '*Bertha's* comin' up but she's well back ...' 'And *Maria* ...' 'And *Foxhound* ...' 'But it's gonna be between *Elise* and *Sunbeam* ...'

Soon the whole of the waterfront seemed filled with a cloud of great white sails as the two smacks raced neck and neck for the line. The sound of the gun was almost unheard as a great cry went up. '*Sunbeam's* won! Pipped *Elise* at the post. Couldn't hev bin ten foot in it. An' after a race of near on twenty-two miles! Good ole Barney. 'E'd skipper a bath tub an' still win!'

A ripple ran through the crowd as the tension of the race relaxed. 'Oh, I did enjoy that!' Cassie straightened her hat, knocked askew in the excitement. 'In fact, the whole afternoon has been great fun, hasn't it, Mama?'

'Yes, but it's all over now.' Hannah turned to go.

'Oh, I'm not going till Luke has received his prize. It's not often the shipwrights win that race, is it, Luke?'

'No, you're right there, Cassie.' Luke chuckled as he put Robert down off his shoulders. 'Uncle George'll be like a dog with two tails, 'cause most of the crew came from our yard, you know. Only two of 'em came from Harveys.'

But Hannah wasn't listening. 'The prizes are given out at

108

the Rose and Crown! Surely you're not going there, Cassie,' she said, shocked.

'I'll only stay until Luke has got his prize. After all, he did captain the team, didn't he?' Cassie didn't give Hannah a chance to protest before she added. 'It's all right, Mama. You can take the children home and ask Lizzy to give them their tea and put them to bed. Not that they'll need much tea, they've been stuffing themselves with cakes and sweets from the stalls all the afternoon.' She handed her mother the push cart and Robert's rein. 'I won't be long. I'll be back in time to see to things this evening.' She straightened her hat and went off with Luke.

They were both in high spirits when they went home, Luke clutching his prize money and the printed winners' certificate and for once he was more than happy to give Tom and Isaac a hand in the bar, full to overflowing tonight, while Cassie was busy in the equally-crowded dining room.

Business was brisk and compliments flowed as freely as beer.

'I never thought you shipwrights 'ud do it agin them brawny sailors,' one said, 'but you pulled on them oars like good 'uns.'

'That you did,' another agreed. 'Now, you hev a pint on me to celebrate, Luke.'

'No thanks. But thanks for the thought.' Luke went to collect glasses and wipe down tables.

'Aw, come on, Luke, bor, thass Regatta night. The Fair is a-blarin' out on Anchor Hill an' everyone's hevin' a high ole time out there. You oughta hev a drink to celebrate, like the rest on us.' Bill Jenks, who had been in the team was already merry.

Luke laughed. 'You want to get me like him so I can't tell a shillun from half a crown, don't you,' he said goodnaturedly. 'But I'm goin' to keep a clear head like Tom an' Isaac here.'

'Tom an' Isaac never won a race today. Close-run thing it

109

was, an' all. I reckon you did right well. Here, Tom, fill up a pint for Luke an' one for Bill over there as well,' Dick Ham shouted.

The tankard came along the bar to him and Luke had no option but to drink it. 'Your very good health,' the shout went up as he drained the mug.

A great many good healths were drunk in the taproom of the Falcon that night. Luke lost count of the number.

Cassie was run off her feet. After the evening meal, the dining room had been opened up as a saloon bar in an extension of the snuggery and it had been filled with yacht captains and owners celebrating the summer's racing and sailing. Captains swapped yarns with captains, races were relived and re-raced – 'I yelled for "water" 'cause I was nearly ashore on the rocks off the Needles but the bugger never took no notice. So I rammed him. Straight through his fores'l with my boom. That made 'im sit up, I can tell ye.' 'Got disqualified, din't ye?' 'No, but there was a rare ole row about it. But 'e shoulda left me room. 'E shouldn't hev hemmed me in.' A hollow laugh. ''E won't do it again in a hurry, the bugger.'

Owners, too were standing drinks to their captains if they had had a successful season – and most of them had. Essex captains were some of the best in the world, so the atmosphere was filled with goodwill and the reek of spirits. Abel Crowther, although no longer an owner himself, knew several of the others and he spent the evening sociably enough with them, whilst Hannah did as much as she considered dignified in administering to the company, leaving Cassie to attend to most things, even to providing extra food where it was asked for, as well as putting an appearance in the taproom from time to time.

At last it was eleven-thirty – an extension had been granted as it was regatta night but only till eleven-thirty because everything must be cleared and tidied before midnight, the next day being Sunday. The taproom had been full all evening and there had been an influx of people when the fair closed down for the night at ten o'clock, with much rowdy singing and the odd scuffle or two, swiftly quelled by the men behind the bar. Now the last of the customers had gone, leaving behind an atmosphere of stale beer and tobacco smoke, and taking with them a trail of sawdust from the floor and bursting bladders that would be emptied against the first available wall as they staggered home, singing and fighting.

'No trouble tonight, Tom?' Cassie said, yawning as she did the last of the glasses.

'Bit of a scuffle at one time, but Luke soon put a stop to it.' He looked round. 'Where is Luke? Come to think on it I ain't seen him this past hour or more. Not since I sent 'im down the cellar to tap another barrel.'

'I reckon 'e went off to bed,' Isaac said, picking up his cheesecutter and settling it on his head. 'An' thass jest where I'm a-goin' now. G'night, all.'

'Goodnight, Isaac. And thank you,' Cassie called.

''Night Isaac, bor.' Tom leaned on the bar and scratched his head. 'Do you reckon Luke's gone to bed, Cassie, girl?'

'There's only one way to find out. I'll go and have a look. I shan't be a minute, then I'll come and help you finish here.'

'He'd had a bit to drink,' Tom called after her. 'Reckon 'e went up to sleep it off,' he muttered to himself. 'I ain't never seen the boy Luke drink afore. Not like 'is old dad. Sat in the corner there tonight, Alf did, waitin' for all an' sundry to buy 'im drinks – which they did – till 'e couldn't see 'is way outa a the door an' had to be pointed the right way to get 'ome. Shouldn't be surprised if 'e fell in the river on the way, an' serve 'im right. He wouldn't be no loss to nobody, an' thass a fact.' All the time he had been muttering Tom had been putting the chairs and stools on the tables ready to sweep the floor and lay fresh sawdust in the morning.

'He's not there.' Cassie came back. 'Where do you think he can be, Tom?'

''E can't still be down in the cellar, surely.' Tom put the last stool on the table and rubbed his back. 'I better go down an' take a look.'

'Yes. He might have got himself locked in.' Cassie followed Tom along the passage to the door under the stairs that gave access to the cellar from inside the house. Tom picked up a stub of candle and lit it and went down the stone steps, calling Luke as he went. 'Ain't nobody here, Cassie,' he said, holding the candle high.

'Oh, yesseris.' A voice came from the depths of the cellar where the candlelight didn't penetrate.

'Luke?' Cassie called uncertainly.

'Luke?' His voice imitated hers. 'I'll give you "Luke", you come near me.' There was a crash in the darkness.

'Leave this to me, Cassie,' Tom said, putting her behind him.

'But what is it? What's wrong? Is he ill?' Cassie followed anxiously. 'Luke's never like this.'

''E's as drunk as a lord,' Tom said, 'an' that sounds as if 'e's turned nasty with it. Now, come on, bor, what are you doin' down here in the dark?'

There was another crash and Luke appeared out of the dimness, red-eyed and dishevelled, as frightening a sight as anything Cassie's imagination could have dreamed up. He was brandishing a bottle. 'Keep away from me or I'll cut yer face to ribbons,' he shouted, smashing the bottle on a beer keg and advancing with the jagged neck in his hand.

'Don't be a fool, Luke.' Tom never swore. 'Put that thing down and come upstairs.'

112

'I'll kill you. I'll kill everybody. I don't care.' As Luke came lumbering towards them Tom thrust Cassie to one side and stuck out his foot. Luke tripped over it and went sprawling on the floor, shouting obscenities. He got to his knees and began to grope for the broken bottle but Tom took him by the hair, jerked his head back and caught him a blow to the jaw that knocked him out cold. 'There. That'll settle 'im,' he said, rubbing his knuckles.

'Oh, Tom, I've never seen him like that before,' Cassie said, tears running down her face. 'I've never seen him even a little the worse for drink.'

'An' thass most likely the reason,' Tom said. "E knows that once 'e starts to drink 'e can't stop, an' that the drink makes him ugly-tempered. Thass why you've never seen 'im touch a drop. But tonight everybody wanted 'im to celebrate, although, give 'im 'is due 'e kept on refusin'. But they overpersuaded 'im an' this is the result. 'E 'on't be feelin' too grand in the mornin', I doubt.'

'We'd better get him upstairs. Shall I take his feet?' Cassie said.

'No. I can manage 'im.' Tom bent down and got hold of Luke and put him over his shoulder as if he was no more than a sack of coal. 'You go first, Cassie an' I'll foller.'

At the top of the steps Tom said, 'Now if you'll lock up, Cassie, I'll take this great mawkes home with me to my shanty. I don't think he'll get violent any more but there's no tellin', an' if 'e does, well, I can deal with 'im. Don't you worry, dearie, 'e'll be all right, 'cept 'e'll hev a head the size of six in the mornin'. But that'll serve 'im right. An' I'll soon sober 'im up, don't you never fear.' He hitched Luke further up on his shoulder. 'Goodnight, Cassie, girl.'

'Goodnight, Tom. And thank you.' Cassie went thoughtfully

113

up the stairs to her own bed, empty without Luke. So that was what had bothered him ever since they moved into the Falcon. He had been afraid that he might be tempted to drink, knowing how violent it could make him. She had always known there was something that worried him since they had come there to live, but she had never guessed it might be anything like this.

Hannah knew nothing of the drama downstairs. She had gone to bed at her usual time, leaving Cassie to see to the last customers and lock up. She heard Abel come up the stairs and go into the room next door and it wasn't long before she saw the handle of the connecting door turn. Her heart gave its customary little leap. Even after all these years he still had the same effect when he entered her room and her bed.

'It's bin a long time, this time, lass,' he said, as he took her in his arms.

'Nearly six months,' she answered. 'I began to think you weren't coming any more.'

'No danger o' that,' he chuckled. 'I have to keep an eye on the way you keep your books.'

She gave him a playful push. 'Is that all you come for, Abel Crowther?'

He kissed her. 'Tha knows different to that, Hannah Jordan,' he said, his voice thickening. 'I get more comfort from you than I've ever had from Charlotte, God knows. She's like ice, that woman. I don't know why I ever married her, except she was a pretty little thing and her father owned the file factory. Well, that's mine now, so I got summat out of the deal, but as for her, she's not even pretty now, and always poorly, always complaining. She's a reet nagging misery, and that's the truth of it. And she hasn't even given me a son to carry on the business. Neither chick nor child have I got, more's the pity.' He drew away and looked down at Hannah in the candlelight. 'Yet all these years I've been coming here and you don't look a day different to when I first saw tha, lass, 'cept p'raps for a glint o' silver.' He put up his hand and touched her hair. 'Things worked out wrong, didn't they? Tha's the one I should have married, not Charlotte.' He grinned. 'I'm getting on, Hannah. I'm the wrong side o' fifty, tha knows, but tha can still make me feel like a young blade on his honeymoon. After all these years, too. But we're wasting time . . .'

When Hannah got up the next morning she looked a little tired, with circles under her eyes but it was nothing to Luke's haggard appearance. Tom had managed to sober him up and he came into the kitchen with a dejected, hang-dog air.

'I'm sorry, Cassie,' he said as he slumped down at the table. 'I'm sorry.'

Hannah looked at him and then at Cassie. So, something *was* wrong between them – really wrong, just as she'd suspected. She busied herself at the stove with her back to them. It was none of her business, up to a point.

Cassie dispatched Florrie and Lizzy to jobs in other rooms and leaned over the table towards him. 'Why didn't you tell me, Luke? Why didn't you tell me this was likely to happen?' she stormed. 'We would never have come here if I'd known what you were like.'

He looked up. 'You know what I'm like, Cassie,' he said sharply. 'What happened last night was not *me*. It was the drink. I knew what could happen once I got drink inside me. That's why I stay late at the Yard – I don't need to, not now, not like I used to – but I thought if I wasn't here I wouldn't be tempted although I vowed long enough ago that I'd never touch another drop. And I wouldn't have, but last night in the bar they

115

kept on and on at me ...' His voice dropped. 'I nearly killed a man, once. You didn't know that, did you.'

She sat down at the table and put her head in her hands. 'So that was why you were so reluctant to move here in the first place,' she said. 'If only I'd known ...'

'Well, you know now,' he said with a sigh that seemed to come from the depths of his being.

Cassie looked round as if looking for a way to escape. 'We shall have to leave here, of course. We can't stay. Not after this happening ...'

Luke nodded. 'Yes, I'll find somewhere for us.' He looked up. 'I believe there's a house going in Queen's Road.'

'For rent?'

'Yes.' He dragged himself to his feet. 'I'll go and see about it now. Oh, God,' he staggered a little, 'my head.'

'Serve you right,' Cassie snapped. 'Perhaps you'll have learned your lesson. Go on, get out, go and see about this house. The sooner we leave here the better for all concerned.'

'Nonsense! I never heard such talk.' Hannah swung round. 'The man needs support, not blame, my girl.'

Cassie's jaw dropped at her mother's surprising intervention and for a moment she simply stood and stared at her. Then she turned away. 'You didn't see him,' she said bitterly.

'I've seen others.' Hannah folded her arms. 'There's no need for you to leave. Luke doesn't have to go near the bar if he doesn't trust himself. It needn't cause any problem; he knows the danger and now so do we.'

Luke slumped back into his chair and looked up, equally surprised at his mother-in-law. He had never expected to be championed from that quarter and he didn't know whether to be glad or sorry. 'And so does poor old Tom,' he said sadly, rubbing his jaw, which was turning gently blue in his ashen face.

He looked at Cassie. She would hate leaving the Falcon again. He remembered how unhappy she'd been before. And now he'd become used to living here he found it was not half as bad as he'd feared. Much to his surprise Hannah had never interfered – until now – and even more surprisingly it had been with him and not Cassie that she had sided. And now the drink problem was out in the open he was sure it would never be repeated.

His mind made up, he sat up straight in his chair. 'Thank you, Hannah,' he nodded briefly in her direction, 'I won't let you down. After all, Tom works in the bar and I've never seen him touch a drop o' liquor so I can do the same.' He turned to Cassie. 'We can stay here at the Falcon quite safely, Cassie. I shan't get into a state like I did last night ever again, I promise you that, in your mother's hearin'. You never need to worry about that.' He got up and went out into the scullery and they could hear the sound of water sloshing. A moment later he came back, his face and head wet from being doused under the pump. 'I'm goin' to the Yard now.'

'Do you feel well enough? You look terrible,' Cassie protested.

'Thass my punishment. I *feel* terrible. But it'll pass. I'll work it off.' He straightened his shoulders and went out of the door.

Without another word Hannah returned to the stove where she was cooking breakfast for Abel Crowther, leaving Cassie to see to the other guests. But Cassie made no move to get up from the table. She hadn't known about Luke's drink problem and fear clutched at her heart. Was this how Alf Turnbull had begun on his road to drunkenness? Would Luke end up like his father? Oh, Edward, she sighed silently, how different things could have been. Should have been. How can I hope to give your son the life he deserves?

'It's no use you sitting there feeling sorry for yourself,'

Hannah said without looking over her shoulder. 'You're not the first wife whose husband's got drunk and you won't be the last. And Luke did have cause to celebrate.'

'I know, but ...'

'But nothing. He's said it'll never happen again. Don't you believe the man?'

'Yes, but ...'

Hannah turned round, still holding the frying pan in her hand. 'I'm sure you don't have to worry about Luke, Cassie,' she said, her voice softer. 'He's a good, hardworking, upright man. So he got drunk. Well, nobody's perfect, are they? I've seen your father when he was so drunk he couldn't stand up. It didn't happen often but when it did I didn't think it was the end of the world. You should be thankful you've got such a good man as a husband. Because he *is* a good man, Cassie, isn't he?'

Cassie nodded. 'Oh, yes, Mama. He's a good man.'

'And he's a good father to the children?'

'Yes.'

Hannah looked at Cassie shrewdly. It was obvious the girl wasn't going to confide in her. 'Nothing in life's perfect, girl,' she said. 'Remember that.'

Chapter Nine

Luke was as good as his word. Although he sometimes took a turn in the bar with Tom he never touched alcohol again. He gained strength both from the fact that Cassie knew his problem and also from Hannah's unexpected sympathy towards him. Even when little Charity was born, three years after Simon, and another child two years later, he celebrated with nothing stronger than tea – although 'celebrate' was hardly the word to describe the events surrounding that baby's birth.

Robert was nearly eight by the time Cassie's fourth child was born. He was a slim lad, tall for his age, with a mane of fair hair that flopped untidily over his forehead. He went to the National School in the High Street, Luke had been adamant about that, although Hannah had wanted to pay for him to go to one of the Academies in the village. Fortunately learning came easily to him. In spite of the monitorial system, where an older child who had learned facts from the tutor came and recited them to small groups who learned to chant them parrot-fashion without necessarily understanding what they were saying, he somehow learned to read and write, knew most of his multiplication tables and could, if pressed, recite passages from Shakespeare. But his favourite haunt was the quay, where he would spend hours either in the water – he could swim like a fish – or larking about in the mud with the other lads. The two boys were totally unlike. Where Robert was fair and fine-featured – just like his mother, people were fond of remarking – Simon was very much Luke's son, with thick brown hair, Luke's thoughtful grey eyes and a figure which, even at the tender age of five, was broad and beefy. There was no guile about Simon. If he wanted something he yelled for it and if he was hurt he yelled louder. He idolized his elder brother and tolerated Charity, his sister, who didn't appreciate his efforts with the wooden building bricks and took a delight in knocking down his carefully-constructed castles. On the whole they were all good children and there were plenty of people at the Falcon to keep an eye on them. Both Lizzy and Florrie were susceptible to their charms so they never went short of a warm cake or a slice of bread and dripping and when Cassie found herself pregnant again before Charity's second birthday she was not dismayed. The two boys had already been moved out of Cassie and Luke's big bedroom to the little bedroom at the front of the house and Charity had been promoted to the truckle bed so the cradle was waiting to be filled again.

Cassie loved her children and so did Luke; sometimes she felt it was the only thing they had in common, for the rest he might have been no more than a permanent guest at the Falcon, except that they shared the same bed and indulged in lovemaking that for her held little love in it. Not that she ever stopped to analyse her life. She was too busy to pause and wonder whether or not she was happy because Hannah did less and less, leaving Cassie to run things while she complained about her arthritis – which miraculously disappeared when Abel Crowther put in an appearance – and sat in her sitting room doing complicated embroidery which she said was for the church but which never got finished. Cassie couldn't help a cynical smile, as her pregnancy progressed, at the way Hannah exhorted her to rest more but never raised a finger to lighten her work load.

In fact, the only thing that Hannah did now to help at the Falcon was to look after the accounts and this task she guarded jealously although it was the one thing Cassie could have wished her to relinquish. Because Hannah was mean. She complained about even the most essential bills and when Cassie asked for money for new sheets she refused to give it to her.

'Why do you need new sheets?' Hannah was sitting in her room with the window closed although there was brilliant sunshine outside.

'Because the old ones are thin and torn.'

'Patch them. That's what I used to do. I don't know what things are coming to, wanting new things at every turn.' She smoothed the skirt of her new dress.

The irony of this didn't escape Cassie. 'They have been patched, Mama. In fact, the sheets on my bed have been patched over the patches. We have a standard to keep up.' She gazed out of the window. 'I'm afraid I shall even have to put a sheet with a patch on Mr Crowther's bed when he comes,' she said, keeping her voice casual.

Hannah looked up sharply. 'Very well. Go and buy some bleached calico. We'll make new.'

'Thank you, Mama.' Suppressing a smile Cassie left the room. She had learned how to handle her mother. And she wouldn't buy calico, she could buy the sheets ready-made. She knew where she could get them at a very reasonable price that would satisfy even Hannah's parsimony.

It was September and the sixth month of Cassie's pregnancy. Lizzy had bathed all the children and put them to bed, Luke was helping Tom in the bar and Millie was just finishing the

121

washing up in the scullery when there was a knock at the back door. Cassie got to her feet. It was one of the rare occasions when she had managed to find five minutes to rest and even that was to be disturbed, she thought ruefully. She automatically went to the bread board and cut off a slice of bread before opening the door. Ragged children often came to the Falcon pleading for a crust and they were never refused in Cassie's hearing.

It was a real autumn evening, misty and growing dusk although it was not much past seven. A girl of about sixteen stood on the step. She was neatly dressed in a dark blue dress with a frill round the bottom that reached just past her calves and her boots were obviously new. Clearly she hadn't come to beg. Cassie peered at the face under the wide-brimmed hat.

'Why, Bella, come in, child. Whatever's the matter?' she said, recognising Freddie Hurst's daughter. She stood aside for the pale, tear-streaked girl to enter. It was not the first time people in trouble had come to the door, either.

'I din't know where else to go, Miz Turnbull.' Bella began to cry again. 'I din't want to go to the work'us an' I thought you might know where I could git work for a bit. Y'see, miz Turnbull, me mum's turned me out.'

'Turned you out!' Cassie's eyes widened in surprise. Bella was the Hursts' only daughter and the apple of her father's eye. 'Why on earth should she turn you out? And what about your father? Does he know?' She frowned. 'Oh, Bella, your mother hasn't turned you out to make more room for lodgers, has she?' she said. Freddie Hurst still sought refuge in the taproom from the constant stream of lodgers his wife housed.

Bella hung her head. 'No, it's not that, Miz Turnbull.' Then, eagerly, 'Yes, thass what it is. There ain't room for me at 'ome. Do you want anybody, Miz Turnbull? I can scrub an' clean like a good 'un.'

'That's not the reason your mother turned you out, Bella, is it?' Cassie drew the girl nearer to the fire as she spoke. 'Now, tell me the truth. I can't help you unless I know the whole story.'

Bella bit her thumb. 'Thass because ... because I'm hevin' a baby,' she said at last and broke into uncontrollable sobs.

Cassie closed her eyes in despair. When she opened them Bella was knuckling her eyes like a child might. The girl wasn't all that bright ... Did she know what she'd done? 'How did it happen?' Cassie started again. 'Do you know who the father is, Bella?'

'Mr Jones, Mum's new lodger.' Bella gave a sniff and Cassie found her a handkerchief. 'Mum was out an' 'e said if I didn't go upstairs wiv 'im 'e'd tell Mum that was me what 'ud stole the money from 'er purse.'

'And was it?'

Bella nodded. 'Well, she never give me any an' I always hev to fetch the water an' wash the dirty saucepans an' clean the shoes, an' that. I wanted a pretty slide for my hair, so I took the money and bought it. That was only tuppence.'

'So you went upstairs with Mr Jones rather than admit to your mother you'd taken tuppence from her purse.'

Bella nodded again, then she shook her head. 'No, 'e made me. 'E shoved me up the stairs an' made me do it. 'E was stronger'n me. I cou'n't stop 'im. But 'e give me sixpence every time, so I didn't mind much,' she added honestly.

'But did you know? Did you understand – about babies, I mean?' Cassie asked, recalling her own ignorance.

'Oh, yes.' Bella nodded vigorously. 'But I never thought it would happen to me. Mr Jones is quite old, you see. I reckon 'e must be thirty or more.'

Cassie drew in her breath sharply. It would be comical if it weren't so tragic. 'But now you find you're having this baby and your mother has turned you out. Does she know it belongs to the lodger, Mr – er Jones?'

Bella shook her head and her tears began again. 'She never even asked who the father was. She jest called me a little slut and said she wasn't hevin' trouble laid at her door and turned me out. I never had a chance to say nuthin'. Not nuthin'.' She gazed round the kitchen. 'I thought me dad might be 'ere,' she gave a despairing shrug, 'not that 'e could do much. Mum don't take no notice of what 'e say. Oh, what shall I do, Miz Turnbull? What shall I do?'

Cassie went over to the stove and poured Bella a cup of tea from the pot that was constantly on the hob. 'Now take that through to the scullery. You'll find Florrie and Millie in there. They'll look after you till I come back.'

She went through to the taproom. As she expected, Freddie was in his usual seat by the window. She took him through to the kitchen and gave him a cup of tea, too. He quickly sobered up when he heard what she had to tell him. 'Bloody lodger,' he muttered. 'Where's Bella now?'

'Through there.' Cassie nodded in the direction of the scullery. 'You'd better talk to her.'

'That I will. I ain't hevin' my girl turned out of the house on account of what some lodger's done to her. The bastard. I'll kill 'im. I never liked this one, shifty-eyed bugger he is.' He put down his mug and stood up. 'Mind you, Mrs Turnbull, I hev to say this, there's never bin anything like this afore. An' whatever people might think, my Annie'd never hev any truck with that sorta thing, that I do know.' He went towards the door. 'Poor little Bella. An' all for a tuppenny hair slide.' He shook his head and his shoulders sagged. 'I don't know wass got into Annie these days, straight up, I don't.' He was quiet for a minute, then he straightened up and squared his shoulders. 'But I shall put a stop to it, you see if I don't. I'm gonna do what I shoulda done years ago. I'm gonna take young Bella home with me an' I'm gonna put my foot down. No more lodgers! I shall tell 'er, she'll hev quite enough to do bringin' up Bella's littl'un 'ithout takin' in lodgers. She won't hev no time for them. Not any more.'

'She might not agree to that,' Cassie said doubtfully.

Freddie's face darkened. 'She'll agree to whatever I say, time I've finished with 'er, Mrs Turnbull,' he said. He went into the scullery. 'Come on, Bella, gal. I'll take you home. You don't hev to worry,' seeing the look of alarm on the girl's face, 'I'll see to it that you're not turned out if I hev to take me belt off to your mother to persuade her. And Mr Jones'll be lookin' for new lodgin's tonight— And a doctor, too, time I've finished with 'im! Thass a good job he's the only one she's got in now, do they'd all be out on their ear.' He took Bella by the arm and went off, muttering furiously.

Cassie sank down in her chair again. She wouldn't relish being in Annie Hurst's shoes tonight! But it was high time the brawny blacksmith asserted himself. It was strange how often it happened that the biggest, brawniest men were the most oppressed by their wives.

Two days later Annie Hurst came to the door with a pot of home-made raspberry jam. 'I jest brought this to thank you for what you done the other night, Miz Turnbull,' she said. She shook her head. 'I never realized ...' her voice was low with shock. 'I've *never* had goin's on like that under my roof, an' never would. My Freddie was quite right to turn the man out.' She simpered a little. 'I didn't know my Freddie could be so masterful. He says I'm not to hev lodgers ever again, and I think he's right. After all, you never know, do you?'

'And what about Bella? Is she all right?' Cassie asked.

'Oh, yes, thanks to you, Miz Turnbull,' Annie clutched her

hands to her breast dramatically. 'If she hadn't come to you . . . oh, that don't bear thinkin' about, do it! But me an' Freddie'll stand by 'er an' bring up the littl'un as if it was our own. There'll be talk, but we'll hold our heads up an' do right by the girl.' She gave a sanctimonious shrug.

'I'm glad to hear it, Annie,' Cassie said dryly.

After that Freddie only came to the Falcon on Friday nights and then only for a pint and a game of dominoes. As for Annie, there were no more lodgers at number four Sun Yard. By the time Bella's baby was born Annie was five months pregnant herself.

November and early December of 1877 were raw and foggy; the men clustered round the big log fires in the taproom and the snuggery lived up to its name. Hannah kept very much to the sitting room, which she had gradually commandeered for her own personal use, and it was Millie's task to make sure the fire was kept bright there. It didn't worry Cassie that the sitting room was virtually out of bounds to her and her family because the kitchen was big and warm and there was plenty of room for them all there. And the servants were snug enough in the scullery, where they had cleaned out the old stove and lit it. With some old rugs and furniture that was no longer needed the girls had made themselves a comfortable retreat for when the work was done.

It was late one afternoon in mid-December. Luke was rowing upriver against the ebb and Martin was sitting hunched in the stern of a small dinghy that had just been finished. Luke always claimed the right to take new boats out on trials, and he and Martin had gone out in this one, made to a new design of Martin's, to make sure the length of the oars was right, to check the stability and how well the dinghy moved through

126

the water. 'Well, she seems nippy enough,' Martin said with a satisfied nod.

'Thass because o' the man on the oars,' Luke grinned. 'The harder I pull the nippier she'll be. But I grant you she's quick to manoeuvre. Is she a bit low in the water, do you think?'

'No, I think she's about right. Watch out, Luke, there's a buoy dead ahead in the water. Pull over a bit to starboard. That's it. Tide's ebbing fast now, I can see that by the rate it's running past the buoy.'

'Yes, it's a hard pull against it.' Luke rowed on, the silence broken only by the creak of the oars in the rowlocks and their rhythmic splash through the water.

'What's that caught up in those posts by the bank?' Martin called. 'Over to starboard, there. It's getting dark but I'm sure there's something there. Can you see? Look, there, between *Fedora* and *Valfreya*?'

Luke turned his head. 'Heap of old rubbish, by the look of it. But we'll go and have a look, if you like.' He pulled on one oar and guided the boat into the bank between the two yachts laid up for the winter. Martin reached out and pulled at the bundle caught up between the posts. 'Hold the boat steady, Luke. Whatever it is is stuck in the mud. Oh, God, Luke it's a young lad!' He heaved the bundle over the side, seeing in the fading light a shock of dark hair and an ashen, mud-streaked face 'Oh, God, Luke, it's young Simon. Your boy! Pull for the shore, man! Quick!'

'Oh, Simon, my lad, what hev you been up to?' Luke said as he rowed frantically for the shore while Martin worked desperately to force the water out of the little boy's lungs and some air into them. 'Do you think he's been in the water long, Marty?'

'Too long, I reckon.' Martin jumped out and made the boat fast and Luke picked up his son and laid him on the bank to work on him again.

'Yes, thass the cold ... He wouldn't need to be in the water many minutes, this time o' year.' Luke broke off, breathless from trying to breathe life back into the little frame.

'Here, let me have another go,' Martin knelt down and took his place.

Luke watched him for some time, then he shook his head. 'Thass no good, Marty,' the tears were running unchecked down his face. 'We can't do it. He's been in the water too long.' He sat back on his heels and dashed his hand across his eyes.

The two men looked at each other and at the inert little body lying between them. 'Do you want me to carry him home, Luke?' Martin asked, his voice breaking on the words.

Luke sniffed, his face working. 'No, Marty, thanks all the same. He's my boy. I'll carry him.' He gathered the little boy up in his arms and got to his feet. 'Come on, laddie, let's take you home,' he said softly, planting a kiss on the cold little forehead.

Martin followed, his head bowed, his hand comfortingly on Luke's shoulder.

Florrie was cutting bread for the children's tea and Charity was sitting on the hearthrug chewing a 'nobbier' – a thick corner of crust spread with butter. Robert came in and went to the table. 'Oh, can I have a nobbier, too, Florrie?' he begged.

'Not till you've washed some of that mud off your hands, my lad. Git you to the sink and clean yourself up.'

'Didn't Simon come in with you, Bobby?' Cassie was near to her time and resting by the fire, a pile of darning by her side. 'I sent him to call you for tea.'

'No, I haven't seen him,' Robert called from the scullery where he was showing his hands to the pump.

'But I sent him down to the quay to find you. Didn't you see him?'

'No. I've been in with Piggy Bartlett, looking at his pipe collection. He's got more than me but his are all in bits. I've got some whole ones so that counts for more, doesn't it? Can I have my nobbier now, Florrie?'

'Oh, here y'are, ye worritsome crittur,' Florrie said with a smile. 'But if you eat that you won't eat your tea.'

'Oh, yes I will.' Robert began tucking into his crust.

'I think you should go and look for Simon. It's getting dark,' Cassie said anxiously. 'He's not very old to be out alone. He only went to fetch you home.'

'Oh, all right.' Reluctantly, Robert shrugged on his coat and picked up his cap. He opened the door just as Luke and Martin reached it.

Cassie was inconsolable. She blamed herself for sending Simon to his death, ignoring the fact that he had done the same errand dozens of times before without harm. No one had seen what happened but it was fairly plain that he had run down Rose Lane to the quay and tripped over a mooring warp and gone headfirst into the water. He would hardly have made a splash and his little body would have been taken with the ebb till it got caught in the reeds. It was not the first time such a drowning had taken place.

'Thass no good blamin' yourself, Cassie girl,' Luke said as he cradled her in his arms in the big bed after the funeral.

'Don't you think I hevn't said to meself a hundred times that if only Marty an' me hadn't stopped to take a walk on Rat Island we'd have been upriver that much sooner? Less than half an hour and the poor little shaver'd still be with us.' The tears ran down his face in the darkness. When he could speak again he went on. 'But thass no good dwellin' on that. Thass happened an' there's no goin' back. That was an accident, pure and simple. It could have happened to anybody's littl'un.'

'But it didn't happen to anybody's. It happened to *ours*, Luke,' she sobbed. 'I'll never forgive myself.'

Luke stroked her hair and comforted her as best he could through his own grief as she clung to him. He felt that for once she was close to him, that her need of him was as great as his need of her. But he knew he had to be strong. 'Thass no way to talk, my girl,' he said firmly, when her tears had begun to subside. 'Life's gotta go on.' He put his hand on her swollen stomach. 'There's another little one to come. We must look forward to that.'

'Please God it'll be a boy,' she whispered.

'Don't matter either way,' he said softly. 'As long as thass healthy.'

But it did matter. Cassie's guilt was twofold now. Not only had she deceived Luke over Robert but she had, however inadvertently, sent his true son to his death. Perhaps this was her punishment. Certainly nothing could have been harder. For the rest of her pregnancy the only thing that kept her sane was the thought that she was carrying another son for Luke.

The baby was born on New Year's Eve after a difficult labour that had lasted a night and a day. 'Is he all right?' she asked Luke as he bent over her when it was all over.

'Yes, Cassie girl, as right as a trivet.' He smoothed her damp hair from her forehead and smiled at her.

'What shall we call him, Luke? Shall he be another little Simon?'

Luke shook his head. 'No, Cassie, dear, he won't be another little Simon. She's a little maid. I thought we might call her Amy.'

'A *girl*!' She turned her head away as tears of disappointment welled in her eyes. 'I wanted so much to give you a – another son. But next time ...'

'There won't be a next time, Cassie. The doctor says no more.' Luke's voice was gentle. 'But I'm satisfied, Cassie. We've got young Bobbie and Charity, and this one's a bonny little maid, look at her.' He put the baby in the crook of Cassie's arm and smiled encouragingly. Cassie tried to smile back but inside she felt nothing but a sense of shame and bitter failure.

Chapter Ten

Cassie took a long time to recover from Amy's birth. She was listless and lacking in energy for so long that Hannah was forced once again to take an active part in running the Falcon. All through January and February Cassie sat in the rocking chair beside the kitchen fire, attending mechanically to the baby's needs and paying scant attention to the petty squabbles between the servants. If she was aware of their resentment at Hannah's high-handed treatment of them she took no notice. In truth, she showed little interest in anything.

Luke worried about her and did what he could to help. Although they were always busy at the Yard he no longer worked such long hours but often came home early enough to help Tom in the bar. In a strange way, now that his drink problem was out in the open it no longer worried him. He didn't even feel tempted by it and it saddened him to watch it rule his father's life.

Alf naturally resented his drinking being watched over by his teetotal son and was often rude and abusive towards Luke, especially when Luke tried to persuade him not to waste his last penny on beer.

'Mind yer own business, ye cheeky young bugger,' Alf would growl, jealous of his son's position both at the Falcon and, even more, at Turnbull's Yard. Alf had never risen beyond a labouring job for the whole of his working life and he resented the fact that Luke was already Yard foreman as well as foreman of the joiners.

Tom could see the difficulty. 'Leave your dad to me, Luke,' he said quietly one evening when Alf was more than usually belligerent. 'You go and look after Billy Bradshaw and his crowd by the window.'

Alf banged his tankard down on the counter. 'Another pint. An' don't give me that muck thass been watered down, neither,' he demanded rudely.

'We don't water our beer, Alf,' Tom said, pulling a frothing pint and pushing it across the bar. 'Not yet,' he added under his breath, 'but if the missus get her way we soon shall. I don't know wass come over her lately.' Luke came back behind the bar. 'I wish young Cassie'd pull herself round, Luke,' Tom said, shaking his head. 'The place is going to rack and ruin since the missus has taken over again. I don't know wass come over her, straight I don't. She's always bin tight with money, that I'll own, but she's got wuss an' wuss, till now ...' he shook his head again, 'she'd scrap a farthin' outa a turd an' not get 'er hands dirty. An' that ain't as if trade was bad. We still get plenty of customers. But we shan't if she insists on waterin' the beer an' thass a fact.'

Luke sighed heavily. 'I'll talk to Cassie again, Tom,' he promised, 'but I doubt it'll do much good. She doesn't seem to care about anything any more.'

'Thass bad, Luke,' Tom said. 'She need suthin' to take her outa herself. Thass what she need.'

'She's still grieving over young Simon. And it didn't help that little Amy wasn't a boy. She can't seem to get over it,' Luke said sadly.

Tom nodded, his face sombre. 'Aye, we all miss that little shaver.' His expression lightened. 'But there's always a next time. P'raps the next one will be another boy.'

'That's just the trouble. There won't be any more.'

'Well, at least you've got one, together. 'Tain't as if they're all girls. And young Bobby's a good boy.'

'That's what I tell her. But it doesn't seem to do any good.'

March came in like the proverbial lion. There were gales up and down the country that sent fishing boats scurrying for harbour, to stay sheltering in their berths until the weather had calmed. At Turnbull's Yard they were putting the finishing touches to a new yawl that had been ordered by Lord Ramsgate for the coming season's racing and she was chocked up on the slip and extra props and blocks had been put in to keep her steady. All hands had been called to work on her, with the consequence that everything else had been left. A 'bogey', a coke brazier that the men had made from a big grease drum to warm their frozen fingers, had gone cold and been left standing, paint kettles littered the place, a pot of glue had been overturned, welding the sawdust where it had spilled into a solid lump, and a heap of timber that had been delivered ready for the next job had been hurriedly stacked in the corner. Sawing-horses stood where they had been used and left and the vats of grease that had been liberally larded on to the slip so that the yacht would slide easily into the water stood empty and evil-smelling.

Luke came down the stairs from the office, ramming his cap on his head and bracing himself against the wind. 'Better get this mess cleared up before Mr George see it,' he shouted over the noise of the gale as he strode through the Yard. 'You boys, clear up these paint pots and take them back to the paint shop.

And get that timber stacked properly. In this wind that'll topple over stacked like that. And get rid of the grease vats. You can put the rubbish into them. Come on, I'll give you a hand ...'

'Luke!' It was Martin shouting from the top of the office stairs, his hands cupped round his mouth. 'Can you come up a minute?' Luke recognised the beckoning gesture rather than heard the words.

It was an hour later before they both left the office. The Yard was clean and tidy and the men and boys all gone, either to the pub or home for their midday break. Even the wood shavings had been cleared away, no mean feat with the wind churning them into eddies. 'Ah, thass better,' Luke said, standing at the top of the stairs and looking around. 'I dunno what Uncle George would have said if he'd seen the mess the place was in. Talk about while the cat's away the mice'll play! And he's only been off a week with 'flu.'

'He'll be back tomorrow,' Martin said hunching his shoulders into his coat and following Luke down the stairs and across the Yard to the gate.

'Haifa minute, Marty.' Luke turned his collar up against the gale. He pointed to a corner of the Yard. 'I'd better just check that timber. I told them to re-stack it, but it might be better if it was roped. In this wind ...' The gale carried the rest of his words away.

Martin followed him. 'Looks all right, Luke. Looks steady enough to me.' He put out his hand and tried it. 'Yes. Steady as a rock.'

'I still think I'd be happier if it had a couple of ropes round it. Thass only got to get the wind underneath one of them baulks and that'll topple. There's some rope in the joiner's shop, I'll go and fetch it.' Luke hurried off, returning in a few minutes with the rope, his tall frame bent against the relentless wind that howled through the Yard. He was halfway back when a sudden gust lifted a twenty-foot length of elm just enough to unbalance it and send it crashing to the ground.

'Watch out, Marty!' he shouted, gesticulating frantically. 'Comin' from the top!'

But Martin didn't hear. He came towards Luke, his hand outstretched for the rope, saying something that the noise of the wind drowned. One more step and it would have missed him. As it was he was caught a glancing blow on the back of the head by a corner of the timber as it hurtled to the ground. He dropped like a stone, his cap, still on his head, slowly turning a dull crimson where the back of his skull was smashed to a bloody pulp.

Luke stared down at him, his eyes wide with horror. 'Marty?' he said, unable to believe the sight before him. '*Marty?* He dropped down on his knees and felt for Martin's pulse. But Martin was quite dead. Luke turned the lifeless body over. Martin's eyes stared up at him, dark and unseeing in a face that was unmarked except for a streak of dust. Luke took off his own cap and bowed his head. 'Oh, no,' he moaned, his grief too deep for tears. 'Not you, too, Marty.' Gently he laid his cousin down again and covered him with the coat off his own back. Then, in his shirtsleeves but heedless of the bitter cold, he went to call for help.

Telling his uncle what had happened was the hardest thing Luke had ever done. George was approaching sixty and Luke saw him age twenty years before his eyes. 'He was my boy. My only boy,' George said over and over again. 'All I've worked for was for him. Now it's gone ... just like that.' He put his arms round his wife to comfort her but his grief was even more terrible than hers.

I'll fetch Hannah,' Luke said helplessly. 'She'll come and stay with you both for a while.'

136

The whole village was stricken. Everyone knew Martin Turnbull and everyone liked him, from the men who worked in the Yard to the members of the Vestry, of which he had been a fair and just member. At his funeral the church was full. People came from all walks of life, and from all the villages along the River Colne, proving what a popular man he had been; and flowers carpeted the graveyard, from a complicated empty chair in red roses from his parents to snowdrops gathered from the hedgerow by the village children. Afterwards Cassie, forced at last to pull herself together, had laid on a sombre meal of home-cured ham and fruit cake in the meeting room at the Falcon, to which everyone was invited. It was a subdued gathering. Even Alf remained sober.

Maisie's grief had made her bitter. Someone had to take the blame for the death of her beloved son and George was the obvious target. 'I never wanted the boy to go into the business,' she said angrily. 'He could have done much better for himself than work in that old Yard. But George would hev him there.' She began to cry again. 'If George'd let him do somethin' else he'd be alive now.'

'It's no good talking like that, Maisie. The boy was as inter-ested in the business as George. You know very well that he wanted to go in with his father,' Hannah said, her voice weary from repetition. 'Anyway, how can you talk like that? You've always been so proud of the Yard and the way George has built it up. I thought you were proud to think Martin was there with his father. For goodness sake, be reasonable.'

But Maisie refused to be reasonable. 'It's George's fault . . . '

'It's nobody's fault. That's no way to talk. George is as] upset as you are. Maisie, you must pull yourself together and think of someone besides yourself.' Hannah spoke in an undertone. 'Whatever will people think!'

'If George hadn't been ill ...'

'If ... if ... if. If wishes were horses, beggars would ride. And if my Reuben hadn't gone to sea he might have been here today instead of drowned in the Irish Sea these nearly thirty years.' Hannah patted her sister's shoulder. 'I do understand, you know Maisie,' she said more kindly. 'But we all have to keep up appearances. And at least you and George have still got each other.'

Maisie sniffed and gave her a watery smile. 'Yes, I know. I'll try and be brave, Hannah.'

When all the company had gone Luke took George and Maisie into the snuggery for a cup of tea and a quiet half hour before they went home. Cassie began to clear up. The pub had been closed for the day out of respect for Martin so everywhere was quiet. The girls, Millie and Florrie, were in the scullery washing up and Lizzy was looking after the children. Hannah had retired to her sitting room to assess the cost of the spread, so Cassie worked alone. She put on a voluminous white overall over her black dress and began methodically to clear and stack the plates and glasses, making several journeys to carry them down the stairs. There was something soothing in restoring order to a room, she had always found this, and as she worked she thought of Martin, cousin to both her and Luke. The two men had been very close; sometimes she felt that Luke had been closer to Martin than his own brothers. Luke would miss him terribly. Suddenly, she banged a pile of plates down on to the tray. It wasn't fair. Fate had already dealt them a bitter blow in the loss of Simon; and now to lose Martin ... She beat her fists on the table in a fit of impotent rage against God, against Fate, against her own helplessness to prevent what had happened. Tears ran down her face, more tears than she had ever shed for little Simon, and God knew she had shed enough for him.

Now she cried for him again, and for Martin, weeping tears of sorrow, of anguish, of anger, of despair, of emotions she couldn't even put a name to. She sank to the floor, her head on the window seat and cried with great sobs that wracked her body yet cleansed her soul. Eventually, she fell asleep. When she woke it was dark except for the light from the gas lamp in the street, shining in through the window.

Slowly, she got to her feet and looked around. Someone had finished cleaning the room although she hadn't heard them moving about. She wondered how long she had slept. It must have been for quite a long time. But it didn't matter, she felt better. The terrible lethargy that had followed Amy's birth had gone, like a weight being lifted from her shoulders, leaving in its place a calm acceptance of what life had dealt her. Simon had gone, Martin had gone. And Amy, poor little scrap, was not the son she so desperately wanted to give Luke. It was her punishment. Punishment for the way she had deceived him. But she knew what she must do. She must give Luke a son. In spite of what the doctor had said she was filled with a calm determination to do this, even if it killed her. She no longer cared about herself, she knew that because she had deceived Luke right from the beginning she had no right to expect happiness. Not that she had ever expected to be really happy, not without Edward. She wondered where he was now. He never came to the village although his father still kept his yacht in the river. Perhaps he was afraid that if he saw her again . . . She shook her head as if to clear it. There was no point in dwelling on what might have been.

She went down the stairs and into the warm kitchen. The children must be put to bed and there were other jobs to be done.

'It's all right, Mrs Cassie,' Lizzy said, 'the childer are both in bed. Did you hev a good sleep, dearie?'

'Why yes, yes,' Cassie looked round in bewilderment. 'But who ... ?'

'I come upstairs an' I see you was asleep so I finished clearin' the table and left you to it. I reckoned you needed that sleep more'n anything. An' Mr Luke agreed with me. You never even roused when 'e come an' stroked your hair.'

'Where is Mr Luke?' Cassie lifted little Amy up out of her cradle where she was just beginning to whimper for food and smiled at her as she put her to the breast. She was very like Simon had been as a baby, for all she was a girl. Cassie bent and kissed the downy little head. It was not Amy's fault she wasn't a boy.

''E won't be long. 'E's jest gone to take Mr and Mrs Turnbull 'ome. 'Is aunt an' uncle, I mean. 'E said if you woke to tell you 'e wouldn't be long.' As Lizzy spoke the back door opened and Luke came in.

Cassie looked at him anxiously. 'Luke, are you all right? Is anything wrong? Uncle George and Aunt Maisie? You look ...'

'No, Cassie,' he shook his head, slowly, as if to clear it. 'Nothing's wrong. It's just that ... I don't know ... I can't take it in.' He sank down at the table and pulled off his cap, twisting it absently between his hands.

'Can't take what in, Luke? I don't understand.'

He looked up. 'What do you reckon, Cassie? Uncle George has just told me he's made me his heir now poor Marty's gone. Everything he's got – the Yard, everything – will come to me when he dies. What do you think of that?'

'But what about Aunt Maisie?'

'Oh, they've got it all worked out between them. Aunt Maisie'll hev the house and enough money to live on for as long as she lives. Then that'll come to me, too. Thass if George goes first, of course. But the Yard'll come straight to me, she says she doesn't want anything to do with that.' He gave a great sigh. 'I don't know, Cassie. I don't know if thass right for me to hev what should've been Marty's.'

'Poor Marty can't have it,' Cassie said quietly. 'And you're the next best thing to a son Uncle George has got. I'm not at all surprised he's named you.'

'Uncle George is certainly more of a father to me than my own ever was,' Luke said sadly. 'But there's another thing . . . '

'Yes?'

'He wants me to go and learn book-keeping so I can help him with the figuring now that Marty's not there to do it.'

Cassie laid the baby in the cradle and went over to him. 'It's a wonderful opportunity for you, Luke,' she said, laying her arm briefly across his shoulders.

'I don't know about that. This is where my skill is, Cassie,' he said, holding out his big, horny hands, 'not in my head. I don't know if I can do it, girl. But how could I refuse the poor old man? He's desperate that I should do it and willing to pay for me to learn. But I don't know if I'm up to it. Oh, I can manage the Yard, that doesn't worry me, me and Martin have looked after that side of it between us for years now. No, it's all the booking and paperwork. I hate paperwork.'

Cassie sank down at his feet and looked up at her husband. For all he was a big man, strong and sinewy, at that moment he looked vulnerable and lost. 'Uncle George will be there to put you on the right road,' she said encouragingly. 'It's not as if you'll have to do it all by yourself, is it?'

'No, I s'pose you're right.' He gave a sigh and stared into the fire. 'Not that Uncle George is much of a book-keeper. He left it all to Marty. Oh, God!' he said savagely, screwing his eyes tightly. 'Why did it have to happen to Marty? He was a good bloke. One o' the best. He'd never done nobody no harm . . . '

141

'Simon was only a little boy. He'd never done anybody any harm, either,' Cassie murmured.

They both sat without speaking for a long time. Then Cassie said, 'Perhaps I'll be able to help. I don't know much about figuring, Mama never lets me near the accounts, but I'm sure I could learn. We'll manage, Luke. I'm sure we shall. And if it's Uncle George's wish you can't let him down.'

He stroked her fair hair, twisted now into a matronly knot on top of her head. 'Thank you, Cassie girl. I don't know what I'd do without you.' He laid his rough cheek against her hair. 'I never expected anything like this, you know. I thought I'd just be a joiner to the end of me days, drawin' me money every week till the day I died. But Uncle George says I'm to hev a good bit more each week and share in the profits as well, so we'll be able to do right by the children and hev a bit to put by.'

She rested her head against his knee. 'You're a good man, Luke. You deserve it. But it'll be a responsibility.'

In late May Stella paid a visit to the Falcon. She had spent the winter with her husband John on Mr Griffith's yacht, sailing in the Mediterranean.

'I came as soon as I could,' she said, sweeping in swathed in a black dress and hat hastily purchased from Colchester. 'We only arrived home yesterday. But why didn't you let me know? I would have come home immediately.'

'We didn't know how to contact you,' Cassie said. 'You didn't leave any forwarding address.' She almost added, 'You didn't even come to say goodbye to us before you went,' but bit her tongue. She didn't want to spoil Hannah's evident joy at the return of her younger daughter.

Hannah had allowed her sitting room to be used in Stella's honour and Cassie viewed the scene with wry amusement as she accepted a cup of tea from her mother's thin, bone china tea service. At that moment she could well understand the chagrin of the prodigal son's brother. All this fuss because Stella had come to visit; Stella, who had hardly put her nose inside the door since her marriage, five years earlier. Cassie suspected that being a yacht captain's wife had turned Stella's head somewhat and to hear her prattling on about sitting at dinner with the Dukes and Duchesses, Lords and Ladies, confirmed her suspicions.

Stella stayed for an hour, alternately dropping names of the people she had been in contact with and the places she had been to – 'Oh, my dears, you should see Vesuvius by night! Such a sight! You've never seen the like! I said to the Duke of Albany ...' and bursting into floods of tears – 'I can't believe it. I simply can't believe it. Cousin Martin. Dead. Do you remember how we all used to congregate on the wall, Cassie? Such a lovely boy ... Oh, and little Simon,' – with renewed tears, 'he was just a baby when I married. A dear little fellow, too. Oh, it's not right, is it, that one so young should be taken.'

Cassie found it all quite wearing and was glad when Stella gathered herself together and prepared to leave.

'Cassie will see you out, Stella dear,' Hannah said as Stella bent to kiss her goodbye. 'Forgive me if I don't come to the door. My arthritis, you understand ...'

Cassie understood, perfectly. Her mother had found Stella equally wearing.

'I suppose John will be off again soon,' Cassie said, as she accompanied Stella along the passage to the door. 'Or has the *Eagle* to have a refit?'

'Yes, John's taking her along to Uncle George's Yard today.' Much to Cassie's dismay Stella sat herself down on the settle near the door. 'But John isn't going to race for Mr Griffith any more, Cassie. Oh, my dear, there was the most fearful row, you'd never believe!' She arched her eyebrows and flapped her hand dramatically. 'These yacht owners are all the same. They think that just because they own the yachts they can tell the captain how to sail them! I ask you! After all, most of them are landlubbers who don't know a warp from a halyard.'

'It must be very difficult,' Cassie said, without much interest.

'Oh, it is. You've no idea.'

'So what's John going to do? Go back to fishing?'

'Fishing? Indeed he isn't,' Stella bridled at the suggestion. 'No, Lord Ramsgate has asked him to captain his new yawl.' She gave a smug little shrug.

'The one that's to be launched next week?'

'That's right. She would have been launched before if it hadn't been for ...' her voice dropped '... poor Martin.' It rose again. 'But it was also the fact that Lord Ramsgate wanted John to be there. And me, of course,' she added. 'John's already started to look for his crew, even though we only got back yesterday. But he knows who he wants and there's no lack of money. Lord Ramsgate's very rich, you know.'

'So I believe.' Cassie nodded.

'I must go.' Stella gathered herself together and stood up. 'I'm truly sorry about little Simon, Cassie,' she said, laying her hand on Cassie's arm. 'But at least you've got three ...' her voice tailed off.

'Yes, I'm lucky there,' Cassie agreed, her voice suddenly becoming brisk to hide the wound that was still raw in her heart. 'It's a shame you haven't got any, Stella. Children can be a great comfort.'

'Pooh, I'm very careful *not* to have any!' Stella assured her. 'If I was saddled with brats I wouldn't be able to go away with John the way I do. John says it's much better that we're childless and I agree with him. I'm *very* careful, I can tell you. I know just what to do to avoid them!' She looked at Cassie. 'I'll let you into the secret, if you like. That is, unless you want more children.'

'No, I don't,' Cassie said slowly. 'At least, not yet.'

'Very well, I'll send you round some of my stuff. It's very good. Never yet failed me.'

Cassie went back to the kitchen. The sophisticated young woman who had just left was a far cry from the young girl who had wanted nothing more than a nice house and nice children. Cassie couldn't help thinking that she had liked the old Stella better.

Her sister was as good as her word. Two days later Stella's maid appeared with a little parcel. Cassie took it up to her bedroom and undid it. There was a sponge and a bottle of liquid together with a note listing its ingredients and saying that they could be obtained from a chemist in Colchester. She looked at it as it lay on the bed. Luke had been sleeping with Robert in the little room the two boys had shared at the front of the house ever since Simon's death, ostensibly to help Robert over his grief, but she knew it was as much to remove the risk involved in sharing the big bed. The doctor had said no more children and she knew that Luke was determined not to take any chances. But Cassie was equally determined that in the fullness of time she would give Luke a son. Until then, with the aid of the bottle and sponge Luke could safely return to her bed.

In the event the decision was forced upon them. A sudden influx of visitors to visit their yachts at the beginning of the season, plus a visit from Abel Crowther, meant that the four guest bedrooms were occupied, and when Jonas Price-Carpenter announced that Edward, his son, would be accompanying him, there was only the little room at the front left to put him in.

Cassie looked forward to Edward's return with a mixture

of excitement and dread. It was nearly nine years since she had seen him. Would he have changed? Would he remember her? What would he say? What should *she* say? Outwardly, Cassie remained her capable, efficient self but inside, her heart pounded and skipped and she felt as uncertain of herself as a young girl.

Chapter Eleven

Edward had changed hardly at all. He was a little heavier, perhaps and there were a few more lines round his eyes and mouth; one or two stray grey hairs in his moustache. That was all. Cassie watched from an upstairs room as he and his father alighted from the trap Tom had taken to meet the train, her hands pressed against her breast to still the thumping of her heart. It was over, she kept repeating to herself, over and done with. Edward had a wife; Cassie was married, too. There was no going back.

Slowly she went down the stairs to greet the visitors. Abel Crowther had arrived by the same train so Hannah was there first, busily ordering the servants to carry the bags in, enquiring after the journey and taking up her old role as mistress of the place.

Cassie waited, her hand on the banister. It wouldn't last. Once Hannah was ensconced in her sitting room drinking tea with Abel Crowther, she would lose interest and it would be left to Cassie to carry on. It was always the same when that man came. Sometimes Cassie wondered if her mother cherished hopes of marrying Crowther, but wasn't there a wife some-where in the background? Cassie couldn't remember.

Edward, standing behind his father, looked up and saw her standing there. She saw his face flush with pleasure and he smiled. 'Why, if it isn't Cassie! It is Cassie, isn't it? And grown more beautiful than ever.'

'Now then, Teddy, m'boy, that's enough of that,' his father growled affectionately, his expression one of pride in his son. 'Remember you're a respectable married man.' He turned to Abel Crowther. 'Always had an eye for the fair sex, that one.' He nudged the other man and nodded towards Edward. 'Chip off the old block, don't ye know.'

Abel nodded and grinned. 'Aye, I know what tha means. When the cat's away . . . '

'More like, when away from the cat!' Jonas Price-Carpenter roared with laughter at his own joke.

'Would you like to come this way, Mr Crowther?' Hannah's tone was icy. 'Cassie will show you two gentlemen your rooms.' Even her black bombazine skirt had a disapproving swish to it as she turned and led the way down the hall.

Cassie went back up the stairs, followed by Edward and his father. She had no choice but to show the older man to his room first because his was the Admiral's room at the top of the stairs. 'You are in the small room at the front, sir,' she said over her shoulder to Edward, hoping he would find his own way. But he didn't. He waited until Cassie had made sure his father had everything he needed and then followed her to his room, closing the door behind him and leaning on it.

'Millie has brought your bags up and she'll bring water for you to wash in about half an hour, if that's all right, sir.' Cassie busied herself straightening the bed cover, twitching the curtain and moving the articles on the dressing table and wash-stand a fraction of an inch. Anything so she wouldn't have to look at Edward. 'Now, if there's nothing else ...' she went towards the door. 'Excuse me, sir.'

Edward didn't move. 'You really haven't changed a bit, Cassie,' he said admiringly. 'You really are just as beautiful as I remembered you. And to think you're still here! I can't believe it! I simply can't believe it!'

'Yes, as you say, I'm still here.' She tried to keep her voice level although her heart was pounding so fast that she was sure he could see it through her dress. 'And extremely busy, so if you wouldn't mind?' She had to escape before her feelings betrayed her.

He put out his hand and touched her cheek. 'Oh, don't be in such a hurry, Cassie.' His voice was pleading. 'It's such a long time since I last saw you. It must be five or six years. No, more than that. Twelve or fourteen, more like. I've never forgotten you, you know.'

She wanted to tell him that she hadn't forgotten, either. That it was exactly nine years since his last visit. She knew, because she had his son to remind her. But she said nothing. Better that he thought she'd done as he'd suggested and got rid of the child – her mouth twisted – if indeed he even remembered he'd made her pregnant. Memory could be very selective on occasion. She managed a smile. 'I hadn't forgotten you either, sir.'

'Oh, stop calling me sir,' he grinned. Then he became serious and took a step back. 'But you're wearing black. I must say it suits your fair colouring but I'm sure that's not the reason.' He looked at her questioningly.

'It's for my cousin Martin.'

'Martin at Turnbull's Yard? I remember him. He wasn't very old, surely?'

'No, there was an accident.'

'Oh, I am sorry. He must have been about my age, too. When did this happen?'

'About two months ago.' She turned away. 'My little son was drowned, too, last December.' She could still scarcely speak of Simon's death without her eyes filling with tears.

'Oh, my dear.' He came and put his arm round her. 'So you're married, Cassie. But of course, you would be, a lovely girl like you wouldn't remain unmarried. And who's the lucky man?'

'His name is Luke.' She fiddled with her heavy gold wedding ring, unable to meet his eyes in case he should detect the feelings he had roused in her.

'Do you have other children?'

'Yes. Three.'

'All boys, I suppose.' His voice was suddenly bitter.

'One boy. Robert.' She was glad his memory was hazy over the years that had passed since they met. That way he would never guess the secret she longed to share with him but knew she never, ever could.

He flung himself across the room and stood looking out of the window. 'Then you've done better than my stupid mare. All she gives me are daughters. Six mealy-mouthed, prissy girls.' She was surprised by the sudden venom in his tone.

'Is your wife well?' Cassie felt on safer ground here.

'Rarely. Spends most of her time lying in a darkened room suffering from a multitude of complaints that people don't die of. More's the pity,' he added under his breath.

'I'm sorry to hear that, Edward.' Cassie went over to him. He looked so sad and crestfallen that she put her hand on his arm.

He covered it with his own. 'It was a mistake. I should never have married Felicity. We were unsuited right from the beginning,' he said sadly. He gave a wry smile. 'But I've made my bed and however uncomfortable it is I must lie on it, as they say.' The expression on his face tore her heart.

'I must go. I've work to do,' she said unsteadily.

'Yes, of course.' He smiled at her, a sad, wistful smile. 'Oh, Cassie, when I think of what might have been . . . ' He sighed. 'But it's too late, now.' He bent his head and brushed her lips so gently with his own. 'Or is it?' He smiled down at her, his eyes warm.

She escaped and hurried down the stairs, her senses in rags. Why had he come back to torment her again? From the few words he had said it was clear that his marriage was a disaster; she remembered him telling her that it had been more or less arranged by his and Felicity's parents. Oh, if only he had cut free and married me, she thought desperately, he would have had the son he so desired. Life would have been so different for us both. She sped along the hallway to the kitchen, pressing her hands against her face in an effort to compose herself. Thoughts like that had no place in her life now. He had already aroused in her feelings that were best forgotten. Luke was her husband. There was no going back.

Cassie was busy serving meals in the dining room when Luke came home from work. He was dirty and dishevelled from a hard day at the Yard and he looked grey with fatigue. He washed at the sink in the scullery and sat down to his meal at the kitchen table.

'I've gotta go and see Mr Herbert tonight, Cassie,' he said, as she came into the kitchen with a pile of plates. 'You hadn't forgotten, had you?'

'No, Luke, I hadn't forgotten.' Mr Herbert was teaching Luke the rudiments of book-keeping.

He ran his hand through his hair. 'I dunno if I'll ever get the hang of it, Cassie. I got no interest in it. Thass got nothin' to do with buildin' boats. I'm like Uncle George, I'm happier workin' on me tools. But he wants me to do it so I must give it a try.'

'Yes, you must. You're all he's got now, Luke. He depends on you.' Her voice was unsympathetic. After talking to Edward, suddenly Luke's Essex drawl grated on her nerves.

'I know.' He sighed. 'One good thing, we've still got all poor Marty's plans. We shan't be short o' designs for several years to come, so we don't hev to worry about that.' He pushed his plate away and got up from the table. 'I'd better be off. Mr Herbert don't like it if I'm late.'

'It's all very well for Mr Herbert,' Cassie said sharply, 'he hasn't had to do a hard day's work. He's been retired for the past six years.' Her voice softened. 'Come in quietly, Luke. Robert will be asleep in here tonight because his room is occupied by a guest. We're quite full up.'

'But what about me? Where shall I sleep?'

'You must come back to your own bed, Luke.'

'No, Cassie.' His eyes filled with alarm and he spoke in an agitated whisper. 'You know I can't do that. It's too risky.'

'It's all right, Luke.' She went to the door with him. 'You don't have to worry. Everything's taken care of. Something Stella gave me ...'

He looked at her uncertainly. 'I may be late.'

'Not too late, I hope.' Her voice rose as Millie came in from the scullery with a stack of clean plates to arrange on the shelves of the dresser. 'Remember you have to do a day's work tomorrow.'

When Luke returned from his lesson Cassie was waiting for him in the big bed, but her thoughts had all been of Edward – neat, handsome and aesthetic-looking, yet so unhappy. He was so different from Luke, with his rugged features and untidy mane of hair and his rough, capable hands. If Luke was ever unhappy he never showed it; sometimes she wondered if he had any of the finer feelings, but perhaps that was a bit unkind, he'd been upset over Simon. And Martin. But he never ever said much, not like Edward. Edward would confide his troubles and ask for comfort. She tossed on her pillow. She still loved Edward, there was no denying it, and what made it worse was the fact that Edward's marriage to Felicity was plainly a disaster. But it was too late. There was no going back. Luke was her husband, she had wronged him once, it must never happen again.

He blew out the candle and as he clambered into bed beside her Cassie, overwhelmed by her guilty thoughts, did what she had never done before, she turned to him and held out her arms.

'It's all right, Luke,' she murmured as he held back. 'I told you, everything's taken care of. There'll be no child from our union, I promise you that.'

She gave herself up to his rough caresses and for the first time found herself responding with a warmth that surprised even herself. But if her thoughts were with Edward it was her secret and one she shared with no one.

The next three days were among the most difficult of her life. Knowing Edward was so near, it took all her self-control not to seek him out.

'Are you avoiding me, Cassie?' he asked with a hurt expression when she mistimed things and met him on the stairs one morning.

'Of course I'm not. You're imagining things.' She tried to pass him but he put his hand over hers as it lay on the banister.

'Come to my room in ten minutes. I want to talk to you.'

'I'm sorry, I can't. The butcher will be here in a few minutes and I have to pay him.'

'Damn the butcher. I want to see you. I want to talk to you.'

153

His voice was low and urgent. 'I'm going home tomorrow, don't you realise that? Have you forgotten what we once were to each other? Does it all mean nothing to you?'

'Let me pass please, Edward. You mustn't talk like that. We are both married now. What's past must stay in the past.'

'But I need you, Cassie. I have to talk to you. Come to my room.'

'*No!*' The word exploded from her lips. 'Now, please let me pass.'

'Oh, Cassie, how can you be so heartless? And after all we've been to each other?' Sadly, he hung his head, but he stood aside and let her pass. She continued on her way, trembling, her legs almost too weak to carry her. She had nearly, so very nearly, given in to his request. Yet her heart sang, because she knew he loved her still.

Edward and his father left two days before the launching of Lord Ramsgate's yawl. Cassie saw them off with relief, yet she had to admit that she hoped Edward would come back. Although he said nothing she was sure that he would. After he had gone she threw herself into preparations for the reception, to be held at the Falcon, that would follow the launch. It helped to stifle the feeling of restlessness, of longing, of regret for what might have been that filled her.

Coming barely two months after Martin's tragic death the launch would be a subdued affair compared with the usual junketings attached to these events, but it would have been unlucky not to have some celebration on such an auspicious occasion.

The Yard had been cleaned and prepared for the launch, and a platform built and draped with blue from which Lady Ramsgate would name the yacht and break the bottle of champagne over her bow. There was great speculation as to what the name would be and such was the secrecy that the painter would have to work from a cradle over the side in order to paint it on after the boat was in the water. A good crowd had gathered to watch the ceremony and Hannah had made little Charity a white, heavily-embroidered dress because she was to hand Lady Ramsgate the bouquet of flowers after the yacht had been named. Cassie had mixed feelings about this. At two and a half Charity was, to say the least, unreliable and to expect her to climb the steps to the platform holding a posy of flowers seemed to Cassie the height of optimism. But both Uncle George and Luke were adamant. There was no other child more fitted to the task.

It was a beautiful day, warm and clear, and the sun shining on the full spring tide scattered it with bright jewels of colour as Lord and Lady Ramsgate mounted the shallow steps to the platform. Lady Ramsgate wore a dress of flowered merino trimmed with magenta satin and her leghorn hat, heavy with flowers and feathers, was trimmed with ribbons of the same colour. She was a small, dainty woman, some years younger than her husband, and her bright costume contrasted oddly with Stella's, who was there as Captain John Jameson's wife but dressed in sober black, as befitted the cousin of the recently-deceased Martin Turnbull. Black didn't really suit Stella. Uncle George, pale with strain, followed with Luke, both dressed in their Sunday suits. The Rector, who would say a prayer of blessing for the safety of the yacht, came last.

Cassie stood at the front of the crowd with Hannah and Robert in a special place reserved for them, the baby on one arm, clutching Charity's hand with the other, ready to send her up the steps with the flowers at the right moment.

The Rector stepped forward and said a brief prayer that no one could hear, then Lady Ramsgate took the bottle of champagne in her hand. 'I name this yacht *Martina*' she said loudly, her voice carrying to every corner of the Yard. 'And may God bless all who sail in her.' A great roar went up as the champagne bottle broke on the bow. The name was obviously a tribute to Martin, who had designed the yacht, and it met with everyone's approval. As they watched, *Martina* slipped, gathering speed as she went down the well-greased ways, her bow dipping in a graceful curtsey as she reached her natural element. It was a beautiful launch and a fitting epitaph to Martin. Suddenly there was a flurry of activity as men waiting in dinghies caught the ropes and, rowing hard, helped to swing her round into mid-stream and there she rested, her topsides gleaming and the paintwork on her hull shining like smooth white silk, a proud and graceful vessel.

Cassie shifted the baby on her arm and bent down. 'Now,' she said to Charity, 'take your flowers and go up the steps to where Papa is standing and give them to the lady.'

Charity looked up at her mother anxiously as she clutched the posy.

'Yes, go on now.' Cassie gave her a little push and Charity began to climb up to the platform. Cassie held her breath but the little girl got safely to the top and immediately thrust the flowers at her father. Luke, scarlet with embarrassment, scooped her up in his arms and managed somehow to transfer them to Lady Ramsgate, to the great amusement of the crowd below.

'She was supposed to curtsey,' Hannah whispered to Cassie.

'Never mind that,' Cassie answered, 'I'm just thankful she reached the top of those steps without mishap! Come on, we'd better go home now. We need to be there when the people arrive.'

'You go on. I'll go and see what's happened to Maisie. She should have been here this afternoon but I can't see her. I expect she thought it would be too much for her.' Hannah was scanning the crowd as she spoke.

'Well, try and persuade her to come to the reception, even if she stays in your room with you.' Cassie turned to go. 'Come on, Bobbie, it's time to go.'

'Oh, can't I stay and come back with Papa?' Robert pleaded.

'Yes, let him stay with me. He'll be all right.' Luke appeared from down the steps, carrying Charity. 'But you'd better take this little madam home with you. I declare if you don't Lady Ramsgate'll put her in a bag and take her home with her. Quite taken with the minx, she is.' Luke gave his daughter a kiss and put her to the ground. 'And pretty as a picture, too. Just like her mother.' He smiled at Cassie, a smile full of love and pride.

Stella came bustling along. 'Really, Cassie, I'm surprised you didn't rehearse that child better than that. Fancy allowing her to make such an exhibition of herself with those flowers. I was mortified to think she was my niece, I can tell you.'

'Luke says Lady Ramsgate ...'

'Lady Ramsgate has breeding. She wouldn't admit how shocked she was,' Stella said loftily. 'But there's no doubt she was, because the child didn't even curtsey, bad-mannered little brat.' She swept off to find her husband, who was deep in conversation with Lord Ramsgate.

Cassie took the children and went home. Charity was beginning to cry. She knew she had somehow offended by her aunt's words but she wasn't sure what she had done. She had climbed those steps in front of all the people and had been relieved to see her beloved Papa when she got to the top. He had picked her up and given her a kiss so he couldn't have been cross with her, and the lady had smiled when Papa gave her the flowers. So what had she done wrong? It was very hard to understand grown-ups. She hoped Mama would let her keep this pretty dress on until bedtime.

Lizzy had organized Millie and Florrie so that everything would be ready for the guests when they arrived. Cassie went up to inspect the meeting room where the food was all laid out. She nodded approvingly. Lizzy was a good girl, reliable and hard-working. She went downstairs to the kitchen. Lizzy would look after things while Amy was fed.

Cassie sat in the rocking chair by the stove while the baby suckled contentedly. Why had Stella made such a fuss over little Charity, she wondered. She looked at the little curly head as Charity played at her feet, the white dress carefully spread round her. She was, after all, barely more than a baby. It must have been quite an ordeal for the little mite. It was a good thing Stella had no children of her own if she was so intolerant.

By the time the baby was safely back in her cradle and Cassie went upstairs the reception was in full swing. She looked round. It was a cause for celebration, and everyone paid tribute to the way the boat was designed and built, but inevitably there was an underlying sadness to the day. This should have been Martin's triumph. The yacht was built to his design and he had watched over it every step of the way. Lord Ramsgate of course had known this, in fact they had had many consultations during the yacht's construction. The naming of it had been an obvious token of his esteem for Martin. As she listened Cassie could hear Martin's name mentioned over and over again and could almost feel his presence tangible in the room and hear his ready laugh. She looked over at her Uncle George. He was finding the afternoon very difficult, she could see that. Several times as she watched he passed his black-edged handkerchief across his eyes. But Luke was beside him, he would look after him.

She turned her attention to the rest of the guests. Lord

Ramsgate was deep in conversation with the Rector. He was a tall, grey-haired man with a loud voice and an imperious manner. Not a man to be crossed, Cassie decided. Half-listening to the conversation she was surprised how often Luke's name – 'young Turnbull' – was mentioned. It was obvious that Lord Ramsgate held him in high esteem and realised with some surprise that Luke, now second in command at the Yard, was regarded as a man of some importance there. It was a new thought and took a bit of getting used to.

As she listened to Lord Ramsgate holding forth to the Rector she couldn't help wondering if he would be equally opinionated when it came to sailing *Martina*, or whether he would allow John Jameson a free hand. She smiled to herself. Yacht owners and yacht captains had an uneasy relationship; the captains knew they were the experts and brooked no interference, regarding the owners as merely playing at sailing; whilst the owners regarded the captains as hired hands, paid to do a job and therefore subject to the whims and fancies of their masters.

Her eyes searched for John and found him talking to Lady Ramsgate. John Jameson was a handsome man, nearer to Lady Ramsgate's age than her husband, Cassie judged. She watched them together for a few moments. The lady was something of a coquette, it would seem, tossing her head in a very affected manner, with a silly little giggling laugh that John appeared to find quite enchanting.

Cassie went over to Stella, helping herself to the last of the smoked oysters. 'John seems to be getting on very well with Lady Ramsgate,' she murmured.

'Oh, yes.' Stella dabbed her mouth with her napkin. 'Well, it's all part of the job, isn't it, being nice to the owner's wife.' She looked over towards Lord Ramsgate and made a face behind her napkin. 'I suppose I'll have to do the same with His

Lordship.' She gave Cassie a glance that was at once superior and pitying. 'We have to mix with all sorts of gentry now, you know. But one gets used to it after a while.' She went off to interrupt Lord Ramsgate's conversation with the Rector.

Cassie watched her go. She hoped Stella knew what she was doing. And more to the point, what her husband might do.

Chapter Twelve

Cassie waited for three years before the conception of her fifth child. They were years in which little Simon was never far from her thoughts, and as Robert grew to be a gangling eleven year old and Charity, fair and fairy-like, reached the age Simon had been when he was drowned, the gap between their ages seemed to emphasise the gap the little boy had left in all their lives. Little Amy, nearly three and a half, was very like Simon had been, with the same serious grey eyes – like Luke's – and unruly brown hair. As she toddled about the house and garden the rush of love Cassie would feel for her was ever tinged with a feeling of desolation for her lost son. Luke's boy.

That Luke shared her grief Cassie had no doubt although they rarely talked about it. Luke was always working: pre-occupied with trying to fill Martin's place in George's life and at the Yard. He had managed to master the rudiments of book-keeping, although he hated it and both he and George put off doing the accounts until the last possible moment and sometimes didn't even bother to do them at all. Occasionally, he would bring home a sheaf of papers for Cassie to help him sort through and she would enter them in the big ledger in her neat round handwriting, so unlike his untidy scrawl. But she was as busy with the Falcon as he was with the Yard and didn't really understand what she was doing.

Hannah did little to help with the running of the Falcon, but criticised much, complaining at the bills, interfering in the dining room, maintaining that helpings were far too large, and refusing to let Tom put down fresh sawdust more than once a week.

'The missus never usta be like that,' Tom complained to Cassie, as they surveyed the taproom floor together. 'I dunno wass come over her.'

'Neither do I, Tom,' Cassie sighed.

'Well, you can see for yourself, gal, can't you?' Tom spread his hands. 'I can't make one spread o' sawdust last a week, not nohow I can't. That stand to reason, feet trampin' in an' out, they cart the mud in an' the sawdust out. An' some of 'em ain't too clever with the spittoons, neither. I ain't never seen my taproom floor in sech a pickle, an' thass a fact.' He leaned his elbows on the bar and shook his head sadly at the scene.

'Look, Tom.' Cassie laid a hand on his arm. 'You must put down sawdust as you need it. Don't worry about Mama, I'll deal with her. It's no use, we shall lose all our customers if she has her way with all this penny-pinching. She gets worse and worse as the years go by. I really can't understand her being so mean. She was always so open-handed.'

She didn't tell Tom, but she often had to dip into her own purse when a bill was larger than Hannah thought it should be and so refused to hand over the money, saying that Cassie would have to make it up by buying cheaper cuts of meat or fewer vegetables in future. Cassie could think only that her mother had been so long out of the day-to-day running of the Falcon that she had become out of touch with reality. In truth, most of the time she behaved as if she were one of the guests that stayed, expecting to be waited on and looked after, without ever lifting a finger to help; yet she still kept a tight rein on the purse strings. It made life extremely difficult for Cassie and she came to dread presenting the bills for her mother to deal with.

'Why must you always order the best coal? You know very well kitchen nuts are cheaper,' Hannah said one day, casting her eye down the coal bill.

'I do order kitchen nuts, but only for the kitchen range.'

'They burn perfectly well in an open grate. They'd do in the bar.'

'Of course they wouldn't Mama, they'd burn away much too quickly. Tom would be forever mending the fire and it would be more expensive in the long run.'

'Not if he collected driftwood and used that as well. There's plenty of it down by the river. He could take the wheelbarrow ...'

'Mama! Tom hasn't time to go and collect driftwood. He's in the bar all day and he has to look after the cellar and take the trap to meet people from the station in between times. Don't forget we open at six in the morning and don't close till eleven at night.'

'There aren't customers in all the time. You could look after the bar while he went. You often do, when he's doing other jobs. He'd enjoy it, I'm sure,'

'I'm not asking him. Collecting driftwood is not what he's paid to do.'

'He's paid to do whatever you ask him.' Hannah rapped on the table as she spoke. 'Don't forget he lives rent free in the cottage. Mr Crowther says ...'

'I don't care what Mr Crowther says. I'm not asking Tom to

go out and collect driftwood because you're too mean to pay the coal bill,' Cassie shouted, losing her temper.

Hannah crumpled. 'Oh, Cassie, you don't understand. It's very difficult to make ends meet these days. You're inclined to be extravagant, you know, dear.'

'I'm not extravagant, Mama.' Cassie controlled her patience with difficulty. She smiled although her teeth were gritted. 'Perhaps if you were to let me have the handling of the day-to-day accounts I could see better where the money went and where economies could perhaps be made.'

'No. No. I couldn't do that.' Hannah shook her head quickly, an almost trapped expression on her face. She took out her purse. 'Very well, I'll pay the coal bill this time. But you must make sure it isn't so big again.'

Cassie left her mother and went thoughtfully back to the kitchen. She had an uneasy feeling that her mother discussed the affairs of the Falcon with Abel Crowther when he came. She had several times nearly let slip his opinion on affairs that shouldn't have concerned him. Cassie wished now she hadn't been so quick to interrupt. Hannah had had a special – relationship? no, that was probably too strong a term – friendship, even that was hardly right either, with the man from Sheffield for as long as Cassie could remember and as children she and Stella often used to speculate as to why he came all the way from Sheffield when he didn't even own a yacht here. They came to the childish but not unreasonable conclusion that he was too mean to buy one and preferred to be taken out in other people's. Cassie's step slowed. *Too mean.* Had her mother become so influenced by Crowther over the years that his meanness had communicated itself to her? She resolved to listen more carefully when her mother began to air Abel Crowther's opinions.

But as she worried over Hannah and the running of the

Falcon Cassie often thought of what her life would have been, married to Edward. Living on his large Buckinghamshire estate she would have led the life of a Lady, with nothing to do but please her husband and give him sons. And she would have given him sons ... more sons. Every spring when the yachts were made ready for the summer's racing and every autumn when they came back to be laid up for the winter she looked for Edward's return to the village. But he never came. Perhaps he felt that it was too dangerous. She tried to put him out of her mind by concentrating on her secret determination to give Luke a son of his own even though the doctor had warned her repeatedly against more children. It was something she knew she had to do; she owed it to Luke. She could never forget how she had deceived him and her guilt still troubled her, even after all these years, especially when she saw Luke and Robert together.

'Roker Wilson says I can go down fishing with him, next time he goes down to the wallet for plaice, Papa. You will let me, won't you?'

'Aye, son, I don't see why not, if your mother agrees.'

But as Luke ruffled the boy's fair curls affectionately only Cassie knew that he wasn't Robert's father, and Robert wasn't his son.

She didn't tell Luke of her decision. She didn't need to. All she had to do was to put aside the little bottle and sponge that she kept locked in the cupboard by her bed and wait for nature to take its course.

It didn't take long.

Strangely, she was reluctant to confess to Luke that she was pregnant again and for a month she tried to brush off his concern for her strained white face by blaming the long cold winter and wet spring.

'I shall be better when the summer comes,' she insisted, trying to calm her perpetually nauseous stomach as she handed him his supper, kept hot over a saucepan because he had been working late.

He picked up his knife and fork, his eyes on her face. 'I think you should see Doctor Banks,' he said anxiously. 'I've never seen you look so peaky. Not since . . .'

She didn't hear the rest of his words because she slipped to the floor in a faint. When she came to she was in the rocking chair and he was chafing her hands. 'This has gone on long enough, Cassie,' he said firmly. 'I've sent for Doctor Banks. It's time we found out what's the matter with you. I knew you weren't right. I could tell.'

Cassie smiled at him. 'You needn't have sent for Doctor Banks, Luke,' she said gently. 'There's nothing the matter with me except that I'm having another child.'

'Another child!' Luke got to his feet as if he been scalded. 'But you can't be! You said . . . You mustn't . . . The doctor told you . . .'He covered his face with his hands. 'Oh, God, what have I done to you?'

'It's not your fault, Luke. I wanted this baby. I planned it deliberately,' she said, looking up at him.

He sat down at the table. 'You'd no right to do that, Cassie,' he said, his voice deadly calm. 'No right at all. I trusted you when you said everything would be all right.'

'Everything was all right, Luke. It was my fault. I wanted another baby.'

'Why, for God's sake?' he shouted, his fist crashing down on the table. 'We've already got Robert and the two girls. Isn't that enough for you, that you must risk your life to bring yet another child into the world?'

She leaned her head on the high back of the rocking chair

and closed her eyes. Tears squeezed out and ran down her chalk-white face. 'I want us to have another son, Luke.'

'Oh, Cassie!' He got up from the table and went across to her. He gathered her to him. 'Do you still miss the little lad that much, Cassie girl?' he said, stroking her hair, his temper forgotten.

'Yes, I do,' she whispered. It was true, she still grieved for Simon, but her grief was made worse by the knowledge that he had been Luke's natural son and she knew she would never be at peace with herself until she had given him another one.

He shook his head, bewildered at the strength of her feelings. 'You should never have taken such a risk. Supposing . . .'

She put her finger over his lips. 'Supposing nothing. I shall be all right, I know I shall. Don't worry, Luke. I want us to have this baby so much that I know nothing can go wrong.'

He bowed his head. 'Please God you're right, Cassie girl.'

The pregnancy was not easy and made more difficult by Hannah, who, in spite of Cassie's assurances that it had been her own fault, continued to blame Luke for behaving, in the words of the prayer book, 'like a brute beast of the field'. In the end she refused to speak to him at all, which upset Cassie far more than it upset Luke, who was much too concerned for his wife's health and safety than for his mother-in-law's vagaries of temper.

As the months progressed Cassie became increasingly lethargic, leaving the girls to carry out the duties of the Falcon, sometimes almost too tired to direct them. Hannah was no help, keeping ostentatiously to her room and demanding more and more service, but Lizzy was a tower of strength.

'Thass all right, m'm. I know wass gotta be done an' I can manage the others jest as long as you're here in case anything go wrong,' she said, bustling about importantly, up to her elbows in flour. 'You jest set there an' rest. Millie, thass time to git the littl'uns their tea. There's some brawn in the meat safe, they like that. An' there's some fruit cake left. Look slippy now, that'll soon be time to start in the dinin' room.'

Cassie was happy to sit and rest. Her ankles were beginning to swell and her hands, too. This had never happened during her other pregnancies. Luke worried incessantly but she refused to be ruffled and told nobody how deathly ill she felt. Everything would be all right, she insisted, as she heaved herself wearily from her chair to her bed and back to her chair again.

The baby was born on a foggy night in early November, nearly three weeks early. It was a difficult birth and she was too tired and weak to do much more than ride the pains that threatened to tear her in half and went on and on until blessed oblivion came to her rescue. Then all was quiet and peaceful. There was no sound anywhere. She drifted in and out of sleep, floating on a gentle sea that stretched as far as she could see into the distance. Once she saw Simon; he was holding the hand of a tall, dark man and they were smiling at her. 'Simon?' she whispered, and held out her arms. 'Papa?' But they shook their heads, still smiling. She fell asleep again and when she woke they were gone, but she could hear Simon crying for her. She frowned. She wished he would stop but he kept on and on until at last she was forced to open her eyes.

The sea was gone and she was in her own bed. Luke was standing beside it holding a bundle in his arms and that was where the noise was coming from.

'Your son is crying for you, Cassie,' he whispered, a break in his voice.

She held out her arms and he laid the baby in them. Already he had a look of Luke about him. She smiled contentedly up at Luke and fell once more asleep, but this time it was a deep, healing sleep.

They told her afterwards that she had hovered between life and death for four days, but she knew nothing of this. She only knew that she had given Luke the son she owed him and that she had seen Simon with Reuben, his grandfather. Her mind at last was easy.

Her recovery, once begun, was rapid. Within a month she had resumed all her duties at the Falcon, working with renewed vigour and enthusiasm, listening to Robert's accounts of his conversations with the fishermen on the quay, giving time to Charity and Amy, who adored their brother, baby Reuben, and still finding time to help Luke with the pile of papers that occasionally found their way home from the Yard and that he found so irksome.

'You're even more beautiful than the day I wed you, Cassie.' Luke looked up from the accounts spread across the kitchen table to where Cassie was carefully entering them in the big ledger.

'That's because you're seeing me in the gaslight.' Cassie grinned at him and pulled forward another sheaf of papers. 'It hides all the lines.' Even after twelve years of marriage she still felt embarrassed by the way he looked at her with such love in his eyes. She paused with her pen in her hand. They had come through a lot in those twelve years and he had never changed. But she had. She was no longer resentful and bitter towards a fate that had tied her to a man she didn't love. She was used to Luke, and she knew him for what he was, a totally honest and upright man. She respected him, leaned on him in times of trouble and felt easy and comfortable with him. The fact that Edward was always there, in her mind, between them was something she had learned to live with. That was how things were and she was resigned to the fact that that was how it would always be. Luke would always be second-best and because of that she felt sorry for him.

Luke leaned back in his chair, always glad of an excuse to

put aside his pen. 'Young Bobbie seems set on going to sea when he's old enough,' he said thoughtfully. 'I'd hoped he might come into the Yard with me. After all, if Uncle George leaves it all to me I'll have to think of who I hand it on to and Robert's the oldest, so he's the one it should be.' He picked up his pen again but only to tap his teeth thoughtfully.

A spasm of apprehension crossed Cassie's mind. 'He's only eleven, Luke. There's plenty of time. He may change his mind when he's been out on the dogger bank a few times,' she said casually, without looking up.

'Of course, it's the yachts he's interested in,' Luke persisted, 'not the fishing. Takes after your father, I reckon.'

'But my father started as a fisherman. That's how they all start. It gives them a good grounding in seamanship.' She tidied the papers in front of her and put them aside before starting on the next pile. She looked up, her expression thoughtful. 'But you're right, Luke, come to think of it. He's never happy unless he's downriver with somebody or other, is he?' She nodded. 'When he gets a bit older we'll have a word with Stella's John. He might be able to find him a berth on his yacht as a cabin boy. He might like that.'

Luke nodded. 'Yes, he might. But it's a pity. I'd hoped he might follow me.'

'There's always Reuben,' Cassie reminded him, looking down into the cradle on the hearthrug. Reuben your rightful heir, she added silently. Somehow, she didn't yet know how, she would have to ensure that her elder son didn't, however unwittingly, rob Reuben of his birthright. But that was in the future. A long way ahead.

'Aye. But he's got a long way to go,' Luke said, echoing her thoughts. 'Who knows where *hell* end up.' He took out his pipe and rammed the tobacco home.

Christmas at the Falcon was very much a family affair. Cassie and the girls decorated the meeting room with holly and mistletoe and everywhere was festooned with coloured paper. A big Christmas tree stood in the corner after the custom introduced by the late Prince Albert. It was Lizzy's responsibility now to cook the turkey and she took the duty very seriously, allowing nobody to interfere.

Cassie and Luke took the children to church on Christmas morning, a bright, crisp, frosty morning and afterwards they went for a walk along the quay before going home. The fishing smacks were there, moored bow on to the quay, some of them with a branch of holly stuck in the old fishing basket left permanently at the top of the mast to warn other boats when they were at sea that fishing was in progress.

'Mr Wilson says I can go stowboating—' he pronounced it *stobbartin'* – 'with him after Christmas,' Robert said as they stood by Jack Wilson's smack.

'Thass rare hard work, fishing after sprats,' Luke told him gravely, 'and thass what stobbartin' is, you know.'

'Yes, I know. He told me. He told me you get frozen to the marrow and your hands freeze to the chains that hold the nets if you're not careful,' Robert said, 'but I still want to go. Can I go, Papa?' He turned to Cassie, 'Mama?'

'We'll see. It's Christmas Day now and nobody's going anywhere,' Cassie said with a smile.

'Except home to eat their fill of turkey, I hope,' Luke added. He lifted Amy up on to his shoulder. 'Look, Amy. Look at all the yachts in the river. They stretch as far as the eye can see. Did you ever see such a sight? And your Papa has had some hand in nearly all of them.'

'Lift me up, Papa,' Charity danced around his feet. 'I want to see, too.'

Without putting Amy down Luke scooped Charity up on his arm. 'There. Can you see all you want to see?' He planted a kiss first on Charity's fair head and then on Amy's chin, which was all he could reach.

'I shall be a yacht captain's wife when I grow up,' Charity announced primly. 'Then I shall be able to go to all sorts of places, just like Aunt Stella. Is she coming to dinner, Mama?'

'Yes. And we'd better go home now. Lizzy will be very cross if we're late home for the turkey she's spent all morning cooking.'

Stella was there when they arrived home; John was somewhere in the Mediterranean on Lord Ramsgate's yacht, so Cassie had managed to persuade her to join the family. A few minutes later George and Maisie came in. They all went upstairs to the meeting room where a huge log fire roared and the table was laid with a white cloth. Cassie looked round. 'Where's Tom?' she demanded.

'Jest a-comin' up the stairs,' Tom's voice called out cheerfully and a few seconds later he came in wearing his best jersey and moleskins and carrying little gifts that he had made for each of the children.

The two girls were beside themselves with excitement as they played with all the toys they had received; the doll's house, the doll's push cart, the pull-along engine for Reuben – who at less than two months old was hardly likely to be interested but couldn't be left out – and the sweets and nuts and oranges they had found in the toe of their stockings. As Cassie watched them and Robert, who was sitting by the window setting up his draught board in the hope that someone would play with him, she was reminded of the first Christmas she and Luke were married, when they lived in the cottage in The Folley. She put her hand to her throat, where the string of pearls

Luke had given her this year was a far cry from the string of wooden beads he had made for her on that other occasion. She wondered where the beads were now – she was sure she hadn't thrown them away.

After the turkey had been eaten and the pudding, brought in flaming, had gone, they all sat round the fire roasting chestnuts that everyone was too full of Christmas dinner to eat.

Maisie and Hannah sat together nearest the fire. 'You're lucky, Hannah,' Maisie said, watching the children playing on the hearth. 'I shall never hev littl'uns like that playing round my hearth. Not now our boy has gone. Nearly four years, it is, since he went. That don't seem possible.' She helped herself to a piece of Turkish delight that was handy. Food was her comfort now and her figure bore witness.

'Yes, I'm lucky to have these four,' Hannah said, 'but I'm still waiting for Stella ...' she looked at her younger daughter over the top of her spectacles.

Stella, who had been trying to interest Luke in a game of cards, looked over. 'Now, don't start that again, Mama. I've told you before there'll be plenty of time for that kind of thing when we've finished travelling all over the world.'

'Hm. So you say.' Hannah turned to Maisie. 'Mind you, they've been to some lovely places. And you should see the things they've brought back. Their house—' she lifted her hands eloquently.

'House ain't a home till thass got childer in it,' Maisie argued.

'And then it's a pig-sty.' Cassie ruffled Amy's dark head as she spoke, her expression belying her words.

At six o'clock Cassie said, 'Come on, Stella, you can come and help me get the tea. I've told the girls they can have the rest *of the* day off so we'll have to wait on ourselves.'

Stella made a face, but she followed Cassie down the stairs.

173

'I'll need a pinafore to cover my dress,' she said when they reached the kitchen. 'It's pure Chinese silk, you know.'

'Yes, it looks very nice,' Cassie said absently, rummaging for a pinafore. 'Ah, that's good, Lizzy's left a pile of sandwiches already made, how thoughtful of her. And there's a trifle in the pantry that we made yesterday. You carry these up, Stella, while I make the tea.' She busied herself at the stove. When she turned back Stella was still standing there. 'What's the matter, Stella?' She looked at her sister in surprise. 'Look, there's a tray, take the sandwiches and the trifle upstairs. Then you can come back for the plates and cups while I get the cake out.'

'Aunt Maisie's right, you know, Cassie. You're very lucky.' Stella picked up the tray and began loading things on to it.

'You mean the children? Yes, I know. But you could do the same, Stella, couldn't you? If you wanted to, I mean.' Cassie poured hot water into the big brown teapot and turned to face Stella as she swirled it around to warm it.

'I wish it was as easy as that.' Stella sat down at the table. 'You see, John doesn't want children. I think he'd leave me if I had a child, Cassie.' She put her head in her hands. 'Oh, everybody thinks how lucky I am. We've got plenty of money – John wins nearly all his races so there's always plenty of prize money. I've been with him to places most people have never even heard of, I have expensive clothes, servants to do all the work so I'm bored stiff most of the time and a house that looks more like a museum than a home. Aren't I the lucky one?' Her voice was heavy with sarcasm.

Cassie sat down opposite to her. 'I thought you were happy, Stella. You always seem so, I don't know, carefree, while I always seem to be up to my eyes in meals or servants or beer crates or auctions or Vestry meetings or helping Luke with his book-keeping ....'

'... or children,' Stella added bitterly. She looked up. 'Maybe *I* could help Luke with his book-keeping. It would give me something to do. I was always quite good at figures when we were at school. I don't suppose I've forgotten it all,' she tailed off, vaguely.

'We'll see what he says.' Cassie gathered the rest of the tea things on to trays. 'Come on, let's take these things upstairs. They'll all be starving and it'll be the children's bedtime before long.'

But watching the way Stella tried to monopolise Luke after tea Cassie was reminded of their young days, and how Stella had hung round him. Surely, after all these years she had got over that! She smiled to herself as she watched Luke move from Stella's side to sit next to Uncle George, and when she followed him, move again, this time on to the floor to play with the children, knowing she wouldn't want to spoil her dress by following him there. There was no doubt what his reaction would be to Stella's half-hearted offer of help with the bookkeeping!

Chapter Thirteen

After two seasons with Lord Ramsgate's *Martina* John Jameson changed yachts yet again. This time he took command of a large racing schooner called *Guinevere*, based on the Isle of Wight.

'That means we shall have to move there. Mr Bracenose – isn't that a funny name? – he's the man who owns *Guinevere*, is a millionaire, too and he's providing us with a house,' Stella said, full of excitement. 'I just had to come and tell you. Isn't it exciting, Mama?'

'Isn't what exciting?' Cassie asked, coming into Hannah's sitting room with the tea tray and setting it down on the table beside her mother's chair.

Hannah moved her embroidery. 'No, Cassie, not those cups. You know I like to use my nice china when Stella comes.' She made a great effort of trying to get to her feet.

'Oh, sit still, I'll get them.' Cassie went over to the china cabinet and got out her mother's best china. 'Although I really can't see what difference it makes. A cup is a cup, after all's said and done,' She was not very good-tempered at having to leave the raspberries she'd been bottling to come and be sociable in her mother's room, just because Stella had turned up, although it had to be admitted that a visit from Stella was, in itself, quite an event these days.

'And there are some of my special biscuits in the pretty tin on the side, there,' Hannah ordered happily. She watched that Cassie did everything to her satisfaction, then said smugly, 'Stella's moving to the Isle of Wight. John's taking command of a new yacht and that's where it's based.'

Cassie raised her eyebrows. 'John's leaving the Colne to go and be based on the Isle of Wight? Does that mean you'll be selling the house in Park Road?'

'Oh, yes, we shan't need that. John says the house we'll be moving to is much bigger. It has six bedrooms and overlooks the harbour at Cowes.' She studied her carefully-manicured nails. 'No doubt we shall be expected to do a lot of entertaining.'

'And no doubt you'll have plenty of servants to help you.' Cassie's voice was only faintly tinged with sarcasm.

'I should hope so!' Stella didn't even notice her sister's tone. 'I could hardly do all that will be expected of me without help!' Her expression went dreamy. 'I wonder if I shall see the Queen. She spends quite a lot of time at Osborne House, I believe.' She smoothed her shot silk skirt and put her head on one side. 'It's a step up the social scale, you do realise that, Mama, don't you, to go and live at Cowes?'

Stella and John moved in the middle of November and they stayed at the Falcon for a week while the removal took place. John supervised the furniture being packed into the specially-made crates and then the big horse-drawn pantechnicon van took it to the railway station to be loaded into the furniture truck in the siding, and taken by rail to Portsmouth and then across the water to the new house in Cowes.

Mistrustful of the ability of the removal men to handle his furniture safely, he was anxious to follow it as soon as possible and contained himself for the few days after it had gone with difficulty. John was a tall, handsome man, with thick, waving dark hair and a neat beard. His eyes, shrewd and calculating, were startling blue in a face tanned from the summer's sailing and his years of captaining yachts had given him a self-assurance that bordered on arrogance. He and Stella made a striking couple; Stella was as slim as a wraith these days and although she would never be beautiful she had an attractive face and knew how to make the best of herself with cheeky little hats and elegant hair styles.

Yet there was something between them that made Cassie uneasy. A look of impatience, almost irritation, on his part at times, when Stella spoke to him, and on hers an over-anxiety to please. Cassie guessed that her sister's longing for a child would never be fulfilled by this hard, ambitious man whom she obviously adored. She looked across at her own husband, deep in conversation with John and wished she could say the same for herself. But although she was fond of Luke, she felt no magic spark such as she had felt with Edward. Nevertheless, she was thankful for the fact that he was a good and loving father to the children, especially Robert. She sometimes felt he had a special affection for him, the firstborn that belonged to another man. She tried to push the last thought away. Would the guilt over that never be gone? After Simon's death she had risked her life in her determination to give him little Reuben so that he should have a son that was really his own, yet still the guilt remained to torment her, sometimes even making her unnecessarily sharp with the boy himself, which wasn't fair.

Robert was with Luke and John now, his young face alight with interest at the talk of yachts. He was thirteen now and his determination to serve on the yachts had never wavered. Every spare moment was spent either at the Yard with his father, learning how they were made, or out on the fishing smacks with whoever would take him, learning how to handle a boat with an aptitude that amazed everyone.

'Takes after your father, Cassie,' Luke would say with a smile. 'Thass a sure thing he doesn't take after me. I get sea sick if I go out beyond Colne Point.'

John was talking to Luke and Robert. The owner of his new yacht was a millionaire by the name of Bracenose and John was anxious that they should not forget this. 'She's called *Guinevere* and she's two hundred and eighty tons. That's a big boat,' he said. 'But Hubert Bracenose can afford it. He's not short of a shilling. Not by any means.' He leaned back in his chair and stretched his legs. 'I've only to ask for something and it's there,' he told them. 'I said the boat could carry two spinnakers and before the words were out of my mouth the order was in at the sailmakers. That's the sort of man he is. No expense spared. And she's a beautiful yacht, Luke, with lovely lines.' He fished in his pocket and brought out a notebook and pencil and began to draw. 'See? That's the shape of her hull.'

Luke leaned forward. 'That's a fine hull.'

John nodded. 'Fine enough, I reckon. She'll cut through the water like a dart. When I get down to Cowes I am going to see about having her made ready to sail for America. She's already having a new suit of sails made, as well as the two spinnakers. Oh, yes, *Guinevere's* going to make a real bid for the America's Cup this time.'

'What is the America's Cup, Uncle John?' Robert asked, his face alight with interest.

John looked up from the rough sketch he was making of *Guinevere*. 'It's the cup that was presented by the Royal Yacht Squadron to celebrate the Great Exhibition 1851,' he said. 'Worth a hundred pounds, so I'm told. The race was round the Isle of Wight and a schooner called *America,* which had been built in America and sent over specially in honour of the Great Exhibition won it. That's how it became known as the America's Cup. Her owners eventually presented it to the New York Yacht Club and now there's international competition for it.' He went back to his sketching. 'And it's time we won it back, to my way of thinking.'

'Well, from what you've told me about this boat and what I can see from your sketch, you should stand a good chance.' Luke stoked his pipe. 'She carries a good spread of canvas and she's got beautiful sleek lines.' He pointed with the stem of his pipe to the top of the mainmast. 'I wouldn't care to be mast-headsman up there,' he said with a smile.

'Oh, I would,' Robert said eagerly. 'It would be really exciting and you'd be able to see for miles.'

'There's more to being a mastheadsman than admiring the view,' John laughed. 'Stuck up on top of the pole some hundred and eighty feet above the waterline for the whole of the race, clearing sails and the topsail yards, lacing the topsail, checking gear – it's no joke, I can tell you. Especially when it's blowing hard in a rough sea.'

'Will you take me on your yacht, Uncle John?' Robert asked eagerly.

John Jameson eyed the boy shrewdly. 'When you've proved yourself to be a good seaman,' he said seriously. 'I only choose my crew from the very best.'

Robert nodded. 'One day you'll choose me,' he said, equally seriously.

The boy's determination to be a yachtsman never wavered. Like the rest of the Colne seamen he began in the fishing smacks, once even playing truant from school to go as cabin boy – an exercise he never repeated after the thrashing his father gave him. But by 1884 when he was fifteen both Cassie and Luke were resigned to the knowledge that the sea was in the boy's blood and they agreed to him being taken as cabin boy on the schooner *Pantomime,* owned by Lord Pathfield and captained by Jacob Goodwin.

Robert was beside himself with excitement and spent all his time at the Yard where the yacht was being made ready for the season's racing, fetching and carrying with a willingness he had never shown his father – a fact Luke was quick to notice and comment on, giving Robert an affectionate cuff as he spoke.

With *Pantomime* safely in the river again, her gear stowed and her paintwork gleaming, Robert was there, doing his captain's bidding, learning the ropes from the older hands, swarming up into the rigging at the slightest opportunity. His ambition was to be mastheadsman on his Uncle John's yacht and he was eager for any experience.

He was halfway up the mast when the earthquake struck.

It was just after nine o'clock on a cloudless morning in late April and the Mate had good-naturedly offered to time how fast the boy could climb the mast. Robert was halfway up when there was a rumble like thunder in his ears and it seemed to him that the whole village rose up and rocked about in front of his eyes. He clung dizzily to the mast and closed his eyes, but he could still feel the yacht swaying crazily beneath him. He wouldn't tell anybody. If they knew he turned dizzy when he climbed the mast they wouldn't let him do it. He'd be all right in a minute if he kept quite still. If only the boat would stop rocking.

'You all right up there, bor?' He heard the Mate's anxious voice calling from below.

He opened his eyes and blinked. He'd been right! The whole

village *had* been lifted up and rocked about! And now it was settling gently down again, to the sound of splintering glass, falling tiles and crashing chimneys. He was relieved to see that the church tower was still standing. Robert looked down at where the Mate, white-faced, was standing on deck, holding on to a stanchion and looking up at him. 'You better come down pretty slippy, bor. Look like there's bin a earthquake or suthin',' he said, his own voice not quite steady.

Robert slid quickly down the swaying mast. He felt perfectly all right now he knew that the shaking and rocking had been outside his head and not inside it. Agitated crewmen were appearing from everywhere, on *Pantomime* and on other yachts anchored in the river and already panic-stricken people were running about on the quay.

'Thass a earthquake,' one shouted, rushing up from *Pantomime's* galley. 'Thass what it is. A earthquake. I mind seein' the same sorta thing once when we stood off Lima. On'y worse'n this. Every buildin' in sight was flattened that time. An' a tidal wave that near sunk the boat.'

'But we don't git earthquakes in these parts,' another less-experienced man argued. 'I reckon that was a gas explosion.'

'A gas explosion? To rock the whole village like that? Don't be daft. Thass a earthquake, I'm tellin yer. I know. I've seen 'em afore, in foreign parts. Come on, boys, we better git ashore. They might need help. An' I wanta make sure my missus an' kids ain't took no harm.'

Even as they argued they were pulling the gig round and getting in, all except the Mate who had no family and was happy to remain on watch. As Robert went to step into the gig the Mate patted his shoulder. 'You'll be all right, bor,' he said. 'You stuck to that mast like a good 'un. In a few years time there on't be a topman to beat yer.'

If he'd given him a sovereign Robert couldn't have been more pleased.

By the time they reached the shore, the gig pitching and tossing as they rowed, the extent of the damage was becoming apparent. The earthquake had lasted some six or seven seconds and had not been severe. Nevertheless, there were gaping holes were chimneys had gone through the roofs of several houses, and the gasworks' tall chimney had completely disappeared. Many of the old dwellings that crowded round the waterfront had been rickety enough to begin with; now they leaned crazily and dangerously against each other, quite uninhabitable. People were streaming on to the quay, shouting and screaming, terrified because they feared this was only the herald of some worse disaster.

As soon as he got ashore Robert ran to the Yard. As far as he could see the yacht on the slip appeared quite safe and another on the stocks in the shed looked all right, but men were running back and forth with buckets of water to put out a fire that had begun in shavings when a bogey had been knocked over in the tremor.

Nobody took any notice of him as he hurried over towards the office. It looked as if the whole of that part of the building had been picked up and put down again. But now the stairs were twisted so they were impossible to climb and the office, although still standing was crooked and twisted, the glass in the window shattered and the door jammed. Two men had fetched a ladder and Robert could see his father talking to them through the gaping window holes. Suddenly, Luke spotted him. 'Bobbie! Go and see if your mother's all right. Tell her I'll come as soon as I can but Uncle George is trapped under a cupboard. He's all right, but thass goin' to be a bit tricky gettin' him out. Thass a bit shaky up here.'

'Can't I help, Pa?'

'No. Do as I say. I want to know your mother's safe. Tell her not to worry, we shall be all right here once we can free Uncle George.'

Robert ran home through the churchyard, keeping an eye out for falling masonry because a jagged crack had appeared in the church tower and great chunks of stonework had fallen and were embedded in the grass between toppled tombstones. Everywhere people were running about, bewildered and panic-stricken, shouting, looking for loved ones, afraid to stay indoors in case worse happened, yet paradoxically reluctant to stray too far from the safety of home. And everywhere the word 'earthquake' was on everybody's lips.

To his relief it looked as if the Falcon had escaped without too much damage.

Cassie, her face white and anxious, looked up when he entered. She was busy helping Lizzy pick up crockery that had been thrown from the dresser and smashed in the tremor. Hannah was sitting hunched in the Windsor chair, a shawl round her shoulders and a tot of whisky by her side, nursing Reuben, who was still whimpering with fear.

'Oh, I'm glad you're safe, Bobbie.' Cassie went over and put her arms round him. 'The girls are home, too. They're all right, except that they got covered in soot when the chimney crashed through the school roof. Millie and Florrie are in the scullery cleaning them up now. It's a miracle but none of the schoolchildren were hurt, thank God.' She brushed her hair back from her face with a hand that still trembled. 'But I haven't seen Papa, Bobbie. I'm worried . . .'

'I've seen him, Ma. He's all right. But the office is a bit shaky and Uncle George is wedged under a cupboard.' He gave his mother a hug. 'Now I know you're all safe I'll go back and tell Pa. I might be able to help.'

'Yes, I'm sure they can do with your help. But first go and ask Tom for some whisky and take that with you. Uncle George might be glad of it. Oh, and tell anyone you meet that there'll be free cups of tea at the Falcon.' She pulled the kettle forward, surveying the crockery still littering the floor. 'Although they might have to bring their own mugs,' she added ruefully. She turned to Lizzy. 'I think we'd better clear the meeting room, don't you? There are sure to be homeless families. We can at least give them shelter here for a night or two if we push the table up against the wall.' She leaned for a moment against a chair, her mind already racing ahead. 'And we'd better make soup . . .'

'Oh, Cassie, I don't think we can do that. We can't afford to feed soup to the entire village.' Hannah took another sip of her whisky and although her hand still shook her voice was remarkably firm.

'Really, Mama! A few bones and vegetables aren't going to ruin us,' Cassie said reproachfully. 'This is an emergency, don't you realise? People have been left with no homes. It's our Christian duty to do what we can to help and give them shelter where we can.'

Hannah shrugged. 'Let them in and they'll rob you blind. The sort of people you'll be sheltering . . . *I* shall keep my door locked.'

'You do that, Mama.' Cassie spoke sharply, annoyed at her mother's attitude. 'In fact, I'll help you back to your room now, if you're not too shaken. Millie's cleaned up the mess in there so it's quite tidy. And no windows were broken.' Cassie took Reuben from her and stood with him in her arms, stroking his hair.

Hannah seemed to shrink in her chair. 'Do you think there might be another one? Earthquake?' In spite of her earlier words she was still obviously white and shaken.

'I shouldn't think so, dear, but you never can tell.' Cassie kept her voice deliberately brisk.

'Then I won't go back to my room just yet, if you don't mind. Just in case.' She looked up at Cassie. 'Perhaps I could sit at the table and peel vegetables for the soup. Make myself useful.'

'That would certainly be a great help, dear.' Cassie relented and smiled at her. 'Millie, fetch Mrs Hannah the stewpot and vegetables.'

It wasn't long before the taproom was full of people drinking tea that was free or beer that they had to pay for, all discussing the earthquake, a calamity unheard-of ever before in England. News was coming in that the tremor had been felt in Colchester and as far away as Peldon and Abberton damage had been reported, but fortunately there was no loss of life. Tales abounded of narrow escapes and heroic rescues that lost nothing in repetition and there was a rumour that a man with a camera from one of the newspapers was travelling round photographing the damage.

Cassie and the girls were kept busy all day and so was Tom. They lost count of the number of bowls of soup that were handed out – some were even heard to admit that they had never eaten so well, but nobody was refused or turned away.

In the middle of the afternoon Luke came in, his face dirty and haggard. Cassie left the girls to carry on with making the soup and tea and sat down at the table. Lizzy poured them both a mug of tea and Cassie realised for the first time how tired she was. 'I'm glad you're home, Luke,' she said. There had been a nagging fear for him at the back of her mind all day.

He gave her a tired smile. 'Yes, I'm all right. We managed to get Uncle George out. He wasn't hurt, but I didn't like the look of him. His face looked a bit funny to me. Anyway, they strapped him on to a plank and carried him home and called

Doctor Squires. I must go and see him shortly, but I had to stay and and get as many of the papers out of the office as I could. They're in a terrible mess, but I think I managed to save everything and shove it all into boxes and an old chest. A couple of the men'll be along with it all before long.'

'Here!'

Luke spread his hands. 'What else could we do with it all? The office'll have to be entirely rebuilt. It wouldn't be safe to leave anything there. And Uncle George won't be fit to do much for a day or two, I doubt.'

'No, I suppose not.' Cassie leaned her elbows on the table and sipped her tea. It tasted good. 'We've made the meeting room ready to take anybody in that's homeless,' she told him after a while. 'And we've only got two guests in so we could put some people in the other two rooms, at a pinch. The Rector called and I told him we could put several families up as a temporary measure. Poor man, he's worried sick what to do with everyone. It isn't safe to house them in the church because of die tower, and I don't know if they're doing anything at the chapel.'

'Trouble is, once you get 'em in, how do you get 'em out again?' Luke asked practically.

'I don't know. But we can't have families with no roof over their heads, Luke, can we?'

'No, Cassie girl, I s'pose not.' He drained his tea and stood up. 'I'd better be gettin' along to see how Uncle George is. He's not as young as he was, and I'm a bit worried about 'im. He was trapped under that cupboard for several hours before we could shift stuff and free 'im. Then I must go back to the Yard again. I'm a bit concerned about one of the boats on the slip. I left some of the men makin' it safe but I must check that it's all right.'

Luke went off to Anglesea Road and Cassie continued making preparations for looking after the homeless families. Liddy was the first to arrive. She had put on a little weight since the last of her children was born, ten years ago, but constant childbearing for nearly thirty years had taken its toll and she looked an unhealthy, pasty colour. Selina, the baby of the family was with her. 'The roof is off our house,' she told Cassie. 'They say people can shelter here at the Falcon if they ain't got a roof over their heads. Is that right?'

'Of course it's right, my dear.' Cassie kissed her. 'But you're Luke's mother. You'd be welcome, anyway.'

Liddy sat down. 'Thank God all me childer are safe. Billy come home from Harvey's Yard an' I sent 'im to make sure they was all right. Emma's in service with Mrs Martin and she told Billy that Mr Martin had jest got outa his bath when the chimbley come crashin' through the roof – right into the bath he'd jest got out of! What d'you think o' that!' She accepted the cup of tea Cassie poured her. 'Goodness know where my Alf is – I ain't seen 'im. But I 'spect 'e's all right. They say the devil look after 'is own, don't they.' She settled down to drink her tea without giving her husband another thought.

It was late and Cassie was tired. She had managed to house twenty families in the end; some of them crowded into the meeting room, some in the Marquis's room, some in Lord Paget's room and the rest making do in the taproom. The Rector paid another visit. He and several others had set up a relief fund for the worst hit.

'A lot of those houses needed pulling down anyway, between you and me, Mrs Turnbull,' he confided. 'But it would have been better if there had been alternative accommodation for their inhabitants first, wouldn't it! But that's how things always seem to work and we must just do what we can. Now, if you can look after these people until tomorrow we'll get tarpaulins to cover the roofs where there's a chance of saving the houses and I'll try and get the rest re-housed where I can. The trouble is, most of them can't afford a realistic rent.' He nodded briskly. 'But I'll see what I can do. At least we should have a little money at our diposal; some of the gentlemen of the village have been very generous.' Cassie accompanied him to the door. As he reached it he turned back. 'I'm sure, Mrs Turnbull ...' he cleared his throat. 'That's to say, you've been very inconvenienced today. You must be reimbursed for your trouble ....'

'Indeed no, Rector,' Cassie said firmly. 'It's the least we can do to help our fellow men. I'm glad to be of help.'

He nodded. 'You're extremely kind.' He hurried on his way, a large, rather dusty figure, with shoulders slightly rounded from poring over his books.

Cassie went back in. Luke still hadn't returned from Uncle George's. She hoped nothing was wrong there. As if in answer to her thoughts the door opened and he came in. She could see from his face that all was not well.

He sat down at the table and put his head in his hands. 'He's had a stroke,' he said, his voice muffled. 'Uncle George has had a stroke. All down one side. Useless. His arm. His leg. The doctor says he'll never walk again.'

'Oh, Luke.' Cassie went over to him and laid her arm across his shoulders.

He looked up. 'It wasn't anything to do with the earthquake. Well,' he corrected himself, 'I suppose it was, in a way. Being trapped under that cupboard for such a long time must have brought it on, although he was all right when we got 'im out. He talked to me right up to the time we got him strapped on the plank.' He shook his head. 'He can't talk now, poor ole chap.

189

Leastways, not so anybody can understand what he's sayin'. Doctor Squires says it might get better. His speech, I mean. He don't hold out much hope for 'im gettin' the use of his arm or leg back. He'll never work again, thass for sure.'

Chapter Fourteen

Gradually the village returned to something like normal. In some ways the earthquake could have been said to do some good because it meant that the worst of the slum dwellings, if they hadn't already fallen or been knocked down, had to be pulled down and their occupants rehoused. Liddy and Alf found a cottage in Paget Road which was far superior to the hovel in Sun Yard where they – or rather Liddy – had reared their family and Liddy did as she had always done and worked in the sprat-canning factory in winter and shelled shrimps in summer to make sure that the rent was paid on time.

But not all the villagers were so fortunate. Cassie, elected to the Vestry after her timely assistance to the homeless after the earthquake was appalled by the apathy of some of the other members of the council to the conditions of the poor.

The Rector, who chaired the meetings, had to be careful not to upset the Churchwarden, Sir Henry Crampin, because there was a tacit understanding that Sir Henry would be generous in the repair of the church tower.

'The cottages on my estate didn't take any harm at all,' Sir Henry said. 'They're well built – I saw to that. It's these 'jerry-built places that didn't stand up to the earthquake.' He blew his nose with a sound like the Last Trump.

'The cottages down by the quay were not so much jerry-built as old, Sir Henry,' the Rector ventured.

'But poor people will always complain. Whatever you do for them they always want more,' Sir Henry continued. 'When was it we put the piped water in? Last year or the year before? Some people are never satisfied.'

'It's not much good having piped water if you haven't got a 'house,' Cassie said quietly. 'And most of the houses that collapsed didn't have piped water, anyway. They still had to fetch their water by the bucketful from the brook.'

'You may be right, Mrs Turnbull.' The people's warden, George Sainty, said hurriedly, clearing his throat and looking warningly in her direction. This was Mrs Turnbull's first Vestry and she clearly hadn't learned to take her cue from Sir Henry.

'Hasn't there been a relief fund set up?' Jim Tyler asked.

'Oh, yes, and there have been meetings in Chelmsford and Colchester as well as in London. Sir Henry and I went to the one in London, didn't we, Sir Henry?' the Rector said.

Sir Henry grunted bad-temperedly. 'We put our hands in our pockets, too. But how long it'll take to get the money distributed is anybody's guess.' He leaned back expansively in his chair. 'But things are never as bad as people make out. People in Wyford can afford to re-house themselves. There's plenty of employment. Two shipyards, fishing, yachting, and that's apart from all those I employ on my estate. And that must number fifty or more,' he added, mumbling into his whiskers.

'There's plenty that can't help theirselves,' Bill Woods the grocer spoke up. 'Them in work's all right. But what about them as can't work? What about them as are too old?'

'Room for them in the poorhouse,' Sir Henry said

importantly. 'That's one of the things you pay your rates for, to keep the poorhouse going for destitute people.'

'You could fill the poorhouse with widows and children of fishermen that have drowned,' Cassie said, 'never mind the elderly and infirm.' She looked round at the assembled company. The meeting room had been cleared and the table replaced in the middle of the room for the Vestry Meeting and nine of them sat round it. The Rector sat at the head, with the churchwarden and people's warden to his left and right. The parish clerk, George Cole, sat on the other side of Sir Henry and it was quite obvious that although the Rector was in the chair it was Sir Henry who was running the meeting. The people's warden, George Sainty, owned three fishing smacks, Jim Tyler was a sailmaker, then there was Bill Woods the grocer, Fred Brown the ropemaker and Tom Last the baker. Cassie was the only woman present and she could tell she was expected to be seen and not heard. In fact her last statement had been received in embarrassed silence and she realised they wished they had never elected her. The thought amused her. They might wish it even more by the time she'd finished with them.

She smiled round at them now. 'Well, something needs to be decided,' she reminded them. 'I've still got four families coming in every night to sleep on the floor in this very room, so it's a good thing these meetings take place in the afternoon. But I can't house them indefinitely.'

Tom Last nodded in agreement. He would never speak up for himself but he was glad to back up Cassie. He knew the plight of the poor. His wife sometimes distributed two-day-old bread at night and she had often met Cassie on a similar errand.

Sir Henry took out his pocket-watch. 'Time I was off. I've a meeting with my bailiff in twenty minutes. Declare the meeting closed please, Rector.'

'But nothing's decided,' Cassie protested.

'Shall we close with prayer?' the Rector said.

Luke had been right about Uncle George. Although Aunt Maisie, nursing him tirelessly, insisted that he was getting better, it was evident that he would never again leave his bed. Luke went to see him every week, and more often if he could find the time, to tell him about progress at the Yard or just to sit with him for half an hour.

He lay between spotless white sheets that Maisie changed at least once every day and sometimes twice, his few strands of grey hair brushed carefully over his bald head, his face carefully shaved and his moustache trimmed. There was a table beside his bed with a little white crocheted cloth on which everything was neatly placed; his glasses, his book, the daily paper.

'You hear what the boy is a-sayin', George?' she would lean over him and shout in his ear. 'The little smack for Harry Bellman is nearly finished.' She would straighten an imaginary crease and turn to Luke. 'There. He heard what I said. Did you see him nod?' But it was wishful thinking on her part and Luke knew it. He came to dread his visits, feeling almost more sorry for his aunt, wearing herself out in caring for him, than for his uncle, oblivious to it all.

Less than a month after the earthquake Luke had a letter from Mr Grimshaw, the manager of George Turnbull's bank in Colchester, asking Luke to go and see him.

'Wonder what he wants?' Luke said, turning an anxious face to Cassie.

'Oh, I don't suppose it's anything to worry about. But since you wrote to tell him that Uncle George wasn't well he knows you'll be running things so he probably wants to meet you and talk things over,' Cassie said cheerfully. 'When do you have to go?'

'Next Tuesday.'

'I'll come with you. I can look for curtain material while you're in the bank with – what's his name? – Mr Grimshaw. The dining room badly needs new curtains – not that Mama will hand over the money for them if I find any, but there's no harm in looking, is there?'

The highly-polished mahogany desk behind which Arthur Grimshaw sat was intimidating and Luke had never realized how loudly his boots squeaked until he walked across the thick pile carpet that seemed to stretch for miles and stood before it.

Mr Grimshaw held out a soft, white hand and Luke shook it in his great, horny one before sitting down on the edge of the chair he was offered.

'You do realise why I've asked you to come and see me, Mr Turnbull?' Mr Grimshaw asked. He was a small man, dwarfed by the size of his desk, with neat grey hair, a neat grey moustache and round gold-rimmed spectacles, which he continually removed, polished and replaced.

Luke twisted his hat round in his hands. 'I s'pose it's because my uncle is ill,' he said. 'I s'pose it's because I wrote and told you I'm responsible for everything while he's laid aside.'

Arthur Grimshaw nodded. 'Partly that, and partly ...' He took off his glasses, polished them and put them back on. 'Well, no doubt you realize that Turnbull's Yard is on the verge of bankruptcy.' The way he said it he could have been merely commenting on the weather.

'Bankruptcy! What do you mean? But that can't be! I don't know what you're talking about!' Agitated, Luke stood up, walked about a bit and then sat down again. 'We've always had work. Two big yachts we've built in the past two years

195

'And never been paid for,' Mr Grimshaw interrupted. 'Most of the money for both those yachts is still outstanding.'

'But one of them was Lord Farley's yacht. We had it back this winter for modifications and now he's gone off round the world in it.'

'So that added even more to his bill. And if he's gone round the world there's no chance of getting him to settle till he gets back.' The glasses had another polish before Mr Grimshaw leaned his elbows on his desk. 'And you can't afford to wait that long, Mr Turnbull. You need money *now*. I think when you go through your books again you'll find your debts piling up at an alarming rate.'

Luke slumped in his chair. 'When my cousin Martin died, Mr Grimshaw, my uncle paid for me to go and learn book-keeping so that I could take it off his shoulders. I learnt quite a bit, although I never liked it – I can do the figuring for boat measurements in my head, you understand, but accounts are something quite different, as far as I'm concerned. I s'pose it's because it's something I've got no real interest in. Anyway, like it or not I learnt it, because that was what Uncle George wanted. But then he hardly let me near the books. He did it all hisself apart from a few bits here and there. To tell you the truth, I've got a great pile of papers at home to be sorted out now – I took them home after the office got wrecked in the earthquake but I haven't had a chance to get at them yet.'

'Well, I don't think you'll find them very encouraging, Mr Turnbull,' Mr Grimshaw said sadly.

Luke spread his hands. 'What am I going to do, then?'

'Well, I can tell you that your uncle was on the verge of selling the row of houses he owns, or rather owned, in Gas Road, when the earthquake struck. But, as you know, the gasworks' chimney fell on them so there's nothing there to sell now. And unfortunately they were very inadequately insured, so that's not much help. There are the houses in The Folley, but they're practically uninhabitable since the earthquake ... How much work have you on hand at the moment, Mr Turnbull?'

Luke shook his head. 'Not a lot. But this is always a slack time. We're busy through the early part of the year, fitting out the yachts for the summer, but once they've gone things always go quiet for a few months unless we've got a big one on the stocks. We're just building a little smack for Mr Bellman, but there's not much else on the order book at the moment.'

'Then I suggest you lay off half your work force. How many men have you got? Twenty?'

'Twenty-four with the apprentices.'

'Well, if you lay half of them off you'll halve your wage bill for a start.'

'No!' Luke sat up in his chair. 'I'm not going to do that if I can help it. Work's not all that plentiful in the place and most of the men have been with us ever since they were old enough to work. I couldn't turn 'em out of their jobs.'

Mr Grimshaw shook his head. 'It doesn't look as if you'll have any choice, Mr Turnbull.' He took off his glasses and polished them thoughtfully, looking myopically at Luke while he did so. 'If you can't afford to pay them. And you have outstanding bills to pay, too.'

Luke pinched his lip. 'How would it be if I put the men to work repairing the houses in The Folley? That would keep them busy and we'd have something to sell at the end of it.'

Mr Grimshaw nodded slowly. 'Yes, that might be a good idea but the men will have to be paid while they're doing the work – you've got no capital, remember.'

Luke stood up and began to pace the floor. He didn't know what to say. This side of the business was a mystery and a worry to him; he'd hated learning book-keeping and had been glad that it had never needed to be put to much use. But now ...

Mr Grimshaw was speaking again. 'And I think I can make you a loan that will tide you over until the houses can be sold. In the meantime, you must give me authority to recover what debts I can for you and I think a wise investment would be a competent man to look after your accounting system, such as it is.'

'That would be a great relief, if only I knew somebody,' Luke said, sitting down on his chair again.

'I think I know the man. I'll see what I can do.' Mr Grimshaw stood up and held out a limp hand. 'I wish you luck, Mr Turnbull. You're going to need it.'

Luke met Cassie outside the town hall. 'The business is in a terrible state, Cassie girl,' he said, taking hold of her arm. 'Come on, let's catch the train and go home. I'm afraid there'll be no new curtains at the Falcon until we get the Yard sorted out.'

'Why? What's wrong with it? You've got work, haven't you?' Cassie asked breathlessly as he hurried her along to the railway station.

'I'll tell you all about it when we're in the train.'

Cassie listened to what he had to say as the train rattled and swayed its way back to Wyford. 'But you should have known all this. You were supposed to be looking after that side of things,' she protested. 'I've helped you, so I know.'

'You only knew as much as I did. And I only knew as much as Uncle George let me see – which wasn't everything.' He sighed. 'You know how it was, Cassie. I didn't like doing it so I was glad there wasn't too much to do. And Uncle George signed all the cheques – which I've now got authority to do. Oh, Lord, Cassie, what a mess.' He looked out of the window. 'Of course, what we need is a really big order. We've got the smack to finish, and if we put the cottages in The Folley in good repair they can be sold. But a nice big boat – a cutter or schooner – that's what we need to put us back on our feet.' He leaned over and put his hand over hers.

She pulled her hand away. 'And what do you think Uncle George will say about all this, when he's well enough to understand?' she said in a tight voice. She felt unreasonably annoyed with Luke for not realizing what had been going on.

Luke stared out of the window. 'I don't think Uncle George will ever be well enough to understand,' he said, 'and I don't know whether I should be sad or glad about that.'

In October Robert came home from his first season racing looking brown and fit. He had grown from a boy to a man in those months and there was even the beginnings of a beard on his tanned face.

'You're growing to look just like your grandfather Reuben, Bobby' Hannah said when he visited her in her sitting room. 'Look, there's his picture, on the table under the window. Can't you see the likeness, Cassie?'

Cassie picked up the picture. It was true. Apart from the fact that Robert was fair where Reuben was dark there was a definite resemblance between the two in the wide brow, the shape of the eyebrows and the determined set of the jaw. She looked at her son. At least there was no vestige of resemblance to Edward. For that she was eternally thankful.

'We raced in the Harwich regatta,' he told them all when his father came home, 'then we went to Dover and did the Dover to Calais, then we raced in the Solent, then we went up to the Clyde and raced there and then Lady Pathfield and the children joined us and we went to the Kyles of Bute and anchored off Tignabruaich – oh, Mama, it was beautiful there.' His face was alight with excitement as he went on, 'Then we went through the Crinan Canal and on up to Mull, but we spent a few days in Loch Aline on the way, which must be the loveliest place – when it doesn't rain.'

'You had a pretty full season then, boy,' Luke said, glad to forget the worries of the Yard in listening to Robert's tales.

'Oh, but that's not all,' Robert laughed. 'When the family left us we sailed back down the Irish Sea and round Land's End ready for Cowes Week! Mind you, we had a pretty rough passage round Land's End and we were nearly late for Cowes Week. But we made it in time and carried off several prizes. Look.' He emptied his pockets and a stream of silver spread across the table.

'You want to look after that, boy,' Luke said seriously. 'You never know when you might need it.'

'I spent some and bought you all presents.' Eagerly, the boy rummaged in his canvas sea-bag and brought out trinkets for his mother and sisters, a plaid shawl for his grandmother and a briar pipe for his father.

'You're really happy now, Robert, aren't you?' Cassie said, searching the boy's face with pride.

'Oh, I am, Ma. I'm doing what I've always wanted to do. Except that I haven't yet been allowed to work at the top of the mast. But I shall. You'll see. I shall.'

'You're full young to be a topman yet, boy,' Luke reminded him. 'You're not yet sixteen. There's plenty of time.'

It pleased Cassie to have all four of her children round the meal-table again, although she knew it wouldn't be for long. Robert would be off with the fishing fleet as soon as he could find a skipper to take him. And that wouldn't be difficult. His two sisters watched their big brother with something akin to awe. They smiled at each other and giggled shyly if they happened to catch his eye.

'Anybody would think I'd been away for five years instead of five months,' he laughed at them. 'You weren't shy before I went away. As I remember you used to pinch the apples out of my bag . . .'

' . . . that you'd been scrumping out of Mrs Tyler's garden!' Cassie said.

'Oh, Ma, I didn't think you knew!' He grinned affectionately at his mother.

The winter was hard and there were weeks when the weather was so bad that no work could be done at the Yard. But eventually the houses in The Folley were repaired and put into good order with a smart coat of paint to add the finishing touch. The men had been happy to try their hands at house-carpentry when Luke had told them the state of things and they had worked with a will.

'You should come and see them, Cassie,' Luke said, when they were finished. 'Even you would be happy to live in one now they're finished. Smart as paint, they are.'

'I just hope they'll sell for a good price,' was Cassie's rejoinder.

It wasn't long before Mr Grimshaw had found a reliable man to take over the accounts for Turnbull's Yard.

'His name's Aaron Wix and he'll be worth every penny you have to pay him,' Mr Grimshaw assured Luke. He patted his shoulder. 'I'm beginning to get things sorted out, Mr Turnbull. Money's still going out faster than it's coming in but I've recovered two large bad debts by dint of an official letter or two and I'm hopeful for several of the others. And the sale of the cottages will help to put things back on an even keel. Just make sure things don't get into such a state again. But there, Aaron Wix will see that they don't.'

'I'm very grateful to you, Mr Grimshaw.' Luke twisted his hat round in his hands. He was never happy in the company of the bank manager; he even found the large, highly-polished mahogany desk behind which Mr Grimshaw sat intimidating. He looked down at his horny hands. 'I'm a craftsman, Mr Grimshaw. I never wanted to be a book-keeper. I've not the head for it.' He lifted his head and met the bank manager's eye. 'But I can turn out a good job, better than most, although I say it myself; I can run the Yard and keep the men happy. We should make a decent profit out of the little smack. Even with the men working on the cottages and then being laid off for those weeks when the weather was too bad to work we're still well up to schedule and there'll be work to do on at least four of the yachts laid up in the river when the smack's off the stocks.'

'You'll need more than that, Mr Turnbull, if you're going to save the Yard,' Mr Grimshaw said bluntly. 'You're not out of the wood yet. Not by any means.' He took his spectacles off and polished them, giving Luke a brief smile. 'But I'm sure you'll make out, Mr Turnbull. You're a conscientious man and although I know nothing about boats, having been and inspected those cottages I know you turn out work of the highest quality.'

Aaron Wix was everything Mr Grimshaw had promised. He was a tall, spare man in his late thirties, with a crumpled shirt and inkstained fingers. As he worked he undid his tie and continually ran his fingers through his hair until it stood on end, giving him an untidy, rakish appearance. But, lost in figures, he was quite oblivious to this.

'Are you quite sure you couldn't cut down on the work force, Mr Turnbull?' he asked one afternoon when Luke came upstairs to the office.

Luke sat down. 'Don't call me Mr Turnbull, call me Luke

202

like everyone else does,' he said absently, scratching his beard as he thought over Aaron's words. 'We lost three men to Harvey's Yard when Uncle George was taken bad,' he said slowly. He sighed. 'Yes, you're right, Aaron, we could cut down. Alf Turnbull has never done a proper day's work in the whole of his life; he's a troublemaker and he drinks too much. We could well do without him.' He gave another heavy sigh and looked at Aaron, 'But you tell me how I can sack my own father.'

Aaron nodded. 'I understand, Luke.'

Luke got up and went over to the window and looked down into the Yard, where Alf was nowhere to be seen but everybody else was busy at work. From where he stood he could hear the ring of the hammer on the anvil just a split second after he saw the shower of sparks and there was a constant noise of caulking hammers and the rasp of the pit saw. 'They're a good batch of men' he said, speaking half to himself. 'I do believe that they'd work without pay to get the Yard back on its feet if it wasn't that they'd have to watch their littl'uns starve. And no man can do that – not that I would ever countenance it.' He didn't add that he himself had taken no wages for several months. The store of money he had saved in his toolbox all those years ago in the futile hope that he could buy a house had never been touched. It had never been needed. In fact, he had forgotten about it until the present crisis when it had come in very handy. It meant he hadn't had to confess to Cassie that he was drawing no money for the long hours he worked.

He turned back into the room and picked up a ledger so he didn't see Cassie hurry into the Yard and up the stairs to the office.

She entered without knocking. 'Oh, Luke,' she said, tears running down her face so that she didn't even notice Aaron, 'it's Uncle George. He died half an hour ago.' She sat down on a bench just inside the door and took out her handkerchief to wipe her eyes.

Luke went and sat beside her, biting his lip. George Turnbull had been more to him than his own father, much more. He had treated him like his own son – after Martin died Luke had *been* George's son. But the real tragedy had been when he'd been stricken down, changing from a happy, forceful, hard-working, cheery man to something little more than a vegetable. Uncle George, as they had known him, had been lost to them nearly a year ago, on the day of the earthquake.

'Don't take on, Cassie,' he said, when he could trust himself to speak. 'I'm sure thass all for the best, you know. At least he never knew the state things had got into, here at the Yard.'

'He was such a good man. And Aunt Maisie was so sure he was getting better,' Cassie sobbed. 'I don't know what she'll do, now.'

'She was killing herself looking after him,' Luke reminded her. 'Come on, we must go and seen her.' He turned to Aaron. 'You'll tell the men, Aaron, won't you. Tell them to pack up for the day as a mark of respect.'

Hannah was with Maisie, who was surprisingly calm, although her eyes were red from tears that she would only shed in private. 'I did what I could for my poor old chap while he was alive and I shall see he hev a good send-off. My conscience is clear,' she said quietly to Luke and Cassie. 'He was a good man, a good husband and father and a good master to his men. He deserves the best I can give him.' She laid a hand on Luke's arm. 'You'll see to it, boy, on't you? The business'll be yours now. You'll see that can stand the cost of a good funeral, I'm sure.'

'What could I say?' Luke said to Cassie on the way home. 'How could I tell the poor soul that we need every penny we can get to keep the bank happy?'

'She wouldn't understand if you did,' Cassie said. 'She never had to think about where the money came from. Uncle George always made sure she had what she wanted – and more besides. If you told Aunt Maisie that money grew on trees she'd believe you.'

'I wish to God it did,' Luke answered fervently.

'I expect the Falcon will foot the bill,' Cassie said resignedly. 'Although getting money out of my mother these days is like getting blood out of a stone.'

In the event Hannah and Maisie between them planned a lavish funeral for George. Hannah, in encouraging Maisie to spare no expense, was quite unaware that she would be expected to pay the bill. It was a blustery day in early March and the plumes on the four black horses that pulled the funeral carriage danced and waved behind the undertaker's mute, contrasting in a way that seemed quite disrespectful with the sombre funeral procession that followed.

It was a long procession. George had been a popular and well-loved figure in the village and men from the Yard left their work and stood with their caps doffed at the side of the street as the cortege passed. Women and children watched, too, the women wiping away a surreptitious tear with a corner of an apron at the passing of a good man.

Luke, helping to bear the coffin that he himself had made as a last gesture to the man he had loved like a father, couldn't help thinking as he entered the packed church that the weight of his uncle's body on his shoulder was nothing to the weight of the inheritance that was now his.

Chapter Fifteen

The next six months were a nightmare. While George had been alive a certain amount of work had come in on the strength of his possible return to work. Now he was dead and yacht captains and owners alike were reluctant to commission work until they were convinced that the Yard wasn't about to close; an event they rendered all the more likely by their very caution.

On the financial side Aaron Wix was a tower of strength, advising when to expand and when to hold back. After Luke had held a meeting with all the men and explained the situation they, too, rallied round and gave him their full support.

All except his own father.

Luke was only too well aware that Alf had never done a hard day's work in his life; it had always been the same and Alf's brother George had accepted this. 'The trouble is, boy,' he had once confided to Luke, 'I never felt I could sack him, not while he'd got all you littl'uns to feed. I should never hev forgive meself to think of you all a-goin' hungry on my account. So I kept him on and tried to make him take some pride in his work. But did he? Did he heck!' He had shaken his head. 'P'raps I done the wrong thing. P'raps I should've sacked him. God knows he spent most of what he earn in the pub. But thass too late now; he's bin here too long for me to turn him out. But he's a real bad penny. I hev to say it, even though he is your father and my brother. What my dear old mother'd say to him now if she was alive I do not know. He was the youngest and her blue-eyed boy. P'raps thass why he was always a lazy sod when we was boys. Never done a hand's turn for nobody. And got away with it, too.' He'd shrugged. 'But 'e's me own flesh and blood so what can I do but keep him on?'

George's words came back to Luke time and again: when the four apprentice boys disappeared and were found in the bilges of the yacht in for repair, where Alf was teaching them to play ha'penny nap, for money, with a pack of greasy cards; when Alf tried to stir up discontent among the men, going around the Yard muttering that there had been new furniture delivered to the office.

'Makin' theirselves nice an' comfortable up there, ain't they? But what about us poor buggers, workin' outside in all weathers? What about a bit o' comfort an' shelter for us?' But as he spoke his backside was never far from the bogey.

The new office furniture had been Aaron's idea. 'It's no good, Luke, we can't run an efficient office with nothing but an old chest of drawers and a kitchen table. No wonder you and your uncle got things in such a state. There's nowhere to file anything, nowhere to keep Martin's yacht plans safe. Your most precious asset and you told me yourself they were never even rolled up until the earthquake forced you to salvage them. And now look at them, stood up in that corner, gathering dust. They need cataloguing properly and keeping in a special chest.'

Luke scratched his beard. 'Can we afford to buy a lot of fancy stuff?'

'I'm not asking for fancy stuff, just plain, good office

equipment that'll make my work easier and the whole office run more efficiently.'

'I'll make it,' Luke decided. 'It'll be cheaper.'

Aaron shook his head. 'False economy. Your skills are more important on the yachts, where they'll bring in the money. You haven't got time to spare to knock up office equipment, and you wouldn't let anyone else do it. And it isn't as if you'd be satisfied with a hammer and nails job, either, you'd make everything into a work of art – and I'm not blaming you for taking pride in your work, don't think that – but that's not what's wanted here. We need reasonable, functional, cheap office furniture. Look, I've got a catalogue here . . . '

Aaron was right. The new furniture transformed the office into a neat, efficient-looking room which impressed the few yacht owners who did come in to enquire about repairs and word soon got around that Turnbull's Yard wasn't going to close, after all. More repairs began to trickle in. But it was not enough.

And Alf's troublemaking continued.

In the end Luke went to see his mother. 'I don't know what to do about him, Mam,' he said, his forehead creased with concern. 'He won't work himself and does all he can to stop the others. If it was anyone else I'd give him the sack without a minute's thought.'

'You know why 'e's like 'e is, don't you, Luke, boy?' Liddy said. ''E's eaten up with jealousy. That was bad enough when 'is brother George did all right an' got 'imself a business, but when the business was left to you, Luke . . . ' She shook her head. 'That was more'n his pride could stand.'

'But surely he didn't think Uncle George would leave Turnbull's Yard to him, did he? He could never have run it.'

'Don't make no difference. 'E never 'ad the chance, did 'e?'

'How would he have felt if Martin had lived? Would he have caused trouble for him, do you think?'

Liddy shrugged. 'That wouldn't have been so bad, if it'd been Marty. At least it wouldn't have been 'is own son 'e was hevin' to take orders from.'

Luke nodded. 'But it can't go on like this. The Yard's already facing ruin if things don't pick up; he'll bring it on faster than it need be.' He scratched his beard. 'I've got to think about the other men, Mam. I've got to keep things going for as long as I can for their sakes.'

'You've spoke to 'im?'

'Till I'm blue in the face. He just shakes his head and says, "You're gettin' above yourself, Luke, boy. Remember thass your father you're a-talkin' to".' He gave an accurate impression of his father's slow drawl.

Liddy laid a hand on his arm. 'If 'e won't listen to reason then you'll hev to sack 'im, Luke. You can't let other men's families starve on account of 'im.'

'But what about you, Mam?'

Liddy gave a hollow laugh. ''E ain't never bin much of a provider as far as me an' the children were concerned so that won't make no difference. Anyway, there's only me an' Selina at home now an' I make sure the rent's paid with me sprat-packin' an' shrimp-pickin'. The others are good to me as well, they all bring me a bit outa their wages, bless 'em. So you don't need to worry about us, boy. You must do what you think's right and forget thass your father you're dealin' with.'

'Thass easier said than done, Mam.'

But a week later things came to a head. It was Alf s birthday and he had spent his midday break in the Ship at Launch, celebrating – he knew it was no use going to the Falcon because Tom would only offer him cups of tea.

He came back brandishing a bottle and shouting to all and sundry to drink with him because it was his birthday. The men tried to calm him down and when that failed they got out of his way.

'So!' He stood swaying in the middle of the Yard. 'Will none of ye buggers hev a drink with me? All right, I'll drink to meself.' He drained the bottle and then picked up an axe. 'An' I'll show ye Alf Turnbull's not a man to be slighted. I'll show my high and mighty son that 'is father's not to be passed by like a heap o' shit, jest 'cause the Yard b'long to him now. That shouda bin *mine*. George was *my* bloody brother, not his. I'll show the bugger 'e can't best me.' He began to lay about the nearly-finished smack with the axe, fortunately too drunk to do much damage. It took three men to overpower him.

The next day Luke had no choice but to pay him off.

Alf received the news with truculence. 'I was gonna leave, anyway,' he lied. 'That ain't right to expect a man to belittle hisself by takin' orders from his own son, you jumped-up young bugger.' He rammed his cap further on to his head. 'But you'll rue the day, you see if you don't. Pride come before a fall an' when you come to it you'll fall bloody hard, you mark my words.'

Luke waited patiently for his father's tirade to finish. Then he said, 'What will you do, Dad? Have you got another job lined up?'

'Mind your own bloody business. I can get a job where I like, jest like that.' Alf snapped his fingers in his son's face.

'I'm glad to hear it, Dad,' Luke said civilly. 'But if you should have any trouble, I hear they're looking for somebody to go round with the night-soil cart.'

Alf sneered. 'Go round with the shit cart! You needn't think I'm gonna lower myself to go round the village emptyin' the bumbies. No bloody fear.'

'No, Dad. I didn't think you would,' Luke said. 'But I thought I'd tell you, just in case ...' He didn't finish the sentence.

'I hated doing it, Cassie,' he told her that night, 'but I couldn't have him going round smashing the place up, now could I? I had to do it for the sake of the other men. They've only put up with him this long because he was Uncle George's brother and my father.'

'How did he take it?' Cassie asked.

'As you would expect my father to take it. He pretended he was going to leave, anyway. I jest hope they'll take him on the night-soil cart.'

'Oh, Luke, being one of the Night Militia is a horrible, stinking job. Working all night, too. Anybody'd have to be drunk out of their senses to take it on.'

Luke sighed in the darkness. 'Should suit my father very well, then.'

'But what about Harvey's Yard – would they take him on?'

'I shouldn't think so. Everybody knows what he's like. But I suppose they might – I know they've got plenty of work.' He sighed again. 'I only wish we had. What we need, Cassie, is one really big order to set us back on our feet.'

'You've got the smack – isn't that a help?' she asked, her voice sharper than she had intended. She had worries of her own.

'Yes, of course the smack was a help. But that's almost finished now. We need something else. Something special, to really set us up.'

'And where do you think you'll get "something special"?' Her voice was impatient.

'I don't know, Cassie. It'd need a miracle, I reckon.'

Cassie turned away from him and thumped her pillow. Miracles were in short supply as far as she was concerned. Life at the Falcon wasn't exactly a bed of roses these days, either. There weren't so many customers in the taproom now, nor guests to stay, because Hannah refused to relinquish her tight hold on the purse-strings and Cassie found it increasingly hard to keep up the high standard she tried to maintain, especially with Luke taking no more out of his business than was absolutely necessary. It meant that Cassie could no longer supplement the Falcon's finances from her own as she had done in previous years.

The only time Hannah became less parsimonious – it would be an exaggeration to say she became more generous – was when Abel Crowther paid a visit. Then she would examine menus and shopping lists to make sure that everything was of the best quality and hand over the money with less than her usual reluctance.

'Aye, tha's a reet clever businesswoman, Hannah,' Abel would say, examining the ledgers, carefully adjusted so as not to show the sudden rise in expenditure. 'But I allus knew tha would be.'

Soon after Robert had begun his third season yachting – he had been taken on the *Venetia* as deck-hand – Edward Price-Carpenter paid another of his rare visits to Wyford. His father had recently died so the ownership and responsibility for *Leander* now rested with him.

'Poor old tub, she's getting a bit ancient,' he told Cassie as she served his after-dinner brandy in the snuggery. She always reserved that task for herself when Edward visited. 'I haven't decided yet whether to keep her or whether to get myself a better yacht.'

'What do you mean, have one built ... sir?' she added as an afterthought, holding her breath for his reply.

He shrugged. 'Have one built. Buy one. I don't know. I haven't decided anything yet.' He stretched out his long legs and slumped down further into his armchair, swirling the brandy round in the glass. 'What do you think I should do, Cassie?' He looked up at her and smiled.

She looked away, her colour rising. 'Oh, I think you should have one built, sir. Then you can have it exactly as you want it,' she replied carefully. A yacht for Edward Price-Carpenter was exactly what Luke needed to put the Yard back on its feet. Only half-formed in her mind was the idea that if only she could engineer it, she would feel she had at last wiped the slate clean and be free from the guilt that had never left her, even after all these years. Ahead of it was the thought that the building of a new yacht would bring Edward to Wyford. Often.

He nodded, blowing a ring of cigar smoke into the air. 'I'll have to think about that one.' He smiled at her and the look in his eyes still had the power to melt her bones. 'Of course, if I were to decide to have a new yacht built, it would mean I would often have to come and check its progress.' He caught her hand as she stood beside him. 'I should enjoy that. I enjoy coming to Wyford and seeing you, Cassie.'

'You don't come very often,' she countered, before she could stop herself.

'That's because I've always had the Guv'nor breathing down my neck all the time. I haven't got that now, although I shall miss the old cove, naturally. But I'm my own master now. I can please myself what I do – within reason, that is.' He grinned at her wickedly.

'My husband could probably help you if you are thinking of building, sir,' she said, putting slight emphasis on the word 'husband'. 'Why don't you ask him for his advice?' She tried to turn away but Edward caught her hand and pulled her back.

'I don't take advice Cassie,' he said softly. 'I do what/want to do.' His gaze swept from her feet to the top of her head, lingering on a level with the locket she wore on a long chain over her high-necked blouse. His voice dropped even further. 'And at the moment what I want to do is take you to bed.'

She snatched her hand away and turned swiftly so that he shouldn't see her flaming face.

'I thought so.' He smiled. 'You've never forgotten either, Cassie, have you? All these years and you still remember. Just as I do.' He picked up his glass. 'Here's to the next time, Cassie.' His eyes were teasing over its rim.

'There won't *be* a next time,' she said fiercely.

'Won't there? Don't be too sure about that. I usually get what I want.'

She hurried back to the kitchen. Oh, what a mess her life was. If only she could pack a bag and follow Edward ... She sighed. Given half a chance she wouldn't even bother to pack a bag. He wanted her, he made no pretence about that and she wanted him, but convention, duty, oh, so many things, tied her to Luke.

That night as she lay awake beside him and listened to his gentle snoring – Luke always snored a little after he had made love to her – she thought about Edward. Somehow she *must* persuade him to have the new yacht built at Turnbull's Yard.

'Have you thought any more about your new yacht, sir?' she asked when she took Edward his early-morning tea the next day. Usually Millie did this but Cassie had made an excuse this morning and had taken it up herself. She put down the tray and drew back the curtains on a bright late May morning.

'Mm?' He opened his eyes and she noticed that even after a night's sleep and needing a shave Edward still looked neat. He sat up in bed and stretched. 'Good gracious, girl, I've hardly had time to give the matter any more thought. Come here.' He held out his hand and she went to the side of the bed. 'Why is it important to you? What difference would it make?' He leaned forward and took her hand. 'Think I might come and see you more often?' he asked, his head on one side. 'You'd like that, Cassie, wouldn't you? You've still got a soft spot for me, even after all these years, haven't you? Oh, it's all right, you needn't be afraid to admit it. I've often thought of you, too.' His gaze held hers. 'But I couldn't keep coming here unless you made it worth my while, you know,' he said softly, allowing his hand to travel gently up her arm. She stepped back as if she'd been scalded. 'Oh, come on. You'll have to be more accommodating than that, my dear,' he said with a mocking smile. 'You were one summer, as I remember. I'm sure you could be again.'

'You know that's not possible,' she said fiercely. 'You're a respectable married man ...'

'Oh, I don't know about that.' He grinned up at her lazily. 'Married, yes. But I was never a great one for respectability.'

'Well, I'm a respectable married woman.' She hurried out of the door.

Edward picked up his tea and leaned back on his pillows, a faint smile on his face. Wyford was a nice little place. He could spend many happy hours here. And one thing he would say for Cassie; she'd kept her figure a damn sight better than Felicity and he didn't think it was all due to whalebone. But that he would find out, in due course. He felt a pleasant stirring of anticipation.

Two days later saw him briskly climbing the stairs to the office at Turnbull's Yacht Yard.

'I'm only making tentative enquiries,' he said, 'but I think I've got a buyer for *Leander,* my father's old yacht and I've a mind to have one of my own built.'

'What sort of yacht did you have in mind, sir?' Luke asked.

215

He didn't like Edward Price-Carpenter and never had. He'd seen too many of his type before, throwing their weight about and pretending that they knew all about yachts and racing when in fact they knew bugger all.

'Something fast.' Edward leaned over the desk. 'To tell you the truth, Turnbull, Lord Felgate, a good friend of mine, is having a yacht built in Harvey's Yard.'

'Yes, I've heard about it,' Luke said. 'She's a two-masted schooner, isn't she?'

Edward nodded. 'And Bunny Felgate says she'll be fast. In fact, the bounder said that when she's finished there'll be nothing to touch her.' He straightened up. 'I want to dispute that. In fact, in my cups at the Rose and Crown last night I was foolish enough to have a wager with him.'

'Wager? What sort of a wager?'

'I wagered him that I would have myself a yacht built that would beat his into a cocked hat.' He shook his head. 'I may have been foolish. I wagered quite a lot of money.'

'And you want us to build you a yacht that will outrace Lord Felgate's,' Luke said thoughtfully.

'Perhaps. I do want a yacht built – but I haven't quite decided who I'll get to build it. I might get Harvey's to do it. Or James at Brightlingsea. Or there's somebody at Tollesbury – I forget his name.' Edward replaced his hat and picked up his cane. 'I just thought I'd come along and put you in the picture. See if you've got any ideas ...'

'We'll look out some plans.' Luke's face brightened. 'My cousin Marty drew up plans years ago for a racing cutter that he swore would beat everything else on the water. But he died and that never got built.' Luke turned to Aaron. 'You'd know where they'd be, wouldn't you, Aaron. You catalogued all Marty's drawings.'

216

Edward nodded. 'Fair enough. I may come and see you in a day or two. I'll see how things go.'

'And they'd better go our way,' Luke said to his retreating back. 'I don't like the bloke, Aaron, but if we could get our hands on his money . . .'

'This order would be just what we need,' Aaron said, nodding. 'I'll look out the plans for you.'

'Is Mr Price-Carpenter still here? He hasn't gone back home, has he?' Luke asked Cassie when Edward hadn't been back to the Yard after three days.

'Yes, he's still staying here, but he's out quite a lot. Why?' Cassie was busy putting the finishing touches to a dress for Amy made over from one that Charity had outgrown.

'He hasn't been back about this new yacht he's thinking of ordering since he looked at Marty's plans. Do you remember Marty's "racer to beat all racers", Cassie?'

She looked up, her face softening at the memory. 'Yes, you had them spread all over the the table, there, poring over them. And Marty had got dreadful indigestion that night. I do remember, Luke. It never got built, did it?'

'No, and now's our chance to build it. If only old P-C would turn up trumps.' Luke prowled restlessly round the room. 'I can't say I like the man, but I want his order. It's what we need. It would put us back on our feet.' He swung round. 'Is he in now? Do you think I should go and have a word with him?'

'He's just finishing his meal in the dining room. After finishing this hem I was going to take his brandy through to the snuggery.' She fastened off and bit the thread. 'There. That's done.'

'I'll take him his brandy. Then I can have a talk to him.' Luke went to the door. 'No, perhaps I'd better not look too eager.

But when you take it, Cassie, ask him if he's made any decision yet. Tell him if he likes to drop by he can cast an eye over the plans again, it'll be easy enough to make any modifications he wants. Yes, that's the best thing. You tell him that. And be sure and give him good measure in his glass tonight,' he grinned as she left the room.

Cassie poured Edward's brandy and took it through to where he was now comfortably sitting in the snuggery. By the time she came out he had made up his mind that Turnbull's should get the order for his yacht.

Luke was elated when he came home the next day and told her Edward had placed a firm order, backed up with a substantial cheque. 'He says there's no hurry. He wants a good job done. He doesn't even mind if it isn't ready for next season as long as it beats Lord Felgate's when it's finished,' he said, rubbing his hands with satisfaction. 'I told him he didn't have to worry about that. Marty's cutter'll slice through the water like a knife through butter. There'll be nothing to touch her when she's done.' He picked Cassie up and waltzed round the room with her, making the three children sitting at the table roar with laughter.

'Put me down, Luke!' She beat ineffectually on his chest, laughing with him. 'You'll drop me.'

'That I never shall. Light as a feather you are, my girl.' And he waltzed her round again.

'My turn, Papa.' Amy danced round with them. 'Let me have a turn.'

'You're too fat. Papa couldn't lift you,' Reuben said, finishing his milk before going to bed.

'I'm not so. I'm not fat, am I Charry?'

'No, dumpling, of course you're not,' Charity grinned.

'Oh, I think you're horrid. Both of you.' Amy flounced into

her chair and folded her arms. But her paddy didn't last long because Luke scooped her up on one arm and gave her a turn round the room. 'There, are you satisfied now?' he said, giving her a big kiss and setting her down again.

'Will you play dominoes with us, Papa?' Charity, always ready to speak up, asked.

'Not tonight, chicken. I'm just going to have my supper and then I've got to go back to the Yard. Aaron is still there and we want to get the order out for the timber for this new yacht tonight, if we can.'

'But what about Aaron?' Cassie said. 'Doesn't he get any supper?'

Luke went and put his arm round her. 'I thought you might put a little something up for me to take back for him,' he said hopefully. 'You know, an old crust ... ?'

'I might even manage to put a bit of dripping on it.' Cassie matched his bantering mood as she ladled beef stew equally on to two plates and set Aaron's on the back of the stove to wait until Luke had eaten his.

Later, when Luke had gone back to the Yard and the children were safely in bed, Cassie slipped upstairs. Edward had said he would be waiting for her and it was with a mixture of excitement and trepidation that she went to him.

If Luke knew that this was the payment Edward had exacted for ordering the yacht he would have torn up the order and thrown Edward into the river, with no hesitation at all. And what he would do to Cassie didn't bear contemplation. But she knew that this order would put the Yard back on its feet. She didn't admit, even to herself, that this was one payment she was willing – even eager, to make.

Edward was waiting for her and his lovemaking was everything she had remembered, and more. But when she left

219

him, looking in on Reuben as an excuse for being in that part of the house, she was far from happy. Already the burden of guilt at what she had done far outweighed any pleasure. And already Edward was speaking about next time ...

Chapter Sixteen

Edward came to Wyford three times between May and Christmas and each time he demanded that Cassie go to his room, reminding her in his soft, conversational way that it wasn't too late to change his mind; he might still receive a better offer and get his yacht built elsewhere. It wasn't true, of course, and if Cassie had stopped to think she would have realized that he had already committed himself too far to go back. But her mind was in too much of a whirl to think rationally and she felt herself torn in two. The thought that she was deceiving Luke sickened her yet she had to go on and she resorted to all kinds of subterfuges in order to satisfy Edward's demands. Indeed, the linen cupboard at the top of the stairs had never been tidied so often before. At the same time the very danger of the situation lent its own extra spice and once in his room he had her under his spell and she was as eager as he to make love. But she was careful not to admit this to him and reluctant to admit it even to herself, telling herself that once the yacht was on the stocks, the keel laid and the ribs beginning to form she would know that the order was safe and these meetings would cease.

*

In January of the year 1887 Abel Crowther paid an unexpected visit to the Falcon. It was unexpected because he didn't usually come between October and April these days. He marched in, unannounced, on a day that was so bitterly cold that the snow clouds lay like a thick grey blanket across the sky, waiting for the temperature to rise a few degrees before the snow could fall. He was carrying his own bag – which sent Hannah into a fluster, apologising because Tom hadn't been at the station to meet him with the trap.

'Blast, woman, how could he meet me? He didn't know I was coming!' he said, shutting her up. He blew on his fingers and beat his arms and stamped his feet. 'By gow, it was freezing in that damn train. How I hate the bloody winter.''Come to my sitting room, Abel. There's a nice fire there.' Hannah fussed round him. 'I'll mull you some ale and Cassie will get you some soup. That'll warm you.'

He ignored Hannah and marched down the hall to the kitchen, where he stood for a moment looking round. Then, without saying anything, he went off into Hannah's room.

Cassie, who had come in behind him, made a face at Lizzy. 'He seems to have come in with the wind on his tail,' she commented briefly. 'I wonder what's brought him to Wyford at this time of the year. He never comes in January. Here, Lizzy, take this bowl of soup in to him. It'll keep him quiet till luncheon.' Even after all these years Cassie still didn't like the man.

She would have liked him even less had she known the purpose of his visit.

He was sitting opposite Hannah in her most comfortable chair, his legs stretched out towards a fire that was halfway up the chimney, his face even more red than usual from the mulled ale.

Hannah on the other side of the hearth, sat with her hands

in her lap, watching his every move. Over the years she had become more fond of this big Yorkshireman than she was prepared to admit even to herself, and her greatest pleasure, apart from that which even at her age he still occasionally gave her in bed, was to see him taking his ease in her sitting room. Just like a married couple, she was fond of thinking. And if it wasn't for his wife, Charlotte . . .

'Charlotte's dead,' he said abruptly, as if he had read her thoughts.

Hannah's heart leapt, but she managed to make her voice sympathetic. 'Oh, Abel. I'm sorry. When . . . ?

'Just after Christmas. Well,' he made an impatient gesture, 'you know she'd been ailing for years. And we're none of us getting any younger. I'm sixty-seven, meself, tha knows.'

'You don't look it, Abel.' It was true. He was heavier, more grizzled these days, but his eyes were still bright, reflecting a brain that had lost none of its shrewdness. And it was his fond boast that he could still manage a ten-mile walk over the hills outside Sheffield, or to Brightlingsea and back.

'Well, I feel it,' he said grumpily and lapsed into silence.

Hannah picked up her embroidery. She wished she was as active and lithe as he was. She was only four years his junior but her arthritis often made it painful for her to move although she tried to conceal this from Abel. She wanted him to continue to think of her as a young woman – as she had been when he first knew her, all those years ago. And in some ways she hadn't changed. Her figure was still trim – she hadn't put on weight like her sister Maisie. Maisie was so fat now that it was a marvel she could still walk about; Hannah had no patience with such gross over-indulgence. And her hair, although it was quite white, was thick and soft, framing a face that was surprisingly unlined. Hannah was never displeased when she viewed herself in the mirror. When Abel asked her to marry him, which he surely would now that Charlotte was out of the way, they would still make a handsome couple.

She sat stitching, occasionally stealing a glance in his direction. He was staring into the fire and it was plain that he had something on his mind because one minute he would give a great sigh and lean back in his chair and the next he would lean forward and rest his hands on his knees. She gave a little inward smile. He was no different from a young swain proposing to his sweetheart. She continued with her stitching, savouring the moment.

'Tha's ollus run this place well, Hannah,' he said at last.

'Thank you, Abel.' She nodded gravely. 'I've always done my best.'

'I'll tek a look at the books, if tha'll get them.'

She got up, trying not to wince with pain and went to the cupboard where she kept them safely locked away. 'Here you are, Abel. They're all up to date.'

He studied them for a long time. At last he said, 'Yes. It should fetch a decent price.'

She looked at him, puzzled. 'Fetch a decent price? What should fetch a decent price?'

'This place.' He gazed round. 'Oh, some of the rooms could do with a lick of paint, but by and large there's nowt wrong. Yes, it should fetch a decent price on the open market.'

She smiled. This was a funny preamble to a proposal. She decided to help him a little. 'You're thinking of selling the Falcon, Abel?' she asked, a touch of humour in her voice. 'Well, of course, that's your privilege. It belongs to you. But what about me? What shall I do for a roof over my head? Have you any suggestions?' She raised her eyebrows indulgently.

He stared at her. 'Oh, I wouldn't expect tha to move out

224

reet away,' he said in some surprise. 'I daresay it'd be three months or more before there'd be any need for tha to move. Plenty of time for young Cassie and Luke to find somewhere.' He nodded. 'And I'm sure they won't see their mother wi'out a comfortable home, not after all tha's done for them, lass.' He nodded again.

Hannah's sewing had dropped into her lap as she listened to his words. Now she looked at him as if she couldn't believe what she had heard. 'After all these years, Abel ... after all I've ... you've ... we've been to each other – are you simply suggesting that I and my family leave the Falcon so that you can sell it? That you don't care what I do or where I go?'

He shifted in his chair. 'Oh, I wouldn't put it quite like that, lass.'

'Then how would you put it? Haven't you any regard for me at all, Abel? You've been here, year after year, sharing my bed, giving me to understand that you lov ... that you had some regard for me. I even thought that when Charlotte went we might ...' She looked down at her sewing and a tear fell on it.

He sighed, blowing out his cheeks. 'Well, I never thought tha'd tek it like that, Hannah. A tumble of a night, which you enjoyed as much as me ...'

'I never said I didn't. Her head shot up.

'But I never spoke of marrying.' He looked into the fire. 'The thought never entered my head.'

If he had thrown her to the ground and spat on her she couldn't have been more insulted. She got carefully to her feet and stood looking down at him. 'What are your plans, then?' she said coldly. 'I need to know so that I can make my own. Will you be staying here tonight?'

'Oh, aye.' He smiled up at her but was met with a stony gaze. 'And I've a man from Colchester coming to look over the place tomorrow. I want to get everything sorted out as soon as I can. If he doesn't make me an offer I shall put the place up for auction. I'll not be beggared about.' He rubbed his hands together. 'I'm selling the file factory, too, and then I'm going abroad. I'm going to travel – see the world, before it's too late. And then I shall settle somewhere where it's warm. I've had my fill of English winters and there's nothing to keep me in England, not now Charlotte's dead.' He leaned forward. 'Tell Cassie this man's coming, so she can give the place a bit o' spit and polish, there's a good lass.'

Hannah went over to the door and held it open. 'You'll be wanting to unpack your bag before luncheon. You'll find it in your room.'

He warmed his hands at the fire. 'There's no hurry, lass.' The door closed. 'Come and sit down by the fire, lass. Tha's not told me about ...' He looked over his shoulder at where Hannah had been standing but the room was empty. He shrugged and leaned towards the fire again. Women were queer cattle.

Hannah said nothing to anybody. She went up to her bedroom and sat there for a long time, wrapped in a shawl against the icy chill of the room. What should she do? Cassie knew nothing about Abel Crowther. Nothing at all. He had been coming to the Falcon for so long that she accepted his visits without question, just as she accepted visits from the various yacht owners. It had never seemed necessary to tell her that the place belonged to him. But she would have to be told now. The question was, when should she tell her? And how much? Hannah rocked back and forth in her chair, not entirely from cold. She just prayed that Cassie would understand that what she had done was for the best.

*

Cassie noticed that her mother looked paler than usual when she took her luncheon in to her in the sitting room. Hannah was sitting huddled over the fire as if she was trying to get warm, although the room was as usual, overheated with a fire halfway up the chimney. 'Is Mr Crowther not eating in here with you today, Mama?' she asked.

'No, he'll be eating in the dining room,' Hannah said, without looking up. She glanced round at the plate on the tray. 'And I don't want all that. I'll just have a little soup.'

Cassie went and stood over her mother. 'Are you not well, Mama?' She felt Hannah's hands. 'Why, your hands are frozen. Do you think you're taking a chill?'

'No. No. I'm ... I shall be all right. I went upstairs to ... to look for something. I got a little cold in the bedroom, that's all.'

Cassie pulled her mother's shawl more closely round her shoulders. Hannah was very thin. 'You should have called me. I would have looked for whatever it was. Did you find it?'

'What? Oh, yes. I found it.'

'Good. I'll go and get your soup.' She went away and came back a little later with two bowls of soup. 'I thought I'd come and have a bite with you, Mama. Lizzy can see to the guests in the dining room as there aren't many in, apart from Mr Crowther. And I'm quite happy to let Lizzy look after *him*.'' She put Hannah's tray on the little table that was always by her chair and sat down opposite to her. 'Ah, this is nice, isn't it, Mama. I don't know why I don't do it more often. It's certainly more peaceful than eating in the kitchen with the children. They come home from school, rushing in like little hooligans ...'

'Cassie, I've something to tell you,' Hannah interrupted.

Cassie looked over at her. She was nervously crumbling bread into her soup. 'What is it, Mama? Are you ill? You don't look well, I said that to you earlier, didn't I?' Cassie's voice was filled with alarm. Her mother was often difficult – autocratic and stingy, but she couldn't imagine life at the Falcon without her.

Hannah shook her head. 'No, I'm not ill. This concerns Abel. Abel Crowther ...'

Cassie's eyes widened. 'You're not going to *marry* him?'

'No.' Hannah shook her head again. 'It's difficult enough, Cassie, without you interrupting.' She stirred her soup around the bowl but made no attempt to eat any of it. 'I don't really know where to begin.'

'At the beginning, I should think.'

'No. I think perhaps it will be better if I begin at the end, Cassie.' Hannah took a deep breath. 'The Falcon belongs to Abel Crowther. He's come here today to tell me that he wants to sell it.'

Cassie's jaw dropped visibly. 'But I've always thought it belonged to us – to you, Mama.'

'I know,' Hannah nodded. 'You were too young to be told anything different at the beginning. And after that you never asked so there never seemed to be the need to tell you. You see, I always thought ...' she hesitated, then looked up at Cassie. 'Now I think it's time. I think perhaps I'd better begin at the beginning, after all.' She looked down at her hands. 'Please, Cassie, try to understand. I did what I thought was best. Remember I had two little girls to bring up.'

'Tell me,' Cassie prompted gently.

Hannah took a deep breath. 'You know your father was a yacht captain. He was one of the best and he won a lot of races. We had – you know that big house in West Street with all the pargetting on the front? Well, that was where we lived, and we had four servants. We were almost accepted as gentry – not quite, of course, we didn't have the breeding – but we had plenty of money and that counted for a great deal. And we lived up to it, I don't mind telling you. Your father didn't believe in saving for a rainy day; not while the sun was shining. And it shone very brightly on us in those days, make no mistake.

'Well, he changed yachts and became captain of *the Aurora,* owned by a Sheffield file factory owner named Abel Crowther.'

'Abel Crowther? A yacht owner?' Cassie said in surprise.

Hannah nodded. 'That's right. I may say I didn't much like the man, but that didn't matter because I didn't have to see very much of him. Only on the odd occasions when he visited Wyford and stayed with us. But I thought he was brash, competitive and a bit ruthless.'

'He doesn't seem to have changed over the years,' Cassie said briefly.

'Perhaps not. Anyway, the season after Stella was born, it would be 1852, when you were four, Abel Crowther went with Reuben on *Aurora* and took his brother Jack as a guest. They were going racing on the Clyde. Reuben wasn't all that happy about the arrangement. He always used to say you needed the owner and his guests on board when you were racing like you needed an elephant, and they were about as much use.'

Cassie smiled. 'Yes, I've heard other yacht captains say that.'

'Well,' Hannah continued, 'I don't know exactly what happened, there were so many conflicting stories, but from what I can gather, they'd had a good month's racing and had won cups and quite a lot of money and they were making passage in the Irish Channel, coming down from the Clyde towards Cowes. The weather was pretty bad, as it can be in the Irish Sea, when Abel's brother Jack got struck by the boom and knocked overboard. From what was – and wasn't – said, it seems to me he should never have been anywhere near the boom, anyway, so it was his own fault. But be that as it may, it seems your father

229

saw what was happening and grabbed the man and tried to hold on to him. Jack Crowther was a big man like his brother and before anyone else could get to help them Reuben had been dragged in with him.' Hannah stopped talking and sat looking into the fire for some time.

Cassie said nothing for a little while, then she touched her mother's knee. 'Yes, Mama? What happened next?'

Hannah shook her head. 'I don't really know. It was in heavy seas, so I was told, and there were dangerous rocks nearby. I'm sure every effort was made to save both men, but it was no use. The bodies were never found.' Hannah stopped talking again and bit her lip to stop the tears that the memory still evoked. 'There was no doubt that Abel felt guilty about it all. If he hadn't taken his brother ... if his brother hadn't been where he shouldn't have been ...' Her mouth twisted wryly. 'I sometimes think if is the biggest word in the English language. Anyway,' she lifted her head and continued, 'Abel was pretty shaken by the whole affair. When they got back he immediately sold his yacht and said he was never going to buy another one.'

'And did he?' Cassie asked.

'Did he what?'

'Did he ever buy another one?'

'No. He never did. After he'd sold the yacht he came to see me. He knew that without Reuben's money I would have nothing except what I could raise on the house – because I certainly couldn't afford to go on living there. But we'd only had it a couple of years and hadn't paid much of it off, so there was precious little to come from that direction. Then he suggested that he should buy the Falcon. We could live there rent-free and it would give me a living.' She shook her head. 'I didn't want to. I didn't know anything about keeping a pub and it was a terrible comedown after the life I'd been used to. But I'd nowhere else to go, so there was nothing else I could do but accept his offer. Remember, I'd two children, one of them still only a baby. At least the Falcon meant there would be a roof over our heads.'

'But what did your family – Aunt Maisie and Uncle George say about it?'

'Maisie thought I was mad. You see, she thought *I'd* bought the Falcon with money Abel Crowther had given me as, well . . . compensation for losing Reuben. She didn't realise that it belonged to him and that I was only here as . . .' she shrugged, 'his landlady, I suppose.'

'But didn't you tell her?'

Hannah shook her head. 'No. I thought it would look better if people thought I'd bought it. Mind you, I'd no idea what I was taking on. If it hadn't been for Tom Bartlett I'd never have survived, but he came along on the day I moved in and said did I want a potman?' Her shoulders sagged. 'God, and to think I didn't even know what a potman was!'

'So that's why Abel Crowther's visited us for all these years. To keep an eye on the place,' Cassie said.

Hannah nodded. 'Mostly. He taught me how to keep the books. Oh, when I think of it I was so ignorant!'

'But you managed, Mama. You made a success of it all,' Cassie said. So many things were falling into place now. If only she had known before she would have understood her mother's insistence that they had been born to better things. She frowned as another thought struck her. 'But why did you always tell us that life at the Falcon was only temporary? It wasn't, was it?' Cassie smiled. 'We've been here over thirty years.'

Hannah looked into the fire. 'I always thought Abel Crowther had a certain – regard for me.' She closed her eyes and went on, 'One of the conditions under which he offered to set me up in the Falcon was that I should share his bed whenever he

231

came to visit.' She flushed a dull red as she said the words. She opened her eyes and looked at Cassie. 'I had no choice, Cassie. That was one of the conditions.' She hung her head. 'Nobody has ever known that until now. I was so ashamed of what I was doing, Cassie, so ashamed.'

'That was why you would never come to church?'

She nodded. 'I couldn't even ask God to forgive such a shameful thing. Especially as I knew that it would happen again and again. I couldn't turn over a new leaf because the next time Abel came he would claim what he considered his just due.' Even now she couldn't bring herself to confess to her daughter that she had looked forward to his visits. 'I thought ... I was quite certain that when his wife died we should be married. He often told me that he was not happily married and I thought that if it hadn't been for Charlotte we should have been married long ago.'

'She's dead now?' Cassie asked.

Hannah nodded. 'Yes, and now she's dead he wants to sell the Falcon and go abroad to live. Suddenly, after all these years, I find he doesn't care tuppence about me. And never has. Oh, Cassie,' she put her hands over her face, 'I feel used. Degraded. I'd come to be very fond of him and I thought he felt the same about me. But I realise now that putting me in the Falcon was only a sop to his conscience and he used me as a little reward to himself for his generosity. And I never saw it like that. It's degrading. Humiliating. I never want to see the man again. Never, as long as I live.' She began to cry, the tears racking her thin shoulders.

Cassie went over to her and put her arms round her. So much had been explained. So much was now clear. 'Don't worry, dear. We'll work something out,' she said soothingly, but in her heart she cried aloud, 'This place has been my home

232

for thirty-nine years and I never realized we were living here on that man's charity! And now we must leave.' She bowed her head. She had never realized just how much she loved the old place.

Chapter Seventeen

For the rest of the day Cassie went about her work in a daze. She could hardly believe what her mother had told her, yet in some ways it all made sense and explained so much of Hannah's behaviour, especially in earlier years. No wonder she had insisted that Cassie and Stella had been born to better things; no wonder she had insisted that they be educated at Miss Fanny Browne's Ladies' Seminary instead of at the National School with the other village children. How else could she convince herself – and them, too – that life at the Falcon was only temporary, the only way she could have borne such a change in her circumstances? It was no wonder, too, that Hannah had put her two girls into the bedroom over the kitchen, where there was no danger of them hearing noises in the night when Abel Crowther visited. Cassie sighed and shook her head. Life had dealt a bitter blow to Hannah Jordan and nobody but she knew what it had cost her in terms of both pride and suffering.

Cassie went upstairs to her bedroom. She could be quiet and undisturbed there to try and think what must be done. She sat down on a low stool and put her chin in her hands, listening to the late-afternoon noises of the Falcon. The children had just come home from school and were clamouring for their tea; Lizzy would give it to them. She pictured the scene in the warm kitchen, the bright steel of the stove, the shining copper of the saucepans and the pretty china that graced the shelves of the dresser. It was a big room and it had seen much of the ups and downs of the family fortunes. She remembered Martin, sitting at the table and drinking rum and peppermint for his indigestion; Robert, shining-eyed, telling them all about his experiences of his first season on a racing yacht; Luke, walking in with the body of little Simon. Quickly, her thoughts shied away from that memory – she kept it locked away because the pain of it even now was more than she could bear. She thought instead of Aaron Wix, sitting at supper with them for the first time. Aaron was a widower, a lonely man, and he had proved a good friend to Luke; a man he could trust.

She heard Tom's voice, raised to the drayman delivering beer crates and her thoughts returned to Hannah's revelations of a few hours ago. The Falcon was to be sold. What would Tom do? Where would he go? Would his cottage be sold along with the Falcon? She couldn't imagine the bar without Tom's ugly face behind it. She couldn't imagine not being at the Falcon herself.

Quietly, she put her head down on her knees and began to weep.

She didn't tell Luke until they were in bed that night. He had long since divided the big room by putting a stout partition with a door in it down the centre, making two quite good-sized rooms. The two girls shared the inner room and Cassie and Luke had the room nearest the stairs. Reuben slept in the little room at the front of the house, except when there were too many guests, when he had a makeshift bed in the kitchen.

Luke was silent for a long time after she had finished speaking. Then he said, 'Shall you mind leaving the Falcon, Cassie?'

'Yes, of course I shall. I've lived here all my life – well, nearly all my life – so I'll miss it. But more to the point, where shall we go, Luke? What shall we do? There are five of us, as well as Mama. The Falcon hasn't really given us much of a living these last few years, because Mama has been so mean that I've had to pay at least some of the bills out of our money. That's meant I haven't had a chance to put anything by for a rainy day. Thank goodness the Yard picked up when it did, Luke.'

'The Yard's picked up, Cassie, but it's not making a fortune, not by any means.' He sighed. 'We shall just have to find somewhere to rent, dear. Thass all there is to it.'

She turned away from him. 'It seems as if we pick ourselves up from one disaster, only to be knocked down by the next. Oh, Luke, will it never end?'

He put out his arm and drew her into its circle. 'We've a lot to be thankful for, Cassie girl. We've both got our health and strength and we've four healthy children. Thass worth more'n anything money can buy. We shall manage. You'll see.'

But Cassie, lying stiffly beside him, couldn't see how.

The next day Hannah was confined to her bed with a chill caught, Cassie was sure, through sitting in her cold bedroom for longer than she'd admitted. Millie had lit a fire in there today and after luncheon had been served and cleared away Cassie went upstairs to sit with Hannah for a while. She looked tiny and vulnerable lying between patched sheets and Cassie felt a rush of love mixed with remorse to think that her mother had had so much to bear over the years and had borne it all in loneliness and in her own private grief, never confiding her worries and fears to a living soul. Cassie picked up Hannah's hand as it lay on the counterpane. 'Forgive me,

Mama,' she said silently. 'Perhaps If I'd known I would have been less impatient. More understanding.' But the barriers of a lifetime are not that easily broken and the words were never said aloud. Instead she asked, 'Would you like a little milk with some brandy in it, Mama?'

'Yes, dear, I think that would be nice.' A ghost of a smile hovered over Hannah's face. 'Don't look so worried, Cassie. I'm not going to die, you know. I'm tougher than you might think.'

'Die? Of course you're not going to die!' Cassie said, as if the idea had never even crossed her mind. She didn't tell Hannah that she had already telegraphed to Stella.

Lizzy brought the milk and brandy. 'I've whipped an egg into it, Mrs Cassie,' she confided as Cassie took it at the door. She looked over Cassie's shoulder to the figure in the bed. 'Look right poorly, don't she. I do hope she'll be all right,' she whispered. 'The Falcon wouldn't be the same without her, would it.'

Cassie smiled. 'She'll be all right, Lizzy. She's tougher than you realize.'

She helped her mother to drink some of the egg-nog and then eased her back on to the pillows. 'That was nice,' Hannah said. She put out her hand. 'There's some money, Cassie – quite a lot. I saved it over the years so that when Abel ... if I ever married again I wouldn't be penniless. I think there's something like a hundred pounds. It's in a mother-of-pearl box in the bottom of the wardrobe. Yes, that's the one. Your father brought it home from one of his voyages. It's a pretty box, isn't it?'

Cassie took the box over to the bed, trying not to think about what she could have done with even a little of the money over the years. 'What do you want me to do with it, Mama?' she asked.

Hannah shook her head from side to side. 'I don't know. But I wanted you to know that it was there. I don't suppose it would be enough to buy the place, would it?' She looked wistfully up at Cassie.

'No, dear, I'm afraid it wouldn't,' Cassie said gently.

Hannah closed her eyes. 'Well, it's there if you want it. It's yours, Cassie. You've been a good girl to me over the years and I want you to have it.'

'Thank you, Mama. I'll leave it where it is for the time being. It's safe there.' Cassie replaced the box where she had found it. When she turned round again Hannah was asleep, but it was a feverish, restless sleep, not a healing sleep and Cassie knew she had been right to send for Stella.

But she wasn't prepared for the fact that her sister would come home with troubles of her own.

'You've brought an awful lot of luggage with you, Stella,' Cassie said with a smile as she met the trap at the door and watched Tom unloading it. 'Had you forgotten, there's not much social life in Wyford? You won't need all those boxes and trunks if you're only staying a week or so.'

'I'm not staying for a week or so. I'm home for good,' Stella said and her voice had a brittle edge to it.

'Coming back to live at Wyford? Oh, that *will* be nice. But you can tell me all about that later,' Cassie smiled. 'But for now, come into the kitchen and have a cup of tea. You must be frozen half to death.'

Watching her sister from the opposite side of the table Cassie noticed with something of a shock that Stella was thinner than ever and her voice had a sharp, staccato edge to it that matched the quick, nervous movements of her hands. It was quite obvious that she was living on her nerves.

'Goodness, the place looks run down,' Stella exclaimed as Cassie showed her up to the room she had set aside for her. Stella was to have Marquis's room, which overlooked the yard at the back. 'Look at the stains in the wallpaper! And the paintwork's all chipped. I shouldn't think you get many people coming to stay with the place in such a state. Are all the rooms as bad as this?'

Cassie gazed round the room, seeing it with fresh eyes. With something of a shock she realized that other visitors would see the room just as Stella did and would notice the stains on the wallpaper and the peeling paint, even though the room itself was spotlessly clean. 'It costs money to buy paint and wallpaper,' she said simply, 'and Mama has never seen fit to spend it.'

Stella swung round. 'But I thought *you* ran things now, Cassie!'

Cassie made a wry face. 'Mama has always kept a tight hold on the purse things.' She shivered. 'Oh, I've got so much to tell you, Stella, but it's freezing up here. Let's go and see Mama, there's a fire in her room. Then we'll go downstairs.'

'You can get one of the servants to light a fire in my bedroom, too. It's so cold in here it feels positively damp,' Stella said, as she followed Cassie out on to the landing. 'Oh, and look at this dreadful carpet. Cassie, what have you been thinking about, letting the place get into such a state? It's dreadful.'

'We may not be here much longer,' Cassie said, to shut her sister up. She was irritated with Stella for pointing out all the things that she, Cassie, had resolutely tried to shut her eyes to. She knew the rooms needed redecorating; she knew the carpets were worn and threadbare; and worse, she knew that the crockery was becoming more and more chipped. In fact, it was difficult these days to find enough whole plates for the dining room. But it had been hard to get money out of Hannah for essential items, let alone replacements. Cassie never had bought the new curtains she needed and now had to draw the old ones very carefully at night to conceal the worn parts. It was all a question of money. Money for the Falcon; money for the Yacht Yard. Even with Aaron Wix's skilful handling the Yard could not be said to be making a fortune, although the men's jobs were safe and there was a steady flow of work. But it was no use trying to explain all this to Stella – she would never understand.

Hannah was worse. Lizzy was sitting with her, wiping her forehead with a cloth every now and then. She got up and left when the girls came in.

Hannah stared up at them, her eyes bright with fever. 'I want the house cleaned from top to bottom,' she said, and although her voice was weak it had an imperious ring to it. 'The master will be home this evening. His yacht comes in today. And I want you to dress Miss Cassie and Miss Stella in their best white dresses . . .' Her voice died away. 'I can't do it, Reuben. I can't manage without you . . . Mr Crowther? Abel? . . . No, I don't want to. I can't do that, it wouldn't be right. Oh, dear.' She turned away and a tear trickled down on to the pillow.

'It's all right, Mama.' Cassie gently wiped her mother's eyes. 'You don't have to do anything you don't want to. Just go to sleep. When you wake up you'll feel better.'

At the sound of Cassie's voice Hannah became calmer and lay with her eyes closed, her breathing weak and uneven. The girls sat beside her for a little while, then Cassie said, 'We may as well go downstairs. She doesn't realize you're here. You can come and see her again later.' She straightened Hannah's covers and followed Stella out of the room.

'What was she talking about?' Stella asked as they went down the stairs. 'She's rambling, isn't she?' She caught Cassie's arm. 'Is she going to . . . ?'

Cassie shook her off. 'I hope not. But she's very ill. And it's partly shock, I think. Come into her sitting room. Millie's lit a fire and it's quiet there, so we can talk.'

240

Cassie told Stella everything, omitting nothing except the fact that there was nearly a hundred pounds in the little mother-of-pearl box in Hannah's wardrobe. She wasn't sure why she didn't tell her about that.

Stella listened, her eyes growing wide with surprise. 'Mama! Sleeping with old Abel Crowther!' she said at last. 'Well, well. I'd never have thought of Mama having a tumble with anyone like him.' She gave a little laugh.

'She didn't have any choice,' Cassie snapped. She didn't like the way Stella had latched on to that particular aspect of the story. 'You'd probably have done the same in her position.'

Stella grinned. 'I might, at that. But not with an old buffer like Abel Crowther.'

'He wasn't always an old buffer. He's only four years older than she is and she was widowed when she was only twenty-eight. You should remember that.'

'Yes, I suppose you're right. I hadn't thought of it like that.' Stella was silent for a while. 'So what are you going to do?' she asked after a bit, giving the fire a poke and then warming her hands at it. 'When old Crowther sells up, I mean?'

Cassie shook her head. 'I don't know. I really don't know.' She stared into the flames. 'It isn't until you are about to lose something that you realise just how much you value it. I simply can't imagine not living here at the Falcon.' Her voice dropped. 'I hated it when I lived in The Folley. It was partly – mostly, perhaps – the fact that it was such a horrible little cottage, but I hated being away from here.' She looked round, hoping Stella wouldn't notice and comment on the hole in the carpet that was only partly covered by the rag rug. She squared her shoulders as if she had suddenly made up her mind. 'But I can tell you this. I shan't give the Falcon up without a struggle.'

'Good for you,' Stella said without enthusiasm. 'At least, I hope you won't give it up until I can get myself sorted out. I need somewhere to lay my head.'

'While you look for another house?'

'While I decide what I'm going to do. You see, I've left John.' Stella's eyes were suddenly bright with tears and she bit her lip hard.

'Left John? But you can't have! Wives don't leave their husbands! What will people say?' Cassie was shocked to the core.

Stella gave a shrug. 'They won't say any more than they do already. At least they won't look at me with pity now because my husband dallies with one pretty woman after another. Oh, he thinks he's being discreet, but everyone in Cowes knows what's going on. And I have to smile and pretend I either don't know or don't care.' Her shoulders sagged. 'But I *do* know and I *do* care. And I couldn't stand it any longer. Your message came just as I was trying to pluck up the courage to leave him.'

'It'll cause an awful scandal in Cowes, Stella.'

'Don't you think the way he's carrying on is causing a scandal?'

'Wives don't leave their husbands. You married him "for better or for worse".'

'Well, there's been too much "worse" just lately. And he hasn't "kept only unto me" for some time. And I'm tired of it all.'

'Does he know where you've gone?'

'He'll guess.'

'Will he come after you?'

She gave a shrug.

Cassie twisted her own wedding ring round on her finger. She noticed that Stella was still wearing hers. 'I don't know what to say,' she said after a bit.

242

'There's nothing to say. I've left John and come home. That's all there is to it.'

Cassie got up from her chair. 'I must go and see to things in the kitchen. Perhaps you'd like to go up and sit with Mama so that Lizzy can come downstairs

But it was obvious that Stella had no intention of moving away from the fire.

On her way to the kitchen, Cassie met Tom going back to the bar with a scuttle-full of coal. She followed him. Someone had to tell him what was afoot. Fortunately the bar was deserted, as it often was at this hour in the afternoon.

'How's the Missus? She any better, Cassie girl?' Tom had never got out of the way of addressing her in the way he had used ever since she was a child.

'Not much, Tom. She's still rambling. We take it in turns to sit with her.'

'She's tough, Cassie girl. She'll pull through.' Tom laid his hand on Cassie's arm.

'I hope so, Tom. But part of her trouble is this place. Abel Crowther wants to sell it. Did you know it belonged to him, Tom?'

Tom's face darkened. 'I half-guessed it might. The Missus was rare anxious not to do anything that might offend him. I never liked the bugger – beggin' your pardon, Cassie girl.'

Cassie smiled. 'I know that, Tom.' She leaned her elbows on the bar. 'What did the man say who Abel Crowther brought to look over the place this morning? I kept out of the way. I couldn't bear ...' She bowed her head, unable to finish the sentence.

'He worn't over-impressed, I don't think,' Tom said. "Specially when he come in here. That was in a bit of a pickle, because I'd got all them old benches in outa the garden an' that

243

ole broken table, 'cause I'd taken the others home to give 'em a bit of a shine up.'

Cassie looked up, smiling in spite of herself. 'Tom! You old devil! You knew what was going on and you did that on purpose!' She laughed out loud. 'I don't suppose you'd emptied the spittoons, either, had you?'

He shrugged. 'Well, a chap can't do everything at once, can 'e?'

Impulsively, she turned to him and gave him a hug. 'I don't know what we'd do without you, Tom.' She became serious. 'But if this place has to be sold ...'

'You ain't goin' to let that bugger sell the place over your head, Cassie girl, are you? I shoulda thought better o' you than that.'

'But what can we do, Tom? It's all a question of money.'

'I got a bit put by,' he said, staring into the distance. 'Ain't a lot by some folk's standards, but thass mounted up over the years. What there is you're welcome to, Cassie girl. That'll all help.'

'Oh, Tom.' She laid her head on his shoulder. 'How can we ever thank you?'

'By makin' that Crowther fella a offer for this place an' lettin' 'im see 'e can't ride roughshod over the likes of us.' He patted her shoulder. 'I'll count up me money an' let you hev it. There was suthin' like eighty pound last time I counted, so there might be a bit more now.'

'Eighty pounds! Tom, where on earth did you ... ?' She stopped. It was none of her business where Tom came by his money although she knew he couldn't have saved much from his wages at the Falcon.

He grinned. 'Oh, I pick up a copper here and there, Cassie girl. Fetching folks from the station, carryin' folks' bags, doin' a hand turn here an' there, you'd be surprised how that mount up over the years.' He spread his hands, they were like great hams. 'I don't spend a lot. I don't smoke or drink an' you provide most o' me vittals. Anyways, that'd be yours in the end. I ain't got nobody else to leave it to, so you might as well hev it first as last.'

'What could I say?' Cassie said, as she lay staring up into the darkness beside Luke that night. The only place they could talk with any privacy was after they had gone to bed. 'A hundred and eighty pounds ...'

'That won't pay for the Falcon, Cassie girl,' Luke said with a sigh.

'It's a start.'

'Yes, but where's the rest of it coming from?'

'I don't know. But I'd feel I was letting Mama and Tom down – Tom even more than Mama, in a funny sort of way – if I don't make some effort.' She turned over and thumped her pillow. 'Oh, why did that dreadful man lead Mama on so?'

'Are you sure that he did?' Luke said quietly.

'What do you mean?'

'Are you sure he didn't set your mother up here at the Falcon to salve his conscience over what had happened to her husband, and then decide that he was entitled to a little perk for his kindness?'

'You mean she was nothing more than a convenience as far as he was concerned?'

'Suthin' like that.' Luke's speech had improved over the years, but at times of stress he sometimes lapsed.

'Oh, Luke. It would kill her if she thought that.' Cassie was silent for a long time. If Luke was right then somehow Abel Crowther must be shown that he couldn't treat Hannah like a puppet on a string, picking her up and casting her aside as the fancy took him. And the only way to show him would be to buy the Falcon. But what with?

'Luke?' Cassie's voice was tentative. 'Could the Yard put up the money, do you think?'

Luke sighed. The Yard was just beginning to pay its way again. The bank had been paid off and things were at last becoming easier. At the moment the Falcon wasn't exactly thriving although it was ticking over. 'You mean mortgage the Yard to buy the Falcon?'

'I suppose so.'

'I don't know if Mr Grimshaw at the bank would agree to that.'

'You could ask him.'

'Yes, I could. But he'd think I was something of a fool to get rid of one millstone only to pick up another, wouldn't he? The Falcon isn't exactly the Ritz, is it now?' His voice in the darkness was sharp.

'It could be, if it had a bit of money spent on it.' Hers was equally sharp.

'Money. It's all bloody money. You must think it grows on trees.'

'I don't – you know I don't. I work just as hard as you do, Luke Turnbull, don't forget that.'

He sighed again. 'I know you do, Cassie. It's just that ... well, you don't know what you're asking.'

'I do, you know.' Her voice was flat. 'I'm asking you to mortgage the Yard to buy the Falcon and I know that if things go wrong we could end up with nothing. No Yard, not even a roof over our heads. But I'm prepared to risk that because of what that man has done to my mother. I refuse to let her be cast off like an old shoe because he's done with her.'

'Hannah's very ill, Cassie.' Luke's voice was gentler now. 'She may never know ...'

'If she knows she won't have to leave the Falcon she'll get

246

better, Luke, I'm convinced of it. Will you go and see Mr Grimshaw?'

'Very well, I'll go and see him. But I doubt he'll agree.' And as he lay awake beside his sleeping wife he almost hoped that he wouldn't.

Chapter Eighteen

After three days, when Hannah showed no sign of improvement Cassie sent a message to Maisie at the house in Anglesea Road where she still lived. Maisie rarely left her house these days because she had grown so fat that she found difficulty in getting about. 'Becca, one of Luke's young sisters, who was twenty-one now and not very bright, looked after her. She had gone as a maid to George and Maisie when she left school after a very sketchy education and had stayed there. Now, seven years later, she ruled her aunt, cleaning and shopping and looking after things in a dull routine that worked so well that Maisie had nothing to do but eat and grow fatter than ever.

'When I heard she was bad I thought I better come and see for mesself,' she said, puffing after each word. 'Young 'Becca didn't want me to come. "No, Auntie," she said, and them was her very words, "no, Auntie. You shouldn't oughta go all that way. Not with your legs. Let me go," she said. But I said, "No, I wanta go and see for meself how me sister is." And here I am.' She sat down heavily at the kitchen table. 'Well, where is she?'

'She's upstairs, in her bedroom,' Cassie said.

'Ain't you brought the bed down? Thass the first thing anybody

248

do when there's somebody ill in the house, git the bed downstairs,' Maisie said, shocked to the core. 'I don't b'live I've been upstairs in my house more'n twice since my George passed away. Me legs, y'know.' She hitched her skirt up slightly to reveal ankles of enormous proportions. She shook her head. 'I don't know if I can climb stairs, Cassie. You oughta brought the bed down.'

Cassie suppressed a smile at the thought of bringing Hannah's bed downstairs so that Maisie could visit and men taking it back up again when she'd gone. 'Mama's really too ill to be moved,' she said gently. 'But I'll tell her you came to see her, she'll be pleased, I know.'

'Oh, I shall go up and see her, time I'm here,' Maisie said, lumbering to her feet. 'I wouldn't hev it said that me sister lay bad an' I never went high nor by to see her. I shall manage. But you might jest hev to give me a push.'

Cassie looked apprehensively at Stella, who had just come into the room, but Stella shook her head. She wanted no part of the operation.

Manfully, Maisie climbed the stairs, hauling herself from step to step with the help of the banister, which shuddered under each onslaught. 'There,' she panted, when she reached the top. 'I done it. I knew I would.'

Cassie, uttering a silent thankful prayer that the journey had been made without mishap, led her into Hannah's bedroom, where a fire burned brightly. Lizzy was sitting by the bed, sewing. Hannah was asleep.

Maisie stood looking down at her. 'Ain't nothin' but a bag o' bones, is she?' she wheezed. 'I don't like the look of her, meself. She's a funny colour, too.' She shook her head. 'Well, I've bin. I've done me duty an' paid me last respects. I doubt I shan't see her no more.' She dabbed at her eyes. 'She was ollus a good sister to me, that I will say.' She sniffed and turned to go.

249

Hannah opened her eyes. 'Is that you, Cassie?' She closed them again, without waiting for an answer.

Maisie's eyes widened. 'Oh, she can still talk ... I never thought to hear ... ' She turned to Cassie. 'She look jest like my George did the day before he,' she nodded, 'you know.' Maisie could never bring herself to speak of anything concerned with death other than euphemistically.

'She's very ill, Aunt Maisie.' Cassie took her firmly by the arm and turned her towards the door, amazed that she could be so lacking in tact. 'But she's going to get better, aren't you, dear?' She laid a brief hand over her mother's as it lay on the sheet.

Getting Maisie down the stairs proved even more difficult than getting her up them. 'I go that dizzy when I look down,' Maisie said, standing at the head of the stairs and clinging to the banister. 'And I don't know if I can bend me knees to git down the steps.'

'Oh, dear, you should never have come up, Auntie,' Cassie said, wondering how on earth she was going to shift her aunt's bulk. 'Look, perhaps if you could just manage to get down one step, you could sit down and go the rest of the way on your bottom. I'll go first, then you won't be able to look down and make yourself dizzy.'

With much puffing and blowing Maisie did as Cassie had suggested and made a slow and majestic progress down the stairs on her backside. 'You shoulda brought the bed down, like I said,' she panted at every step. 'You can't expect folks to climb stairs, not when they get to my time o' life.'

She reached the bottom and Cassie managed to heave her to her feet. 'I'll get Tom to take you home in the trap,' she said, trying not to think of the difficulties getting her up into it would present.

'Thank you, Cassie dear. I should appreciate that. Young 'Becca'll be that riled with me if I go back wore out. She look after me like she was me own daughter. Oh, Stella,' as they came back into the kitchen, 'I'm glad you thought fit to come back. Thass a shame to see your pore mother lyin' there lookin' so bad, ain't it.' She went to the overmantel and adjusted her hat, although there was no need; it was nailed on to her head with so many vicious-looking hatpins that nothing short of a riot could have dislodged it. 'How long are you home for?'

'Stella will stay at least until Mama's better,' Cassie said quickly.

'Then she might be here for a long time,' Maisie said gloomily. ''Cause I don't like the look o' Hannah, that I don't. I don't like the look of her at all.'

Luke had a long talk with Aaron the next day and then they both went to see Mr Grimshaw and had an even longer talk with him.

'It'll probably go for auction,' Mr Grimshaw said. 'That's how these things usually work. And the brewers will be sure to want it. Why don't you let them buy it and keep you on as tenant landlord?'

'But supposing they don't?' Luke asked.

'Supposing they don't what? Put in a bid? Oh, they're sure to. The breweries are buying up as many pubs as they can, nowadays.'

'No – supposing they don't want to keep us as tenants? After all, it's in Hannah's name at the moment, and she's in no fit state to take it on.'

Mr Grimshaw pinched his lip. 'Give me a week to decide how much you can afford to bid,' he said at last, 'but I'm making no promises that it'll be a worthwhile proposition. You're only just

251

beginning to pull round, you know. You can't really afford to start speculating at this stage.'

'We'll have to tighten up a bit more at the Yard, Luke, if he does agree,' Aaron said, as they travelled home in the train. 'We're not doing too badly now we're getting on with the cutter. It's looking good and it's helped us a lot. We've got a full order book, too. It's true, you know, success breeds success. As soon as word got round that we'd taken the order for the cutter from Mr Price-Carpenter the other orders started coming in. But if you do manage to buy the Falcon you'll need to spend quite a bit of money to put it into better shape. It's got a bit run-down these past few years, if you don't mind me saying so.'

'Mm. You're right, of course.' Luke scratched his beard, a habit when he was thinking. 'We don't get so many people staying there, these days. Oh, you can't blame 'em, not when there's the Station Hotel and the Grosvenor, all smart and modern, where they can put up. We get filled up when the yacht owners come down at the beginning of the season, of course, but sometimes that side of it is quite dead.' He grinned. 'What we need are a few permanent lodgers – paying guests.'

Aaron was silent for a while. Then he said, 'I shall be looking for somewhere to live in a month or so.'

'You?' Luke looked at him, amazed. 'But I thought you had a room with old Mrs Oliphant in Alma Street.'

'Yes, I've lived there for years. Ever since my wife died, in fact. But her son and his wife are coming back from America in April and she's told me she'll need my room for them. Oh, I don't blame her, blood's thicker than water after all's said and done, and to tell you the truth she's getting a bit past looking after herself, let alone me, so I shall be quite glad to get out. But I wondered if perhaps I might rent a room at the Falcon, Luke. It'd be permanent; a regular, dependable source of income and it would suit me very well. A bit of company in the evenings – not that I'm a heavy-drinking man – and three meals a day and a warm bed, that's all I need.' He laughed. 'And I promise you I won't get under your feet and talk shop in the evenings, Luke.'

Luke grinned back. 'Wouldn't matter if you did. I don't seem to talk about much else, meself.' His grin faded. 'But we're a bit ahead of ourselves, aren't we? Mr Grimshaw hasn't given us the go ahead to put in a bid for the Falcon yet.'

Cassie had been right. The moment she told Hannah that Luke had been to see the bank manager with a view to buying the Falcon she began to rally, although her recovery was slow.

Abel Crowther had gone. He left while Hannah was hovering between life and death, without saying goodbye to her, without even asking after her. He left his solicitor to deal with the sale of the Falcon, giving him instructions to auction it so that it would fetch the highest price. There would be no concession because Luke Turnbull might be after it. All Abel Crowther wanted was to be rid of the place for the highest price that could be obtained with the least trouble and as quickly as it could be arranged.

The sale of the Falcon was fixed for the twelfth of April, nearly two months ahead. Mr Grimshaw had given Luke a figure beyond which he must on no account bid and which, even with the money Hannah and Tom had given Cassie, was hardly likely to be enough. Cassie was despondent. She even mentioned it to Edward when he visited.

'Then we shall just have to find somewhere else to meet, my lovely Cassie,' he said, drawing her into his arms before he had even unpacked his luggage.

'No, Edward ... not now. There isn't time.' She tried to free herself.

'Of course there's time. It won't take a moment. I've missed you, Cassie.' He pulled her down on to the bed.

He was right. It was over very quickly. So quickly she had no chance to respond. She felt used.

And Edward had offered no solution to – had not even been interested in – the problem of the Falcon.

She resolved to finish their affair once and for all. Edward's yacht was growing on the stocks and he was obviously delighted with its progress so there was no danger he would cancel the order. She had settled any debt she might owe him over and over again.

But it wasn't that easy. And of course she had to go to his room to tell him.

'Oh, no,' he said with a lazy grin when she had said her piece. 'You're not getting away that easily, my lovely Cassie.' He caught her arm in a vice-like grip and began to unbutton her bodice. 'If you think that now my yacht is safely ordered you can back down on your part of the bargain you're very much mistaken.'

Tears glistened in her eyes; tears of temper and frustration. 'Some bargain!' She tried to struggle free of his grasp. 'It was only going to be the once. That's what you said ...'

'That's what you *thought*' he said, his expression hardening as she resisted. He pulled her close, his face stony. 'Now, be a good girl and stop making a fuss. Or shall I tell your husband how many times you've pleasured me? Do you think he'd like to know?' He looked down at her, watching her dawning horror.

'You wouldn't ...' she breathed.

'Try me.'

But she daren't risk it and once again she succumbed to his demands.

'And let's hear no more nonsense about finishing the affair,'

254

he reminded her when it was over. 'I wouldn't like to have to tell Luke how much I enjoy making love to his wife because *he* might feel inclined to put a stop to it and that would be a pity, wouldn't it, Cassie?' He put out his hand and began to caress her again. She got up quickly before her body could betray her into responding and went to the door, pausing to check that there were no tell-tale signs before opening it just a crack to make sure that the coast was clear before slipping out. At that moment Millie came out of the meeting room with a duster in one hand and a book in the other. If it hadn't been for the fact that she was surreptitiously peeking into the book – a waste of time, since she couldn't read – she couldn't have failed to see her mistress looking furtively out of a guest's bedroom door. Cassie closed the door quickly and stood leaning against it, her heart thumping.

'Nearly caught?' Edward laughed, still reclining on the bed.

'It's all very well for you,' Cassie hissed. 'Your reputation isn't at stake, is it!' She opened the door again and slipped out along to her mother's empty bedroom, where she splashed water from the ewer on to her burning face before going back down the stairs. She hated herself for being under Edward's spell.

The days dragged on. Aaron Wix moved in with no fuss. Cassie had felt justified in taking a little of her mother's money to buy paint and wallpaper and had herself redecorated Lord Paget's room in readiness for him. Lord Paget's room was the larger of the two rooms overlooking the yard and when she had finished it looked fresh and bright although it got no sun. Rummaging about in the attic she found a box of velvet curtains that her mother had never mentioned, even when she'd seen the ones in use falling to pieces as they hung there. It only took a good shaking and some careful altering and one pair was ready for Aaron's room, as it would now be called.

In spite of his untidy, rakish appearance Aaron turned out to be a perfect lodger. He kept his room spotlessly neat and tidy and made his own bed every morning. He had brought with him an armchair and a desk from his room at Mrs Oliphant's and Cassie always saw to it that a fire was lit for him if the day was chilly, in case he wanted to stay upstairs. But usually, after his evening meal in the dining room Aaron would spend time in the bar, making half a pint last most of the evening as he talked or played dominoes or cards with the men, many of whom had forsaken the Falcon for the Ship at Launch when the beer became what they called 'thin', but had come back as soon as word got round that the beer at the Falcon had 'gotta bit o' body in it agin''.

'He's a decent bloke,' was Tom's verdict. 'An' he never mind doin' a hand's turn behind the bar when we're busy. And we do get busy now, Cassie girl. Thass not like it used to be these past few years. Thass gettin' jest like ole times.' And he grinned at her, his ugly face lighting up happily.

As for Cassie, she had never been busier. What with keeping an eye on every aspect of the Falcon, making sure that her mother was looked after and caring for the children, she had precious little time to herself. Charity was fourteen, now. She could have been useful in helping at the Falcon but she had set her heart on becoming a school-teacher and neither Cassie or Luke could bring themselves to discourage her. She was a clever girl, good with her younger brother and sister and good with the class that she already taught as monitor at school. 'I'll be glad to take her on as a pupil teacher,' Miss Jones, her teacher, told Cassie. And so it was arranged, much to Amy's annoyance, who declared that she didn't want to be taught by her sister. Reuben remained quiet. He didn't want to be taught by anybody. He wanted to be a blacksmith in his father's Yard and make the sparks fly and the iron ring on the anvil. Although sometimes, when his big brother Robert came home, bearded now and weatherbeaten, with tales of life as a topman aboard the yachts, his ambition at last realized, telling of the places he'd seen and the things he'd done – carefully watered down in his mother's presence – Reuben was sometimes torn between the blacksmith's forge and following his brother. But Reuben was still only eight. He didn't have to make his mind up yet.

Stella was no help to Cassie.

'What are you going to do, Stella?' she asked one day, coming into the kitchen with a trayful of dirty crockery from the dining room. 'Have you written to John?'

Stella looked at her in surprise. She was sitting in the Windsor chair, close to the fire. 'No. Why should I write to John? He hasn't written to me.'

Cassie frowned. 'But surely you don't want simply to stay here ...'

'Why not? This is my home. I'm very happy here.' And she smiled over at Luke, who was just finishing his supper at the table.

'Thass nice to know,' Luke said, 'and you're very welcome to stay with us, Stella.'

'While we're here,' Cassie reminded them. 'And that may not be for much longer.'

'Well, then we'll have to go somewhere else, won't we?' And Stella smiled at Luke again.

'Are you going back to the Yard tonight, Luke?' Cassie asked, her voice sharper than she'd intended because she felt excluded.

He pushed his plate away and yawned. 'No, I don't think so. I think I'll stay in and read the paper.'

'You could give Tom a hand in the bar, if you're not too tired. There seems to be quite a full house in the taproom tonight.'

'Shall I come too, Luke?' Stella started to get up out of her chair.

'You? You wouldn't know a tot of rum from a pint of porter,' Cassie said. Stella was always running after Luke these days and Cassie didn't like it. 'If you want something to do you can take this milk up to Mama and make sure she's settled comfortably for the night.'

Luke put the newspaper down and went through to the bar. He was quite glad to go, for he didn't want to become involved with Cassie and Stella's bickering. They didn't seem to get on well, these days. In fact, Cassie was sometimes very hard on her sister. He felt sorry for Stella after the way her husband had treated her and tried to make her feel at home, but Cassie seemed to go out of her way to pick on the girl. It was very strange. And not like Cassie at all.

There was a lot of raucous laughter going on in the taproom. 'What's the joke, Tom?' Luke said as he slipped in behind the bar. 'Everybody seems in good fettle tonight.'

'I shouldn't stay in here if I was you, Luke,' Tom said, and his face was serious. 'I hoped you wouldn't come in tonight. Anyways, I've got plenty of help with Aaron, here.'

Luke frowned. 'Why, what's the matter with everybody?' Joe Toliday came up to the bar. 'Yore ole man got his comeuppance, today then, Luke,' he said, and dissolved into laughter.

'I dunno about comeuppance. Falldownance, I reckon,' somebody shouted from the other end of the room and there was another gust of laughter.

Luke turned to Tom. 'What are they on about, Tom?'

Tom sighed. 'Well, you'll hev to know, in the end, so you may as well know now. Your dad had bin round with the night cart with Scrappy Welham. He was drunk, as usual, and when they'd finished, about five o'clock this mornin', him and Scrappy climbed up on to the seat o' the cart to drive the old hoss up to the farm and empty the cart. Well, Scrappy set the hoss off before Alf was ready an' he overbalanced and fell backwards into the cart.'

'They had to tip 'im out with the muck when they got to the farm,' Joe spluttered, nearly helpless with laughter at the thought.

'I don't reckon 'e come outa that lot smellin' o' roses!' someone else shouted.

Luke sighed and shook his head. He didn't laugh. All he could think was how much lower could his father sink.

Suddenly, the bar went silent as the door opened and Alf came in. He was cleaner than anyone had seen him for years. Even his hair had been washed. It was plain he was in an ugly mood. He swayed up to the bar and leaned over it.

'Gimme a pint, you,' he said to Luke.

'No, Dad, you've had enough, I can see that,' Luke said quietly. 'I'll go and get you a cup of tea.'

'I don't want your bloody tea!' Alf banged his hand on the bar. 'Gimme a pint.'

'No. You've had enough.'

'I've had enough o' the likes o' you tellin' me what to do.' Alf's voice dropped. 'What happened last night was your fault, Luke boy. Dropped your ole dad right in the shit, didn't ye. Givin' an honest man the sack an' tellin' 'im to git hisself a job on the shit cart. An' now you won't even give me a drink to slake me terrible thirst.' He thrust his face right up to Luke's and his expression was ugly. 'You done the dirty on me, boy. You done the dirty on yore ole dad good an' proper. But you'll pay for it.' He slammed his fist down on the bar and the glasses rattled. 'By God, I'll see you pay for it. Nobody make Alf Turnbull a laughin' stock an' git away with it.' He turned away, lost his balance and fell over. Luke hurried round the bar to help him up. 'Git away from me. You're no so o' mine.' He got to his feet and staggered out of the bar.

There was an embarrassed silence after he had gone. Then, one after another, the men came up to Luke and patted him on the shoulder, wordlessly showing their sympathy, their regret at what had turned from a joke into an ugly scene, and left.

Luke leaned his elbows on the bar and bowed his head. 'I must go after him. He might do himself a mischief, the mood he's in.'

'I'll go,' Tom said. 'If 'e sees you it'll be like showin' a red rag to a bull, Luke boy.'

'Yes, he's in an ugly temper. I reckon he's been to every pub in Wyford to get as drunk as that, because they'd only serve him with one pint apiece, I made sure of that.'

'Do you want me to come with you?' Aaron asked as Tom went to the door.

'No, you look after Luke. This business has upset 'im, I can see that.'

Tom went out into the cold night air. The river was the obvious place to go first. He wouldn't put it past Alf to drown himself to spite Luke and the tide would be well up. He hurried through the churchyard and down Rose Lane to the quay. There were not many people about on this chill March night, although there was plenty of noise from the three pubs along the quay, and shafts of light spilled frequently across the water as the doors were opened and closed and the men went to relieve themselves in the dark water of the river.

But there was no sign of Alf.

Tom walked the length of the quay from the Ship at Launch to The Folley but there was no sign of Alf. Perhaps he had gone home, or out on to the wall. He hurried past the now smart cottages in The Folley. Out past Turnbull's Yard was the quickest way on to the river wall. But as he passed the Yard he was aware of a glow coming from the boat up on the stocks. He began to run.

The fire was in the cabin of the new cutter. Tom could see the flames already beginning to lick round the skeleton of the coach roofing. He dashed back along the quay to the Rose and Crown. 'Fire!' he yelled in at the door. 'Fire at Turnbull's Yard!'

Everyone spilled out of the pub. One man ran to tell Luke while another ran along to the Anchor and the Ship at Launch to fetch more men. They came running, some carrying lamps, others buckets, then they smashed in the Yard gates, fetched ladders and formed a human chain with buckets of water from the river. Inside the yacht was an inferno and flying sparks started other, smaller fires in the shavings.

Luke came hurrying up with Aaron and watched the burning yacht helplessly. There was nothing they could do except watch the chain of men, working like an efficient machine, passing buckets of water along the line and up the ladders to the men trying to dowse the flames, their faces glistening in the heat. 'Thank God the tide's full,' Luke breathed. 'At least there'll be no shortage of water.'

At last the danger was over and the fire was extinguished. Two men took lamps and climbed into the sodden, smouldering cabin to make sure there was no danger of the fire flaring up again.

'Thass a good job I came to look for your dad,' Tom said to Luke, wiping a grimy hand across his even grimier face. 'Else that might hev bin another hour afore anyone noticed the fire. It musta started down in the cabin.'

'Did you find him?' Luke spoke absently. He was walking

round the yacht with Aaron. At that moment his thoughts were for the burned cutter, not for his father.

'No. I was on my way to see if he'd gone out on to the wall. But I never got there.'

'No. I expect he went home to take it out on poor old Mam. He was too drunk to go anywhere else. I'll go and see him when we've finished here.' He turned to Aaron. 'The hull doesn't seem too badly damaged, does it? Most of the fire was contained below deck, thanks to Tom.' He climbed up the ladder still propped against the hull. 'Oh, my Lord, there's a mess in there,' he said, climbing over on to the deck.

'I shouldn't come any further if I was you, Luke.' One of the men, Luke recognised him as Mark Vince, a shipwright who had been working on the cutter only that day, came slowly out of what was left of the cabin.

'I can see the damage is pretty bad,' Luke said, going towards him. 'I want to have a closer look.'

'No, Luke, it's not that.' Mark came forward and put his hand on Luke's shoulder. 'Don' go in there, boy. We've jest found your dad.'

Chapter Nineteen

Alf's body – or what was left of it – had been found among the smouldering rubbish left by the fire. It was a bitter blow to Luke to think his father had felt so vindictive towards him that he had set fire to the yacht that was to have been the salvation of Turnbull's Yard. At the same time he felt sad at such a futile waste of time – both in the living and in the dying. Luke had never understood his father, never been close to him, and with something of a shock he realized that nobody had been close to Alf Turnbull, not even his brother George. What a lonely, pathetic man he had been.

Of course there was an inquest. The yacht was examined minutely and traces of paint and varnish were found splashed around on parts of the deck that the fire hadn't reached. Clearly, Alf had gone aboard the yacht with the purpose of spoiling, not destroying, the work that had been done. But since he was never without his old clay pipe it was plain what must have happened. It would only need a drop of red-hot ash and the whole lot would go up like tinder, especially with all the shavings that lay about. And in his fuddled state Alf wouldn't have known what to do, but probably blundered around making matters even worse. A verdict of accidental death while the balance of mind was disturbed was brought in.

'Don't take it too hard that he died, Luke,' his mother said, after the funeral. 'I know we shouldn't speak ill o' the dead, but your dad was a bad lot, through an' through, and we all know it. The on'y good thing 'e ever did for me was to give me you childer – an' that was on'y for 'is own pleasure. Not that I welcomed you at the time, that I hev to admit, but you've all bin a blessin' to me in the long run.' She looked round the small room at her family. All eleven of them had managed to get home, although they made no secret of the fact that it was to support their mother rather than to mourn their father that they had come. Selina, at twelve years old the baby of the family, still lived at home and would probably remain there. Unlike the others she had no reason to wish to escape now.

Liddy busied herself about. She had arranged the funeral herself, giving her husband more dignity in death than he had ever had in life. And afterwards she had ham and cake in her own house, small though it was.

She was full of plans for the future. 'I can please mesself what I do, now,' she said happily. 'An' the first thing I shall do is go to Mrs Bates' shop an' get some pretty china like these Cassie's lent me today. I can hev pretty cups and saucers now there ain't no danger he'll chuck 'em at me an' smash 'em all. 'Nother cuppa tea, Hannah? Maisie?'

'No, thankee, Liddy, but I will hev another sliver o' your fruit cake. Thass a rare nice cake.' Maisie held out her plate. 'I'm very partial to fruit cake, y'know.'

'Becca, sitting beside her and looking after her like a mother hen, said disapprovingly, 'I hevn't found any food you *ain't* partial to, Auntie.'

Maisie nodded and shrugged. 'I don't stint meself, that I'll own,' she said, taking a large bite. She turned to Hannah, sitting on her other side. 'An' you shouldn't neither, Hannah,' she said, spraying crumbs as she spoke. 'You're as far through as a fourpenny rabbit. You want buildin' up after your illness.' She leaned over. 'I never thought to see you outa that bed, you know. When I come to see you I thought you were a gonna.'

Hannah smiled at her but said nothing. She had a slightly puzzled look about her, as if she wasn't quite sure what was going on and why they should all be crowded together in this little room. She had watched the funeral service in the churchyard from her sitting room window because she was not yet strong enough to go out in the cold, but it hadn't meant much to her. She had watched funerals from her window so often over the years that one was very like another. Tom had looked after her and had brought her to Paget Road in the trap when the funeral was over, carefully wrapping her in shawls and blankets for the short journey. She looked round for Cassie. 'What is it, Cassie?' she asked in a plaintive little voice. 'Why are we here?'

'It's Uncle Alf s funeral, Mama. He died last week. I told you, dear.'

'Did you? Oh, yes.'

Cassie patted her mother's hand. That was another worry to add to all the rest. The illness seemed to have left Hannah's mind weak.

When it was time to leave Luke said, 'Let's go for a walk along the wall, Cassie. I don't want to go back home yet, there's too many people about. A man can't think straight.'

Cassie looked at him in surprise. They never went for walks together; there was never the time. 'I'll just settle Mama in the trap ...'

'Oh, can't you let Stella do that? It's little enough she does to help.'

'Yes, all right, Luke.' She buttoned her coat and picked up her gloves. 'I'm ready.'

They both kissed Liddy and left. Cassie waited for Luke to speak but they had walked for some time and had reached the cottages in The Folley before he said anything. 'These houses are a jolly sight better now we've done them up than they were when we lived here,' he said, stopping in front of their old cottage. He looked down at her. 'I was happy living there with you, Cassie, when we first married. Happier than you were, I know.'

'I missed the Falcon,' she explained lamely.

He began to walk on. 'I'm afraid you'll have to miss it again, Cassie,' he said quietly.

She caught him up. 'What do you mean?'

'I mean there'll be no money to bid for it now.' He walked her quickly past the Yard, where there was still a faint acrid smell coming from the burnt yacht. 'Not after the fire.'

'But weren't you insured?'

'Not enough to cover all the damage that was done. And Mr Price-Carpenter won't pay us any more until the damage has been made good and the yacht's finished. He agreed to pay us in three stages and the fact that one stage has to be done again is no fault of his.' They reached the river wall. The late afternoon air was cold and damp with mist hanging in the marshes, giving the trees and bushes a grey, ethereal appearance. The tide was at its lowest ebb and the whole scene looked cold and colourless; even the yachts in their winter shrouds were no more than grey silhouettes stretching into the distance. Cassie pulled her coat collar up round her ears but said nothing.

'I can't believe ...' Luke began again, 'I can't believe how my father must have hated me to do what he did.'

266

'He didn't mean to, Luke. 'We know now that he didn't mean to set the yacht on fire. He only meant to …'

'Only meant to what?'

Cassie shrugged. 'Like the Coroner said, he only meant to make a mess.'

'He still must have hated me, even to do that.'

They walked on in silence for some time. Then Cassie said, 'What are we going to do then, Luke?'

'About what?'

'About the Falcon.'

'Nothing we can do, dear. We can't bid for it, Mr Grimshaw has already made that quite plain. We'll just have to find somewhere else to live. It's a pity we had to sell the houses in The Folley, we could have …'

No! I wouldn't go back there – I'd rather sleep in a field.'

Suddenly, Luke burst out laughing. 'Oh, Cassie, I don't really think you would, dear. But it won't come to that. In fact, I've got a house in mind that we can rent. Come on, we'll turn back now and I'll show you where it is.'

They retraced their steps back along the river wall, past the Yacht Yard and up the hill by the Black Buoy pub to the house on the corner of Alma Street and Love Lane. It was a big, double-fronted house with an impressive front door. 'It wouldn't be so bad living there, would it, Cassie?' Luke asked, watching for her reaction.

She shook her head. 'I suppose not. But doesn't Mr Penfold live there?'

'Yes, it's his house, but he's gone to live with his daughter in Scotland. He doesn't want to sell the house until he knows whether he'll like it up there, so it's to be rented out, at least for a time.'

Cassie sighed. 'It's a nice house,' she said without enthusiasm, 'but isn't there *anything* we can do to save the Falcon?'

Luke shook his head. 'No, Cassie. Nothing. And I think it will be best if we don't even attend the auction.'

'I don't see how I can avoid it, since it's to be held in our own meeting room,' Cassie replied. She sighed. 'Mama won't like having to move.'

'Will she even understand?' Luke asked gently.

Cassie shook her head. 'I don't know. I really don't know. She's certainly not been herself since her illness. She never even knows what day of the week it is.'

'I daresay she'll improve when the weather gets warmer.'

'I certainly hope so.'

When they reached home Edward had arrived. He had come as soon as he could get away to see the damage done to his yacht.

'Is she beyond repair, Turnbull?' he asked anxiously.

'Oh, no, sir. The hull itself was barely scorched. The damage was all inside. And of course she'll have to be dried out before work can start on her again. Half the river went inside her to put that fire out, I think.' Luke scratched his beard. 'So she won't be ready to race this season, I'm afraid.'

'Never mind that. As long as she's fast when she's finished. Fortunately I didn't put a time limit on my wager and as long as Bunny Felgate knows my yacht's on the stocks he'll be happy to wait. His new one's to be launched next month and he's already boasting that she'll be a world-beater.'

'Being launched next month, is she?' Luke said. 'That's good. We'll be able to see how she shapes up in the water. It's always nice to be able to see what the opposition is. Are you coming down for the launch, sir?'

'Ye-es, I think I will. I'll get you an invitation, too, Turnbull. I'm sure you'd like to see what we'll be up against.'

'I would indeed, sir.'

Edward stayed for nearly a week. He spent much of his time at the Yard with Luke and Aaron but sometimes after his midday meal in the dining room he would say to Cassie – in the hearing of whoever happened to be within earshot – 'I shall be working in my room this afternoon, Mrs Turnbull. I should be glad if you would bring me tea about four. And bring it yourself, if you don't mind. Those maids of yours are not too careful about slopping the tea as they pour it.'

'You'd think I'd got nothing better to do than to sit and pour tea for him,' Cassie would complain, back in the kitchen. 'I don't know why he can't do it for himself.'

But she obeyed his command because she feared what he would do if she refused him. She felt trapped and hated herself for what she was doing yet was powerless to end it. She wondered what Edward would do when the Falcon was sold and dreaded to think what he might plan.

Afterwards she slipped through the door connecting Edward's room to Hannah's and busied herself tidying drawers and cupboards. Then she went downstairs with an armful of Hannah's stockings.

'Here you are, dear.' She took them into where Hannah sat in her sitting room. 'You can sort through these and mend those that need it, can't you? I'll just go and ask Millie to collect Mr Price-Carpenter's tea tray. He should have finished by now.'

The day of the auction drew ever nearer.

'What are you going to do, Stella?' Cassie asked her sister for the umpteenth time. 'You won't be able to live here, you know. Unless you stay on as a paying guest, like Mr Wix.' She looked up from mixing pastry. After all these years she was resigned to the fact that pastry-making was a task she couldn't delegate. Nobody could make it as light as she could herself.

'Mm. I might do that,' Stella nodded. 'But you'll be moving to quite a big house. I could come and live with you, couldn't I?'

'No, you couldn't.' Cassie's voice was definite and she banged the rolling pin down to reinforce her words. She didn't like the way Stella fawned round Luke, calling him 'brother-in-law, dear,' in a most un-sister-in-law-like fashion. And what was more, Luke seemed to enjoy it. 'Mama will have to come with us, of course, so there won't be any room for you. Anyway, you've been here over a month, now. Don't you think it's time you went back to John?'

'Go back to John? I'm not going grovelling back to John. He's the one who was unfaithful, not me. Well ...' she put her head on one side, 'I wasn't often unfaithful to him.'

'Stella!' Ironically, Cassie was quite shocked at her sister's words. 'Do you mean to say ... ?'

Stella got up and went over to the window. 'I don't mean to say anything,' she said firmly. 'But if your husband was away for months at a time you might find you'd get lonely. That's all.'

'Aren't you lonely now?'

Stella turned and flounced down into her chair again. 'Oh, no, there's plenty going on here.' She put her head on one side. 'That Mr Price-Carpenter, for instance. He's rather nice, isn't he? Wasn't he the one you were so keen on, oh, years ago? I seem to remember you used to meet him by his father's yacht. Wasn't it him? Or was it someone else?'

Cassie shrugged elaborately. 'I really don't remember. Of course, you were too young ...'

'Well, I'm not too young now.' Stella smiled wickedly. 'And do you know, I think I'd only have to give him half a chance and ... well, you know ...'

Cassie put her head down and kneaded the pastry furiously

and far too long so that Stella shouldn't see the way her face flushed. 'I'm sure you're imagining things,' she said.

Stella yawned. 'You may be right, but I don't think so. Anyway, I don't see how you'd know. If a man made eyes at you you'd never even recognize what he was after, would you?'

'No, I don't suppose I would,' Cassie answered briefly, wondering what Stella would say if she knew even half the truth.

That evening Luke was helping Tom in the bar. There was an air of gloom and despondency over the taproom because in two days' time the Falcon would be sold and nobody knew what would happen after that.

'And to cap the lot we've run outa beer!' Tom joked, holding a glass under an empty pump and pumping away.

'It's all right, I'll go and tap another barrel,' Luke laughed as the men clustered round. 'I don't think the pub's run quite dry yet.'

He went off down to the cellar. The new barrel was at the far end and he took the candle with him. When he had finished he started back to the stairs but was surprised to see a pale, ethereal-looking figure at the foot of the stairs.

'Who's there?' he asked, holding the candle higher. There were tales of ghosts in the Falcon, just as there would always be in houses as old as this, but he had never believed in them and certainly never thought to see one. The skin on the back of his neck began to prickle. 'Who is it?' he repeated, his mouth dry.

'It's me, Luke.' Stella's voice came out of the darkness.

'You, Stella! You frightened the life out of me. What in the world are you doing down here?'

'I saw you come down and I followed you, Luke,' she said, coming towards him. 'We never get a chance to talk, do we? Not to talk properly, I mean.'

'Talk? What do you want to talk about, then?' Luke stopped

271

in his tracks. What on earth was the woman on about? Was she ill? Her voice didn't sound quite right.

'Us, Luke. You and me.' She came up to him, a wraith-like figure in white, her hair a cloud of gold in the candle-light.

'There's nothing to talk about, Stella. I don't know what you mean,' he moved to pass her but she stepped into his path again.

'Oh, Luke, don't be so obstinate. Do you think I haven't seen the way you look at me when Cassie's not there?' She laid her hand on his arm.

He nearly dropped the candle. 'I don't know what you mean, Stella,' he said again.

'You married Cassie but it was always me you really wanted, wasn't it?' She smiled up at him and her eyes were like huge dark pools in the shadow of her face.

Luke swallowed. 'What are you driving at, Stella?' he asked, but he didn't need to ask and already his body was beginning to respond to her invitation.

Stella wound her arms round his neck. 'She trapped you into marrying her, didn't she, Luke?'

'No, no, that's not true.' He knew what was wrong with her now; he could smell spirits on her breath. He tried to free himself with one hand while holding on to the candle with the other. He had the irrational idea that as long as he could keep the candle alight he was in control of the situation.

She turned her head and blew it out. 'There,' she said, 'now you've got both hands free.' She pulled his head down and began to kiss him, guiding his hand to her breast at the same time.

'There,' she whispered again, her mouth close to his. 'Isn't that what you want? Isn't it what you've always wanted? And what I've always wanted, too?' She pressed herself against him, tangling her free hand in his hair.

272

He nearly succumbed. The pure animal instinct in him nearly got the upper hand but at the last minute he caught her hands in a vice-like grip and held her away from him.

'What do you think you're trying to do, Stella?' he said, his voice stern. 'Have you no shame?'

She tried to struggle free. 'I want you, Luke. I've always wanted you. You must know that.'

'What about your own husband?'

'Why should I worry about him? He doesn't bother about me. Anyway, it's you I love, Luke.'

'You're lonely and you're missing John. And you've had too much to drink. That's the truth of it, Stella. You don't really love me, any more than I love you.' His voice became gentler. 'You know it's true, Stella. Why don't you go back to John?'

She turned away from him and began to cry. 'I wish I could. But I don't think he wants me, Luke. If he wanted me he would have at least written to me before now, wouldn't he?'

Luke re-lit the candle. Stella's face was tear-stained and woebegone in the soft light. 'Have you written to him?'

She shook her head. 'It's up to him to write first.'

Luke sighed. 'Over something as important as this I don't think it matters *who* makes the first move as long as one of you does. Do you still love him? Really love him, I mean?'

She sank down on the cellar steps. 'Oh, yes, I love him, all right. If I didn't love him would I have put up with his flirtations with all those other women for all these years?' She dried her eyes on the hem of her dress. 'Oh, I understood why he did it. After all, he's only human. A yacht captain is quite a glamorous figure, isn't he? In command of a huge, beautiful sailing vessel, winning races all round the country and even farther afield. Looked up to and respected by everyone, especially the wives of the rich owners, who've got too much time on their hands anyway. Oh, it can be a glamorous life ashore, if not afloat for a yacht captain. I wasn't surprised that his head was turned by all the ladies who fawned over him.' She leaned her head against the wall. 'I suppose I thought that if I left him he would realise that it was me he really loved. I called his bluff She gave a little hiccupping laugh. 'But it didn't work, did it? He didn't even bother to write to me.'

'Are you sure he knows where you've gone?'

'He'll guess. After all, where else would I go? I've got nowhere else.' She dragged herself to her feet. 'I suppose you'll say I must leave the Falcon after my exhibition down here tonight.'

'That's up to you. Cassie and I will be moving out within the next few days, I reckon. We shan't be able to stay on here after the place is sold. So, there's no reason why you shouldn't stay on, if you want to.'

Stella's mouth twisted wryly. 'Whoever buys it might even take me on as barmaid. That would be a turn-up, wouldn't it? And Mama never allowing us anywhere near the taproom.'

'Well, you've only got to wait until the day after tomorrow to find out.' Luke followed her back up the stairs and went back to the taproom. Stella was a silly little mawther. It was a good thing she hadn't tried her tricks on someone less strong-willed. She might have got more than she'd bargained for.

Chapter Twenty

It was the night before the sale. Stella was upstairs helping Cassie to get the meeting room ready for the auction the next day, moving the table to one end and putting rows of chairs where interested parties could sit.

'There,' Cassie said, surveying their work. 'Twenty chairs. That should be enough, I should think.'

'If there are any more people they'll just have to stand round the sides,' Stella said. She sat down on the nearest chair. 'I wonder who'll buy it.' She looked round the room with its dirty cream paint and cracked linoleum. 'Whoever it is will need plenty of money in order to put it into good order again. This room alone wants new curtains and new linoleum as well as new chairs. The only thing in here that's worth saving is the table.'

'Well, it'll be somebody else's worry. Not yours or mine,' Cassie said, her voice sharp to cover the hurt inside her. 'Now, I'm going to see if Lizzy's got Mama settled in bed. You can go down and make her some cocoa. She always likes a drink after she's in bed.'

Stella went downstairs and a minute later Cassie heard a

scream of delight. Lizzy came up a few moments later with a mug of steaming cocoa in her hand.

'Whatever was all that noise about, Lizzy?' Cassie asked.

Lizzy beamed. 'Mrs Stella's husband's jest arrived, Mrs Cassie. She was ever so surprised to see him.'

'So I heard,' Cassie said with a smile. She gave a sigh. 'I hope now John's come they'll manage to sort out their problems.'

With Hannah settled Cassie returned to the kitchen but John and Stella were nowhere to be seen. Seeing her look of surprise Lizzy cocked her head in the direction of Hannah's sitting room. 'In there,' she mouthed, although the walls were sufficiently thick that they couldn't have heard her. 'They wanted to talk and it's still warm in there. You know how Mrs Hannah likes to keep a good fire right up till the time she goes to her bed.'

Cassie nodded. She gave a yawn. 'I suppose we'd better get on with making pies for tomorrow. No doubt there'll be quite a lot of people wanting a pie and a pint.'

'The meat's all cooked and cold on the slab in the larder,' Lizzy said. 'Shall I fetch it?'

'Yes, go and fetch it. It's as well to keep busy. Doesn't give us so much time to think, does it.'

She busied herself with the pastry while Lizzy filled the pies. The first batch was in the oven and cooking before Stella and John came back into the kitchen. They were hand in hand and looked very happy.

Cassie went over to her brother-in-law and kissed him in greeting. 'It's nice to see you, John. You're looking very well,' she said, careful not to show any surprise that he had arrived.

He covered Stella's hand he was holding with his other one. 'I'd have been here before but I've been in the Mediterranean for the past month. I was contracted to go so I couldn't get out of it. Not that I tried,' he admitted. 'I didn't know Stella wasn't coming back. I knew she'd come home because her mother was ill, but I'd no idea she didn't intend to return. When I got back from the Med. and found she was still away . . . ' He shook his head. 'It gave me quite a jolt, I can tell you.'

'We've had a long talk,' Stella said and her voice held a maturity that Cassie had never heard before. 'We realize how stupid we've both been.'

'Yes.' John sighed. 'I let my position go to my head, I'm afraid. And I must admit I enjoyed the fact that Stella was jealous. It made me feel safe, somehow, as if it didn't matter what I did. She would still be there because while I had the power to make her jealous I knew she still cared.' He bowed his head. 'It was callous of me, I can see that now.'

'You didn't like it when I played the same game, did you?' Stella reminded him softly.

'No, you're damned right I didn't.' He gave a rueful smile. 'And when I realized you'd left me and weren't coming back . . .' He shook his head. 'That was when I saw what a silly damned fool I'd made of myself over these past years.'

'So what now?' Cassie was glad they finally understood each other but they'd said nothing so far about the future. She could envisage the whole process beginning again once they returned to Cowes.

'We're not going back to Cowes,' Stella said, as if she'd read Cassie's thoughts.

'And I'm leaving the yachts,' John added. 'I've had over twenty years at sea and I've enjoyed every minute of it, but I'm forty now. I've a nice little nest-egg that I've earned racing over the years and I think it's time I settled down to be a landlubber so I can spend more time with Stella.' He smiled at her and his expression softened. It was obvious he was still very fond of his wife, in spite of everything.

'Are you coming back to Wyford to live, then?' Cassie asked.

He nodded. 'Yes, I think so.' He grinned. 'I thought I might put in a bid for this place. I've always fancied running a pub.'

Cassie was astonished at the fierce stab of jealousy that shot through her. It seemed to take all the strength from her body and reach right down into her fingertips. 'But how can you have decided so quickly? You've only just come home. You didn't even know it was up for auction,' she said weakly.

'That's true, but I first saw the posters when I reached Colchester and I thought, "That's Stella's old home. If she says she'll take me back I'm damned if I won't put in a bid for it – if she's willing." And when I suggested it to her she thought it was a marvellous idea.' He smiled at Stella again. 'Of course I might not get it,' he added carelessly and Cassie had the idea that he wouldn't really mind one way or the other.

'You'd better take a look over the place. You might change you mind when you see the state it's in,' Cassie said, trying not to let her voice betray her feelings.

'Yes, come on, I'll show you.' Stella stood up and caught his hand. 'It's in dreadful need of repair . . .'

'The roofs sound,' Cassie put in quickly.

'Yes, but look at the paint and paper . . .' Together they left the kitchen.

Cassie sat down heavily in the Windsor chair. She didn't want Stella and John to buy the Falcon. Stella didn't care about it, she never had, and it was only a whim on John's part. It was bad enough having to part with the place at all, but somehow a stranger taking it over would be more bearable than seeing it go to Stella and John. True, John had the appearance of a man who knew what he was about. Yacht captains ran a tight ship and that would be good discipline for running the Falcon. All the same . . .

She sat for a long time, staring into space, until the smell of burning roused her and she removed the batch of charred pies that had been forgotten. Automatically she began to make another batch to replace them, wondering how Stella would cope with this aspect of Falcon life. Her pastry had always been like concrete.

The auction was at two o'clock the next day. As Cassie had predicted, both the dining room and the taproom were full for luncheon and there was a steady tramp of feet up the stairs to the meeting room. Soon more chairs were needed and finally people had to stand round the walls. But most had only come to watch, not to buy. Cassie couldn't bear to see her home fall under the hammer and so she left before the sale began and went down to her mother's room.

'What's going on?' Hannah asked petulantly. 'There's an awful lot of noise. Is there a sale on upstairs?'

'Yes, dear, that's right.' Cassie stared out of the window.

'Is it a wreck sale?'

Cassie didn't answer, although she was tempted to say yes. Yet if only there was money available she could make the Falcon into a beautiful place. She could see it in her mind's eye – the colours she would use, the curtain materials ... Resolutely she turned back to her mother. 'I'll go and make you a cup of tea,' she said.

She made the tea and took it in to her mother. Luke came in as she went back to the kitchen. 'I thought you might be feeling a bit bad, Cassie,' he said quietly, 'so I came home to be with you.'

'Thank you, Luke.' Her eyes welled with tears and she bit her lip. 'I don't know if I could bear it if John and Stella buy the place, Luke. Somehow, it wouldn't seem quite so bad if

279

it went to strangers. But Stella ... she's never cared tuppence about it ...'

Luke put his arm round her. 'Thass no good being jealous, Cassie. That'll only eat into you and make you bitter. You've got to look forward, dear. Have you started thinking about the Corner House?'

She shook her head. 'No. I've kept thinking – hoping – something would turn up so we didn't have to go there.' She poured a cup of tea for herself and Luke and they sat either side of the kitchen table drinking it, hoping for some miracle that would mean they could stay.

'How long do you think it'll take?' Cassie said after a while.

'Not long. Should be over soon.'

As if on cue the door burst open and Stella and John nearly fell in. 'We've got it! We've got it!' Stella shouted, capering round the kitchen. 'The Falcon's ours!'

John wiped a bead of sweat off his handsome brow. 'It was a near thing,' he said, sitting down at the table. 'If they hadn't accepted my last bid that would have been it. I couldn't have gone any higher.'

'Oh, but you didn't have to!' Stella gave him a resounding kiss. Then she kissed Luke and Cassie and went on to kiss the door, the window, the dresser and even the coal hod – leaving a smudge of coal-dust on her nose. 'It's ours. All ours. I've always loved the old place and now ...' she raised her arms and danced round the table, '... it belongs to us, to John and me.'

Cassie felt the jealousy twisting up her insides and she felt sick. It wasn't fair. They shouldn't have it. They didn't love the place, not like she did.

Luke got to his feet and went over to John. 'Congratulations, boy,' he said, shaking him by the hand. 'I wish you well.' He kissed Stella very briefly on the cheek. 'You'll have your work cut out now, Stella,' he said with a grin. He turned to Cassie. 'Cassie girl?'

Cassie nodded and managed a ghost of a smile. 'Yes, congratulations, both of you. There's a cup of tea in the pot if you'd like one.' She left Stella to pour it.

There was a tramp of feet on the stairs and then silence. After a little while Lizzy came in. 'They've all gone, Mrs Cassie,' she said, and Cassie could see she had been crying. 'Shall me an' Millie start to clear up?'

'Yes.' Then Cassie checked herself. 'You'd better ask Mrs Stella,' she said, her voice unsteady. 'She's going to be mistress here now.'

Cassie and Luke moved into the Corner House a week later, taking a tearful Lizzy with them. The children were excited and they happily carried pictures and smaller items of furniture to their new home, making endless journeys through the churchyard from the Falcon to the Corner House. Then they ran from room to room, admiring everything and getting in everybody's way.

Cassie worried about Hannah. She didn't really understand what was going on and Cassie felt that as the Falcon was still in the family it would be less upsetting for her to stay on there. Millie would have been quite happy to look after her. But Stella refused to even consider this. They would need Hannah's sitting room for their own use, she pointed out, and her bedroom would make an extra one to let. Already Aaron Wix was a permanent guest, so that was one bedroom they couldn't let out at a higher rate: they couldn't afford another such one.

So Hannah was brought to the Corner House and Cassie made her as comfortable as she could, with all her own possessions round her, in a room on the first floor that had a view of the river.

'Oh, this is very nice,' Hannah said. She walked round the room, touching her possessions. 'I always knew we should come back, you know. But I think the china cabinet would look better on that wall, don't you, dear? We'll get the maids to move it. I'll ring the bell.'

'There's only Lizzy, Mama.'

'Only Lizzy? That was very silly of you, Cassie, to give the others the day off. On moving day, too. They should all be here, helping.' She sat down in her armchair by the window. 'Oh, this is nice. I can see the boats on the river. I shall sit here and watch for Reuben's boat. Ask the girl to bring me my tea, will you, dear?' Hannah picked up her sewing.

'I do believe she thinks she's back in the house in West Street,' Cassie told Luke when he and Tom came from the Falcon with the last load of furniture on the cart. They had brought all the pieces from Hannah's private rooms and all the things Luke had made but the rest they had left; John would have to buy quite a lot to fill the gaps at the Falcon and Mr Penfold had left a good deal of his furniture in the Corner House so the arrangement suited them all. 'She seems quite happy to be here.' She turned to Tom. 'Would you like to go up and see her, Tom?'

Tom shook his head. 'I'd best be gettin' back, Cassie girl,' he said. 'Mr John said not to be too long.'

Cassie laid a hand on his arm. 'I hope you won't find it – difficult, Tom, after all these years.'

Tom swallowed noisily. 'Well, that ain't never gonna be the same now, is it?' he said. He climbed back into the cart. 'Here, Luke, ketch hold of the other end of this box. Thass the last bit, then we're finished.'

They all settled down to their new lives. The children loved the new house, partly because it was different and children are always ready to embrace the new and different. But even they confessed that they missed talking to Jack and Major, the two great drayhorses, and feeding them lumps of carrot while they nuzzled their hands with their warm, wet, gentle noses. As for Cassie, she missed every aspect of life at the Falcon and couldn't bring herself to go back there once she had left. Whenever she saw Stella in the street, which wasn't often, she would make an excuse so that she didn't have to return as a guest to her old home. That was something she didn't think she could bear. Not yet. Not until she began to feel that the Corner House was home. It was a strange feeling – for a while she felt she was in limbo. She didn't belong anywhere. The Falcon was no longer her home and the Corner House was not yet home although she lived there. She, who had always been so busy that there were never enough hours in the day, now had time on her hands. And sometimes it hung heavy.

But when the Vestry met at the end of May she was forced, as a member, to attend and it was with some trepidation that she made her way through the churchyard to the meeting held, as usual, at the Falcon. She had left Hannah sitting in the garden. Her mother was much stronger now and sometimes took little walks by herself, mostly into the churchyard, where she would sit and wait for funerals because she liked to see all the people and the flowers. When he saw her there Tom would go and sit with her for a while before escorting her home. Cassie often wondered whether Tom was happy with John and Stella. He never said.

It took all Cassie's courage to push open the door at the Falcon. She didn't know what she had expected, but she was amazed at the transformation. The passage that ran from the front to the back of the house had been painted a light cream

283

and there was a new mulberry-coloured carpet runner on the floor and up the stairs.

Stella came to greet her. She had a vast pinafore on and her arms were floury; Cassie had never seen her look so happy. 'Oh, it's lovely to see you, Cassie. Don't you think we're making the place look nice? Of course, it'll all take time but we're doing it as fast as the money will allow.' She kissed Cassie. 'Oh, I can't tell you how happy I am, Cassie,' she said, giving her a hug and leaving floury marks on Cassie's merino jacket. 'And John's taken to the life of an inn-keeper like a duck to water. He loves it. Really loves it.'

'I'm glad you're happy, Stella,' Cassie said and tried to sound as if she really meant it as, deep down, she did. But she wished Stella could have been happy somewhere other than at the Falcon.

'We've already redecorated three of the guest bedrooms and the meeting room,' Stella prattled on. 'Of course, John does all the painting and decorating himself – he's very good at it, you know. Oh, and we had that Mr Price-Carpenter in again last week, but I expect you know that. He came to see how his yacht is progressing after the fire.' She nudged Cassie. 'Quite a man for the ladies, isn't he? Not over-fussy, either, from what I can gather.'

'I don't know what you mean.' Cassie looked at the watch hanging on her lapel. 'I must go up to the meeting. They'll be starting without me.'

'Stay and have a cup of tea with me afterwards,' Stella called. 'And don't forget to notice the new chairs in the meeting room. John bought them in a job lot at a sale last week.'

Cassie made her way slowly up the stairs. So Edward had been back to the Falcon. Things had happened so quickly that she had had no time to warn him of the changed circumstances.

She wondered if he had asked her whereabouts – after all, it wouldn't have been difficult to discover where she had gone, he need only have asked someone when he went to the Yard to check the progress of his yacht. But he had made no attempt to seek her out. She was disappointed. She missed him. After all these years part of her was still in love with him and still hoped ...

The Vestry meeting dragged on, but at least it gave Cassie an opportunity to study the changes John and Stella had made to the meeting room. There was still a smell of fresh paint about it and the old curtains had been replaced with a light, chintzy fabric. There was new green oilcloth on the floor that nearly matched the seats of the chairs John had bought and even a new picture of the Queen over the mantelpiece to replace the old one. I could have done all this, if only I'd had the money, Cassie couldn't help thinking. She brought her mind back to the meeting. They were discussing plans for the Queen's Jubilee the following month. 'I think we should at least decorate the streets in honour of Her Majesty's fifty years as Sovereign,' the Rector was saying.

'Have we got bunting?' George Sainty asked.

'There are a few old flags in the vestry at church. We had them for the celebrations at the end of the Crimean War, I think.'

'They'll be pretty mouldy by now, then,' Sir Henry Crampin said self-importantly. 'We must have new.'

'Who's going to buy them?' Cassie asked.

Sir Henry gave an elaborate sigh. 'I suppose I'll have to put my hand in my pocket.'

'Not much use putting a lot of flags up when people hang all their washing out on the street. You can't get along the road sometimes for sheets flapping in your face,' George Cole pointed out. As parish clerk he was responsible for the notices put up round the village telling people not to commit this nuisance and he took it as a personal affront that the notice was largely ignored.

'The women have nowhere else to hang their washing. The yards where they live aren't big enough to hang a handkerchief to dry,' Cassie said.

'That's not up for discussion today,' Sir Henry snapped. 'God knows we spent long enough over that at the last meeting. We're talking about the Jubilee celebrations.'

'I should think a procession, with the town band, and then tea on the quay,' the Rector said firmly. 'We must provide a good tea for the villagers, they expect it when there's something to celebrate.'

'And who's going to foot *that* bill?' Sir Henry said grumpily.

'We'll go round all the shopkeepers and pubs, that's what we usually do. And I'm sure Sir Hector Rebow will be generous.'

'He gave ten pounds last time,' George Cole said, leafing back through his Minutes.

'And I gave twenty, as I remember,' Sir Henry said, tipping back expansively in his chair.

After the meeting Cassie declined Stella's invitation and hurried home, on the pretext of having left her mother too long. When she got back Lizzy was busy in the kitchen, complaining that she still didn't know where everything had been put, so she went through to the garden. Hannah's chair was empty.

Cassie hurried back to the kitchen. 'Where's Mrs Hannah? Have you seen her, Lizzy? Is she in her room?'

'No, Mrs Cassie, I ain't seen her since I took her a drink about a hour ago,' Lizzie said, wiping her hands on her apron. 'Shall I go and look for her?'

'No. No, I'll go. You carry on with what you're doing.' Cassie pinched her lip. Wherever could her mother be? She hadn't gone back to the Falcon because Cassie had just come from there, and she hadn't been in the churchyard watching for funerals, like she did sometimes.

Cassie called the children, just home from school and sent them to look for their grandmother, then she hurried back to the Falcon to see if Tom could be spared to join in the search.

Hannah had gone indoors soon after Cassie had left for the Vestry meeting. It was a lovely afternoon, too nice to sit in the garden. She put on her best hat, she'd almost forgotten that hat, but it had come to light when they moved to this nice house. She'd worn it when she and Reuben were married. She was very lucky to have married a yacht captain; it meant they were much better off than most of the people in the village. But it also meant they had a duty towards those less well-off than they were themselves. Hannah took up a basket and went out.

She walked out along the river wall, humming to herself. Reuben would soon be home again. She shaded her eyes with her hand and looked downriver; the tide wasn't right yet for his yacht to come up. Perhaps he would come tomorrow. Happily she scrambled down the bank and began to pick sea lavender, making it into little bunches that she tied with bits of grass and then laid carefully in her basket.

It was Tom who found her. She was in Sun Yard, giving out her bunches of sea lavender to the ragged urchins who lived nearby as if she was Lady Bountiful bestowing gifts on the poor. The children were laughing at her.

'Come on, dearie.' Tom took her by the arm. 'Thass time you was a-goin' home. I think you've done enough for one day.'

She looked up at him, puzzled. 'Reuben? I wasn't expecting you home today.' She frowned and then her face cleared.

'No, you're not Reuben, you're Tom. I forgot. Yes, let's go home. I don't remember why I came here. Liddy doesn't live in Sun Yard any more, does she?' Happily, she allowed Tom to take her home.

Chapter Twenty-One

As he had promised Edward made sure that Luke was invited to the launching of Bunny Felgate's yacht *Victorious* with him. It was a brilliantly sunny day and Harvey's Yard at the other end of the quay from Turnbull's had been cleared and swept, bunting fluttered from every available flag-pole and post and was strung wherever there was enough space to hang it. Crates of beer stood ready for the workmen's celebrations afterwards and the Town Band was murdering *Life on the Ocean Wave* happily on the platform.

Edward and Luke walked round *Victorious* as she stood on the ways waiting for the chocks to be knocked away.

'She's got a fine, deep keel,' Edward said.

'Mm, but I wonder how well she'll point. She's a bit full in the lower sections,' Luke said thoughtfully. 'None the more for that she's a fine yacht.'

'Beat mine, will she?'

'Not a chance. But of course it'll all depend on the way she's sailed. I see Jim Pickering is here. Is he going to captain her?'

'Yes, I believe he is.'

'He's a good bloke. Doesn't lose many races, I'm told.'

'I'll have to start looking round for my captain, then.' Edward turned away. 'Ah, Bunny. Fine yacht you've got here, but not as good as mine will be when she's done.'

'It'll be a while, won't it, Teddy? Sorry to hear about the fire, old fruit.'

They went off and Luke stood where he was to watch the yacht launched. He could tell a lot by the way the hull took the water. He scratched his beard. *Victorious* was certainly a beautiful boat with long, sleek lines but Luke was confident in his cousin Martin's design. Edward Price-Carpenter's yacht would outstrip this one, sailed by the right crew.

Thomas Harvey, the owner of the shipyard came up to him. They were not rivals in the normal sense because usually Harvey's Yard built bigger boats than Turnbull's. 'I was sorry to hear about the fire on Price-Carpenter's yacht, Turnbull,' Thomas Harvey said gruffly. 'That was a bit of bad, for you. Your father, too. I'm sorry.' He cleared his throat and nodded towards *Victorious*, now floating gently on the tide. 'All I can say is these two buggers must have more money than sense to wager the amount of money they have. Do you reckon the yachts are evenly matched?'

'Yes, I don't think there'll be a lot in it. But as I've said before it all depends on the captains and crews.'

'Absolutely. Who's going to captain Price-Carpenter's?'

'He hasn't got round to finding a captain yet. The yacht won't be done much before the end of the season, so there's plenty of time.'

Thomas Harvey nodded. 'One thing about it, these two yachts have given our yards work and kept our men employed, although I'll hazard a guess that our wage bill for them won't anything near match the amount of money they've wagered on the race between the two boats.'

Luke nodded. 'I reckon you're about right, there, too, Mr Harvey.'

Preparations for the Jubilee celebrations gathered momentum. The Rector had made a record collection from the wealthier members of the parish, increased by dint of dropping judicial hints as to the generosity of business or political rivals. Over the years he had learned to manipulate as well as tend his flock.

'You'll be giving Stella a hand at the Falcon, I daresay, Cassie,' Luke said, pulling off his boots at the end of his day's work. 'Tell John I'll come and help Tom in the bar if he wants me to.'

'No.' Cassie shook her head quickly. 'Stella hasn't asked me to help.'

'Well, dear, haven't you offered? You know how busy it can get, times like these.'

Cassie shook her head again. 'I'll help if she asks me, but I don't think she will. She manages very well. I'm surprised, really.' She smiled a shade too brightly at Luke. 'I'll get your supper. It's all ready.'

Luke shook his head. He had known Cassie would miss the Falcon, but he had never realized quite how much.

As for Cassie, after always having had too much to do she now found that she had too little, although once Hannah had become mobile again and taken to wandering off she found she often had to go searching for her. Sometimes Hannah would take things from the pantry to give away, sometimes she would pick the flowers and berries from the hedgerows. If she could find nothing else she would pick up stones and pebbles. But the pattern was always the same. She would go to the poorest parts of the village and knock on doors, saying, 'I've brought you a little something to tide you over, dear,' just as she had done when she lived at the Falcon and took the leftover bread and pies round after dark, a habit Cassie had continued. Only now the children laughed at her and the rest merely pitied the little wizened figure with her basket.

The move to the Corner House seemed as if it had put an end to Cassie's meeting with Edward. She hadn't seen him at the Falcon, even though both Stella and Luke had spoken of him visiting Wyford. She was relieved, yet in a way she had to admit that she missed the excitement of their stolen meetings, although of late he had been less ardent, less eager and she had been more on edge since the day they were nearly discovered by Millie. Yet, perversely, she couldn't help feeling slighted, especially since Stella had hinted that he was nothing more than a philanderer. But Stella didn't know – or did she? Had she, Cassie, been no more to Edward than a passing fancy?

She busied herself plumping cushions to stifle the thought and then went over to the window and stood gazing out at the river. No, she couldn't believe that. True, Edward had blackmailed her into the affair with him, but only because he understood her so well that he knew there was no other way to get her to agree. In fact he had probably only given the order for his yacht to Luke because he saw it as a way to get her back into his bed. He had made it quite clear that Luke wouldn't get the order if Cassie didn't go to him. And being totally honest with herself she had to admit that in the beginning she hadn't been at all reluctant. It was only afterwards that she realized that he expected the affair to continue and that there was no escape.

She sighed and moved away from the window. Thank heaven it looked as if it was all over now.

She sat down in an armchair and gazed round the room. It was a pleasant room on the first floor, next to Hannah's, enjoying the same view of the river. Mr Penhale had left quite a lot of his furniture for their use and it was all of the best quality. It was quite a step up in the world to live in a house like this, she appreciated that, and she tried very hard not to hanker after the hustle and bustle, the smell of stale beer and tobacco smoke, the noise of the bar and the warmth of the kitchen at the Falcon. But it was hard, she missed it all and sometimes she felt that taking her away from it was the final punishment that fate had dealt her; especially as Stella, who didn't care two straws for it, was living there and making a success of it into the bargain.

Stella didn't ask for any assistance from Cassie so she contented herself with making mountains of sandwiches, cakes and pastries for the party that was to be held on the quay as part of the Jubilee celebrations.

It was a very hot day at the end of June. The band leading the procession could be heard coming nearer and nearer, the sweat pouring down the faces of the bandsmen as they marched in their thick, braided uniforms blowing with a good deal more enthusiasm than talent their version of Sousa's march *The Liberty Bell.* They had paraded from the Cross, at the other end of the village, and following the band were some villagers in fancy dress; some, like the members of Ancient Order of Buffaloes and the Ancient Order of Foresters marching with the dignity that befitted their ceremonial regalia, others tagging along behind, happy just to be a part of the celebrations.

Cassie was in charge of the tea, lavishly spread on long tables that reached half the length of the quay. It was a public holiday so Luke was there, too, helping to carry chairs, plates of sandwiches and tins of cakes, while the children waited impatiently for the procession to arrive so that tea could begin. Hannah had been settled in a big wooden armchair on a platform a little apart from the proceedings, where she could see everything but wouldn't be frightened by the crowds.

'That'll suit you very well, Hannah,' Luke said as he handed her her parasol. 'You'll feel like the Queen yourself, sitting up there.' He gave her a smile.

Hannah smiled happily back. 'Yes. And I shall be able to watch for Reuben's yacht to come upriver from here, too. He should be home soon.'

Luke patted her knee and went off. He had become fond of his mother-in-law over the years and it grieved him that her illness had turned her from the efficient, capable woman she had once been to this child-like creature, living in a world of fantasy much of the time.

The noise of the band grew louder and more discordant as the procession approached. It was about twice as long now as it had been to start with and everybody was in holiday mood, marching or prancing more or less in time to the band and singing more or less the same tunes. Once on the quay the procession dispersed for tea, but this couldn't be served until Sir Henry Crampin had said a few words and proposed a toast to Her Royal Majesty on her fifty years as monarch.

The crowd became a little impatient at Sir Henry's inability to be brief, for they were far more interested in the food on the tables than in his rhetoric, but he finally stopped talking and after some liquid refreshment the band struck up again, this time playing unrecognisable tunes from light opera, and the party began in earnest. Cassie was kept busy dispensing sandwiches and cakes, while Lizzy looked after the tea urn. One or two enterprising people had set up stalls on the quay but nobody was buying cockles and shrimps when they could have their fill of meat paste sandwiches free. The tide was full so there were boats, too, giving trips up or downriver and racing against each other just to add to the fun, but without the fierce competition that attended the regatta.

Now and again Cassie glanced towards Hannah. Her mother was still sitting happily watching what was going on, smiling at all and sundry, and Cassie breathed a prayer of thankfulness that she hadn't chosen today to wander off.

After they had eaten as much as they could the crowd began to disperse, making their way to the Fair on Anchor Hill.

'Can I go, too, Mama?' Reuben came and asked.

Cassie looked down at her son. He was very like Luke. 'Yes, you can go if the girls promise to look after you, Reuben.'

'I don't need looking after,' he protested.

'Oh, come on, Ben, don't argue.' Amy caught his hand. 'At least Mama is letting you come with us.'

'And you'll be sent home, right quick, if you don't do as you're told,' Charity, very much the elder sister, said, leading the way.

Amy and Reuben looked at each other and made a face behind Charity's back as they followed her.

When most of the clearing up was done Cassie spoke to Lizzy, saying, 'I'll take Mama home now. She's been very good, she's sat there all the afternoon. You did make sure she had some tea like I asked you, Lizzy, didn't you?'

'I did go and ask her but she said she wasn't hungry.' Lizzy shook her head sadly. 'She said she could see Reuben comin' upriver with his yacht and she was gonna wait and hev some tea with him.'

'Oh, dear,' Cassie sighed. 'This is one of her bad days. Some days she's really quite sensible. I'll go and get her.'

She went over to where her mother was still sitting, watching the river, a gentle smile playing round her lips. 'Come on, dear, it's time to go home now. Have you enjoyed your afternoon?'

But Hannah didn't answer. She had died quietly and peacefully among the crowds in the sunshine.

295

'I like to think she saw Papa's yacht, at last,' Cassie said, weeping quietly as she and Lizzy laid Hannah out, a tiny figure now, hardly recognisable as the tall, hard-bitten woman who had ruled the Falcon, keeping her own counsel and her own dark secrets over so many years. 'Life wasn't easy for her. Thank God death came gently to her. The doctor said the heart attack was swift. He said she wouldn't have known a thing about it.'

Cassie went to see her aunt. Maisie didn't go out at all now, she had grown so fat that it was as much as she could do to get from one room to the other in her own house and she was always short of breath.

'Oh, dear. My pore sister,' Maisie wiped her eyes. 'I never thought she'd hev gone first. Look at me, I've got so many different complaints that the doctor don't know which one to treat first yet here I set, still jest about alive. But there, they say a creakin' door last the longest, don't they? And young 'Becca look after me that well – she 'on't let me hev chocolate now, although you know how I used to love a bit o' chocolate, don't you?' But she say, "No, Auntie, that ain't good for you, not in your state," so I hev to abide by what she say. She's a good girl.' Maisie helped herself to a third piece of gingerbread that 'Becca had brought in with the tea when Cassie arrived. 'I shan't come to the funeral, Cassie girl. You understand, don't you? My legs ...'

'Oh, yes, Auntie. I understand.' Cassie was glad. She remembered the last time her aunt had visited, when Hannah was ill. She didn't want to risk a repeat of that performance.

Cassie missed her mother more than she admitted to anyone, but not the child-like Hannah of the past year, she missed her sweeping imperiously about, giving orders in her brisk voice and when she was feeling particularly despondent she would imagine Hannah saying 'Now pull yourself together, my girl. Life's for living, not for moping about.' And she would smile at herself through the tears that were never very far from the surface these days.

Throughout the summer Edward Price-Carpenter's yacht once again took shape. The charred timbers were all removed and replaced and by the end of the summer she was finished and ready to be launched. Luke wanted her off the slip as quickly as possible because he was anxious to get the keel laid of the new schooner that would provide his men with plenty of work for the winter.

'She's to be launched the week after the Regatta,' Luke told Cassie as they sat in the garden late one evening at the end of the summer. This was something quite new to them both; they had never had a garden to sit in before and would never have had the time to sit in it if they had. 'Young Bobbie should be home by then. I reckon he's had a good season. The weather's been ideal.'

'I wonder what he'll think of his new home?' Cassie mused. Their son had gone to sea before they moved out of the Falcon.

Luke smiled. 'Yes, I wonder. Not that he'll spend much time ashore in it, knowing Bobbie. He's no sooner on dry land than his feet are itching for a heaving deck. The sea's really in his blood, and that's thanks to his grandfather Reuben, I reckon.'

'Who's to perform the ceremony when the yacht's launched?' Cassie asked, bending over her knitting. She had a sneaking hope that she might be asked herself. It would be fitting, as wife of the builder, and only she and Edward would appreciate the deeper significance.

'Oh, he's bringing his wife down for it. Didn't I tell you? He thought it would be nice as he's having the yacht named after her – *Felicity*, it's to be called. Funny name, isn't it?' Luke picked up the newspaper and began to read it.

'Felicity? No, you've never said.' She concentrated on picking up the stitch she'd dropped. So Edward was bringing his wife to Wyford . . . She felt a pang of jealousy mingled with surprise and wondered what she would be like, this mealy-mouthed, ailing creature that Edward had so little time for. No doubt he was naming the boat for his wife as a sop to his conscience. Poor thing. Cassie felt sorry for her. She made a mental note to order flowers for Amy to hand to her after the launch.

Robert arrived home during the last week in September. He was eighteen now, with a man's deep voice and a thick golden beard. Cassie could see the striking resemblance to his grandfather and she wished Hannah could have been there to see it, too.

They had telegraphed news of Hannah's death to him but the reality didn't strike until he saw her empty chair, her walking stick and her work table, the piece of embroidery she had been working on still there because Cassie hadn't had the heart to put it away.

'I took it for granted that she'd always be around,' he said, shaking his head. 'Perhaps I should have spent more time with her . . . I never seemed to talk to her much.'

Cassie smiled gently at him. 'There's no need to feel remorseful, Bobbie. We all feel we should have done more, but we're all only human, with ordinary human failings and we don't always do what we should. And Grandmama was happy enough, just knowing you were there. She was very proud of you, you know. And the more so because you're so like your grandfather.' She surreptitiously wiped away a tear that always threatened when Hannah was mentioned. 'Now,' she smiled brightly, 'tell us all about the places you've visited.'

On the day of die launch it rained all the morning, but by two o'clock the clouds had lifted enough to show a patch of blue sky although the sun was nowhere in evidence. A chill wind dried the bunting that adorned the Yard and the boat and draped the launching platform.

Cassie dressed carefully for the launch, wanting Edward to see her at her best. She put on her ottoman silk dress – black, of course, as Hannah had only been dead four months – bemoaning the fact that since leaving the Falcon she had put on several pounds in weight and no longer had the tiny waist she had taken for granted, but relieved that black suited her colouring very well. Her hair was still thick and fair and she wore it in a loose bun that, unlike some, was all her own hair and owed nothing to padding. She had bought a new hat with a high crown and swathed in wide, pale grey ribbon. With it worn slightly tilted over one eye she felt quite dashing.

Luke had been at the Yard all morning but he slipped home to change into his best suit before the ceremony. He kissed her before he left. 'You look a treat, dear,' he said admiringly. 'You're a credit to me and I'm proud of you. You'll come along with Robert in a little while?'

She nodded. 'Yes, we shan't be long.' She could hardly tell him that she had taken so much trouble over her dress not for his sake, but to impress Edward.

Cassie and Robert joined Luke in the office, kept very tidy and clean by Aaron, to meet the other members of the launching party. Besides Luke and Aaron, the Rector was there – he was always invited to give a Blessing to boats before they were launched – Lord Felgate, who had come, as he put it, 'to view the opposition', and Edward with his wife and two of his daughters.

When Cassie saw Felicity Price-Carpenter she could hardly believe her eyes. Where was Edward's 'stupid mare' who suffered from a myriad of complaints that people don't die of?

Here was a strikingly beautiful woman, with jet black hair, large dark eyes and a silky, pale complexion. She was expensively dressed in a wine-coloured dress, and Cassie noted enviously that it was nipped in at the waist to show that even after six children she still had the figure of a young girl. Her hat was pink and wide-brimmed, trimmed with a host of stuffed birds and animals that all seemed to be jockeying for position among the flowers and ribbons. She carried a pink parasol that had a cat's head on the handle and two mice hanging from it in the very latest fashion. She looked the picture of health.

Cassie was so shocked she could only stand and stare. How could Edward have said such things about this elegant, self-assured woman in her elaborately expensive costume? Against her Cassie suddenly felt dowdy and dull, despite the fact that she had dressed with such care.

Felicity came over to her. 'So you're Mrs Turnbull,' she said in a low, well-modulated voice. 'Teddy's often spoke to me about you. You used to keep the Falcon, didn't you? He's told me you make the most delicious meat pies.' She smiled and turned away. 'Isn't that right, Teddy?' she called over her shoulder.

Edward came across straight away although he had been deep in conversation with Luke and Aaron. 'What's that you say, my love?' He put his arm round her waist and smiled into her eyes.

'I've been telling Mrs Turnbull how you always rave over her meat pies.'

'That's right. The best I ever tasted.' He gave a brief, impersonal smile in Cassie's direction. 'Excuse me, my love, I have one or two things to discuss with Turnbull and his man.' He kissed Felicity on the tip of the nose and went back to Luke.

Cassie felt sick. She couldn't believe this was happening.

Edward was treating her with total indifference, almost to the point of rudeness. And the way he fawned over his wife . . . and after all the things he'd said . . . It was like some stupid charade. She turned away, shocked and disgusted at his behaviour.

It was a perfect launch. *Felicity* slid into the water, gathering momentum as she went, with hardly a splash.

Luke, standing beside Cassie, said, 'Marty would have loved to see her go down like that. She'll be a fast boat, there's no doubt about that.'

'I hope you're right, Turnbull,' Edward Price-Carpenter had overheard Luke's remark. 'I've a great deal of money hanging on the speed of this boat.'

'She's certainly a smart craft,' Bunny Felgate admitted. 'Got a good, sharp bow.' He shook his head. 'But she'll never outrun my *Victorious*?

Edward laughed. 'I'm confident she will. How long before she'll be ready to race, Turnbull? A fortnight?'

Luke looked at him in surprise. 'I hadn't thought you'd be expecting to race her this season, Mr Price-Carpenter. I can have her ready in a fortnight or so, if necessary, but the weather's beginning to close in. All the yachts are coming back. The season's finished, you know.'

Edward slapped him on the back. 'Well, we'll argue about that back at the Falcon. The landlord and his wife are putting on a spread for us. We'll talk over a glass or two.'

The meeting room at the Falcon was ready. The table was laid for thirty and a four-course meal was served; soup, roast beef, trifle and finishing with cheese and fruit. It was delicious. Cassie, sitting between Edward and Luke was in turn full of admiration at the way Stella and John were handling things and then jealous to think that they could manage perfectly well without any help from her. She had plenty of time to think and to watch what was going on because although Luke tried continually to include her in the conversation Edward persisted in ignoring her, either turning his back on her to attend to his wife or talking across her to Luke. Cassie became increasingly annoyed. Why was he treating her like this? Surely he didn't think she was likely to make a scene?

She tried to pretend she didn't notice what he was doing by studying the other members of the party. Charity and Amy were in their best dresses, both looking charming and Reuben was behaving himself, fortunately. Amy had handed the bouquet of flowers Cassie had ordered for Edward's 'poor' wife, to Felicity with great composure; Felicity still had it with her, Cassie noticed. Then she saw Robert. He was sitting beside Edward's eldest daughter, Marian, and they seemed to be getting on very well together. Too well, in fact. She watched them in dawning horror. Marian was what, sixteen or seventeen? Too young to fall in love, surely. But although they had only recently met there was an unmistakable air about the two of them. They had eyes for nobody but each other and they made a handsome pair. Cassie pushed the plate away, her pudding only half-eaten. What if they *did* fall in love? What if they wanted to marry? Could she bear to shatter their happiness and ruin the lives of those around them? Or would she dare to keep her dreadful secret? She felt sick. This was a problem she had never ever contemplated.

Chapter Twenty-Two

'Well, what do you think then, Turnbull? Can you have *Felicity* ready to race in a fortnight? My friend Bunny Felgate here is anxious to lose his money. He can't wait to race against her.' The table had been cleared and people were standing or sitting about in knots, relaxed after a good meal and unwilling to end the celebrations.

Luke scratched his beard. 'I don't see why not, sir. The sails are all finished, except for the second spinnaker, and I can't think you'll be likely to need that, not at this time of the year. The mast can be stepped tomorrow so that'll mean the riggers will be able to finish off. Then it's only a matter of trials and the fine tuning of her. Yes, I think a fortnight should do it. She's pretty well complete inside. And we sometimes get some very nice weather in October. "St Luke's little summer", they call it.'

'Then get the men working overtime on her. I'm sure they'll be happy to find a bit extra in their pay packets.' Edward slapped Luke on the back.

'You've got your crew, of course?' Luke asked.

'Ah! Well, no. Not exactly. I was hoping you might be

able to help me there,' Edward said. He cleared his throat. 'I would have asked Captain Chaney but he prefers to stay with *Leander.*' He pinched his lip. 'I suppose he might sail *Felicity* in her first race as a sort of one-off,' he said doubtfully.

John came along with a tray of sweetmeats. 'Why don't you ask *him*?' Luke laughed, nodding towards his brother-in-law. 'He sailed *Guinevere* for Hubert Bracenose till he gave up sailing and took the Falcon on.'

'Oh, really? I've heard tales of *Guinevere* and her skipper,' Edward said with interest. 'He sounds just the man I'm looking for.'

'Are you talking about me?' John said, deftly manoeuvring with his tray between the people standing about with an expertise learned on the deck of a heaving yacht.

'Yes. How would you like to go to sea again?' Luke asked.

'No. Not me. I'm a landlubber now.'John shook his head and made to move on. 'It'd have to be an exceptional craft that would tempt me now I've got a taste for having my feet under my own table.'

'Would *Felicity* tempt you?' Edward asked.

John put his tray down on the nearest table and thought about it. '*Felicity.* Now *that* might be worth thinking about.' Then, after a minute, he picked up the tray again. 'No,' he said, 'I couldn't spare the time to spend a season racing. I've got plans for this place. Anyway, Stella wouldn't like it, and it wouldn't be fair to leave her to run things without me. We're still getting the place on its feet.'

'I'm only asking you to skipper her for one race,' Edward said, 'against my friend, here. He owns *Victorious.*'

'*Victorious!* Now there's a fine yacht. Fast, too. I raced against her out of Cowes, earlier in the summer. There was nothing to touch her. Except *Guinevere,* of course. And then it was a pretty close run thing – we nearly beat her but she pipped us at the post.'

'Well, I'm expecting *Felicity* to beat her,' Edward told him, 'and I have a lot of money at stake. So – what do you say? You're a crack skipper. How about making sure I win my wager?'

John was silent for several minutes. Then he said carefully, 'I'd need to have a word with Stella. If she agreed I'd want to pick my own crew.'

'That's fine by me. You go ahead.'

'It's quite a good time of the year,' John said thoughtfully, 'Most of the men are back from the season's racing so I would have the pick of the bunch.' He nodded and held out his hand. 'All right. You're on. I'll win your race for you.'

Edward Price-Carpenter shook it. 'Good man. You and your crew will be well-rewarded, I promise you that. I stand to win a lot of money on this race. Bring another bottle of wine, landlord – or should I say, skipper? – and let's drink to our victory.'

I'll bring you another bottle, sir, but I won't drink – not until we've won the race.'

'Oh, come on, skipper. You've more faith in yourself than that, surely.'

'Oh, yes, I've faith in my skills. But I never drink to a race until it's won. Call it superstition, if you like.'

John Jameson left nothing to chance. He accompanied Luke and his men downriver when the yacht went on its trials and suggested various small modifications to the rigging. Robert went, too. His Uncle John had agreed to let him go as mast-headsman as the boat was only on trials. John took the helm. 'Let's see what we can get out of her,' he said with a grin. 'You lads, look lively when we go about or you'll be over the side.'

He craned his neck to where Robert was busy aloft. 'Are you fit up there, boy? We're going to move,' he yelled.

Robert signalled that he was ready. 'Ready about!' John shouted. 'Lee oh!' As the boat swung round there was a mad scramble to release sheets and the crack of the mainsail as it flapped across and filled with wind. 'Harden in the sheets!' John commanded. 'Come on, look lively there!'

Felicity creamed through the water with the wind on her beam, leaving a foaming wake behind her. 'She'll do,' John said at last. 'Mind you, I'll get several knots more out of her when I've got my own crew. It makes all the difference, a crew that knows exactly what's expected of them. Not that I'm complaining, Luke. I wouldn't expect your men to be as nippy. But she's a nice boat. A very nice boat. Your cousin knew what he was about, designing her.'

'You'll take me on as topman, Uncle?' Robert said when they arrived back at Turnbull's quay. 'I did all right, didn't I?'

'Yes, boy, you did. But I need a man with a bit more experience for this race. And I know who I want. Monkey Miller is the man I'm after. He lives at Brightlingsea and I think he's back. He's been in the Med.'

Robert's face fell. 'Why won't you take me, Uncle?'

'I never said I wouldn't take you, Bobbie. I said I wanted Monkey Miller for my first topman; he got his nickname because he climbs like a monkey and is as sure-footed. But I've got you down as second topman, if you'd like to come. The boat can take two; she's a big yacht. And don't forget we shan't be sailing on the village duck pond. It's been a bit choppy today, but by the time we get ten or fifteen miles out the sea's likely to be fairly unfriendly this time of the year.'

Robert's eyes lit up. 'Oh, thank you, Uncle John. You needn't worry about me. I've sailed in some pretty rough weather, picking up seaweed on the mast, at times. I know how to look after myself.'

The next fortnight was frantically busy for Luke at the Yard. He worked long hours because he had always made it his rule that he would put in as many hours as the men who worked for him.

John paid several visits, bringing crew members to see what the yacht was like and what conditions they would be working under.

Cassie made the most of the days that Robert was at home. She knew only too well that if it had not been for this race he would have been seeking a berth on one of the fishing boats. If Robert was not sailing he would be fishing, for he was never happy on dry land. However, she noticed that he spoke less about who had offered him a berth on the cod smacks than about Edward Price-Carpenter and his yacht. And always, somehow, the conversation would be steered towards Edward's pretty young daughter, Marian. She would be coming down with her parents for the race and had promised to kiss every member of the crew – without exception, Robert stressed, his face colouring under its tan – when the race was won. Again, it was a pity that neither Charity nor Amy had got brown eyes. Blue eyes were so dull, didn't Mama think? Marian had brown eyes and they went well with her fair hair. She was a very pretty girl, wasn't she? And all this was delivered in a matter-of-fact, throw-away style that deceived no one, least of all Cassie, who worried and fretted and felt the hand of cold fear clutching round her heart.

'Robert seems very taken with Mr Price-Carpenter's daughter,' she said lightly to Luke when he arrived home one evening. 'He hardly talks about anything else – apart from the race, that is. Have you noticed?

Luke nodded. 'Mm. He does seem to have taken a fancy to her.'

'He's a bit young, don't you think?'

'Oh, I don't know. I had my eye on you when I was ten, as I recall.'

'That was different, Luke.'

'Aye, you're right.' He sighed. 'But maybe it's only a passing fancy. I think young Robert's given most of his heart to the sea. In any case, I'll be surprised if young Miss Marian's father hasn't already got some earl or duke lined up for her and I doubt she'll have much choice in the matter.'

'I wonder if Bobbie realizes that. I wouldn't like him to get his heart broken, Luke.'

'No, Cassie, neither would I.'

'Perhaps we should nip it in the bud.'

Luke smiled at her. 'There really isn't anything to nip yet, dear, is there?'

'But if there should be?'

'We'll keep an eye on things, dear. We can't do more than that at this stage.'

But Cassie still worried. If Robert and Marian fell in love it would not be only *their* lives that were ruined.

It was the day before the yacht's departure for the Isle of Wight and the Price-Carpenters were due back at the Falcon. Edward had insisted on going on the race, despite John's attempt to dissuade him.

'It all adds to the weight, sir,' he said, with his tongue in his cheek. 'Every pound counts, you know. And with all due respect, you're not really a racing man, are you?'

'Not really a racing man, you insolent tyke! Of course I'm a racing man. Who do you think raced *Leander* for my father?'

'Captain Chaney, sir?' John knew he was being impertinent

but he didn't care. He could get away with it. Edward Price-Carpenter wanted him for this race.

'Cheeky bugger.' But Edward grinned at him. He wagged a finger. 'I've raced more times than you've had hot dinners – and I'm *not* missing this one, the devil I am! Bunny Felgate will be on his boat so I shall be on mine. I want to be on hand to collect my wager at the first possible moment.'

John sighed and inclined his head in defeat. 'It's your yacht, Mr Price-Carpenter.'

Weather permitting, the yacht wouldn't be away much more than a fortnight. She was to sail to Cowes, where *Victorious* was already waiting, and then the two yachts would race over the Royal Yacht Squadron's course round the Isle of Wight, after which they would return to Wyford to lay up for the winter. There was a good crowd to see *Felicity* go downriver just before the top of the tide and already the twenty-eight strong crew that John had picked so carefully were working well together, although John would use the journey to get them and the boat into proper racing trim.

'She'll need that experienced crew,' Luke remarked to Aaron. 'Look at the sky. There's some rough weather coming, if I don't miss my mark, the way those clouds are building up.'

'That yacht will weather a hurricane, Luke,' Aaron said with a smile.

Luke didn't return his smile. 'I hope she won't have to,' was all he said.

Cassie hadn't gone to the quay to see the yacht leave. She had said goodbye to Robert and given him the St Christopher medal she found among her mother's treasures and that had once belonged to his grandfather. She wanted no part of the flag-waving and cheering that would accompany the yacht slipping

309

its mooring. Of course Felicity would be there, waving to her husband, so she wouldn't be missed, Cassie decided bitterly. She was beginning to have doubts about Edward's love for her. With his wife's presence she had understood that he would have to be circumspect, but there had surely been no need for him to ignore her completely. And he had never once sought her out since she had left the Falcon – something she found hard to understand after all they had been to each other. Yet she still couldn't bring herself to accept that he really didn't care for her, and she looked desperately for some other explanation. But she could find none.

She picked some chrysanthemums and took them to put on her mother's grave in the churchyard. There was already a jar of asters there. She frowned. This was not the first time she had come to put flowers on Hannah's grave and found someone had been there before her. She found another container and put her flowers in it, then sat on a seat in the late-afternoon sunshine, pulling her shawl round her for warmth against the chill of the autumn air.

She thought of her mother and Abel Crowther and how Hannah had spent all those years deceiving herself into thinking he would marry her one day. It was very sad, really, because once she discovered the truth her life had simply collapsed. Cassie sat gazing at the flowers she had put on the grave and a sudden unpleasant thought struck her. Had she been doing exactly the same thing with Edward? Had *she* spent *her* life deceiving herself into thinking that he would have married her if he could? She thought back to her meeting with him on the river wall, the night before he sailed off with *Leander*, when she had told him she was pregnant. She remembered the occasion with perfect clarity now, even the bits that she had suppressed from her memory all these years. Edward had told her to be rid of the child; he had given her money for the purpose and as far as he was concerned, that was the end of it. Oh, he had said that he loved her, and that was what she had clung to, but had his words been empty? If he hadn't been engaged to Felicity would he have married her? She shook her head. Of course he wouldn't. After all, when he came back to the Falcon all those years later, he never once asked what had happened, whether she did indeed get rid of the child. In fact, he had probably forgotten the whole incident, except insofar as he remembered that she was ... she no longer shirked from the truth ... an easy conquest. Cassie buried her head in her hands. Was this really the truth? Had she spent nearly twenty years of her life doing exactly the same thing as her mother had done for all those years – had she been chasing a dream that never existed? She shook her head. Edward couldn't be as callous as that ... but at the same time a voice inside her asked, couldn't he?

'You all right, Cassie girl?' She pulled herself together with difficulty and lifted her head at the sound of Tom's voice.

'Yes, Tom, I'm all right.' She gave him a wintry smile and patted the seat beside her. 'Why don't you come and sit down for a minute?'

He did as she suggested. 'I often come an' set here when I got a minute to spare,' he said. 'I miss your ma, you know.' He cleared his throat noisily.

'So it's you, Tom.' Cassie's face cleared and she smiled at him. 'It's you who puts the flowers on her grave.'

He nodded. 'Thass right. Thass all I can do for 'er now.'

'You were very fond of Mama, weren't you, Tom?'

He looked straight ahead. 'She was everything in the world to me. I'd hev gone through fire an' water for 'er.'

'Did you ever ask her to marry you, Tom?'

He turned to her in surprise. 'No, 'course not. That worn't

311

my place. She was a yacht captain's wife. She wouldn't never hev looked twice at a feller like me.' He shook his head. 'But that didn't matter. That was enough that I was there and she was there. I never asked for more.' He spoke with a quiet dignity.

Cassie laid her hand on his gnarled one. 'You looked after her, Tom. She knew that. She told me she could never have managed without you.'

Tom's old face flushed and Cassie knew she couldn't have said anything that would have pleased him more.

'You don't come and see us much, these days,' he said after awhile. 'Ain't we good enough for you now you've come up in the world? Livin' at the Corner House an' all that?'

'Oh, Tom, do you really think that?' Cassie said. She shook her head. 'It's nothing like that, you know it couldn't be. It's just that,' she bit her lip, 'the Falcon belongs to Stella now, Stella and John. It's nothing to do with me. I wouldn't like Stella to think I was trying to interfere, or pry into the way she runs things.'

Tom sniffed. 'Shall I tell you suthin'?'

'What?'

'Young Stella'd be on'y too pleased if you was to go an' see her an' offer to lend a hand now an' then. I've seen her weep with worry an' despair when she didn't think anyone could see.'

'Then why doesn't she ask me?'

'For the same reason you don't offer, I reckon. She's too proud.' Tom got up from the seat. 'I must be gettin' back. The folks will soon be back from seein' the yacht off an' some of 'em might want a drop o' porter. An' now John's away Stella won't know which way to turn if she don't get a bit o' extra help.' He stomped off down the churchyard in the direction of the Falcon.

Cassie sat where she was for a little longer, then she got up and pulling her shawl round her more closely followed him.

Stella was in the kitchen basting a joint of beef, her hair

escaping from its pins and her face red from the stove, while Millie and Florrie scuttled about like rabbits. She put the joint back into the oven and then leaned her head on the mantelpiece, her whole body drooping with tiredness and despair.

'Would you like an extra pair of hands, now that John is away?' Cassie asked quietly.

Stella straightened and turned round, her face lighting up. 'Cassie!' She went over to her sister and gave her a hug. 'Do you really mean that?'

'Yes, of course I do. I would have come before, only ... well, I didn't want to butt in.' Cassie took off her shawl. 'Now, what would you like me to do?' She looked enquiringly at Stella and they both said together, 'Make pastry?' and burst out laughing.

'Well,' Stella said, 'Mama always said there was nobody who could make such light pastry as you and she was right.'

Cassie rolled up her sleeves. 'You should have asked me to come and help you before, Stella,' she said. 'I would have been happy to come. I miss the old place, you know.'

Stella busied herself peeling apples. 'I didn't like to ask you because I thought you might resent the fact that John and I were here instead of you. You hardly ever come to see us except when there's a Vestry Meeting.'

'It's true. *I* hated to see you here instead of me. And when I realised what a success you were making of the place – well, you obviously didn't need me. That meal after the launch of Price-Carpenter's yacht ...'

'Ah, you don't know the half about that,' Stella said ruefully. 'John and I were both up all night preparing it. We didn't get to bed at all. And we were so worried in case things went wrong!'

'No one would ever have known,' Cassie smiled.

'To tell you the truth I've been worried sick as to how I'd manage without John here,' Stella admitted, 'but I daren't let him know or he wouldn't have gone, and I knew how much he wanted to go on the race. But now you've come, like the answer to a prayer,' she hugged her sister's arm. 'And will you help me prepare the celebration meal ready for when the yachts get back, too, Cassie?'

'Of course I will, silly. I'll be glad to.'

'Good. I'll put the kettle forward and we'll have a cup of tea. Get the cups down, will you?'

Later, as Cassie made her way home she sang to herself. It was a good thing she had seen Tom. Stella would be glad of her help and she would be glad to give it. And she knew Luke wouldn't object – he knew how much she missed her old life.

Cassie spent a happy fortnight helping Stella while John was away and Stella confessed that she would never have managed without her sister, especially with the party to prepare for the yachts' return. Felicity Price-Carpenter and her daughter Marian had come down to Wyford with Edward and were staying at the Falcon. Sometimes they would come into the big, warm kitchen where Stella and Cassie were working, simply for a little company and to have a chat.

'Has your Robert worked as a mastheadsman before, Mrs Turnbull?' Marian asked one day, 'or is this his first trip?'

'Oh, no, this isn't his first trip by any means. He spent the whole of last season on Mr Theobald's yacht as topman,' Cassie told her. 'Mind you, it wasn't such a big yacht as your father's and the mast wasn't so tall. But it was still a long way up. Why do you ask?'

Marian flushed a little. 'I wouldn't want him to get hurt,' she said shyly.

Felicity smiled at Cassie. 'I think your young Robert has rather stolen Marian's heart,' she remarked, with a teasing look in Marian's direction.

'Mama! How can you say such things!' Marian got to her feet and hurried from the room, her face flaming.

Felicity watched her go. 'Young love's a wonderful thing, isn't it?' she said dryly. 'I remember when I was in love like that ... Maybe the dream would have lasted if I hadn't married him and found out what he was really like.' She looked up quickly at Cassie. 'Not that I'm suggesting that your Robert ...'

Cassie shook her head. 'No, of course not. I understand that. But you ... ?' She was anxious for Felicity to continue.

Felicity shrugged. 'Edward swears he is faithful to me and when we are in company he fawns over me till it makes me sick, because I know only too well that he will lift the skirts of any woman who will let him as soon as my back's turned. And it doesn't matter to him whether she's a duchess or a dairymaid. He's no better than a rutting stag.' She sighed. 'I shouldn't say all this to you two ladies, should I? I should keep up appearances, but I don't care any more – why should I? He doesn't care about me and I did my duty by him and nearly ruined my health by giving him six children. It was hardly my fault they were all girls. Anyway, I have my own lover now, although Edward doesn't know it.' She shook her head, smiling wryly at Cassie and Stella. 'I expect you think it must be a wonderful thing to have plenty of money, beautiful clothes, expensive yachts ... but it isn't wonderful at all, really. It's all a matter of keeping up appearances and papering over the cracks. I'd give it all up tomorrow for a happy marriage like you both have.'

'I guess we all have our share of problems,' Stella said gently. 'John and I have had difficult times, too.' She nodded towards Cassie. 'My sister, here, is the only person I know whose marriage hasn't hit a rocky patch at some time or another.'

Cassie managed a smile but she felt far from happy inside. If only they knew! But when the race was over and the yachts

315

returned they would probably find out ... because if Robert and Marian looked like becoming too fond of each other she would have no option but to tell them all the secret she had kept for nearly nineteen years. There would be no other course open to her.

Chapter Twenty-Three

Bunny Felgate and Edward had agreed that whoever won the race would foot the bill for the party at the Falcon and that there was to be no lack of either food or drink. They also swore that whatever happened on the race they would remain good friends.

'I hope they'll be able to keep to that,' Luke said one morning at breakfast when the yachts had been gone for a week. He gazed out of the window at the lowering sky. 'It looks to me as if the weather's going to roughen. It won't be much fun round the Needles if it gets any worse.'

'Perhaps it's not so bad where they are,' Cassie said. 'Or perhaps they'll put the race off till the weather improves.' She was not anxious for the yachts or their crews. Only Robert's safety concerned her.

'I doubt thass not going to get better. They were too late to catch St Luke's little summer last week and now it looks as if the weather has clamped down good and proper.'

'Well, then they should put it off till next season. Surely it wouldn't matter. Do you know which day they intend to go?'

'The first one that's favourable, I guess.'

'They hope to be back here by next Friday, don't they?'

'Thass right. But I shouldn't bank on it. They could be there a fortnight just waiting for the weather to clear. And then they'll have to wait till their heads have cleared.'

'What do you mean?'

'Well, I guess they'll all have a drop to celebrate before they ever start back here for the proper party.'

'I think the whole idea was stupid,' Cassie said irritably, 'two grown men wagering like that. Do you know how much money's at stake?'

'Several thousand pounds apiece, from what I can gather.'

'They must have more money than sense. I've no patience with them,' Cassie said in disgust.

Luke grinned at her. 'Then I suppose you won't be bothering to come down to the quay to see them dock when they come back?'

'I'll see. I'm helping Stella all day. I might be too tired.'

'Not you. You're never tired. You'll be there – if you want to, that is.'

Luke went off to work and Cassie did what she had to do at the Corner House and then went along to help Stella at the Falcon. 'Just as I used to when I lived in The Folley,' she said to herself as she slipped through the kissing-gate into the churchyard. Only now she didn't hate her own home. In fact, Luke had written to Mr Penfold to ask if he would be willing to sell them the Corner House, because it didn't look as if the old man was ever coming back to Wyford. Mr Penfold hadn't yet replied but Cassie hoped very much that he would agree. She was beginning to like living there.

In the event, *Felicity* was back earlier than expected. Instead of arriving on the Friday, she came up on the midnight tide on Thursday evening. *Victorious* was not with her and it was a subdued crew that put the boat to bed and made their way wearily ashore at just after eleven o'clock.

John hurried home to the Falcon, where both Cassie and Luke were helping Stella with the last clearing up before going home to bed. They had all spent the evening in completing as many of the preparations as they could for the party that they hoped would take place the next day.

'Oh, John, you're back! I've missed you!' Stella flung her arms round her husband's neck. 'Well, did you win the race?'

Gently, John released himself from her grasp. 'No, we bloody didn't,' he said, his face like thunder. 'I saw to that.' He nodded in the direction of the joints of beef and hams still on the table. 'And we shan't be needing all that, either. There'll be no celebrating here, I can tell you.'

Luke poured out a glass of whisky and put it into John's hand. 'Here, boy, get this inside you. You look about all in. Then you can tell us what went wrong, for it's a sure thing something did.'

John sank down into a chair at the kitchen table, swallowed the whisky in one gulp and rested his head in his hands. 'Oh, yes, Luke, you're right there,' he said, his voice savage. 'Something went very wrong.'

The door opened and Edward Price-Carpenter came in. John immediately stood up. 'Get that bastard out of here. Don't let him near me. I'll kill him. I swear I'll kill him with my bare hands.' He struggled but Luke restrained him and he slumped down at the table and began to weep like a child.

'Whatever is it? What's the matter with you both?' Cassie frowned impatiently, looking from one to the other, while Stella tried to cradle John's head in her arms.

Edward glared at John, his face full of a fury that he seemed to be controlling with great difficulty. 'He knew that half my estate was on this wager,' he said angrily, 'but he lost the race. *He deliberately lost the race*. And all because of the accident. God knows there are enough of those at sea.'

'Accident? What accident?' Luke said sharply, just as Cassie said, 'Where's Robert? Why isn't he here?'

John looked up, his face wet with tears. 'Robert isn't here because that bugger sent him up the mast when it wasn't fit. He countermanded my orders and sent him up there to free the tops'l shrouds in a screaming gale and the poor kid fell to his death in the sea round the Needles. Monkey Miller had already got a broken arm and a gashed hand through trying to do it and I said leave it till the wind dropped a bit, or at least till first light. But no, he couldn't wait.' He leaned across the table to where Edward stood and wagged a finger at him. 'I told you before we ever started that there could only be one captain giving orders on my ship and that was going to be me! If you hadn't been so bloody pig-headed that boy would be here now.' He turned away. 'I don't want to talk to you. You're not worth wasting breath on.'

'I'm a ruined man,' Edward said, his voice bordering on a whine. 'We could have won. We were well ahead ... You deliberately lost the race.'

'You're dead right, I did. And serve you bloody right. I'd have wrecked the bloody boat into the bargain if there hadn't been men's lives at stake.' He shook his head. 'God, how I stopped myself from chucking you overboard I'll never know. But I'll tell you this, *Mr* Price-Carpenter, you'll be wasting your time if you ever come again to the Colne for a crew. There's not a man on the whole river will sail with you when word gets round what you did.'

Edward turned to Cassie and Luke, standing together,

shocked into near-incomprehension at the news of Robert's death. 'It's not true, Edward. Say it's not true,' she was saying over and over again.

'Yes, Cassie, I'm afraid it is,' Edward said, his voice more sympathetic now. 'Turnbull, I need to talk to you.' He threw a glance in John's direction. 'Due to him I'm practically ruined. I shall have to sell the boat, there's no question of that, but I'm sure we can come to some financial arrangement over the loss of the boy.'

Luke had been standing with his arm round Cassie. Now he deliberately put her from him and walked over to Edward. 'I need to talk to you, too, Mr Price-Carpenter. Can we go into Hannah's room, Stella?'

Stella nodded. She was sitting with John and holding his hand.

Luke went to the door. 'You stay here, Cassie, we shan't be long. This way.' He gave Edward no title but indicated the way with a sharp toss of the head.

Edward followed and Luke led the way into Hannah's old sitting room. 'I can't tell you how sorry I am that this happened, Turnbull, but I think Captain Jameson is treating the whole thing in a rather dramatic way. These accidents happen, you must know that . . .'

'I'm prepared to abide by the story my brother-in-law has told,' Luke said, his voice wooden. 'He said the boy's death was your fault and I believe him.'

Edward waved his hand. 'Let's leave aside fault, if fault there was. Look, as I said, due to Jameson's bad seamanship we lost the race and I'm practically ruined, but I'm sure I can offer some satisfactory financial compensation over the loss of your son . . .'

''*Your* son, Mr Price-Carpenter,' Luke said quietly.

321

'What do you mean, *my* son?'

'Robert was your son, not mine – although God knows, I couldn't have loved him more if he had been of my getting. But he wasn't. He was yours and you sent him to his death.' Luke watched as Edward crumpled into a chair and covered his face with his hands. 'Yes,' he went on, 'it's a bitter pill, isn't it? You've got six daughters, haven't you, by your wife? And it's been a constant source of disappointment to you that you never had a son. Well, you did have a son. Cassie's son, Robert. And a finer boy never lived.' Luke's voice broke on the words but he went on, 'And that's your punishment, Mr Price-Carpenter. Knowing that you sent your own son to a watery grave for the sake of a stupid wager, made when you were too drunk to know what you were doing.' He was silent for a moment, letting the words sink home. Then he said, 'I don't want your money, Mr Price-Carpenter. Nothing can compensate me and Cassie for the loss of that boy. But I'm telling you this,' his voice rose and he clenched his fists so hard that his knuckles showed white, 'if you aren't out of Wyford by the morning, by God I'll thrash you and once I start on you I won't be responsible for the consequences. How I'm keeping my hands from your throat at this minute the good Lord only knows. Now, get out of my sight and my life and don't let me ever see you again.' He went over to the door and flung it open and nearly fell over Cassie, on her knees outside, the tears streaming down her face.

He helped her to her feet. 'I told you to keep out of the way,' he said sternly. 'You should never have been listening at the door.' Then his expression softened a little. 'Come on, dear, I'll take you home. We'll talk in the morning when I've cooled down a bit.'

'So you knew! All the time you knew!' Cassie kept repeating as she stumbled home beside him, half-blinded with tears, trying to keep up with his stride. Her thoughts were in a turmoil. In all these years Luke had never given any hint that he knew Robert was not his son; nor that he knew that Edward Price-Carpenter was the boy's real father. He had made no secret of the fact that he didn't much care for Edward over the years, but he had always treated him with politeness and courtesy. Remorse choked her as she remembered how she had allowed Edward to blackmail her over the building of *Felicity*. She was ashamed now at how she had been taken in by him – at how she had thought she was in love with him. She knew now she had never been in love with Edward – not the *real* Edward. She had been in love with an Edward who didn't exist – had never existed – outside her own mind. The real Edward had given her Robert in the casual conquest of a country innkeeper's daughter and taken him away from her in a mad determination to win a wager that would never have been made had he been sober. She prayed to God that she would never have to set eyes on the man again. And all the time Luke had known her secret. Her heart swelled with something that she couldn't put a name to; a warmth and a feeling of deep gratitude that he was by her side.

They went inside the house and Luke pulled the kettle forward on the stove and made a cup of tea. 'I can see this won't wait till the morning so we might as well get it over now,' he said gently as he poured her a cup. 'Yes, Cassie, I knew Robert wasn't my son. I knew he belonged to Edward Price-Carpenter.'

'But how? And why didn't you tell me?' She blew her nose hard, trying desperately to pull herself together.

'Why didn't *you* tell *me*?' he asked.

'Because you would never have married me.'

He smiled. 'Cassie, I told you, I would have married you at any price.'

'Did you know, then, right at the beginning?'

'No. I thought, well, that night in the cattle shed ... I felt guilty and ashamed over that. But then, it was something Stella said ...'

'Stella? But she didn't know.'

'No, but you know how furious she was when she knew we were to be married.'

'Yes, she always wanted you, didn't she?'

He gave half a smile. 'She never stood a chance against you, Cassie. But she was so mad with me that she tried to make me jealous by saying that you'd been meeting Edward Price-Carpenter as well as me and coming home late at night. Well, I didn't think much about that until Robert was born because she didn't know the whole story and anyway, I knew what a spiteful little cat she could be. But I'd seen enough new-born babies in my mother's house to know whether a baby was full-term or not and as soon as I saw him it didn't take me long to do the sums and realize that Robert wasn't my child.'

'But you even chose his name,' Cassie said, wonderingly.

'Yes. I made up my mind never to think of him as anything but my own boy.' He shook his head. 'And I never did. Until tonight.'

Cassie began to cry again and he took her in his arms and wept with her over the son they had both loved so dearly. A long time later, when their tears were spent Luke made some fresh tea and gave Cassie another cup.

'Why did you do it, Luke?' she asked as she sipped it.

'Why did I do what, dear?'

'Why did you accept Robert like that and never say anything?'

He looked at her in surprise. 'Why, because I love you, Cassie girl.'

She looked down into her teacup. 'It wasn't much of a bargain, was it, Luke? You knew I didn't love you.'

'Maybe not when we married, dear.'

She looked up sharply. 'What do you mean?'

He smiled. 'Oh, Cassie, do you really need me to tell you? Don't you know what love is? It's not just a tumble under the sheets, is it? Put it like this – would you have stayed with me all these years? Would you have lived in the cottage at The Folley with never a word of complaint? After little Simon died would you have risked your life to give me Reuben – a son that was really mine – if you hadn't loved me? That's not the sort of thing people do out of duty, is it? Think about it, Cassie. We've been through a lot together. Isn't that what love's all about?'

She looked at him. His face was lined and weatherbeaten and his hair was turning iron grey but he was the same Luke she had married and till now she had never realized that the thread running through her life with him, a life made up of small troubles and big ones, of joys and sorrows, had not been one of duty as she had led herself to believe, but of love. Real love, deep and lasting.

She smiled, a watery smile. 'I never realized, Luke. To think, all these years and I never realized.'

He leaned across the table and took her hand. 'Didn't you, dear? Well, as long as one of us did that's all that matters.'